JOHNNY McCABE

Brad Dennison

Author of
THE LONG TRAIL and *WANDERING MAN*

PUBLISHED BY PINE BOOKSHELF
BUFORD, GEORGIA

Johnny McCabe is a work of fiction. Names, characters, places, and incidents are either the product of the author's imagination or are used fictitiously. Any resemblance to actual persons, living or dead, events or locales is entirely coincidental.

Copyright 2016 by Bradley A. Dennison
All Rights Reserved

Editors: Martha Gulick
          Donna Dennison

Copy Editor: Loretta Yike

Cover Design: Donna Dennison

In Memory of
Leon Shook
Many thanks for the inspiration, encouragement and guidance. You are truly missed.

PART ONE

Christmas

1

Montana, 1881

THE BOYS HAD gone into the ridges and come back with the biggest, grandest Christmas tree Bree had ever seen. It was so tall it had to be cut a little so the angel could perch on top of it and not bump its head on the ceiling. And it wasn't just that the tree was tall, but it was full. Its boughs extended out into the parlor so much that it had to be cut back a little so people could get through the doorway into the kitchen.

The family decorated the tree, which really meant Bree, Aunt Ginny, Haley and Temperance decorated. Josh and Dusty had good intentions about decorating. But they ended up drinking whiskey and smoking cigars, and talking with Sam and Charles about everything from hunting to cattle to the weather, and didn't get much actual decorating done.

Aunt Ginny and Sam were living in town these days, but they came out for the decorating of the tree.

"I wouldn't miss our evening of working on the tree," Aunt Ginny said.

Bree was in a gray blouse and a floor-length skirt, and her hair was tied back in a long braid. She was hanging a decoration that was actually an old pine cone Pa had made for her years ago.

She said, "It seems so strange without Pa here. And Jessica and Cora."

"They'll be here," Josh said. "They're coming out Christmas Eve."

"I can't believe how many people we're going to have here. The house is going to be so full. Fuller than it's ever been before."

Aunt Ginny nodded. "That it will be."

They had decided to turn this year's Christmas into a full-family event. Matt and Peddie would be here. Mister Harding and his wife had been invited. And the best part of it, Bree thought, was Jack and Nina were home from Boston and would be here.

Jack was out of town for the moment. He was off in Helena, meeting with a judge. But he would be back in time for Christmas.

When the tree was finished, Bree took a step back and admired their work. She was admiring it again, later in the evening. Aunt Ginny and Sam had turned in. Dusty and Haley and Jonathan had gone home. Temperance was in the kitchen, doing a final clean-up before she went to bed, and Josh was out on the porch getting a breath of evening, winter air. This left Bree and Charles alone by the tree.

Every Christmas tree struck Bree as a thing of wonder, but none quite as much as this one.

"Oh, Charles," she said. "It's so grand."

He came up behind her and wrapped his arms around her. She leaned her head back on his chest.

"*You're* grand," he said.

This got a smile out of her. She looked up at him and got a quick kiss.

She said, "I think Christmas is the greatest time of the whole year."

He nodded. "We never had a Christmas like this when I was growing up. I'm realizing I missed so much."

"Well, you're part of this family, now."

They stood for a while looking at the tree. Some of the decorations had been made by Pa or the boys, and others brought from San Francisco by Aunt Ginny. And little flames flickered and danced on the candles, giving the tree a magical look.

After a time, Charles said, "I'd best be turning in. Tomorrow starts early, and even though Christmas is almost here, the work goes on."

"Are you still planning on riding out to the line cabin tomorrow?"

He nodded. "Being ramrod has its responsibilities. I'll be back before Christmas eve."

"Well, come on. I'll walk with you out to the porch."

They found Josh still out there, a glass of whiskey in hand. Now that Josh was the man of the house, and Pa, Jessica and Cora had moved out to the cabin in their little canyon north of the valley, Josh had taken to standing on the front porch and looking off at the night. He greeted the morning on the porch, too. Just like Pa always had.

The sky was clear and the stars seemed extra bright, the way they did during the winter. A quarter moon was out, and the floor of the valley was awash in pale moonlight. They had a good view of the covered bridge down by the river.

There had been a few light dustings of snow, but they had all melted away. The ground was a gray-brown color in the moonlight.

She said, "If we don't get snow soon, then there won't be any for Christmas. We just have to have snow for Christmas. I don't think I ever remember a Christmas without snow."

"We'll have it," Josh said.

Bree decided it was too cold for her to remain out on the porch, so she gave Charles a goodnight kiss and went inside.

Josh said to Charles, "Are you still planning to ride out to the line cabin tomorrow?"

Charles nodded. "Unless you have something else for me to do."

"Once you're out there, make sure the men are loaded up with firewood, and then high-tail it back here. We've got some hard weather coming."

Charles glanced at the night sky. "Looks crystal clear up there, Boss."

"It looks that way. But when you've lived in these mountains long enough, you develop a sort of feel for the weather. The wind has shifted. It's coming from the north. And more than that, there's a feeling in the air. We're gonna be hit with snow, and we're gonna be hit hard."

2

JOHNNY STOOD on the small porch of the log cabin. Ahead of him was the canyon floor. The far canyon wall was rocky, and out beyond the canyon was a cliff covered with pine. From where he stood, he could see a rocky peak off to the north, hazy in the distance.

Johnny had a cup of coffee in his hand, and his gun was buckled into place. He stood in the morning air, enjoying the crispness.

Frost covered the brown grass just beyond the porch, and the canyon floor was silvery with it.

Thunder was down there, frolicking about in the coldness of the morning. The stallion seemed to love cold weather. A small herd of mustangs was with him. And Old Blue stood, chomping contentedly on the morning grass. The old steer didn't seem to care if there was frost or not.

Johnny heard the door opening behind him, and Jessica came out. She was in a heavy wool coat, and a kerchief was pulled up and over her hair. She had a cup of coffee in one hand.

"It's so cold," she said.

Johnny grinned. He stood in a flannel shirt and a vest. "It's just right."

"You worked really hard on the woodpile yesterday. I meant to ask you about it last night, but I got distracted."

He looked at her and she was giving him a wide smile, and her eyes were sparkling a little. The way a woman does when she looks at the man she loves.

"Distracted?" he said. "Seemed to me you were really focused."

"Now, Mister McCabe. I *am* a lady."

"A very focused lady."

"I'll give you that." She took a sip of coffee, and then wrapped both hands around the mug to keep them warm.

She said, "But about that wood."

"We've had no real snow yet, but there's snow coming. A lot of it, and soon. I want to make sure the wood shed is as full as it can be."

"Well, you have two more days before we leave for the main house."

Johnny shook his head. "We're leaving today, around

noon."

She looked at him as if to say, *huh?*

Johnny looked off toward the distant peak. "See that white cloud that looks like it's sort of wrapping itself around that mountain top?"

She nodded. "Looks kind of pretty."

"It is. But it's a sign of death."

She blinked with surprise. "A Shoshone thing?"

"Just something I learned from a lot of years in these mountains. That's the sign of a storm coming, and it's coming fast. I want to be at the main house before it hits, or at least before it gets bad. I want you to pack enough things for a week."

"A week?"

He nodded. "It'll be at least a week before we'll be able to get back through the passes to this canyon."

"Maybe we shouldn't go."

"I know Josh and Dusty. If we don't arrive at the main house, they'll come looking for us. The storm'll be hard for riders to be out in it."

He shifted his gaze from the distant mountain back to her. "How about you? Are you and junior up to riding?"

She nodded. "I'm fine. Granny Tate says the pregnancy is as good as any she's ever seen."

Then Jessica gave him a questioning kind of grin, like she just realized what he had said. "*Junior?* What makes you think it's going to be a boy?"

"Just a gut feeling."

"If you're right, and that doesn't mean I'm agreeing that you are, but *if* you're right, do you want to name him Junior? John McCabe, Junior?"

"No." He shook his head. "We don't seem to have any juniors in the family. But I was thinking, they say the first McCabe in the country was named Peter. The father of the man I talk about a lot, the first John McCabe."

"Peter McCabe."

Johnny nodded. "What do you think?"

"Has a nice ring to it."

"Or we could go with your father's name. Caleb."

"But what if it's a girl?"

Jessica had talked about her mother, and her mother's name. Johnny said, "How about Abigail? Maybe Abigail Virginia?"

She smiled. "You are good with names."

He looked back at the mountain. She followed his gaze.

She said, "Has that cloud gotten a little bigger?"

He nodded. "It's going to come fast. Let's get moving. I'll go get the horses."

"I'll start packing."

She turned and went back into the house, and Johnny could hear her calling to Cora.

Johnny looked down at the canyon floor. Not quite a quarter of a mile, but further than a cowboy wanted to walk.

He gave a long, hard whistle that echoed against the far canyon wall. Thunder lifted his head and looked up toward the house, then started trotting up.

3

DUSTY WAS in his buckskin shirt with a thick denim jacket over it. Haley had knit a long scarf for him, and it was wrapped around his neck.

He had come to town in a buckboard to meet the stage.

Jack was due back today. He had gone off to Helena to assist in a trial because the local prosecutor had to recuse himself for whatever reason—Dusty found legal stuff boring and didn't really pay attention when Jack was telling him. Judge Mack had recommended Jack.

Dusty decided against waiting outside. It was too danged cold. He went into the Second Chance for a cup of hot coffee.

"Storm coming," Mr. Chen said. "Feel it in my bones."

Dusty nodded, sipping from a ceramic cup. "That's what Josh says. I'm tendin' toward believin' him."

Hunter brought some more wood in and loaded it into the stove at the center of the room.

Dusty said, "You both still coming out to the ranch for Christmas?"

It seemed like Bree had invited almost half the town this year.

Hunter nodded. "That we are."

"You better come on out this afternoon. If Josh is right about the storm, we got a blizzard coming. The passes might be impassible before the day's done. This town will be under three feet of snow before morning."

Chen said, "My bones say Josh is right."

Dusty heard the stage coming in.

He said, "That should be Jack."

He drained his coffee and set the cup down on the bar and headed out.

The driver was hopping down from the seat. He had a white beard that touched his chest, and his face was deeply lined. He was in a heavy wool coat, and a scarf that wrapped under his chin and went up and over his hat.

"Howdy, Ned," Dusty said.

"Hey, Dusty."

"You look about half-frozen."

"That's how I feel. I'm headin' over to the Second Chance for some hot coffee in a couple of minutes. I'm not takin' the stage any further today. Not with this storm comin' in."

Ned pulled open the stage door and Jack stepped out. He was in a fur hat with earflaps that folded down and a heavy wool coat.

"Jack," Dusty said. "Nina would've been here, but I convinced her not to come. It's too danged cold. She's at her folks' farm. We'll pick her up on the way to the ranch."

Jack nodded, glancing up at the sky. "We've got a storm coming. A real one."

The sky had been clear at sunrise. Now a cover of grayish-white clouds hung low and filled half the sky. The wind was strong and trees branches were waving about.

Dusty said to Ned, "No other customers today?"

Ned shook his head. "Didn't expect many. With this storm coming, they're gonna be closed for a while. Folks are hunkering down for the winter."

They climbed up into the wagon.

Dusty said, "Josh sent Charles off this morning to the line cabin to make sure the line riders were set for the storm. But when he saw the clouds and how fast the storm was coming, he saddled up himself and went out to fetch Charles back. Josh is expecting the snow to hit hard by this afternoon."

Johnny had built a small barn for Old Blue against one end of the canyon. He was going to have to leave the steer in a stall, with enough grain in a bin to last for a few days. The stall was open so the bull could step outside the barn when he wanted to, but the opening was angled so the cold wind wouldn't touch him.

Johnny said, "I'll be back when I can. You hang tough until then."

Johnny stepped outside the barn and looked up at the sky, and he saw the clouds were now blanketing it. The wind was strong and icy.

Thunder was waiting for him. Johnny swung up and into the saddle and said, "The storm's going to come fast, old friend. We'd better move even faster."

He rode back up to the cabin, then got Jessica's horse saddled and fit a second horse with a pack saddle.

He found Jessica in the kitchen, kneeling in front of Cora. The little girl was in a heavy woolen coat with a hood, and Jessica was wrapping a scarf around her neck. Johnny said. "We've got to be going now."

4

BREE WAS on the porch watching for any sign of riders coming from across the valley. Charles and Josh, in particular. If they didn't get in ahead of the storm, they might be snowed in at the line cabin for days. They would miss Christmas. Or worse, they might be caught in the storm. Men had died in these mountains that way.

The sky was now covered with a heavy, white cloud. Like a giant, down-stuffed quilt. It would have been pretty, Bree thought, if she didn't know what it meant.

Then the snow began. The wind was coming hard from the north, and the flakes didn't twitter and dance their way down in the magical way some snowfalls have. These flakes went whipping past. Then more followed, and within seconds the snow was coming heavy and hard. Bree realized visibility was dwindling and she couldn't see much past the covered bridge.

Aunt Ginny and Sam were at the house. They hadn't gone back to town, not after Josh told them about the coming storm. Ginny stepped out on the porch with two cups of steaming tea and handed one to Bree.

Ginny said, "It seems like we're always standing and waiting for these men."

Bree nodded. "Comes with the territory, I guess."

She took a sip of tea. Earl Grey.

She said, "Aunt Ginny, what happens when one of them doesn't come back?"

"We'll deal with it then, child. But it's not going to be today."

There was movement at the bridge. At first Bree thought she saw two riders, but then her heart fell when she saw it was a wagon. Then she felt guilty for being disappointed, because she knew it was Dusty coming in from the Harding farm with Jack and Nina.

Aunt Ginny gave Jack a long hug, and said, "So, Jackson, how does it feel to be traipsing about the country on legal business? Cavorting with judges?"

"At the moment," he said, "mighty cold."

Then it was Bree's turn. She wrapped her arms around her brother and said, "It never feels completely like home when you're gone."

He said, "I've been gone a lot, over the years. But Nina and I plan to be here, from now on."

There was a trunk full of presents that Jack and Dusty hauled in. Then Temperance and Haley were giving Jack and Nina hugs, and Dusty was warming his hands by the hearth. Sam offered Jack and Dusty a glass of whiskey each.

This left Bree and Aunt Ginny on the porch.

Ginny said, "Aren't you going to go in? Warm up a little?"

Bree shook her head. "I think I'll wait just a little longer."

An inch of snow was already on the ground, and the wooden bridge now seemed to be lost in what looked like heavy fog.

Then Bree saw two riders. She jumped in the air and almost ran down the stairs to greet them. But as they grew closer, she saw it was another buckboard. The man driving it was really tall, even more so than Charles, and someone was beside him on the seat. Bree realized it was Carter and Emily Harding.

Again, she felt guilty for being disappointed.

Josh hadn't hired a new wrangler yet, so Dusty said he would take care of their horses.

Harding said to her, "Your Pa here yet?"

She shook her head. "Don't know if he's coming, what with the storm."

Harding opened the door, and saw Bree was still standing by the railing, looking off toward the valley.

He said, "You coming in?"

"No. Not yet. I'm still waiting for Josh and Charles."

"They'll be along. Them's two of the toughest I've ever seen."

5

THUNDER LOVED to run in the snow. One time a few years ago, Johnny had given Thunder his head after a storm had dropped two feet of powdery snow on the valley floor. Thunder stumbled and they fell and slid sideways. Johnny's leg was trapped under Thunder but he was still hanging onto the saddle. Thunder scampered back to his feet with Johnny still hanging on and then they took off running again. Johnny's leg was a little bruised up from the fall, but he was laughing too hard to care.

But at the moment, Thunder seemed to know that they had to get Jessica and Cora to safety. They had left the canyon with the wind blowing strong and cold, and as they rode down into the valley, the first flakes started falling. And then the snow turned into sleet, whipping about them in the wind.

Jessica could ride and she was sitting strong in the saddle, and Cora was bundled up and riding on the saddle in front of her. Johnny was leading a pack horse that was carrying everything Jessica had packed.

The snow was up over Thunder's hooves when they reached the wooden bridge. Visibility was now so bad because of the snowfall, Johnny could see only a faded hulking shape ahead, and he knew it was the ranch house. Within an hour, he didn't think the house would be visible from a distance even half as far away as the bridge.

They rode up and Bree came running down from the porch to greet them. Ginny was with her.

Ginny said to Jessica and Cora, "Let's get you two inside and thawed out."

Johnny said, "This storm is going to be a bad one. Is everyone here?"

Bree shook her head. "Josh and Charles are still out there."

Dusty stepped around from the side of the house. He said, "I'll take care of the horses."

Johnny nodded, then he said to Bree, "Who's here?"

She said, "Sam's here. And the Hardings. And Jack and Nina. Uncle Joe's here, and Uncle Matt and Peddie. Mister Chen and Hunter just got here a little while ago. Tom's staying in town. He figured the marshal should be there."

"Go get the men. Tell them we're going to build a big bonfire."

Bree had long ago learned not to question her father. She did what he told her. She went and got the men.

"A bonfire?" Jack said. He was standing in the living room by the hearth.

Harding nodded, shouldering into his coat. "In this kind of snow, you could get lost just a quarter mile from the house. Your pa's thinking it'll help the boys out there find their way home."

Bree followed them outdoors.

Dusty called out to Pa over the wind, "We can't use the firewood. We have enough for maybe a week in the wood shed. If we use that, we won't be able to heat the house."

Johnny said, "Is the bunkhouse empty?"

Bree nodded. "Old Ches and Kennedy are out at the line cabin."

"Then, once the storm is done and the snow is cleared, we're going to have to build a new one."

They cleared the bunkhouse out. Charles had little in the world, which Bree found ironic because his family had enough money to buy the entire territory. Bree was able to stuff everything Charles owned into a pair of saddle bags, and Aunt Ginny and Temperance pulled sheets and blankets and pillows away from the bunks and hauled them to the main house.

Dusty said, "Will they be able to see this? With the snow comin' down so thick?"

Johnny said, "It's getting dark soon. The fire will look like a dull orange glow through the snow. It won't be visible from much more than a mile out, but I hope it's enough."

When the building was empty, what little daylight there was had faded to darkness.

"All right," Johnny said. "Let's hope this works."

He took a match to one mattress. The fire caught fast. It wasn't long before flames were dancing along the roof.

Bree was standing with Pa, Dusty and Jack a few yards back from the bunkhouse. Against the freezing winds of the storm, the heat of the fire felt good. But she was so filled with fear for Charles and Josh that she wasn't able to enjoy it.

If anyone had thought Pa's plan was a little excessive, Bree would have challenged them, because there were now three inches of snow on the ground and it was coming down faster than ever, and her brother and her man were both out there somewhere.

Bree would have stood out in the blizzard until she froze, but Pa ordered her inside. She removed her coat and stood in front of the fire with a cup of tea.

Temperance was pacing back and forth from the hearth to the front windows. She would look out a window, then come back toward the hearth.

Nina was on the sofa. She said, "This place is keeping out the wind real nice."

Bree nodded. "Pa built it tight."

But her mind was only partially on what she was saying.

The men were outside, making sure the fire didn't spread past the bunkhouse. Bree wondered what would happen if Charles and Josh weren't home by the time the fire was done. There was nothing left to burn.

But then she heard Pa's voice calling out from the porch. "Riders coming!"

Bree ran for the door. She didn't even bother to grab her coat.

6

CHARLES FELL out of the saddle, and Jack and Carter caught him. Josh tried to swing out of the saddle, but he ended up sliding off and Dusty tried to catch him. Both wound up in the snow.

"They're half-frozen," Johnny said. He had to call out over the roar of the wind. "Get 'em inside!"

Ginny opened the door and said, "Get 'em on the sofa. In front of the fire."

Charles and Josh were conscious and tried to make their legs work, but ultimately had to be dragged into the house.

Their coats were covered with ice and snow. Dusty and Haley tried to work the buttons of Josh's coat, but the buttons were under a layer of ice, so Dusty gave the coat a pull and tore the buttons loose. Jack and Carter were doing the same with Charles.

Bree and Temperance stood back. Bree had her hand over her mouth and tears were flowing. Temperance was doing the same.

Aunt Ginny said to them, "They'll be all right. I've been through this before. Remember when your Pa was caught in a blizzard that time, coming in from the range?"

Bree nodded. She remembered. She said to Temperance, "It was before you came to live with us."

Johnny pulled a glove from one of Josh's hands. "His fingers have frostbite. Probably Charles does, too. Likely in their toes, as well."

Ginny said to Sam, "Go get some buckets of snow. We'll have to warm their hands and feet gradually so they won't lose their fingers or toes."

Temperance said, "Snow?"

Ginny said, "You warm them up gradually. If you don't, tissue will die and gangrene will set in. First snow, then cold water, then room-temperature water. Then warm water. One step at a time."

Jack said to Sam, "There are buckets in the tool shed. Come on. I'll go with you."

A couple of hours later, Charles sat with a cup of hot

coffee in one hand and a blanket wrapped around his shoulders. Josh was beside him.

Charles said, "I still feel a little chilled. Isn't that strange?"

Josh shook his head. "It's normal, as frozen as we were."

Charles held out a hand and made a fist, and then opened his hand again. "My fingers hurt."

Josh said, "It's to be expected. We both had frostbite all the way to our knuckles."

Johnny was in a rocker. "My fingers still don't feel right, from that time I had frostbite. And that was maybe five years ago."

Bree sat on the arm of the sofa, and she reached down and pulled Charles in for a hug.

She said, "I was so afraid I'd lost you."

"I'll admit, I was a little worried for a minute or two, myself."

Temperance was on the sofa beside Josh. He opened the blanket and let her inside with him, and he wrapped an arm around her.

He was in a flannel shirt and jeans. He was wearing socks, but his boots were gone.

He said, "I'll miss that pair of boots."

Johnny said, "We had to cut 'em off. No other choice, or you would have lost your toes."

Josh grinned. "I'll choose my toes over a pair of boots, any day."

Josh had caught up with Charles at the line cabin. Old Ches and Kennedy had a stack of split wood and enough supplies for two weeks.

"We'll be all right here," Ches said. "We'll sit and feed the fire and talk about women and drink whiskey. We'll be fine."

Josh and Charles had then lit out, trying to race the storm back to the valley. The storm had won.

Josh had said to Pa, "That fire you started saved our lives. Visibility was so bad, if not for that fire, we might have ridden right on past the house and never even seen it. You wouldn't have found us till spring."

Pa said, "Such a thing has happened before, in these mountains."

Charles looked at Bree and said, "You crying?"

Bree wiped the tears away and shook her head no, but more tears followed.

Charles said, "There's no need to cry. Josh and I are all right."

Bree nodded. "I know."

Temperance and Bree looked over at each other. Temperance's face was wet, too. They both laughed.

7

CHRISTMAS MORNING, the place was alive with laughter and smiles. Santa Claus had left a pile of presents, and Cora and Jonathan stared with wonder at the sight of them.

Presents were opened. Dusty had a small wooden antelope Hunter had carved from a chunk of pinewood.

"Hunter," Dusty said. "I didn't know you could do work like this."

Hunter grinned. "I'm a man of mystery."

Carter gave Charles a revolver. It looked a little like a Smith and Wesson, but not quite.

Carter said, "A new shootin' iron for you. It's a Merwin-Hulbert. Forty-four-forty. It'll take the same cartridges your Winchester does. Let's hope you never have to use it."

Chen had a glass of eggnog with a touch of rum in it. "Everyone here. This is nice. They don't have Christmas in China, but I think maybe that should change."

When the presents were opened, Charles stood looking at the tree, with a glass of warm eggnog in one hand. Bree had both arms wrapped around him and her head was resting against his chest. He was too tall for her to reach his shoulder.

The storm had been three days ago and was followed by another. The snow had drifted up over the side of the house to completely cover the windows. Jack and Dusty had shoveled out a path to the outhouse, and then had gone out on snow shoes and come back with a deer.

Venison stew was simmering away on the stove, filling the house with a smell that made Bree's mouth water.

She said to Charles, "I'm just so glad you're home safe. Both of you."

Charles grinned. "That was three days ago. Aren't you ever going to put it behind you?"

She shook her head. "Never. I could have lost you so easily."

Aunt Ginny was walking past. She said, "You men put yourselves in danger and then when it's done, it's like it never happened. But for us women who are left behind here, always waiting and never knowing if you're coming back alive, we never really put it behind us."

That evening, with a fire roaring in the hearth, Aunt Ginny sat in her rocker by the fire, a glass of Chablis on an end table next to her. Johnny had taken his chair out to the cabin, so he sat on the sofa with Jessica beside him, and Cora was asleep in her lap. Bree sat on the floor in front of him.

Charles was leaning one elbow against the hearth, and in one hand was a glass of bourbon. Jack had gotten a bottle for Christmas and was sharing it. Jack sat at the foot of the hearth, and Nina was with him. Josh was sitting beside Bree with his back against the sofa and a glass in one hand, and Temperance was beside him. Uncle Joe was standing off behind the sofa with a glass of scotch. Everyone else was scattered about. Some were on pallets that had been pulled together with blankets and quilts on the parlor floor.

It was a sleepy time and a good time. Family and friends gathered all about.

Jessica leaned into Johnny and he put one arm around her and pulled her in closer.

Harlan Carter said from somewhere behind the sofa, "You sure built this place good, McCabe. The heat from that fire fills the whole room right good."

Johnny nodded. "The first winter we spent here, we had only the small cabin."

Ginny said, "Oh, I remember that winter all too well."

"What's now the kitchen," Johnny said, "was the cabin. It was what we built first. The boys were young, and Bree was just a little tyke."

Josh said, "She still is."

Bree elbowed him.

Joe said, "Them were the days. We had just ridden all the way up here from California and got the cabin built in time for the first snow."

Ginny said, "That seems so long ago, now."

She said as the thought occurred to her, "I remember when I first saw you, John, back in San Francisco. You didn't have your long, Shoshone hair back then."

Johnny nodded. "I wore it short like you, Jack, back then."

Jack was grinning. "Hard to imagine."

Joe said, "I remember that long ride we had 'cross country, just a few years before that. Just you, me and Matt.

Remember that?"

Johnny nodded. "So long ago. And yet, it seems like just yesterday in some ways."

Bree looked over her shoulder and back at her father. "That was when Grandpa was killed, right? And you and Uncle Joe and Uncle Matt came west looking for the killer."

Johnny nodded. "That's how it was."

Josh looked back at him. "That was when you first come west? Then when did you ride with the Texas Rangers?"

"That actually wasn't when I first came west. I had ridden with the Rangers a while before that."

Ginny said, "John, you've told your story in bits and pieces over the years, but have you ever told the children the whole thing? From start to finish?"

Johnny gave a look that said, *oh boy,* and said, "That's one long story."

"And a great way for us to spend a cold, winter's eve together."

Bree looked back at Johnny again. "Come on, Pa. Tell us."

Johnny looked over at Joe and said, "Where's Matt? He was a part of this, too."

Joe nodded his head toward the center of the room. "He's sawin' 'em off over there."

Johnny grinned. He didn't really want to talk about himself, or those days before Lura. And yet he found his thoughts drifting back to that time. Back when he was about the age of Josh and Dusty. He realized he wasn't very tired. Maybe he was in the mood for a long story, after all.

Dusty strolled over, a glass of scotch in one hand. He said, "What was it like back in those days, Pa?"

"Well, for one thing, the land was more open. More wild. The town of Cheyenne wasn't here, then. None of the railheads. The only real settlement north of Texas was Fort Laramie, and there wasn't much between the two. A few trading posts, and that was about it. The buffalo—there were so many of them. A herd could blacken the entire countryside. And the Indians. They were riding free, like they were meant to. The Lakota. The Cheyenne. The Shoshone."

Dusty said, "Were Uncle Matt and Joe with you in the Rangers?"

Joe shook his head, and Johnny said, "No. Uncle Matt served in the Navy. And Joe..." He looked over at Joe.

Joe said, "I was a scout for the Army out of Laramie."

Johnny knew those were hard days for Joe, and decided to let Joe say as much or as little as he wanted to. Joe said nothing more.

And so, Johnny began talking, telling about what life was like when he was with the Rangers. Chasing down Mexican border raiders, Comanches, Kiowas, and gangs of outlaws. And then after the Rangers, he had spent a few months roaming about the border towns, drinking too much tequila and generally getting into trouble.

"And then," he said, "I got a letter from Ma telling me Grams had died. I decided it was time to go home. Back to Pennsylvania."

"That's what we called our grandmother," Joe said. "Grams. I got a letter from Ma, too. So I decided to head home for a while. Visit the family."

"And we met up on the trail."

And everyone sat and listened while the fire roared in the hearth, and the icy winter winds shook the window panes. They sat and listened while Johnny talked of a time long ago, when he was young and the land was wild.

PART TWO

Returning Home

8

Kansas Territory, 1856

JOHNNY McCABE REINED up near a small gulley where a stream cut through. It was August and he found the stream to be little more than a trickle, which was what he expected. But the banks were high which told him the water ran deep in the spring.

A few small trees grew. Alder and some birch. The sun was trailing low in the sky, and Johnny thought this was a good enough place to camp for the night.

The water in the tiny stream wasn't anything he would drink. Shallow surface water wasn't. But it would be fine for coffee.

Johnny had ridden all the way from Texas, and he did so without a pack horse. All of his supplies were rolled up in his bedroll or tucked into his saddle bags. A shirt and an extra pair of pants and some ammunition. A coffee pot and a couple bags of coffee. Three or four extra bandanas—an old Texas Ranger he knew said always carry extra bandanas. A few other things, including two cans of beans. He didn't need a lot of food supplies because he could shoot his supper better than any man he knew.

He was twenty years old, and his jaw was covered with sparse, fine hair. He was in a range shirt that had been blue when he first got it, but the sun and dust had turned it to a sort of desert gray. He wore a flat-brimmed, gray sombrero and cavalry pants. Holstered at each hip was a Colt .44 revolver, and an eight-shot Colt revolving rifle was tucked into the saddle boot. His guns were all Texas Ranger issue.

The horse he rode was a gray stallion that stood a little over fourteen hands. Caught wild by a mustanger a year ago, and Johnny acquired it from him in a poker game. It was only half broken and the mustanger had been glad to part with it, but Johnny liked the horse's spirit.

He called the horse Bravo because the poker game had

been in a cantina in a small town that was on the Mexican side of the border. The Mexicans called the Rio Grande the *Rio Bravo*.

Johnny picketed Bravo and then gathered some birch sticks from a deadfall to start a small fire. Then he rubbed down Bravo, which he was sure was Bravo's favorite part of the day.

As it grew dark, he dug into his saddle bags for a can of beans and a skillet, and he set about cooking himself some supper.

He had taken a shot at a rabbit earlier in the day, and it was one of those rare times that he missed. Nothing he was happy about. He would have to do with beans tonight.

He sat by the fire, stirring the beans every so often and waiting for the coffee to boil. He was thinking about home, about the farmhouse back in Pennsylvania. He hadn't seen Ma and Pa in three years. He had written letters and they had written back, but it took months to get a letter from Texas all the way to Pennsylvania.

When he got the last letter, four months ago, they told him Grams had died and he decided it was time to head back. At least for a visit.

He loved Texas. The place had taken hold of his heart and was threatening to never let go. He doubted Ma and Pa would understand, because the farm had been in the McCabe family for three generations and they couldn't imagine calling any other piece of land home. Pa had said once that the family was as tied to the land as the land was to the family. He recommended his sons go out into the world to learn, to gain experience, but it was always with the idea that one day they would return to build their lives in Pennsylvania.

Johnny knew when he got home, Ma and Pa would want him to stay. And he wondered if it would be too easy to do what they wanted, to fall back into the life of a farmer. If once he was back on the farm, his years in Texas would begin to seem like a fading dream. As he sat with the fire crackling before him and the beans warming in a skillet and the coffee pot boiling, he wondered if he would really ever see Texas again.

He didn't stare directly into the fire. One of the first things he had learned with the Rangers was to look away from the flames. The moment or two it would take for your eyes to adjust to the darkness was all a Comanche would need to come up on your fire and stick a knife into you.

Not that he expected to meet a Comanche here in eastern Kansas, but he didn't want to develop careless habits.

Johnny had picketed Bravo, and the horse was standing with his head drooping. But then Bravo lifted his head quick and looked off to the darkness. Something was out there. Probably just a coyote, but Johnny had learned with the Rangers not to take chances. He slid a revolver from his holster.

Then a man called out, "Hello, the fire!"

Johnny thought he recognized the voice. A voice he hadn't heard since he had left home. But no, it couldn't be.

He called back, "Come on in."

He watched as a man came in on foot, leading a horse. When the man stepped into the firelight, Johnny saw he had dark hair dropping to his shoulders and a bushy beard that swallowed the lower part of his face. He was in a buckskin shirt and a wide-brimmed cavalry hat that was faded and tattered. The buckskin shirt fell to his hips and he had a belt around his middle, and a pistol was tucked into the front of the belt. He wore cavalry pants and buckskin boots. Sticking up from the top of one boot was the hilt of a knife.

The man had changed a lot, but Johnny would know him anywhere. He knew the slope of his shoulders and the way he walked. You don't forget a man you grew up with.

Johnny rose to his feet. He said, "Joe."

The man stopped and squinted. "Johnny? That you?"

They ran toward each other, first shaking hands and then hugging.

Joe said, "Let me tend to my outfit, and we can talk. That coffee you got goin' smells mighty good, too."

After Joe had stripped off the saddle and picketed his horse, he sat down to some beans. The coffee was ready so Johnny poured him some.

"What're the odds of meetin' you out here?" Joe said.

Johnny shook his head and shrugged his shoulders. "I wouldn't even dare guess. What brings you here? Last I knew you were stationed up at Laramie."

Joe said, "Left the Army a while back. Lived with the Cheyenne for a time. Then I got a letter from back home telling me Grams had died."

"Yeah. I got one, too."

"Thought maybe it's time I went back and saw the folks."

Johnny nodded. "Been havin' the same thoughts."

"Look at us, though." Joe grinned beneath his beard. "Wonder if they'll even recognize us."

Johnny wondered at Joe's beard. Johnny was two years older than Joe, but Johnny's beard was still thin and wispy.

Johnny said, "I wonder if the old farm will feel like home."

Joe was silent a moment, then he said, "I been through some hard times. I wonder if any place'll ever feel like home again."

Johnny waited, but Joe said no more.

Before they had come west, Johnny's little brother was never reluctant to confide in him. But they were no longer farm boys, and Johnny realized Joe was no longer his little brother. They were now men of the West.

Johnny was a seasoned tracker and scout, and people were calling him a gunfighter. Joe was very evidently a frontiersman, a mountain man. And it was not the way of men of the West to pester each other with questions, so Johnny asked none and Joe said no more about it.

After they ate, Joe climbed into his bedroll and was soon asleep. Johnny unrolled his own blankets. Johnny had seen some men use a saddle for a pillow, but he seldom did. He pulled a jacket from his saddle bags and rolled it up, and he would use it as a pillow.

He left his boots on, something he had learned down in the border country. The last thing you wanted was to step into a boot in the morning and find a scorpion there waiting for you. You could always shake your boots out first, if you remembered. But he knew a Ranger who had forgotten to, and paid the price. The man couldn't step down on his foot for days, and he had cramping in his stomach and spent a full day in the outhouse, unloading from both ends.

Johnny unbuckled his gunbelt and set it on the ground beside his blankets, and then crawled in.

Then he drew a pistol and held it in one hand as he rested his head back on his jacket.

He looked up at the stars, and as he waited for sleep to take him, he wondered about Joe. How different he was from the last time Johnny had seen him. And how different he himself probably was now. How different they would seem to Ma and Pa.

And he thought about the girl he had left behind, and wondered if she would still be there.

9

JOHNNY AND JOE RODE overland, not taking any trails. Sometimes they rode in silence, and other times they chatted.

Johnny told him of his time with the Texas Rangers. Chasing Mexican border raiders, and how he one time made an impossible shot with his Colt rifle, ricocheting a bullet off a rock to plug a raider who thought he was safely behind cover.

"Naw, you didn't," Joe said.

Johnny nodded. "Like playing pool."

"And you got him?"

"Plugged him in the back of the head."

Joe shook his head. "If that don't beat all."

And Johnny talked of his life after the Rangers, drifting from one border town to another. One particular gunfight he got into.

"I knew he could clear leather faster than I could, so as he began drawing, I jumped to one side and did a headfirst somersault. He missed, and I came up shooting. Got covered in mud, but I plugged him."

Joe chuckled. "People talk about that kind of thing, though. A story like that grows, from one saloon to another. Among cattle camps and Army posts. I heard talk of you, you know, all the way to Laramie."

Johnny blinked with surprise.

Joe said, "Oh, yeah. People asked me if I was *the* Johnny McCabe's brother. They were calling you the *Gunman of the Rio Grande*."

"They weren't."

Joe nodded. "Yes, sir. Gunman of the Rio Grande. That's you."

Johnny rode along in silence for a while, then said, "I don't know if I like the idea of people talking about me, especially all the way off in Nebraska Territory. What I did was what I did at the time, but I like to think what I'm doing affects only me and the people involved."

Joe shook his head. "Life is like a still pond. You drop a stone in the water, you don't know how far the ripples will reach."

Johnny gave his brother a look. When they were kids, it wasn't unusual for their brother Matt to launch into poetry or philosophy. Matt was always the silver-tongued one. But Joe was quiet, and when he spoke it was usually with few words.

Joe saw Johnny's look and chuckled. "I got that from an old Cheyenne shaman I knew."

They came out of the woods a hundred miles south of the farm, and onto a trail that cut through a pass between two hills. The hills were wooded with maples, birch and alders.

"Might as well follow this along for a while," Johnny said. "Normally I like to travel overland and not by trails. Makes me feel more free, I guess. But now I'm thinkin' I'd like to get to the farm. See Ma and Pa. We'll travel faster if we take the trail."

Joe nodded. "Yeah. Me too."

The trail took them to a stretch of land where the hills were clear-cut and grassy. Cows were grazing and two silos stood tall in the distance.

Johnny said, "This land is so different than Texas. I had almost forgotten."

Joe nodded. "More humid."

He had already pulled off his buckskin shirt and was riding in a range shirt that was a faded gray.

The trail topped a hill, and down below and a little ways ahead, they saw a man walking. He was tall and thin and was in dark clothes, and carrying some sort of heavy looking pack over his shoulder.

"Don't look like no farmer," Joe said.

Johnny shrugged. "I'm not sure what he looks like."

They rode ahead, and as they drew closer, Johnny realized he recognized the man's gait and the set of his shoulders.

"Could it be?" Johnny said.

"Cain't be. But I think it is."

They reined up beside the man afoot. He looked up at them. He was taller than either of them would be, were they standing on the ground. His shoulders were narrower, but not frail. He was in a dark blue navy shirt and matching pants that flared wide at the cuffs. He wore a dark cap, and the pack over his shoulder turned out to be a duffel bag.

"Matt?" Johnny said.

Matt squinted up at them, not sure just what he was

seeing for a moment.

Then he said, "Johnny? Joe? Is that you?"

Joe was grinning beneath his beard, and tossed a glance at Johnny.

Joe said, "You never know what you might happen upon, on the trail."

Matt was giving a wide grin. "Why, I don't suppose you do. You two look like hooligans from the Wild West."

"Well," Johnny said, "I suppose that's just what we are."

Johnny and Joe swung out of the saddle and gave Matt hugs and handshakes and slaps on the back.

Matt said, "What are you both doing here?"

"We both got letters sayin' Grams died," Johnny said. "Decided it was time to visit home."

Matt nodded, now a little somber. "Yeah. I got a letter like that from Ma."

Johnny said, "So, we decided it was time to come east and visit the family."

Johnny looked at Joe. "Well, we can't just leave this Navy swabby on foot here in these hills. This ain't really a frontier anymore, but it's still some pretty remote country."

Joe squinted one eye and rubbed his beard. "Do you suppose a swabby might be able to sit on the back of a horse without falling off?"

Johnny said. "We've got to try, I suppose. We can't just leave him out here."

Matt said, "Funny, you two. I should be able to sit a horse just fine. I've been out at sea for the past three years. You ever hear of sea legs?"

He handed his duffel bag up to Joe. Johnny then pulled a foot out of the stirrup and Matt pushed a foot in, and then took Johnny's hand and swung up and onto the back of the horse, behind the saddle.

To Matt's credit, he knew which foot to push into the stirrup so he wouldn't spin around as he swung into the saddle and wind up sitting backwards on the horse. Johnny had seen it done before.

Johnny looked back at him but didn't realize he was grinning until Matt said, "What are you laughing at?"

"Nothing. I'm just glad to see you know which end the head is on."

"Hey, don't you laugh at me until you can tell me

which end of a ship is the bow and which the stern."
 Joe said, "Come on. Let's ride. We got us a lot of miles ahead of us."

10

THEY CAMPED for the night off the trail, near the edge of the woods.

Matt said, "Elizabethville is only a few more miles down the road. I wish we had money for a room."

"Not me," Johnny said as he unrolled his blankets. "I haven't slept in a bedroom for three years. Every single night has been under the open sky. Or when it was raining, in a tent or under a wagon. I don't know if I'd feel comfortable with a roof over my head."

Joe nodded. "Same here. I think a room would make me feel all closed in."

With the fire crackling low and stars coming to life overhead, Johnny walked off to the edge of the camp and stood, looking off toward the road.

Matt walked up to stand beside him. He had rolled a cigarette and the smoke wafted gently past Johnny.

Matt said, "Anything wrong?"

Johnny shook his head. "Not really. It's just that this would be a terrible place to camp, back in Texas. We got probably five hundred feet to the road, and then it's open all the way back another couple hundred yards to some woods out yonder. We're wide open here. People will be able to see our fire for miles."

Matt slapped Johnny on the back of the shoulder. "We're not in the Wild West anymore, little brother."

Johnny nodded. "Ain't that the truth. I don't know if that's a good thing, or not."

Johnny turned and walked back into the camp. Matt stood looking at him, wondering exactly what Johnny meant. It wasn't his words, but his tone of voice.

Johnny fished through his saddle bags and pulled out a can of beans. He said, "Joe and I were busy talking today and we didn't shoot us any supper. 'Fraid it's just beans tonight."

Matt watched Joe dig out a long wooden spindle of some sort and sit by the fire. Joe then pulled from the fire a twig that had a tiny flame dancing on the end, and brought the fire to a small cup-shaped section toward the end of the spindle.

Joe said, "Not to complain about them beans, but I

have to admit, I cain't wait to taste Ma's cookin' again."

Matt was watching Joe curiously. He said, "Just what is that thing you're holding?"

Joe held it up. "A pipe. A Cheyenne pipe."

"Cheyenne?"

He nodded. "An Indian tribe I trucked with for a while. A long while, actually."

"You *trucked* with them?"

Joe nodded. "Lived with 'em for a time."

Matt gave his brother a long look. "You lived with Indians?"

Joe nodded again. "Hunted with 'em. Fought with 'em. Almost married one of 'em."

"But aren't they..." Matt was trying to be polite, but he was a little horrified and was having a hard time keeping it from showing. "But aren't they savages? I mean, do they even cook their food?"

Joe chuckled and looked over at Johnny.

Johnny said, "In a lot of ways, they live a cleaner, truer lifestyle than we do. I've met some Indians. Comanche and Kiowa, mostly. Fought some of 'em. But I've known many white men who strike me as being just as savage, or even more so."

Joe took a draft of smoke and let it drift from his mouth. "Highly religious folks. Clean, too. Washed in a river or lake every single morning. Not many white folks can claim that."

Matt gave Joe another long look. Johnny thought maybe Matt wasn't sure if Joe was joking. Johnny chuckled and went back to heating beans in the skillet.

Matt said, "Everything I've ever heard about Indians..."

Johnny shook his head. "Hearsay is not the same thing as learning. Didn't Pa use to say that?"

Joe said, "Believe he did."

"I can't speak for the Cheyenne, but I found the Comanche and the Kiowa much different than anything I had ever heard about them."

Matt said, "Cheyenne? Kiowa? Aren't they all the same people?"

Joe shook his head. "No, sir. Every bit as different as them people in Europe."

Johnny said, "The Germans, the French, the Swiss. They all live on a tract of land not much bigger than

Nebraska Territory. And yet look how different those cultures are."

"But," Matt said. "It's not the same."

"I've found people are about the same, anywhere. They might dress different and have different languages, but they all laugh when they find something funny. Cry when they're sad. They love their children about the same way. They all need food and shelter."

"But," Matt said, "it couldn't have been the same, living with them. You were an outsider. Their ways are different. Primitive."

Joe shook his head. "I weren't an outsider. I joined their tribe."

Matt was left staring, speechless.

But Johnny said, as he stirred the beans, "That so?"

Joe nodded.

Johnny said, "An old scout I knew lived with the Apache one time and joined them. Told me a lot about it. A lot of folks call him Apache Jim."

Joe nodded again. "Apache Jim Layton. Heard the name a time or two. At least once his name was tied together with yours. Is it true what they said, 'bout you and Apache Jim riding into Mexico after border raiders to rescue a woman that got herself captured?"

Johnny nodded. "Yeah. About six months ago."

"They say you shot ten Mexican raiders with eight shots."

Johnny shook his head. "Got five, with four shots. They were on horseback, and when one fell he knocked the one beside him off his horse, too. I was using that Colt rifle in my saddle."

"They also say you got ten Comanches once with ten shots."

Johnny shook his head again, as he stirred the beans. "Five with five shots. That was nothing, really. I was standing on the ground and they were riding down on me. I was still with the Rangers, then. A fellow Ranger was wounded and on the ground behind me. I just drew and shot. No harder than shooting cans off a rail fence. Folks make more out of it than they need to."

Joe grinned. "Folks are talking about you all the way to Laramie."

Matt was listening, but saying nothing. Johnny

thought his big brother was finding himself feeling lost.

Johnny said, "A lot has happened, Matt. We're not the same boys who grew up on the farm beside you, all those years ago."

Matt nodded. He then sat on the ground beside Joe and draped his arms across his knees and looked into the fire. Johnny thought Matt looked a little distant.

Johnny noticed a difference in his two brothers. Matt, who sat on the ground like it was something new to him. And Joe, who sat cross-legged on the ground making it look like the most natural thing in the world.

After a while, Matt said, "I'm not the same boy, either."

And he let it go at that. Matt had always been the one to talk, to express his thoughts. But now he was strangely silent. Johnny decided to leave him alone, following the way of men of the West.

The three sat in silence while the fire crackled away, until Johnny said, "Beans're done."

Joe said, "Dish'm out."

Matt took a couple of blankets from his duffel bag and spread them out on the grass.

He said, "I don't know how well my back's going to take to sleeping out on the open ground."

Johnny had already stretched out. He had pulled a jacket from his saddle bags and rolled it up and was using it as a pillow. His gunbelt was beside him.

He said, "I prefer to sleep on the ground, under God's open sky. I've come to feel the most at home sleeping this way. I haven't slept on a mattress since I don't know when."

Joe was tucking his pipe back into his saddle bags. He said, "The closest I've come to sleeping under a roof in years is in a Cheyenne lodge."

Matt said, "So, tell us what it was like to sleep in a lodge that belonged to an Indian."

Joe was silent a moment. Joe's voice was deeper than it had been when Johnny last saw him and he had a wild juniper bush of a beard, and he had picked up a bit of an accent. He said *cain't* instead of *can't*. But one thing that hadn't changed was he had been a boy of few words, and now he was a man of few words.

Johnny had learned there was often deep meaning in Joe's silence. You learned to read that silence, and Johnny was catching sadness in it now.

Then Joe said, "The lodge was mine."

Matt propped himself up on one elbow. "The Indian lodge was yours?"

Johnny had a feeling Matt was going to pursue it further, and that Joe didn't want it pursued, so he said, "Let's get some sleep. I'd like to make it to the farm by tomorrow."

Matt settled into his blankets. Joe climbed into his own.

Then a stick broke somewhere in the darkness beyond the fire. Johnny sat up and a pistol was in his hand.

Matt was looking at Johnny like he had lost his mind. "It's probably nothing," Matt said.

Johnny held up his hand for silence.

Joe hadn't drawn any weapons, but he was sitting up in his blankets and listening.

Johnny looked over at where the horses were picketed nearby. Joe's horse was looking over toward the woods, but then it apparently decided there was nothing to worry about and went back to dozing. Bravo hadn't looked up at all.

Johnny looked at Joe and nodded. Joe settled back into his blankets and Johnny did the same.

"What's going on?" Matt said. "There was nothing out there. Maybe a small animal, but that's all."

Johnny said, "Once you've been shot at a few times, I guess you just get a little jumpy."

Now Johnny had Matt's full attention. "You've been shot at?"

Johnny didn't really want to talk about it, but said, "We've talked about some of the men I've shot. But sometimes they tend to shoot back. We chased lots of men, when I was with the Texas Rangers. Mexican border raiders. Outlaws. Occasional renegade Indians."

Joe said, "Guess they haven't heard of the legend, out to sea."

Matt was now intrigued. "Legend? What legend?"

Johnny said to Joe, "Will you stop?"

Joe chuckled, but said nothing more.

Matt said, "I have a gun, too, you know. A Colt thirty-six. It's in my duffel bag."

Joe said, "Won't do you no good there."

"Well, I don't expect to need it here. We're not on the

high seas, and we're not in your Wild West."

Joe said, "I ain't packin' mine away."

Johnny slid his gun back into its holster, but he kept it within reach. "Old habits die hard, I guess."

11

THE FOLLOWING MORNING, Matt rode with Joe, and Johnny had the duffel bag tied to the back of his saddle. It rode atop his bedroll.

Fences lined the trail, and at either side corn fields stretched away into the distance. Occasionally the boys saw a farmhouse, along with a barn and a small grouping of silos.

The afternoon passed and the sun fell below some sharp ridges to the west.

Matt said, "Want to make camp?"

Johnny shook his head. "We're too close to the farm."

Joe looked over at Johnny and said, "Let's keep on ridin'."

"I don't know about you boys," Matt said, "but I've been out to sea for three years and not used to sitting on a horse. My backside is about done for."

Johnny said, "You'll have time to recover, once we're at the farm."

Joe grinned, and they continued on.

The sun was soon gone, and the sky overhead was darkening when they topped the crest of a hill, and they could see a lighted window below.

Johnny reined up and looked down at the house. Joe reined up beside him. It wasn't fully dark yet and they could see the house and the yard.

"There it is, boys," Matt said, from over Joe's shoulder. "First time we've seen home in three years."

The house looked like it always had. Two floors, a peaked roof. A chimney made of brick. White clapboards. An old oak tree stood tall twenty feet from the kitchen doorway. A wooden swing had been suspended from the tree by ropes when Johnny was a child. He and Matt and Joe had climbed the tree more times than they could ever count.

The house and the yard didn't seem to have changed, and yet, Johnny had been gone so long that the daily sense of familiarity you have when you live in an area was gone. In a way, Johnny felt like he was looking at it for the first time.

"What do you think we'll find?" Johnny said.

Matt shrugged. "Ma and Pa, I suppose. A little older than we remember them. But otherwise, not changed much, I suspect. Life here in farming country doesn't change much.

One day to another, one year to another, is pretty much the same."

They were silent a moment.

Then Joe said, "Maybe they haven't changed, but we have."

Johnny nodded. "I wonder if we'll seem like strangers."

"Only one way to find out."

Matt nodded. "Indeed."

And still they hesitated.

Matt said, "It has been said you can never really go home again, once you've been away for a while. You've changed, but the people have also changed. It'll never entirely be the way you remember it, and you'll not be the way they remember you."

Joe pulled off his hat and shook out his long hair. It had become matted down under his hat. "The thought of everyone lookin' at me like I'm a stranger won't feel very good."

Matt shook his head. "No, indeed."

Johnny thought of Becky Drummond. The girl he had left behind. The first girl he had ever kissed.

He had kissed many in the years since, in the back rooms of saloons throughout southern Texas and in Mexico. In fact, he had done more than just kissing. But it had all been in the throes of tequila-induced passion. When he had kissed Becky, there had been an element of sweetness to it. A feeling of adventure. A feeling of stepping into territory he had never before been. Like he was some sort of pioneer.

She had been fifteen. When he saw her in his mind, he saw her with freckled cheeks and a long brown braid. She had green eyes that would come alive with mischief, like when she suggested they sneak off behind the barn at a community picnic, which was where the first kiss happened.

But she was no longer fifteen. A girl can change a lot in three years. She was probably not so much a girl now, but a woman. Would she be the same? Would she still look at him like she did then? Or was she married by now? For all Johnny knew, she could be a mother. In his letters home, he had never asked about her and Ma had never commented.

He thought about the changes in himself. He had been a farm boy when he left. Now he had fought border raiders, outlaws and Comanches. He was a gunfighter they were talking about in saloons throughout south Texas, and according to Joe, all the way to Nebraska Territory. He wondered if there was any of that farm boy left in him. He wondered what Ma would think of that. If she would be ashamed of what he had become. He was starting to wonder if he really wanted to find out.

Maybe coming home was a bad idea, he thought. But it was too late, now.

A dog began barking from somewhere outside the farmhouse.

"Well," Johnny said, "they know someone's here now."

Matt nodded. "They'll be expecting us. Or me, at least. I wrote to tell them I'd be coming."

"I suppose we might as well ride on down," Joe said.

Johnny gave a reluctant nod of his head and nudged his horse forward, and Joe fell into place behind him.

12

THE DOG CAME RUNNING out of the darkness, up the trail to meet the riders. Some sort of lab mongrel. Johnny remembered the dog well.

Johnny reined up and swung out of the saddle.

"Ol' Jeb," he said, and the dog's barks of warning became yips of delight. The dog was wagging his tail so hard his entire back end was swinging back and forth.

Johnny knelt and the dog ran toward him. The dog flicked a lick at Johnny's face, then Johnny began rubbing the dog's head and neck. The dog's tail was fanning away.

Johnny said, "I see you're still around, you old coon dog."

Old Jeb was a little heavier than Johnny remembered, the skin around the neck and chest a little looser. Three years can be a long time in the life of a dog. The same for a person too, he supposed.

"Come on, Jeb," Johnny said, swinging back into the saddle. "Let's go see the folks."

The dog, yipping and prancing, led them the remainder of the way down the hill to the farmhouse.

Matt dropped down from Joe's horse, and stood with his feet apart and his knees stiff. He said "I don't think I'll be able to walk for a week. I hurt in places I didn't know I even had."

The old farmhouse had a front porch that overlooked the yard, and Johnny and Joe tethered their horses to the railing. Johnny climbed the steps to the porch and took off his hat, and he raised his right fist to knock on the door.

Before his knuckles could make contact, the door opened and a man stood in the glow of a kerosene lamp. His hair was now completely white and the flesh under the jaw looser than Johnny remembered, and trailing from the eyes were more lines than what had been there three years ago. But he was the same man Johnny remembered.

"Pa," Johnny said, extending his hand.

Thomas McCabe ignored his son's hand and pulled him in for a hug.

A woman spoke from behind Pa. "John?"

Johnny looked past Pa to see Ma, her auburn hair now streaked with white and her face rounder than it had once

been.
　　Tears streamed down her cheeks as she looked at her son, and Johnny went to give her a hug.
　　Matt and Joe were with Pa, joining in one big three-way hug. Then they went to Ma. She threw her arms around Matt's neck and then turned her attention to Joe. She gave him a hug, and then stepped back and reached a hand up to his bearded face.
　　"Don't they have razors in the West?" was the first thing she said, and the boys and their Pa broke out laughing.
　　A voice came from the doorway to the parlor. "Johnny! Matt! Joe!"
　　The voice was deep, the voice of a man, and Johnny didn't recognize it. He looked to see a young man standing there, almost as tall as he was and with a crop of wild red hair and a freckled nose and long arms and big hands.
　　Johnny said, "Luke?"
　　The boy smiled, and extended his hand to his brother. Johnny grasped the hand, pleased with the strength of his little brother's grip, then pulled him in for a hug.
　　"You were just a little kid when I left," Johnny said.
　　Luke nodded. "Now I'm almost a man."
　　Johnny looked his brother in the eye. "No *almost* about it."

　　Johnny removed his gunbelt, and slung it over one corner of the twin bed. The same bed he had slept in as a boy.
　　Ma had stared at his guns and he knew she didn't like the sight of them, but she had said nothing about them. Joe's pistol was tucked into the front of his belt, and if she had looked at it with concern, Johnny didn't see it. But she looked at his guns with a little furrow between her brows, which meant she was worried but trying not to comment. Maybe it wasn't so much that Johnny was wearing guns, but that he wore them like they were a part of him.
　　Maybe Ma was right to look at these guns the way she did, he thought. They were in a way kind of symbolic of the changes in him. Changes he was sure she wouldn't like. Changes he wasn't sure he liked.
　　He peeled off his shirt and stepped out of his pants. Wearing only his long handled union suit, he climbed beneath the covers of his bed.

He had thought the bed might feel like it always did. Like it was his. And yet it felt somehow different. Alien.

On the other side of the room was Matt's bed. Matt was under the covers and already snoring away.

He and Matt had shared this room as children. Joe and Luke shared another.

Johnny thought the room hadn't changed much. He expected the room to have been closed up, or to have been used for storage. But the beds were freshly made and waiting for them, as though they hadn't been gone three years. The furniture was dusted and the floor swept.

"Ma has kept this room ready for you and Matt ever since you left," Luke had said when Johnny stood in the doorway, looking at the old room. "Pa said she shouldn't bother keeping it up because you three wouldn't be home for a while, but she said she wanted your beds ready in case you came home unannounced. She said it wouldn't do for a boy to return home and not have his bed ready for him."

Johnny pulled the covers to his chest. As his head sunk into the pillow, he looked up at the exposed timbers of the room's ceiling. Moonlight crept in through the window and created shadows that filled in the gaps between the timbers.

Johnny drew in a long breath, savoring the scents. Smoke, from the wood stove in the kitchen downstairs, and a smell of dry wood from the floorboards. All as it had been years ago. Even the sounds were the same. An occasional creak of the ceiling overhead. Matt sawing 'em off in the bed across the room. And yet, something felt wrong.

Maybe he was what was wrong, he thought. Maybe he had killed too many men, had been shot at too many times. Had drained too many bottles of tequila and consorted with too many women his mother would have turned pale at the thought of. He had slept too many nights listening for any sound in the night that might indicate a Comanche was sneaking up on him. He had played cards and swilled whiskey and tequila with hard men. Enough years of this and you start to become like these men.

He was sure the farm boy he had once been was still there, buried somewhere deep inside him. He just wondered if it was possible for this boy to ever again rise to the surface.

Johnny turned over on his side and closed his eyes. He tried not to think about Becky Drummond, but he had to

45

admit, the thought of seeing her again scared him every bit as much as the thought of a Comanche sneaking up on him.

Johnny waited for sleep to take him, but it didn't. He became aware of an uneasiness, and he knew what it was. It wasn't the unfamiliarity of his own bed, or even the thought of Becky Drummond.

He climbed out of bed and grabbed a wooden upright chair from the corner and placed it by the headboard. Then he grabbed one of his pistols and placed it on the chair. Now, as he stretched out in bed, it would be within reach.

Old Jeb came walking over, his head hanging like a dog's head will when he's concerned. He curled up beside the bed. Johnny reached down and scratched him behind the ears.

"It's mighty good to see you again, old boy," Johnny said.

The dog had been like a friend when Johnny was growing up. Always at his side. The dog belonged to the family, but somehow it was Johnny the dog seemed to take to the most. And here the dog was, once again at his side. At least that much hadn't changed.

13

JOE CAME DOWNSTAIRS for breakfast a changed man. The beard was now gone, and he had used scissors and given his hair an improvised cut. His hair now fell in uneven lines to his collar.

With his beard gone, Joe looked a lot like Johnny. Except Joe was a little taller, his jaw was a little stronger, and his hair was a deep brown where Johnny's was more auburn.

"Well," Johnny said with a taunting smile. "You look almost human."

Matt said, "I had thought our little brother was somewhere underneath all that fur."

Johnny and Matt were sitting at the table, taking their old places across from each other as though it were somehow written in stone that when in this house, you sit in these designated places. Pa was at the head of the table, and Ma sat across from him.

Ma said, "Now boys, leave your brother alone."

Joe pulled out a chair beside Johnny, and sat.

Matt said, "Is this the first time you've shaved in three years?"

Joe shook his head. "I always kept shaved when I was with the Cheyenne. Otherwise they call you *dog face*."

He gave a quick glance to Johnny, like he was wondering if he should have said that. Pa gave a glance to Ma—they seemed to have no idea what he was talking about. Johnny just gave a slight nod to Joe and said nothing.

Ma had prepared eggs, bacon and toast, and a coffee pot was hissing away on the stove.

"Ma," Joe said, "I ain't smelled anything this good in I don't know how long. Three years, I guess. You can smell this food all the way upstairs."

He reached for some bacon.

"Josiah," she said, "we still wait for the blessing."

He stopped and glanced once at Johnny. Joe had mentioned as they rode that he had taken most of his meals for the past three years in front of a fire, roasting venison or rabbit on a wooden spit. He hadn't sat at a table and said a blessing for so long, it felt alien to him. He had done Cheyenne prayer songs, but not a traditional, white-man blessing. Johnny realized his brother felt as out of place here as he did.

They all joined hands, and Pa spoke in a deep baritone that filled the room. Johnny thought it could have filled a theater.

"Dear Lord, we humbly thank Thee for the blessings Thou hast so generously bestowed upon us, and for bringing our sons home safely to us. And for this wonderful meal thou hast provided for us, and for Ma, the incredible woman who did the cookin'. Amen."

"Oh, Thomas," Ma said with a smile, embarrassed to have been mentioned by name in prayer.

Johnny hoped to one day find a woman who could love him like Ma loved Pa. His thoughts were brought back to Becky Drummond.

Johnny had reluctantly left his guns upstairs. This was the first time he had gone so great a distance without them strapped to his hips in three years. He had felt strangely off balance as he walked down the stairs. His steps felt unnaturally light. A gunbelt with two pistols can be heavier than people realize. But even without his guns, he couldn't help but wonder if the changes in him would be evident by the way he carried himself, the things he said. Even the look in his eye. He wondered how it would feel if Becky looked at him like he was a stranger.

He had never mentioned Becky in his letters to Ma because he was never one to want to discuss his personal feelings, but as he sat at the table this morning, he considered asking about her. Trying to find some way to slip a question about her into conversation without it seeming obvious. But he knew Ma had liked Becky and Johnny didn't want her getting any thoughts about grandchildren. Ma was one to forever put the cart before the horse. And he knew his brothers would have too much fun taunting him about it. So he pushed the thought from his mind and decided to focus on the breakfast Ma had made.

"I will say, Ma," he said, "in all my wanderin's throughout Texas, I never found anyone who could cook up bacon like you can."

She gave the smile all mothers give when their children like their cooking. "I'm just glad you're home, John. Not wandering through Texas anymore. And I'm glad your brothers are home, too."

The door opened and Luke stepped in. He had been

out feeding the chickens and slopping the pigs. His sleeves were rolled up and there was some color in his cheeks. It was still a little cool outside this morning. The month was May, and the days could become downright hot in the Pennsylvania foothills, but the nights and early mornings could still make a man want a jacket.

Luke said, "I hope you boys ain't eating all that bacon yourself."

He sat down and began scooping bacon onto his plate, and a couple scoops of scrambled eggs. The plate of bacon was now empty.

Pa said, "Eat up boys. We have a big day ahead of us."

"Now, Thomas," Ma said. "The boys have just gotten in. They might want to rest up a little. Don't go putting them to work right off."

"No, that's all right," Johnny said. "I don't mind pitching in. I've been away from the farm for three years. It'll be good to get my hands dirty."

It would also give him a chance to focus his mind on something other than how much of a stranger, an outsider, he felt in the place that used to be home.

Matt said, "Speak for yourself. I'm still sore from sitting on the back of that horse."

Joe said, a grin cracking to life at one corner of his mouth, "It'll be good for Matt to do some real work. All that sailin' around on a boat can make a man soft."

Matt held one hand out before him, so Joe could see the palm. "Look at those callouses. You don't get that lollygagging around. Working on a ship is real work, boy."

Joe threw a wink at Luke from across the table and said, "Sure it is. I bet they worked you right hard."

Luke was giving a wide smile. He glanced at Pa, who was chewing a mouthful of eggs. Pa returned the smile back to him. It was good to hear the banter about the table again.

"Hey, Johnny," Luke said. "You tell 'em. Workin' on a boat ain't men's work."

Johnny thought it was good to hear the voices of his brothers as they prodded each other, like they had in the old days. But he still couldn't shake the sad feeling he had deep inside because he felt like a stranger in the place that had once been his home.

He decided to pitch in a little. Might make him feel a little less like a stranger.

He said, "I knew me a gambler once who got fearsome calluses on his hands from all the cards he played. But he never did get out of a chair."

Matt looked at his brother with raised brows, as if to say, *What, you too?* Then he rested an elbow on the table and pointed a finger at Johnny. "I saw that stack of wood outside, waiting to be sawed into stove lengths. Pa, you still have two buck saws?"

Pa nodded. "Sure do."

"Then, little brother, I'll match you log for log, and then some."

Johnny said, "What's the winner get?"

Matt held up both hands. "The glory of knowing he won."

Johnny chuckled. "All right. You're on. I could use a little glory. That is," he looked at Pa, "unless you had something else that needed doing."

Pa shook his head. "Not at all. We got three cord of firewood out there ready to be cut and split. I'll take Joe and Luke with me out to the field. You two can have at the wood."

Johnny peeled away his shirt and tossed it aside. He pushed up the sleeves of his union suit and grabbed one of the buck saws. With a four-foot-length of oak lying across a saw horse, he went at it with the bucksaw. Matt was doing the same at a second saw horse. Suspenders were in place over Matt's shoulders, and his sleeves were rolled up.

Johnny pulled the saw blade through the wood, let it fall back into place with a gentle push, then pulled again. Fast. Again and again. It sounded like Matt snoring at night. The saw bit into the wood, and saw dust drifted to the ground.

Johnny bulled his way through, and a chunk of wood a foot and a half long fell to the ground. Sweat was already beading up on his back, beneath his undershirt.

He stood and wiped some sweat away from his forehead. "I forgot about the humidity, here in the East."

Matt dropped his first chunk of wood to the ground, and straightened up. "Same here. Out at sea, the winds are strong, and the air is clean and often crisp. Not like this."

"The winds are strong in Texas, too. Kind of crisp in the winter, especially in north Texas, and dang hot in the summer. But it's a dry heat."

"I guess we were just used to this as kids. Never thought much about it."

Johnny pulled the log into place and began working on it again, cutting a second chunk of stove-length wood. Matt did the same.

When the second one fell to the earth, Johnny stood to let the muscles in his back stretch a bit. He had worked hard in Texas. Sometimes twelve hours in the saddle. But it was a different kind of work.

Matt's second piece of wood was on the ground too, and he was rubbing the palms of his hands.

Johnny said, squinting into the sun, "What about them callouses you built up scrubbing all them decks on that boat?"

"They're different kinds of callouses, apparently. Not the same you get from farm work. And," Matt threw his brother a sidelong glance, "it's a ship, not a boat, and I wasn't a deck hand. I was the first mate."

Matt hitched the log into place and began sawing again. Johnny did the same. Matt's final two pieces of firewood fell to the earth, and seconds later Johnny's joined them. They were each done with their first four-foot-length.

"First mate, huh?" Johnny said. "That's not exactly Navy terms, is it?"

Matt gave a glance toward the front door. The house was maybe two hundred feet away, and the door was shut. He gave Johnny the impression he didn't want Ma hearing what he was going to say.

"I wasn't exactly in the Navy."

This had Johnny's attention. "Do tell."

"I started out in the Navy," he pulled a handkerchief from his back pocket and dabbed sweat away from his forehead, "but, well, things happened. I got a position as a deck hand on a commercial freighter, and worked my way up."

"And you never told any of this in your letters home, apparently."

Matt shook his head.

Johnny said, "Because, let me guess, what happened to get you kicked out of the Navy wasn't something you wanted to share with Ma and Pa."

"No."

Johnny reached for a canteen. The one that had been

51

on his saddle, that he drank from many a time under the hot Texas sun. "That gun you mentioned, in your duffel bag. Apparently that's not Navy issue?"

Matt shook his head. "It is, but that's not where I got it. I won it in a card game when we were anchored in Manila. We sailed in dangerous waters. Pirates set upon us more than once. A man needed a gun."

Johnny knew. He could tell by the look in Matt's eye. "You've killed a man."

Matt nodded. "More than one. Been shot at a few times, too. In fact, one time, a bullet took some skin off of one of my shoulders. But I did most of my fighting with a cutlass."

"A cutlass?"

Matt said, "Got pretty good with one. I gave it to the pilot of our ship when I left. I couldn't very well bring it home. There'd be a lot of questions."

"Don't worry," Johnny said, and tossed the canteen to Matt. "Your secret's safe with me."

Matt took a chug of water and replaced the cork. "What about you? As I remember, you were going to join the cavalry. But from what Joe was saying, it doesn't sound like you did."

"Well..." Johnny's turn to fess up. "I did join the cavalry. But I wasn't with them very long. Something happened."

"Something you'd rather Ma and Pa didn't know about."

Johnny nodded. "I joined up with the Texas Rangers and rode with them for a while. Then, for the past eight months—maybe a year—I've been just kind of on my own. Taking jobs here and there. Worked as a cowhand for a time. Rode shotgun for a stagecoach company for a while. Served as a marshal of a small town for a few weeks." He chuckled. "Me, with a badge. Can you imagine?"

"Did you really ride into Mexico to bring back a kidnapped girl?"

Johnny nodded his head and chuckled. "That's a story in itself."

"So, that's what Joe was talking about. The legend. You got into some scrapes and people started talking about you."

Johnny nodded.

Matt said, "You always were spectacularly good with a gun."

"And yet, it's not being showy with a gun that saved my life. It was the fact that for some reason, I seem to be able to hold a steady hand when bullets start flying at me. Few men can do that."

"I experienced that, too. One time pirates boarded our ship, and I just stood there on the deck and unloaded my pistol on them. I brought three of them down. Then I went at them with my cutlass and got two more before the rest turned and ran. Must run in the family."

Johnny leaned the saw against the horse and said, "You know, I'm kind of in the mood for something a little stronger than water."

Matt was smiling. "Just what do you have in mind?"

"I got a little something I brought with me from Texas. In my saddle bags. Come on."

Johnny started away, toward the barn. With a smile, Matt dropped the canteen to the ground and followed.

In the barn was Johnny's saddle. He had brought his bedroll up to the house, but his saddle bags were still tied to the back of the saddle.

He reached into one of the bags and produced a bottle. It was filled with a light, golden liquid.

Matt said, with a curious smile, "Now what, pray-tell, is that?"

"Tequila. They like it better than whiskey, down Mexico way. I developed something of a taste for it, myself."

"Do tell."

Johnny pulled the cork and took a mouthful. "Heaven on Earth."

He handed the bottle to Matt.

"Careful, now," Johnny said. "The bite's a little different than whiskey."

But Matt was tipping the bottle. He took two plugs, then wiped his mouth with the back of his sleeve.

"Oh, yeah," he said. "Very different."

"Not sure if you like it?"

"Well, I'm not one to jump to a rash judgment. I think I should give it a few more trials."

They stretched out on some hay in the loft. The loft doors were open, and though the air was humid, the breeze was a little cooling. Something about hay tends to be a little cooling, too. Johnny had discovered that when he was growing up. He and Matt and Joe would stretch out in the hay up here, sometimes. He and Matt would talk. Of dreams, religion, philosophy. Joe was never much of a talker, but he would listen and sometimes throw in a thought of his own.

Now there was a bottle of tequila with them. Johnny said, "I bet this is the only bottle of tequila in all of Pennsylvania."

"Now, that would be a downright shame," Matt said, holding the bottle. He had just taken a chug and was relishing the feeling as it traveled its way down.

Ma and Pa were always death against drinking alcohol. There had never been any on the farm. Johnny's first taste of it had been when he joined the Army. His first taste of tequila had been when he joined the Rangers.

Apparently Matt was no stranger to drink now, either, because he took the first belt of tequila like it was water. Johnny said as much.

"Well," Matt said, handing the bottle back to Johnny, "on a ship, rum's a big favorite. And scotch. I dare say I've developed a bit of a taste for both. Something else I wouldn't want to share with Ma and Pa."

Johnny took a drink from the bottle. "Of course, there's gonna be hell to pay if we come back into the farmhouse smelling like tequila."

"Tell me something," Matt said. "What happened with the Army? Did you get kicked out?"

Johnny nodded. "I beat up an officer. I was lucky I got kicked out and not thrown in the stockade."

"Dishonorable discharge."

Johnny nodded again.

"Want to talk about it?"

"Not really. But," he shrugged, "why not? There was a town near the fort where I was stationed. And there was a girl in town, and I'd ride in to see her once in a while."

Matt shook his head. "Add a girl to any equation, and trouble seems to brew."

"It did this time, that's for sure. Seems she was also seeing a lieutenant. A West-Pointer, by the name of Samson."

Matt laughed. "Samson? No kidding. Did he have long hair?"

Johnny chuckled. "No. But he was right full of himself.

A West-Pointer, and he was oh so proud of it. He was all upright and held his head high. He ordered me to stay away from his girl. He did it like he was ordering me to saddle his horse. But it was just him and me. There was no one else around, so I told him I was off duty and he had no business ordering me anywhere. He then slapped me across the face, like a girl would do. I think he might have been trying to challenge me to a duel, or something."

Matt was chuckling. "No kidding. What'd you do?"

Johnny shrugged. "What'd you think I'd do? I slugged him in the face."

Matt was now laughing outright. "No. You didn't."

Johnny was laughing, too. Something about tequila made things seem extra funny. "I did. A right hook. Caught him right square in the cheekbone. His knees, they buckled, and he went down. To make matters worse, we were in the livery barn in town. When he landed, his shoulder went into a pile of fresh horse droppings."

Matt was now hanging onto his stomach, he was laughing so hard.

Johnny said, "You should've seen this guy. His uniform was always clean and neatly pressed. Well, it wasn't so clean, afterwards."

"So, that's what they kicked you out for?"

Johnny nodded, and handed the bottle back. "That's about it."

"Striking a superior officer. How did you manage not to get thrown in the stockade?"

"When he got to his feet, with horse dung on his shoulder, he was so furious I thought he was gonna cry. He stood there, face all red. Eyes all waterin' up. I don't think any of his West Point training ever prepared him for getting slugged in the face in a barn and falling into a pile of horse droppings."

"What'd he do?'

"Well, he just stood there for a minute, huffing at me. I said to him, 'Well, are you gonna swing at me, or not?' He said, 'I'll see you thrown out of this man's army.' I said, 'You'd best clean the dung off your shoulder, first.'"

Matt took a swig of the tequila.

Johnny said, "I guess he figured he wanted me as far gone from there as possible, so I couldn't tell the story of how the West Point lieutenant almost cried after getting hit and falling into a pile of poop. I never did see the girl again. I'd met a couple Texas Rangers when I was in town on furlough, and I showed them all how I could shoot and ride. They told me if I ever needed a job to look 'em up, and they'd take me to their captain. So I did, and they did. One of 'em was a feller by the name of Zack Johnson. Became one of my best friends."

Matt said, "You always were too good with a gun for your own good. You were always practicing with Uncle Jake's guns."

Their Uncle Jake was Pa's brother and had been a Texas Ranger back in the thirties, in the war between Texas and Mexico. He had gone west for a taste of life beyond the farm, fought in the war and returned with a pair of Paterson Colts. When Johnny was fourteen, Uncle Jake started showing him how to use them. Johnny practiced with them until he could make trick shooting look easy. Pulling stunts like having Matt throw a silver dollar in the air and plugging it clean through with one shot before the coin hit the ground. Or lining up cans on a fence, and drawing the gun and getting all five with five shots. Uncle Jake had shown him how to execute a border shift, and with a week of practice Johnny could do it like he had been doing it for years.

Uncle Jake said he had never seen anyone able to handle a gun like Johnny. Matt had tried some target practicing with one of the pistols and he wasn't a bad shot, but Johnny handled those guns like it was second nature. After a time Uncle Jake gave the guns to him, something Ma never approved of.

Matt said, "You took those guns with you when you went West, didn't you?"

Johnny nodded. "I had no idea how the Army worked. I thought they'd let me carry them. But everything was Army-issue, including the weapons."

"Do you still have 'em?"

Johnny shook his head. "Lost 'em in a poker game, down in Corpus Christi. Not one of my finer moments."

Matt held up the tequila bottle, now half full. "You know, Pa's gonna kill us."

"No he won't. Come on." Johnny slapped him in the shoulder and got to his feet, and he climbed down the ladder from the loft to the barn floor. Matt followed.

Johnny reached into his saddle bags and pulled out a

half full sack of coffee and a beaten-up tin kettle. "We can go out into the woods and make us a little camp fire and have some coffee. That stuff Ma makes is so weak compared to the trail coffee I got used to out in Texas. That stuff could take the rust off a nail."

Matt nodded with a smile. "That's the way we used to make it on the ship. Let's go."

The land was a series of low ridges that rose and dropped. The woods behind the house were mostly poplar, oak and maple, some of them standing tall, and the ground was covered with dry leaves and underbrush.

Pa had been told by many farmers in the area that he should have clear-cut these woods to make more room for pastures or crops, but Pa's father had given him a love for the forest, and so he had let a couple hundred acres of trees remain. They still had almost a thousand acres for corn, which was Pa's main crop. More than enough, Pa had said often.

Even though Johnny and Matt had been gone only three years, they found the land had changed. One outcropping of bedrock seemed more pronounced, and another was partially covered over with dirt, grass and leaves. A long alder had fallen across a small stream, and another log that had been across that same stream years ago was now rotted and had fallen into the water.

They found a section near the stream and built a small fire. Unlike the Texas countryside Johnny had grown so accustomed to, the earth here was covered with a few inches of dried leaves. Tinder that an errant spark could catch onto and bring down half the forest. Johnny cleared a circle five feet in diameter, all the way to the bare ground.

Also unlike the Texas countryside, this land was damp once you got below the top covering of leaves. It rained often here, and water was close to the surface. It was also prime country for mosquitoes, critters you didn't see much of in the arid drylands of central Texas.

Johnny and Matt used some dry leaves for tinder and found some small sticks for kindling. A deadfall provided some old, weathered oak branches that were easily snapped into a useable size, and they had wood for the fire.

Johnny dipped the small kettle into the stream to fill it with water, then dumped in some coffee and stood it in the fire to set it to boiling.

Matt sat on the ground, his arms resting across his knees. "I have one question for you. Becky Drummond."

Johnny snickered, and shook his head. "That's a name, not a question."

"It's also a question. I didn't want to ask you back at the house, because you've always been private. Not as much as Joe, maybe."

"No one's as private as Joe. With him it's more about what he doesn't say than what he does."

"I also knew Joe and Luke would needle you about it."

"And you would have, too."

Matt raised his brows with mock innocence and said, "Whatever do you mean?"

Johnny grinned. He was on one knee, using a broken branch as a poker to stir the fire. "What made you think of Becky?"

Matt shrugged. "Back before we left home, it was hard to think of you without thinking of Becky Drummond. You two seemed almost destined to be together."

"Isn't that exaggerating a little?"

"Nope."

"And here I thought Becky and I were being discreet."

Matt shook his head. "We all saw it. Ma and Pa talked of it. You two were always at each other's side, even when you were little kids. Catching frogs and lightning bugs together in the summer."

Johnny nodded, smiling a little at the memory. "She always was a tomboy."

"Then she got older, and started looking quite fetching in a dress, if I remember correctly."

Johnny nodded again. "She wasn't such a tomboy then."

"Did you ever write to her?"

Johnny shrugged. "I wrote her a letter once I arrived at Fort Kiowa. But the postal service out there is so sketchy. It can take sometimes months for a letter to get from one place to another. If it arrives at all. I never knew if she got it, and I never got one from her."

The water eventually boiled. He took it off the fire and let the water calm down a bit, then he returned the kettle to the flames. "This is the way we make it out there. When it boils over three times it's ready."

Matt chuckled. "Not much different than the stuff we drank on the ship."

"So," Johnny said, "how'd you get kicked out of the Navy? What'd you do?"

"It's not common knowledge, outside the Navy itself, but there are what they call hazing rituals. Abuse given to young sailors. It's a way of unofficially initiating them into the ranks. I saw a sailor, a shipmate of mine, beaten to death. They decided I was fair game but I'm our father's son, and I wasn't going to stand for any of it. And I have our mother's temper. I beat the hell out of three of them. Threw one of them overboard. He almost drowned. The captain decided he'd had enough of me, and he had me locked up until they reached shore, which was Fort Sumter in South Carolina. They set me ashore with a dishonorable discharge, and I signed on with a merchant ship."

"But, you were in the right."

"I was. But I was trying to buck a long established tradition, right or not. I was viewed as a trouble-maker. It would shame Ma and Pa to have a son bearing the label of trouble-maker. Society seems to be less interested in right and wrong, and more interested in labels."

Johnny snorted a bitter chuckle. "Well, maybe I belong carrying the label. I could have handled my situation better. I didn't have to try and show up that lieutenant. I could have just said *yes, sir*, and let it go at that. But I couldn't. Pride, I guess. Ma and Pa raised us better'n that."

Matt nodded. "Maybe. But you figure, farming is the kind of job where you work for yourself. You answer to no man. True, you answer to the weather and to the price of crops, but there's no overseer telling you what to do. You take two farm boys who grew up in an environment like that and put us in the military, where it's all rules and regulations. Where it seems like they not only fail to respect independent thought but discourage it. Add into the equation Ma's temper and Pa's backbone, which we both seem to have, and you have a reputation for disaster."

"Maybe we should have seen it coming."

"So. You never answered the question."

"What question?"

"Becky Drummond."

Johnny gave a shrug. "That's a question I don't know if I know an answer to. I'm not the same man I was when I left.

She may not be the same girl."

"We all change."

"But if we had stayed, then she and I would have changed and grown together. By doing it apart, we may have grown in such different directions we might not even recognize each other. I know I'm not the same."

"No, you're not. Neither one of us is. Even if Joe hadn't got you talking about those raiders and Indians you killed, I would know you've killed a few men. I can see it in your eyes. Your manner."

"I've killed more than a few."

Matt hesitated a moment before asking the next question. "How many have you killed?"

Johnny shrugged again. "I've lost count."

Matt let the weight of that statement settle in.

Johnny said, "Been shot at a few times too many, too. That's what my friend Zack says. That's why, even out in these woods, I feel uneasy without a gun. I know in my head there's no renegade outlaw out there waiting to ambush us. But I'm constantly looking about us. Constantly listening to every sound the woods make."

"Well, you won't know about Becky until you see her."

"Yeah, I know."

Matt smiled. "You can't hide out here on the farm, forever. You have to go into town eventually. Come Sunday, Ma will be dragging us to church."

Johnny said, "I saw a Chinaman eat this way, once. With two sticks. He would trap his food like that and lift it off the plate. Neat as you please. As easy as you or I would use a fork."

"Yeah, I've seen that too. We docked at a port in Asia, more than once."

"And he was hell on wheels in a fight. He was running a small farm in east Texas. Not many Chinamen in Texas. You see more in California, or so I'm told. I saw him lay out three highwaymen one time. Neat as you please. Used his feet, too, and made it look almost like a dance. Showed me a couple things about fighting."

"You were always top notch in a fight, yourself. As good with your fists as you ever were with those guns."

Johnny nodded. "He showed me a thing or two about fighting, and I taught him how to shoot."

They sat in silence for a moment, while the coffee

boiled in the kettle.

Matt said, "Johnny, you've seemed kind of ill at ease since we've been home."

"Guess I have."

Matt waited, to see if his brother would talk.

Johnny was silent a moment, listening to the coffee stir and hiss inside the kettle.

He said, "This place used to be home. I guess it hasn't really changed any, but I have. When I was out there, that wide open country somehow snagged hold of my heart. I don't know just how. But there are places where you can sit in the saddle and see the land stretch out before you. Not like it does here, for maybe a half mile in some places, but for miles. *Miles*, Matt. And when the wind is just right, the grass blows in waves, almost like an ocean of grass. For miles all around you. In the spring, the grass is green, and wild flowers grow.

"And the sky, Matt. The horizon is so low, and that big, blue sky rises up from one side and all the way down to the other. And at night, the stars are so big you feel like you can almost reach up and touch 'em."

Matt said, "It's like that at sea, too. I would sometimes stand at the bow. That's the front of the ship, for you land lubbers."

Johnny laughed.

"And I would just look off to the horizon. All that water, rising in swells that would just flatten out, and then rise again. More than once I would see porpoises out there, just frolicking. We saw whales, more than once. One time, a whale came to the surface just a few yards from the ship. It let out this honking, wailing sound. Like nothing I've ever heard before. More incredible than music from the finest instrument. A bunch of us were standing there, watching it. Then it dove back down, its tail slapping the water hard on the way down, and soaked us. It was wondrous."

"I guess I just feel like an outsider, here. An outsider in the place that was once my home."

"You don't consider it your home any longer?"

"I want to. I used to. The whole time I was in Texas, I thought of this place as *back home*. Whenever I talked about the farm, that's what I called it. But now, I'm realizing my home has become that open, wild land, and wherever my horse took me."

"I think I know how you feel."

The kettle began boiling over for the third time. Johnny grabbed his two sticks and pulled it from the fire. "Coffee's on."

14

JOHNNY AND MATT RETURNED to work in time to saw up a couple more logs each before Pa, Joe and Luke came home from the field.

At supper, Pa said, "I will admit, the way you two were pestering each other about work, I figured to find you had cut a cord, each."

Luke chuckled.

Matt said, "Sorry, Pa. We wound up sitting in the barn, talking. A lot to catch up on, I guess."

Ma said, "I'm glad. You boys shouldn't have to be put back to work as soon as you get here. There's plenty of time for that."

Johnny said, "We'll do better next time. Of that, I promise."

Matt nodded. "Definitely."

Ma had baked up a load of chicken and potatoes. She had also fixed a huge plate of biscuits. Johnny brought one, oozing with butter, to his mouth and chewed into it. One thing was true—he had never found cooking like this on the frontier.

Pa said, "I'm heading into town tomorrow, to get some supplies. Your mother's kitchen is a little barren, and we're going to have to stock it good if we're going to keep feeding you boys."

Ma said, "I had forgotten how much four growing boys can eat."

Pa glanced to Johnny. "It wouldn't hurt you to come along, too. Get a haircut. You still look like a wild man from the frontier."

Johnny's hair had last been cut months ago. It covered his ears, and fell to his collar in back.

Pa then turned his gaze to Joe. "Wouldn't hurt for you, either. You look a lot less like a savage than you did when you first got here, but a good haircut is what you both need."

Johnny didn't take to the idea of going to town, because that might mean a chance meeting with Becky Drummond. He glanced at Matt, and the look in Matt's eyes said he understood. But Johnny decided to say nothing.

"There you go, Johnny," Fred Whipple said.

He was a man of about Pa's age, but with a balding

head, a round soft stomach, and a bubble of flesh beneath his chin. He wore a bushy mustache that rose at the corners to meet two bushy sideburns. He was the only barber in Sheffield, Pennsylvania.

Johnny removed the white apron Whipple had tucked under his chin and looked in the mirror. His hair was now short cropped and combed away from his face, exposing a high forehead that seemed a little higher than the last time he had sat in this chair.

"I look downright civilized," he said. "First time I've looked civilized since I don't remember when."

Matt was sitting in a chair by the window. He had a newspaper open. "Why, Johnny, you'll never look truly civilized."

"Well, you have to give Fred an A for effort."

Johnny stepped out of the chair, and placed his hat on his head. It fit a little looser than it had when he walked in.

Joe sat beside Matt. He had picked up a paper and read a bit, but had dropped it back to the stack of papers on the window sill. Joe was not a reader. He was often too restless to simply sit and read.

Fred had worked on Joe and Matt before he started on Johnny, and since the shave Joe had given himself the day before hadn't been all that clean, Fred had gotten out the razor and now Joe's jaw was smooth.

They paid Fred and then stepped outside. Johnny slid his hands down his hips to check his guns out of habit, but found they weren't there. It was now Day Two of no guns. It still felt unnatural not to have them buckled on, and he wondered if he would ever grow used to it. He had thought about wearing them today, but Matt had said he would scare the good citizens of Sheffield to death if he did.

Pa was at the grain and feed store. The boys were to head down there and help him, as soon as the haircuts were done. Afterward, they were going to the cemetery to visit Grams' grave.

"You boys go on ahead," Johnny said. "There's something I gotta do."

Matt was following his train of thought. Matt said, "Are you sure?"

Johnny said, "Yeah. Gotta get this over with."

"Come on," Matt said to Joe. "We can help Pa."

Johnny strode along the sidewalk, his pants tucked

into his riding boots, his hat pulled down over his head. He was wearing a dark blue, double-breasted shirt he had rolled up in his bedroll. A shirt he had picked up in Texas. A lot of the men wore them, there.

People looked at him out of curiosity. He realized he looked as out of place as he felt. Some recognized him after a first glance and gave him a greeting or a nod of the head. The town had grown a little, and there were some folks Johnny didn't know.

A woman with a deeply lined face, and gray hair protruding from under her bonnet, nodded at him and smiled. "Good morning, John. I had heard you and your brothers were back. It's good to see you again."

Johnny touched the brim of his hat. "Good to see you too..." What was her name? Oh, yeah. "Mrs. Goodson."

They had ridden in only two nights ago, and already people had heard they were back. News sure traveled fast, Johnny thought.

Johnny stepped into the doorway of the general store, the heels of his riding boots clicking on the floorboards and his spurs jingling a little. He removed his hat and reached up to flatten his hair, only to be reminded Fred Whipple had cut most of it off.

A man stood behind the counter. He was somewhere near Pa's age. A white apron was in place, and arm garters held the sleeves from drooping. He was bent at the shoulders, which put him maybe an inch shorter than Johnny.

The man looked up at him and said, "Johnny McCabe."

"Mister Drummond." Johnny walked over to the counter and extended his hand and Drummond grasped it firmly.

The man said, "We had heard you boys were back among us."

"Yeah. Word travels fast."

Drummond nodded with a smile. "It surely does. I suppose you're looking for Becky."

"Well," Johnny gave a half shrug. "It'd be nice to say hello."

Drummond nodded with a knowing smile. It struck Johnny the man smiled a lot. He hadn't noticed years ago. Pa had often said, beware of a man who smiles too much.

Drummond said, "I'll get her for you."

"Thank you, sir."

Drummond stepped out through a doorway to a back room, which Johnny knew to be a store room. Within a few moments, she stepped out into the room. Becky. Her face lit with a smile.

"Papa told me I had a visitor," she said. "I was hoping it would be you."

Johnny took in the view that was Becky Drummond, comparing the Becky who stood here now with the Becky he remembered from three years ago. She seemed like she had lost a little baby fat in her face, which made her cheekbones seem more pronounced in a way that struck Johnny as classy. The freckles were still there. But her eyes, which had once danced with the joy of life as a young girl, were now glowing with the sensuality of a woman.

Her hair was a chestnut brown, and where it had been usually tied in a braid or just falling free in times past, it was now wrapped into a bun at the back of her head.

"Hello, Becky." He didn't really know what else to say.

She said, "We heard you and your brothers had come home."

Johnny nodded. "Word travels fast."

"It sure does."

He wondered how many more times he would be saying that today.

She stepped toward him, tentatively at first and then more hurriedly, and stretched up onto her toes to plant a quick kiss on his cheek. He was not tall, but even still she rose barely above his cheekbones.

"It's so good to see you," she said. "I was so hoping you would come by the store."

"I had to come by and say hello." There was so much he wanted to say, and yet he didn't know quite how to get it all out. It was like there was an invisible wall between them. A wall created by an absence of three years.

He remembered how she had cried when he told her he was leaving to join the Army. He remembered their final night together, a moment stolen in the back of Pa's buckboard on a dark, wooded trail. How she had rested in his arms and told him she would wait for him, for as long as it took.

He hadn't waited for her. The more time that passed, the more distant his life in Pennsylvania seemed to become.

As time went by he had thought of Becky less and less. At one time, he wasn't even sure if he would ever return to Pennsylvania.

He wondered if she had truly waited for him. Part of him hoped not, because the boy she said goodbye to and said she would wait for had never really come home. That boy didn't exist anymore. What stood before her was a gunfighter. That was the word for it. He had stood among gunfighters, fought beside them and against them, and rose to stand among the best of them. And he wasn't ashamed of it. He was what he was. He hoped Becky was living her life, not waiting for some boy who could never really return.

She said, "So, are you going to the dance?"

His brows rose questioningly. No one had mentioned a dance.

He said, "There's a dance? When?"

"Saturday night."

"Well..." He wasn't sure how to phrase what he wanted to say. Matt was so eloquent, but words often didn't come easily to Johnny. "I don't know if I have a right to ask this, but..."

"Yes," she said, her eyes dancing. "If you were going to ask to be my escort to the dance, then the answer is yes."

He couldn't help but grin. She had gumption, but never crossed the line into brazenness. The thought occurred to him that she was more woman than he had ever deserved.

"The dance starts at seven," she said. "A barn dance. At Logan Everett's farm."

Johnny knew the name Everett well. He had gone to school with a couple of the Everett boys. When he was fourteen, he and Pa and Matt had pitched in for a barn-raising after the Everett barn had burned to the ground.

He said, "I'll pick you up then at, say, five-thirty?"

She nodded. "That would be most fine."

"Give us a little while to talk."

"I'll see you then."

He looked at her long. There was so much he wanted to say. So much bottled up inside him. He wanted to tell her she looked beautiful. He wanted to say he was sorry for becoming something that could probably never belong in a small farming town like Sheffield.

What he managed to say was, "It's really good to see you, Becky."

He left the general store and headed to the grain and feed store. He found himself thrilled that Becky was still unmarried, and yet he was afraid that once she got to know him as he was now, she would be disappointed. The thought gave him an ache down deep inside. He found himself wishing he had never come back home at all.

15

ONCE THEY WERE back from town, Johnny and Matt attacked the woodpile. Johnny worked in silence, focusing on sawing the wood. Cutting every log into stove-lengths. Hauling it by the armload to the woodshed, which was a small lean-to built onto the side of the barn. He would then grab another log and lay it across the saw horse and have at it again. He wore his hat to keep the sun from his head, but he had peeled off his shirt, and his undershirt was soaking with sweat.

He realized Matt had stopped sawing and was watching him. Johnny stopped and looked at his brother and said, "What?"

"Tell me about it. How'd it go?"

"How'd what go?"

"Becky Drummond."

Johnny looked back to the log he was halfway through cutting. "Come on. Let's talk over some tequila. There's still a little left."

Matt took a swig and handed the bottle back to Johnny. They were stretched out in the hayloft again.

Matt said, "You know, Pa's really going to kill us. The second day we were supposed to attack that stack of wood, but here we are."

Johnny said, "We can go back to work after a while."

"Full of tequila?"

"It can be done." Johnny took a pull from the bottle. "What you do is drink a lot of water, and work like there's no tomorrow. You sweat it out of you. I've done it before."

He handed the bottle back to Matt, who took another drink. Matt said, "This tequila grows on you. Beats rum all to pieces."

"I got so I was drinking a little too much of it, back in Texas. That old scout I mentioned, Jim Layton, sort of took me under his wing and offered me some advice. One piece of the advice was to get out of the life I was leading. Stay away from tequila and go home. I was considering his advice when I got the letter from Ma telling me Grams had died."

Matt handed the bottle back to Johnny. "So, you took his advice and here you are. Except you're still drinking tequila."

69

Johnny nodded, looking at the bottle. "Become a habit, I guess. But I think I'll make this my last bottle for a while. I keep a flask of corn squeezings in my saddle bags, but that's to prevent infections in case of a bullet or an arrow wound."

Matt was grinning. "Seriously?"

"The captain I rode for in the Rangers is where I got that idea from. I saw a man take a bullet in the forearm. It broke the bone. That wasn't really a problem, because if it was set properly and splinted, he would be back in action in maybe six weeks. The problem would be if infection set in. If that happened, he'd be dead in four or five days. That's the most common form of death in wartime, you know. Infection from wounds. And there's nothing the doctors can do except stand by and watch."

Johnny took a pull of tequila, and handed the bottle back to Matt.

Johnny said, "Well, that man who got the bullet in his arm, the doctor wanted to saw his arm off in an attempt to prevent infection. But what the captain did, he had a couple of us hold the man down, and he dumped a couple ounces of corn squeezings into the bullet wound."

"No kidding," Matt said, looking at Johnny wide-eyed.

Johnny nodded his head. "I can tell you, that man did holler. He screamed like a banshee. You would'a thought Comanches were working on him. He bucked and screamed. But he kept the arm and infection never set in. The captain said it works every time. I said, can I have some? He handed me an old metal flask he had and filled it from a bottle."

"You ever use it?"

"Only once. A friend of mine. That Ranger I mentioned, Zack Johnson. He caught a Comanche arrow in his leg. I pulled the arrow out, then sat on his chest and poured corn squeezings into the wound. He kept his leg. That was the time I had to shoot those Comanches. Zack was on the ground behind me with that arrow in his leg."

"You didn't answer the question."

"What question?"

"Becky Drummond."

Johnny chuckled and shook his head. "All right. Becky Drummond. I'm taking her to the dance Saturday night."

"The question is, though, where do you stand with her?"

"I guess the answer to that question is...I don't know.

On one hand, if she'd have me, I could build us a farmhouse and raise children. Pa's offered me a section of land."

Matt nodded. "He's offered one to each of us."

"Becky's a one-of-a-kind woman. As great as she was at fifteen, she's double that now. But..."

"How can there possibly be a *but?*" Matt said.

"Because of that land out there. What we were talking about yesterday. The wide-open land. Long, low grassy hills that stretch for as far as the eye can see. And in southern Texas, you get canyons and desert ridges. It's a hard land, but it's a beautiful land. As beautiful as it is hard. And the desert's not a dead place, like people think it is. It's alive. Little bushes and wild flowers. Little animals."

"But it's dry. There's no water."

"Oh, yes there is. If you know how to find it. I listened to men like the captain I rode for, and that scout, Apache Jim. That Chinaman I mentioned told me about roots and stuff you can dig from the ground to eat. And I learned from an old Kiowa scout. They talked and I listened."

"That land to you is like the ocean is with me," Matt said. "It got a piece of your heart."

"I think it got more than a piece. I've been gone from it for only a few weeks, but it's like I can feel it calling to me. I could marry Becky, if she's foolish enough to have me, but could I ever really be happy here?"

Matt still held the bottle. He looked at it thoughtfully. "I suppose you could always take her with you. Build a home out there. Cattle, or something."

"If she would go."

"You could always ask her."

"I spent a lot of time with her when we were growing up. I practically grew up alongside her. Somehow, I don't think the girl I knew would want to go."

Matt handed him the bottle. "There's something I have to tell you. Something I heard at the feed and grain store, yesterday. After Joe and I went back to help Pa, and you went to see Becky."

Johnny waited. He took a belt of tequila. His head was starting to swim a little bit, so he figured this would be his last belt. He planned to get back to working on the wood, and making good headway with it before Pa got back from the fields.

Matt was hesitating, like he didn't really want to say

what he had to, but felt he should. "I'm not sure I should say this because it's something I'm not sure you're going to want to hear. But you're going to hear it sooner or later. Might as well be from me."

"Well," Johnny said, "don't keep me in suspense."

"It seems Becky has been seeing someone over the past year. Trip Hawley. No one knows how serious it is, but he seems to escort her to every dance, and most of her dances are with him. And he stops by the store a lot. He's had dinner with the Drummonds more than once."

So, Johnny thought. She hadn't waited for him, after all. He felt a little relief, because this sort of released some of his guilt. And maybe if Trip was in the picture, then it might make things a little less complicated between him and Becky. While Johnny was now something of a stranger in this little farming community, Trip belonged here. Trip could build a life with Becky, and maybe devote himself fully to her and their children.

And yet Johnny realized he was also feeling a small twang of jealousy, as irrational as it was.

"Come on," Johnny said, getting to his feet. A little unsteady, because of the tequila. Maybe it was best to focus his mind on something else. "Let's get some water into us, and get back to work."

16

WHEN JOHNNY AND HIS BROTHERS HAD LEFT home three years ago, he had left his Sunday go-to-meetin' suit hanging in the closet. It was made of a gray woolen material, and it had fit nicely when he was seventeen. Now he was twenty, and was finding the jacket was too tight through the shoulders, and the trouser legs were about an inch too short.

Matt laughed. "Looks like you're ready for a flood."

Johnny said, "And what are you going to be wearing to the dance?"

Matt produced from his duffel bag a folded suit. Charcoal gray with little pinstripes. With a smile of triumph, he said, "A while ago, I decided to buy a suit that fit. As first mate of a merchant ship, I expected to be going into business. I'd been saving money, hoping to buy an interest in our ship. A business man needs a suit."

They were alone, so they could talk freely.

Johnny said, "I never thought much beyond the day ahead of me. The job at hand. I blew all my money on cards and tequila. And women. Now I have no suit for Saturday night and no money to buy one with. I rode in with not much more than just the clothes on my back."

"I'm sure Ma can alter that suit before Saturday night."

And she did. With a measuring tape, a pair of scissors and a needle and thread, she worked her magic. Come Saturday night, the suit fit like it always had.

He didn't know how to tie a tie, so he turned to Matt for help.

As Matt worked on the tie, and Johnny stood with his chin held up to give Matt room, Matt said, "One thing a businessman learns is how to tie a tie."

"I'm not a businessman," Johnny said.

"That's right. You're a wild and woolly gunfighter."

"Not so woolly, maybe."

Johnny had to borrow one of Pa's white shirts. He wore a pair of black shoes he had left behind three years ago. They still fit.

He found Ma and Pa in the parlor. Matt had come down ahead of him and was standing in the suit he had bought.

"Well, now," Matt said. "You look downright civilized."

"I'm hearing that a lot lately. Don't quite know how to take it."

Ma was beaming a smile. "My, don't you look dapper. Don't listen to your brother."

"I try not to."

Johnny noticed his parents weren't dressed for the dance. Pa was in a work shirt and suspenders and had a book in one hand. A pipe was in his mouth. Ma had a piece of cloth suspended inside a wooden hoop and was embroidering a picture of flowers. Looked like she was working on a pillow case.

Johnny said, "Aren't you two coming to the dance?"

"Not this time," Pa said.

Ma said, "Your Pa's back is acting up, and I'm going to stay home with him."

Luke came bounding into the room. He had a suit the color of Johnny's. "Hey, Matt, I need some help with this tie."

"Where's Joe?" Pa said.

Johnny nodded with his head toward the stairway. "He's still upstairs. Tying his own tie."

Matt said, "How does he know how to tie a tie?"

Johnny shrugged. "Beats me. He's a man of mystery."

"That's your brother," Ma said. "Always the silent one. Silent and mysterious."

"So," Pa said, looking at Johnny. "Are you meeting Becky there?"

Johnny shook his head. "I'm picking her up at the Drummond house."

Pa nodded with approval. "That's what a gentleman should do. You don't meet a girl at a dance. You meet her at her house and escort her to the dance."

Joe came down the stairs. He was wearing his buckskin jacket over a white shirt he had borrowed from Pa, and a string tie was in place but listing to one side. His pants were the same faded cavalry pants he had worn when he first rode in. Looked like he might have dusted them off a bit.

"Joe," Matt said, "you're not among savages now. You should have a suit to go to a dance."

"I'm not gonna to climb into a monkey suit for anyone," Joe said, glancing at Johnny. "And I'm not gonna be there to dance. Only for the beer."

Ma threw her hands in the air, in a gesture of

resignation. "I didn't hear that."

"Ma," Matt said, bending down to give a peck on her cheek, "with this crowd, there's probably a lot you don't want to hear."

Pa was chuckling.

The boys stepped out the door. Johnny and Joe had grabbed their hats. Joe's was tan colored, and it was floppier and more tattered than Johnny's. He wore it tilted back a bit on his head so the drooping brim wouldn't block his vision. There was a small rip in one side of the hat's crown.

Matt said, "You're not wearing those things into town, are you? You'll look like a couple of desperadoes."

"We *are* desperadoes," Joe said. "Let's ride."

Johnny and Joe had saddled their horses already, and hitched a team to the buckboard. Matt climbed onto the wagon seat, and Luke landed beside him.

"Here," Matt said, handing the reins to him. "You're almost a man, now. You drive."

"Yes, sir."

"Don't go calling him *sir*," Johnny said. "It'll go to his head."

They rode down the long driveway to meet with the road that would lead them into town.

Luke said, "Hey, Joe, is that a bullet hole in your hat?"

Joe nodded. "A Blackfoot bullet. Took the hat clean off my head. Took a little skin with it, too. I got me a scar. My hair covers it."

"What's a *blackfoot*?"

"An Indian."

Matt said, "And Ma and Pa don't need to hear about that, either."

Luke shrugged. He held the reins in his hands and drove along.

The Everett farm was ten miles away. At about the halfway point, the road leading to their place split off from the main road to town.

"Hold up," Matt said to Luke.

Luke gave the reins a tug, and a call of "Whoa!" He brought the wagon to a stop.

"What's wrong?" he said.

"Not a thing. But you can't expect Johnny to bring Becky Drummond to the dance on the back of a horse."

Johnny swung out of the saddle. He said, "A lady would never be caught riding astride a horse. Though I've known a few Indian women who did it. Didn't seem to hurt 'em none, or make 'em any less proper."

Joe snorted a chuckle.

Matt climbed down from the wagon.

Joe also dismounted, and he handed the reins of his horse to Matt.

Joe said, "I'd better ride Bravo. That stallion is only half-broke."

"How am I gonna ride?" Luke said.

"With me." Joe stepped up and into Johnny's saddle, then extended his hand down to Luke, and Luke put a foot in the stirrup and swung up to sit behind Joe.

Johnny climbed into the wagon. "I'm not sure how I'm gonna feel after riding a few miles on this hard, wooden seat."

Matt said, "I would think after three years in the saddle, you'd have calluses built up where it counts."

"Different kind of work," Johnny said with a grin. "Different kind of calluses."

Matt caught the joke and shared the grin.

"Come on," Joe said. "Let's get goin'. I got me a hankerin' for some beer."

Johnny gave the horses a click and a snap of the reins, and he was off to town.

The Drummonds had a house just outside of Sheffield. A white clapboard two-floor structure, with a carriage house attached. Built onto the front of the house was a porch with an overhanging roof. Johnny had gotten a kiss from Becky more than once on that porch after dark.

The sky overhead was blue with only a few thin clouds, and there was a light breeze. But this dang humidity, Johnny thought. There was a fine layer of sweat along his back and the side of his ribs. Though, he had to admit, the humidity was probably only part of the reason for the sweat. His inner turmoil over Becky was eating at him.

Johnny knocked at the front door and was greeted by Becky's father. Even though cowboy etiquette allowed a cattleman or a scout to keep his hat on at all times, etiquette which Johnny usually followed, he had to remind himself this was not Texas. He removed his hat and said, "Good afternoon, sir."

"Hello, Johnny. Come on in. I'll go tell Becky you're here."

Johnny stood in the entryway while Drummond climbed the stairs. Johnny found he had to wait only a few minutes.

Becky descended the stairs with grace, one hand gliding along the banister, and her face was alight with a smile. Her hair was coiled atop her head, giving plenty of exposure to a long, willowy neck. Her dress was a light, summery blue, with a white lace neckline that fell just off of her soft shoulders. Clutched in one hand was a drawstring purse of the same material as her dress.

Becky said to her father, "Will you and Mama be coming along soon?"

"Shortly. I have to hitch the wagon."

Johnny thought he noticed a slight edge to Drummond. Like he was a little miffed about something but wasn't talking about it.

Becky said, "We'll see you there, then."

Johnny held the door for Becky and followed her out onto the porch. He replaced the hat on his head as he stepped out into the sun. As he walked along beside her to the wagon, he was reminded about how awkward he felt without a gun at each hip.

He took one of her hands as she climbed up and onto the wagon. He then leaped up.

He looked at her, and she gave a smile.

He said, "You look beautiful, in case I hadn't mentioned it."

"You hadn't, but thank you. And you look great, including the hat."

Johnny took the reins and with a gentle snap, the horses began moving. "Matt says I look like a desperado."

She gave him a mischievous smile. "I kind of like desperadoes."

The road to the Everett farm took them through some woods. The land rose up in hills at either side and was too steep and rocky for crops or for good pasture land.

A wooden bridge crossed a small stream, the same stream Johnny had made coffee from a few days ago, if you followed it along far enough. The iron shoes of the horses made a sort of clattering sound on the old boards of the bridge.

"Johnny," Becky said. "Will you do something for me? There's a small logging road that should be coming up on our right."

Johnny nodded. He knew of it. He had passed it on the way into town.

She said, "Could you pull in for a moment?"

Johnny looked at her with a question in his eyes.

She said, "I would just like some time alone with you. A chance to talk, before we get to the dance. Once we're there, I won't have you alone for the rest of the night."

Johnny saw the opening among the trees to their right. A small grassy patch. He turned the horses in, and they came to a thin trail with a grassy hump running down the middle. The trail was littered with dried leaves and sticks.

"Looks like this old logging road hasn't been used in a while," he said. "When I was here last, Charlie Wheeler was still using it. He sold a lot of firewood."

"Old Charlie died maybe a year ago. His wife and his daughter own the place. His daughter lives outside of Philadelphia, now. Has a family there. His wife has gone to live with her. His place is setting untended right now."

Johnny barely remembered Charlie's daughter. He didn't remember her name. She had married before he was even ten years old and moved away.

Johnny said, "A man could make a go of it there. Charlie's place is small, but there's good land there for tilling. And there's firewood."

She nodded. "The right man, in the right situation."

Again, Johnny thought about the potential opportunity opening its door right in front of him. If only it wasn't for the open land further west tugging at his heartstrings.

He said nothing, and he followed the logging road along for a short distance.

"This far enough?" he said.

She glanced back toward the road. It couldn't be seen from here, so there was a fair chance anyone traveling along wouldn't see the buckboard.

She said, "Yes, this is good."

Johnny gave a tug of the reins to tell the horses to stop, and lifted one knee and placed his foot on the brake lever, and pushed it down. The rear wheels locked up.

He glanced about and thought there was enough room

at either side of the trail for him to turn the wagon around.

"We shouldn't stay long," Johnny said. "Your parents will be by, shortly. It wouldn't look good for us to leave the house before them but arrive at the dance after them."

"I really don't care what anyone thinks. Not after three years." She reached a hand to his jaw. "I have missed you, Johnny."

Her mouth found his. They kissed long and hard. His hands were at the back of her neck and on her bare shoulders. Her neckline slid down her shoulders an inch or two, which just ignited the passion inside him more.

The kiss ended and his mouth was on her neck and shoulder, and she was breathing like she was running long and hard up a hill. She reached to his tie and gave it a tug, and it came undone. He would never get it tied again, but he didn't care. His hat tumbled away, bouncing off his shoulder to land somewhere on the ground below.

"Do you think this is wise?" Johnny said.

She answered by starting to work on the buttons of his shirt.

"People will know," he said. "We don't show up to the dance until later, people will know."

"They'll know anyway. Anyone with eyes can see how we always were when we were together. I never felt more alive than when I was with you, Johnny. When we were together, the way a man and woman are supposed to be. I've been waiting for you for so long."

She had finished on his shirt and gave the tails a tug, and they came loose from his pants. He was wearing no undershirt, as a way of trying to combat this danged humidity. She slid her hands over his chest. He reached behind her and began to unfasten her dress.

When the back of the dress was loose, he gave a glance to the back of the buckboard and then looked at her with a question in his eyes. It wasn't like they hadn't danced this dance before. And it wasn't like they hadn't christened this buckboard before, either. They knew the cargo bed was just their size.

He stepped over the seat into the bed, and with her hand in his and the back of her dress hanging open, she followed him.

17

MATT HADN'T left a girl behind like Johnny had, but he had escorted a young lady to a couple of dances and there had been a kiss or two. Sylvia Roberts was her name. He sought her out now, thinking he might ask her to dance. They could talk. Get reacquainted.

But as he asked for her, he found her name was now Sylvia Barnes. Mrs. Chet Barnes, to be exact. Sylvia was standing with Chet. She was holding the hand of a child old enough to walk.

Matt shook his head with amazement. In his mind's eye, Sylvia was still seventeen. Smiling in a shy but flirty way that made Matt uncomfortable in a good way. But here she was. Twenty, married and a mother.

Life had gone on without him. He had been off at sea, fighting pirates and storms and learning the sea the way Pa knew farming. Matt knew that none of the folks in Sheffield would suspend their lives and wait for his return, but it was still kind of strange to see how much some of them had changed since he had last seen them.

It was like two ships at sea, he thought. Sailing side-by-side. You look away for a little while, and when you look back, the other ship has changed its course and is now halfway toward the horizon.

He felt out of place. A stranger in a place he had once called home. He wasn't as torn up about it as Johnny was, because he hadn't left behind a woman like Becky Drummond, but he understood the feeling.

He started making an active search for unmarried women to dance with. He happened upon Trudy Larkin, who had been in his class in school before she dropped out to help her parents with their farm.

Trudy had never struck Matt as particularly intelligent or charming, but she had the misfortune to fill out her blouse ahead of the other girls in school and was too polite to refuse a request. Matt had escorted her to the woods behind the barn at a dance once and learned the shy farm girl wasn't so shy, after all.

He found Trudy at the punch bowl. She now had a child for every year he had been gone and another on its way. She was married and still apparently doing what she did best.

Matt continued to wander about.

A girl was standing alone by one wall. A girl Matt didn't recognize, which struck him as odd. In a town as small as Sheffield, he expected to know everyone. The girl's hair was as blonde as corn silk and tied behind her head in a ponytail. Her complexion was light, almost pale, and her eyes were the color of a clear summer sky.

Matt felt he should remember a girl this pretty. Maybe she was new to the area. The town had grown, so he figured maybe he shouldn't be so surprised to see folks he didn't know.

A girl this pretty shouldn't be standing alone. Matt figured he would remedy that.

"Excuse me," he said to her. "Could I have this dance?"

She turned her blue eyes to him and smiled. "Of course."

The band was playing a waltz. As close to the Vienna Waltz as a fiddle, a banjo, and a guitar could come. Matt took the girl's right hand in his left and placed his right hand behind her left shoulder, and she fell into place with him as they glided across the barn floor to the music.

"Should I call you Mister McCabe?" she said. "Or may I call you Matthew?"

"You know who I am?"

She gave a smile that was one part shy, and one part flirtatious. "But of course."

He had to admit, he was starting to realize there was something about her he thought he should recognize. "You do look a little familiar. But I can't quite place you."

"Hmm. I remain a mystery."

Matt laughed. "Isn't that the job of a woman? To be a mystery?"

"I thought it was to drive men mad."

"I bet you do that easily enough."

Her brows rose a notch. "Maybe. Maybe not."

It was then that the curve of her face, the shape of her nose and jaw, seemed to bring a name to mind. Not a particular first name, but a family name. "Everett. Are you one of the Everetts?"

"And we have a winner."

"Amy? Aggie's little sister?"

She said, "And the man is two for two."

"But it can't be," he said. "Aggie was a year ahead of me in school. She got married before I left town, if I remember right. But her little sister is just a child. Or, at least, she was when I left."

"Sixteen," she said. "I'll be seventeen next November. You've been gone a long time, Mister McCabe."

The last Matt remembered, Amy was a skinny young kid with bare feet and a turned up nose. Now she was marrying-age. Matt surely felt old.

The song ended, and the crowd of dancers applauded politely. Matt thanked Amy for the dance. He could probably have gotten a second dance out of her, but he had trouble getting the image of the barefooted, skinny young girl out of his mind. He headed to the punch bowl.

With a cup of punch in hand, he stood on the sidelines and watched the dancers. At one side of the barn a man was sawing away on the fiddle, another was plucking at the banjo, and a man with a guitar was strumming chords. The song was *Sally Gooden,* and couples were wheeling about the dance floor. People were laughing. Folks standing along the side were clapping to the rhythm of the song.

Matt stood and watched. He realized if he were not here, if he were still at sea, this dance would be progressing exactly as it was. His presence here was about as insignificant as it could be. Except for the dance with Amy Everett. And she was now dancing with a boy Matt didn't recognize, just as she probably would have even if Matt were not here.

He had come home hoping to find home. He had been gone so long. He wanted to reconnect with that certain feeling of sanctuary Ma and Pa's farmhouse and the town of Sheffield had always given him. And yet he felt like nothing more than a stranger. He felt...

"Insignificant." He said the word aloud. "I feel insignificant."

A man was scooping punch into a cup. He looked at Matt and said, "Hmm?"

Matt shook his head. "Nothing."

He turned and headed out the barn door. The dance continued on without him.

18

MATT FOUND Joe outside the barn, standing with cousin Thad and a couple other boys. Thad was talking. Thad loved to talk, and when he did, it was like he was holding court. He had the gift of charismatic speech, but not theatrically, like Matt did. Thad's gift was more like that of a politician. The gift of poetic bull, Pa had once said. It wouldn't surprise Matt if Thad ran for office one day.

"You should have seen those red savages run," Thad was saying, his voice carrying across the barnyard, his toothy grin in full form. "Never did see a red devil who had what it took to face a man in a fair fight."

Thad was a year younger than Johnny and about as tall as Matt. His hair was the color of buckskin, and it was thick and usually looked windblown. He had pronounced cheekbones and a wide smile. Matt suspected Thad practiced his smile in front of a mirror.

Thad had headed west shortly after Matt and his brothers left. He joined the cavalry and was stationed at some fort out west. Matt forgot which one. He had learned the story in a letter from Ma. In a skirmish with Indians, Thad took an arrow and spent a few weeks recuperating, and then he was sent home. His military adventure ended after eight months.

Thad was apparently regaling everyone with a story from his days out West. Matt knew Thad enough to doubt there was a lot of truth to what Thad was saying. Generally what Thad said was more about Thad saying it than anything else. Matt thought Pa had nailed the proverbial nail on the head.

The sun had set, and the sky overhead was gray. A string of lanterns hung outside the barn and had been lit.

Joe was looking off toward a hayfield beyond. Even though he was with Thad and the boys, he was still standing alone. A tin cup filled with beer was in his hand and he was smoking a hand-rolled cigarette. He stood in his buckskin jacket and his faded cavalry pants, and his floppy, wide-brimmed hat. His tie was long gone. He looked about as out of place here as Matt felt.

Matt walked over to Joe. Joe glanced at him and said, "What's in the punch?"

Matt hadn't even tried it yet. He took a sip. It was

sweet. "Lemon juice, I think."

Thad had said something else—Matt wasn't paying attention—and the boys were laughing long and hard.

Joe said, "He's full of hot air, you know. The Indians I knew are a strong and noble people. They have courage coming out of their ears."

Matt said, "Thad's always been full of hot air. I sometimes wonder why we keep him around."

Joe shrugged. "Because he's family, I guess. Like it or not."

"Have you seen any sign of Johnny?"

Joe shook his head. "Don't really expect to. Not for a long while, at least."

Matt nodded his head in agreement. If Matt had been with a girl like Becky Drummond, he wouldn't be here, either. Nothing more needed be said.

Except one thing. Matt said, "Folks will talk."

Joe said, "Not if they know what's good for them."

Johnny stretched out in the back of the buckboard. He was wearing absolutely nothing. Becky was wearing nothing but an opal ring she had inherited from her grandmother, and was lying beside him. He was thankful no mosquitos seemed to be out.

He was on his back, and he had rolled up his suit jacket to serve as a makeshift pillow. Her head was on his shoulder, and he had one arm around her back. Her hair had come loose, and with Johnny's free hand, he was alternating between playing with her hair and gently sliding his fingers over her shoulder.

The sun had gone down, and they were surrounded by the dark woods. The sounds of the woods had changed from the chirping, lively sounds of day to the more hushed sounds of the night. Crickets. The gentle hoot of an owl somewhere off in the distance. A breeze slipping through the trees and shaking the leaves a little.

Becky's dress was somewhere on the ground. Johnny hadn't seen where it landed, and he had been too busy to care. She had tossed his shirt away, over the side of the wagon. He figured they would be searching for their clothes by match light.

She said, her voice kind of sleepy and dreamy, "I've missed this."

Johnny said, "Me too. I guess I hadn't realized how much."

The women he had been with in those border towns—being with them was nothing like being with Becky.

Her eyes opened. He could feel one lash brush against his chest. "Johnny, I have something to tell you. I don't really know how to tell you, but..."

He said, "Trip Hawley."

"You know?"

He nodded. "I keep my ear to the ground."

She seemed conflicted. Her breathing became kind of short, and he felt her tense up a bit.

"You have nothing to apologize for," he said.

"It's just that I feel I owe you some sort of explanation."

"I was gone for so long. You must have been starting to wonder if I would ever come back. It isn't fair to expect you to wait forever."

She nodded. "I got only one letter from you. It arrived three months after you sent it, based on the postmark. But I got it, and I wrote back."

"I never got that letter. Out west, the mail service sort of creeps along, and it's not organized well. Sometimes letters just don't arrive. Your letter must have gotten lost."

"Trip's a good man."

Johnny said, "Yes, he is. I remember him well."

He had the feeling he wasn't the only one with a lot to say but unsure of how to say it. He thought Becky seemed torn.

Pa had said more than once sometimes the best way to say something is just to say it. He decided to go first.

"I'm not the man I was when I left."

She jumped in. "You're a good man, Johnny. Don't let anyone ever tell you different."

He shrugged. "Maybe. I don't know if I'm any better or worse than when I left. But I'm different. Not the same farm boy you knew."

She hesitated, and then almost reluctantly said, "No. In some ways you're not. I mean in some ways you are, and you're a good man..."

"It's okay." He chuckled. "I'm not hurt. Really. I've had those thoughts right along, and it's best to get them out in the open. Show all our cards."

She grinned. He could feel the grin against his chest. "We've sort of done that already."

He chuckled again.

She grew serious. "A lot of folks don't know this, but Trip's asked me to marry him. I haven't given him my answer yet."

"Do your folks know?"

She nodded. That would serve to explain her father's sort of edgy mood earlier in the afternoon. Trip had proposed marriage, and here she was running off to a dance with her old beau. A dance she and her old beau had never arrived at. Johnny wondered briefly how Trip would feel about it.

"Johnny," she said. "Are you staying? Are you going to stay here in Sheffield, or are you going West again?"

"Part of me wants to stay," he said. "I think I probably should stay. Ma and Pa want me to. But..."

"I can see it in your eyes. I could see it at the store the other day. I could see it today. You're here, but you're not really here. A part of you is still out there, and probably always will be. It's not like you've come home. It's more like you're just here for a visit."

He let her words settle on him. He couldn't deny any of it. The intention hadn't been to necessarily leave again, but maybe his heart knew all along that he wouldn't be staying.

She said, "Say the word and I'll marry you. If you're going to stay, I'll marry you. If you'll have me."

"Becky," he gave a chuckling sigh. "Only a fool would say no to you."

"Then, say the word. If you really can build a life here, if you could really give me your full devotion. But I can't marry a man if I know he'll always be looking off to the horizon. If he'll be standing on the porch at night looking off to the west, and wondering *what if.* If you can say the West has no hold on you, that you never want to go back. That you've had your adventures there and are done with it. If you can say that, then I'll tell Trip *no.*"

Johnny said nothing. He had to let everything she said jostle around inside him. After all, this was not idle talk. These were weighted words they were sharing. Decisions were being made in the back of this buckboard. Decisions that he knew would ripple down through the years.

"I can't make that promise," he found himself saying. "I want to, but I can't."

She nodded.

He said, "I surely want to, Becky. You're a treasure, and I know it. But that land out there, it somehow has a hold of me. I can't explain it. It's not you or anything you've done, believe me."

"I know that."

He continued anyway. "You're the best woman a man could ever have. And it's not like there's anyone out there waiting for me. There's no one who could compare to you. But it's just that the land out there has a hold on me."

"You're going back."

He nodded. "I guess I am."

He realized a decision had been made as he said the words. A decision he supposed he knew in his heart had already been made, but his head was just now realizing. He wasn't sure how he would break the news to Ma and Pa, or even if they would understand, but he was going back to Texas.

He said, "Have you ever thought about going west? I've thought I might want to start a small cattle ranch, one day. We could build a life there. Raise children there."

She shook her head. "My life is here. My family is here. I want to raise my children here."

He nodded. He understood.

They were silent a moment.

Then she said, "I'm going to miss you."

"Promise me one thing."

"Anything."

"Promise me you'll have a good life. The life you're meant to have. Marry Trip. Have children. Raise them to be good men and women. Raise them to make a difference. Build a life with Trip. A life that, when you're old and looking back on it, will give you no regrets."

She shook her head. He felt a dab of wetness against his chest, and realized she had let a tear escape. "No regrets."

"And sometimes, not very often but sometimes, in the evening when you look off to the setting sun, think of a gunfighter you once knew. Because whether I want to admit it or not, that's what I am. Think of a gunfighter you once knew, and know he'll be standing on a porch sometimes and looking off to the eastern horizon and thinking of you."

"It's a promise. All of it."

They rested in silence for a while. The crickets chirped,

and he could feel her heart beating against his chest.

Through the trees, he could see a pale, golden light. The moon was rising.

"It's late," he said. "We should be getting to the dance."

She shook her head. "I don't want to move. I want to stay here a while longer and indulge in what might have been."

Johnny couldn't help but say it. "What about Trip? Is this fair to him?"

She rose from his chest to hover over him, her hands at either side of him, her arms straight. Her hair was hanging down and touching his face.

She said, "I needed this, Johnny. I'm not ashamed to admit I longed for it. I never feel more alive than when you and I are...shall we say, dancing. Don't think poorly of me for it."

He shook his head. "I could never think poorly of you."

"And I think I need one more dance." And she dropped onto him, her mouth landing on his.

19

THE LANTERNS LIGHTED UP the barnyard. Many of the wagons had gone, and a couple people milled by the door. The musicians had long since gone home.

Matt had a pint bottle in his hand. Martin Everett, the eldest Everett boy, had gone to his bedroom and come back with a pint of rum—God bless him.

Joe liked beer, but the beer had run out, so he was sharing the rum with Matt. Any port in a storm.

Martin had joined them for a couple mouthfuls of rum, then went off to see a girl home. A girl he knew from school and said he was hoping to marry. A girl he would build a life with, here in farming country.

Matt took a swig of the rum and handed the bottle to Joe. Joe took a pull from it.

Matt said, "Ma's going to turn inside out when we come back smelling like rum."

Joe said, "She's got to expect it. Like it's always been said, we have Pa's backbone and Ma's temper. Them's ingredients for a whole passel of trouble."

Outside, beyond the edge of the lantern light, crickets were chirping. The night had turned off cool, a welcome break from the heat of the day, but there was a dampness to it. Matt could smell wet earth.

Matt said to Joe, "You lived among Indians for a while? And you almost married one?"

Joe nodded. He said nothing.

Matt said, "I think all three of us have lots of secrets we don't really want to tell Ma and Pa about. Things they just wouldn't understand."

Joe nodded. He still said nothing.

"Will you talk to me about it when you're ready?"

Joe said, "Yup. When I'm ready. A lot happened I'm not ready to talk about just yet."

"Understood."

They were silent for a few moments. Matt had the bottle again. He took another sip of rum. He hadn't realized how much he had missed it. On the ship, he had usually taken a shot or two of rum before bed. When he played cards with the other men, there was often rum involved. When he thought of his life aboard ship, he thought of the salty spray of the sea, the rolling horizon, the sails billowing and snapping in the wind, and the taste of rum.

Matt said, "Did you see the look on Trip Hawley's face tonight? He was watching for Becky and Johnny to arrive."

"And they never did."

"Oh, I think they arrived, but not here."

Joe chuckled, and took another pull of rum.

Matt said, "What do you think Trip's going to do?"

"I think he's gonna want to beat the stuffin' out of Johnny."

Matt shook his head. "It'll be his mistake. I really don't think there's a man alive who can whip Johnny."

20

MA INSISTED the boys take Sunday off and attend church with her and Pa. Matt's head was aching because of all the rum, and all he could think about as the preacher rambled on was getting ahold of a cup of Johnny's thick, strong coffee.

Come Monday, Matt and Johnny attacked the wood pile again, and this time they worked with furious abandon and got all of the four-foot-lengths sawed into stove lengths.

They didn't split them. Wood splitting was done just before the wood box was loaded. Some chunks of wood would be split into thin pieces and used in the early stages of building a fire. Other chunks would be split into halves only and placed in the fire once it was hot enough to catch a larger piece of wood on fire.

Come Tuesday, they decided to head into town. Even though it was a farming town and mostly everyone attended one of the two churches in town—Baptist or Methodist—there was also a saloon. Matt had decided he had missed the taste of rum more than he realized and had a hankering for some.

Johnny figured, even though they wouldn't have tequila, he would tag along.

Pa had said to them, "Your Ma won't approve, but what the hey. You're young, and you boys worked hard. Go into town and have a drink. If Ma balks, I'll deal with her. You're grown men. You should be able to have a drink if'n you want one."

He slapped Joe on the shoulder and said, "Go with 'em, boy. Have a drink with your brothers."

Luke was smiling. "I can drive the wagon."

Pa shook his head. "In a few more years, you can. But today, you're heading out to the fields with me."

Johnny and Joe saddled their horses. Matt didn't want to be the odd man out and there was a beaten-up English saddle in the barn, so he saddled the old mare that served as the family horse. She shook her head and gave a couple of whinneys, letting it be known that she wasn't accustomed to a saddle and didn't like it.

Joe was grinning. "Won't be surprised if she tries to buck you off."

Matt said, "She's too old to do any bucking."

Turned out he was right.

He couldn't ride like Johnny and Joe. They moved with

the horse, like they were one with their horse. Matt bounced along in the saddle and Johnny figured Matt would have a bruised back-side before the day was through. But to Matt's credit, he never fell out of the saddle.

They swung down from their saddles in front of the saloon. Of course, this wasn't really a saloon, not as Johnny understood the word. It was a drinking establishment. Kinsey's Tavern. Once they were inside, they were greeted by a mahogany bar, and there were no whores waiting to try to sell their wares. No card sharks waiting to start a faro game and cheat you out of your money.

They bellied up to the bar, and Matt ordered a shot of rum.

Johnny said, "You don't have tequila, by chance?"

The bartender shook his head. Johnny didn't know him. Apparently another newcomer to town.

Johnny said, "Southern bourbon? Corn squeezings?"

The bartender shook his head.

"Scotch, I suppose."

The bartender nodded. "That, we have."

Joe ordered a beer.

"So, here we stand," Matt said. "We went off to see the world, to learn more about what lay beyond the confines of Sheffield, Pennsylvania, so when we returned we would have worldly knowledge. Pa didn't want us to build a life for ourselves here because it was all we knew. He wanted us to do so because we chose to, after having seen some of the world."

Johnny looked to Joe. "Give him just a taste of rum, and he gets more wind than those sails on his ship."

Joe chuckled.

Matt ignored them. "I suppose what I'm getting at is that the intention was for us to serve in the military for a little while and then come back here and find wives and have children. And push a plow into the earth and attend church on Sunday."

Johnny nodded. "That seems to be the way of it."

"But what happened was the world changed us. Johnny, you became a gunfighter. Me, I sailed the seven seas and fought pirates. At times, I have to admit, I was little better than a pirate myself. And you..." Matt looked to Joe.

Joe shrugged. "What can I say?"

Joe took a sip of beer, and said to Matt, "They talked

about our brother, you know. His name is mentioned in saloons and around campfires."

Matt said, "You mentioned that once."

Johnny shut his eyes. "I don't want to hear this."

"What're they saying about him?"

Joe said, "They say he drinks hard, lives hard, and shoots hard. They say he shot the gun clean out of a man's hand."

Matt looked at Johnny. "That true?"

Johnny nodded. "Yes. But it's not what they say."

They waited while Johnny took a sip of scotch. Not bad, he thought, but it sure wasn't tequila.

Johnny said, "The man challenged me to a gunfight. This was last winter, sometime. It's hard to tell, south of the border. They don't really have winter down there. I was in a cantina, that's what the Mexicans call a saloon. I was in there, and there was a senorita who worked there that I had taken a shine to. A little too much tequila, and Sheffield starts to feel like it's a long ways away, and the values you might have learned tend to go out the window."

Joe and Matt were both waiting for him to continue. He noticed the bartender was, too.

"Well," Johnny said, "there was this man by the name of Walker. Never did get his first name. He decided to challenge me to a gunfight. Was calling me all sorts of names. Well, you can't just let a man get away with something like that. Folks'll think you're a coward, and then your reputation will be no good. If you want to build a life in the West, you have to have respect. And you can't have respect if folks think you're a coward.

"Walker stood out in the street calling to me. I left the cantina, and stepped out to meet him."

The bartender, enthralled with the story, took a bottle and refilled Johnny's glass.

Matt said, "So, you just met him out on the street to have a gun duel?"

Johnny nodded. "Now, keep in mind, I had too much tequila in me. Walker—he's standing there shouting to me. Calling me a coward and other names. I said, *Put your money where your mouth is, and go for your guns!*"

"Did he?" the bartender said.

Johnny nodded. "Oh, yeah. He went for his, and I went for mine. Now, he was standing maybe fifty feet away. A shot

I could make almost every time. But not after all that tequila."

He looked at his audience. He said, "Walker reached for his gun first but I was faster. We got both of our guns out at about the same time. He fired first and missed. Just barely. I felt the wind of the bullet as it went past my ear.

"I fired next, and I was aiming dead center on his chest. But I was too filled with tequila to make the shot. My bullet caught his hand and knocked the gun clean out of his grip."

"No kidding," Matt said.

"The bullet ruined his gun. Broke the handle and knocked the cylinder clean out. It also took three fingers off his hand."

Joe was grinning. "You're making that up."

"No I'm not. Swear to God. The last I knew, they've started calling him Two-Finger."

Matt was shaking his head. "Incredible."

Johnny said, "That's the way it happened."

Joe said, "They say you outdrew Monkey Bob Donovan, in a town south of the border. They say he drew on you and got off one shot but missed, and you put one between his eyes."

Johnny nodded. "That really happened, too. Just like they said. I was down there with Zack. Monkey Bob, he challenged me. I had a little too much tequila in me then too, but not enough that I couldn't shoot straight."

Johnny glanced at the bartender, then at Matt. "They called him Monkey Bob because he had a face only a mother could love."

Matt said, "Johnny, you really are a desperado."

Johnny looked to Joe, who had again taken to staring off into a distance only he could see. Johnny noticed Joe seemed to do that a lot, these days.

Johnny said, "All three of us have done some hard living these past three years, I think. Done some things I don't think any of us would want Ma and Pa to know about, or the people here in Sheffield. They just wouldn't understand."

Matt said, "I killed a pirate captain with a knife once. We were being boarded. He had a cutlass in his hand, and I had lost mine. I pulled a knife I wore on my belt. He swiped at me and I ducked, and then I cut him from his belt to his jaw. One long, fast and hard swipe. I kept that knife sharp. I have it with me. It's in my duffel bag at the house. Won it off a Persian sailor in a card game. I didn't want to show up with it on my belt, but I don't like to be far from it."

Johnny said, "Like me and my guns."

Matt nodded. "Something like that, I suppose."

Joe said, still looking distant, "I lived among the Cheyenne. Two years."

Matt and Johnny both looked at him. They remained silent while they waited for him to continue.

Johnny drained his shot glass. Funny thing about scotch, he thought. The more of it you drank, the better it seemed to taste. Matt finished his rum, and the bartender refilled both glasses.

Joe said, "I was with the Army when they rode down on a small village of Lakota. What the white men call the Sioux. I was the scout. There weren't no warriors there. Just women and children, and a few old men. I didn't know the Army was going to do that. I was told to scout the village, so I did. It was the Army. They gave orders and I followed 'em. But these soldiers, they rode down on 'em. They shot and killed every one of 'em. There was one girl, maybe no more'n fifteen. Three of the soldiers surrounded her, and they were intending to have their way with her. I pulled my gun and told 'em the first one who touches her will get one right betwixt the eyes. They shot her instead. Then they burned all the lodges."

A tear was running down the side of Joe's face. "I just rode away. I never looked back. I guess I'm officially a deserter. But I rode away. Found myself up in the mountains, in Nebraska Territory. I passed myself off as a hunter and a trapper. Pretty easy to do, after a few weeks on the trail. I gave my name as Joe Reynolds. I took the name from Taffy Reynolds. The first girl I ever...let's say the first girl I ever knowed."

Johnny smiled. He remembered Taffy Reynolds. A girl who was kind of short and had dark hair. She had been maybe a year behind Joe in school, and shyness had never been one of her problems. By the time Johnny and his brothers had left Sheffield, Taffy and her family had moved out to Ohio, but her legacy still remained.

Joe continued, "I met some Cheyenne warriors and began spending time at their village. They had set up their village for the winter in a valley. There's a river runs through there, they're startin' to call the Salmon River. Stayed there two years, and while I was there, I met me a Cheyenne woman. Fell in love. But then she chose to marry another warrior. That was when I decided to maybe ride east.

"I swung into Fort Laramie, figuring they probably wouldn't remember me, or know me. I looked a lot different than I did in my Army days. That's when I found the letter from Ma, at a trading post waiting for me."

The bartender said, "You three all left here probably not much different than any of the other farm boys around here. But your life's experiences changed you. You came back different men than when you left."

Johnny nodded. He said, "I think we're seeing that, more and more, the longer we're here."

The discussion didn't go any further, because Trip Hawley walked in.

Trip was a couple inches taller than Johnny, but longer and thinner. He had a shock of hair the color of mud and a nose that was a little too long. But he was an honest boy who worked hard and was greatly respected for it, and now he was madder'n all get out because he thought the woman he loved had been wronged.

"Johnny McCabe!" he bellowed. "I want a word with you. Right now!"

Johnny shook his head, and said to his brothers, "I guess I should have seen this coming."

21

TRIP HAWLEY STRODE across the empty barroom floor to stand behind Johnny.

He said, "I know you was with Becky Drummond Saturday night. I know what you was doing."

Johnny turned to face him. "Slow down, Trip. I don't want to fight you."

Trip said, "You got no right being with my woman. I asked her to marry me. You got no right touching her."

Johnny said, "Have you talked with Becky?"

"I ain't. There's nothing she can say."

"Trip, she loves you. Go talk to her."

Trip said, "Not till I have defended her honor."

Johnny sighed with resignation. He knew where this was going.

Trip stepped back to build momentum, the way a country boy will do before he throws a punch, and then he let loose with a blow he figured would lay Johnny out on the floor.

Johnny stepped to one side and Trip's fist found nothing but air. Johnny grabbed Trip by the shoulder and belt and gave him a shove toward the bar. Trip lost his footing in the process and the mahogany bar caught him on the chin, snapping his head back. Trip dropped to the floor and stayed there for a moment or two, blinking his eyes and shaking out the cobwebs. Then he got to his knees, but rose no further. A purplish bruise was already rising on his chin.

Joe said to Johnny, "That was slick."

Matt said to Johnny, "That Chinaman teach you that?"

Johnny nodded. "Sometimes it's best not to meet an attack head on, but to sidestep it and help it along its way."

Joe said, "Looks a lot like Indian wrestling I seen among the Cheyenne."

Trip tried to get to his feet, but stumbled back to his knees.

Johnny said, "Trip, you gotta relax. You asked Becky to marry you, and I think she's gonna say yes."

Johnny and Joe each grabbed Trip by an arm and helped him to his feet. Johnny said to the bartender, "Can you fetch him a whiskey? It'll help with the pain."

"Rum," Matt said.

Johnny said, "Whichever's cheapest."

The bartender set a shot glass on the bar in front of Trip and poured a mouthful of whiskey into it.

Johnny said, "Drink that down. It'll make your chin not hurt so bad."

Trip downed the shot, and then his eyes widened and Johnny thought Trip was going to spew the whiskey right across the floor. Johnny realized it was probably the first time Trip had ever tasted whiskey. Probably would be the last, too. Trip was coughing like his throat was on fire. Johnny slapped the boy's back a couple of times.

Funny that Johnny thought of Trip as a boy. Trip was Johnny's age. Trip was a little taller than he had been three years ago, and his shoulders filled out his shirt a little more. But otherwise he was still the same farm boy he had been. Whereas Johnny and his brothers were so different from what they had been when they first left Sheffield.

Trip leaned his elbows on the bar. "You done broke my jaw."

"No, I didn't," Johnny said.

Johnny turned his back to the bar and leaned his elbows on it.

"I love Becky," Trip said. "For the longest time, all us boys stayed away from her. We knew she was just waiting for you. But time went by and she didn't hear from you. So I got brave and I asked her to a dance. She's a great girl, you know."

"The catch of a lifetime," Johnny said.

"But then you come back, and you take her right out from under me."

"Listen to me, Trip. Becky's a good girl. I don't want you to ever think different. And she loves you. She knows you're a good man. We talked long about that. I think if you rode over there right now, she'll tell you yes. She's gonna marry you."

Trip looked at Johnny. "You think so?"

Johnny shrugged. "I'm not a gambling man. Well, not too much. But if I was to lay odds, I'd say, yes. I think she's gonna marry you."

Trip smiled, but the smile hurt his jaw, and he winced and brought a hand up to it.

"Listen, Trip." Johnny gripped him by the shoulder. "I need you to promise me something. Always take good care of her. Make her happy. Build a good life with her. Bring children into the world, and raise 'em right."

Trip nodded. "I'll do that."

"Have you thought about the Wheeler farm? I hear it's available. If you offered the Wheeler widow the right price, she'd probably sell it to you."

He nodded. "I'll admit, I've thought about that place."

"Your family is well respected in town. I'm sure the bank would be willing to work with you. Now, if you think your jaw will hold together, go on over there and see Becky. Right now."

"But, I ain't had a bath. I'm still in my farmin' clothes."

"Trip, just go over there. She's gonna see you in your farming clothes a lot, over the years."

Trip's eyes lighted up. "I'm heading over there right now."

Johnny said, "Treat a girl like that right, Trip, and you'll never regret it."

Trip nodded. He turned and headed out the door.

Matt said, "I think that's one of the greatest things I've ever seen a man do."

Johnny said nothing. He turned back to the bar and waved one hand toward his empty whiskey glass. With a big smile, the bartender filled it.

22

IT WAS toward the end of September. The corn in Pa's fields now stood tall and was ready to be harvested. The humidity of summer had died away, and there was a smell of dryness to the air, meaning autumn was just around the corner.

A gunshot cracked sharply and an empty can leaped away from a fence rail. The shot died away into the distance like a roll of thunder as the can landed in the grass. Thad McCabe held a pistol, and smoke drifted from the muzzle.

Thad was grinning wide and looked at Johnny.

"Not bad," Johnny said. "A hundred feet. Not bad shooting at all."

"Not bad?" Thad snorted a chuckle. "Pretty good shooting is what it is."

Johnny stood behind Thad, and Matt and Joe stood alongside Johnny. They waited while Thad drew a bead on a second can and plucked it off with another shot.

Thad was using a Colt .44 he had acquired during his short time in the Army. His Army-issue holster was buckled around his waist.

Johnny was wearing his guns. Dang, but it felt good to have them back where they belonged. He hadn't worn them in the three months he had been home. He still slept with a pistol on a chair beside the bed, but this was the first day he had actually buckled his gunbelt on.

Thad had come over and they decided to do some target practice. Joe had his gun tucked in front of his belt, and Matt had his Navy Colt in one hand.

Luke was there also. "Let's see you take two, now. Shoot one and then the other, without stopping."

Thad gave Luke a look as if to say, *watch this*, and fired two shots. One can leaped away and the other went spinning and dropped to the ground.

"You only nicked one," Johnny said.

Thad looked at him. "I'd like to see you do better."

Matt smiled. "Show him what you can do, Johnny."

"It'll be hard to beat that," Thad said, nodding with his head toward the fence rail. "I been practicing every day out behind the house. Ma hates the shooting. The noise and all. But I have to do it."

Matt said, "Why?"

"Because I'm going back. West, that is. I'm going

west."

"Have you conned the cavalry into taking you back?"

Thad gave him a look that said he didn't appreciate the comment.

He said, "The cavalry is behind me. I'm going west, anyway. I'm staying home for Christmas, then come spring, I'll be gone."

Johnny said, "What'll you do out there, if you're not in the Army anymore?"

Thad shrugged. "I can work cattle. Or maybe look for gold. There's a ton of it out there, you know. A fortune waiting to be dug up. There's prospectors out in western Utah Territory, working a piece of land they call the Washoe. And there's other places. The gold's just waiting to be found."

Thad aimed his gun at another can standing on the rail, squinting one eye as he aligned the pistol's sight with the can.

"There's plenty of gold right here, Thad," Matt said. "In the soil. You won't find soil richer than this anywhere. And your home is here."

"I don't consider trying to beg a living from the land to be the same as gold. I'm seeing my father grow old doing it, and it's not for me. The west is practically awash in gold."

Matt said to Johnny, "You ever see any gold in Texas?"

Johnny shook his head. "Met a man who had a gold watch once. That's all I ever saw."

Thad said, "And in the West, mainly in California, communities are growing. They need leadership. Men to run for office."

Johnny said, "I should've figured that would be in there somewhere."

Thad ignored him. "I figure maybe that's where my gold truly lies."

Thad squeezed the trigger for emphasis, the gun cracked, and one more can leaped from the fence rail.

Thad looked to Johnny and to Joe. Thad said, "You boys were out West. You know why I want to go back there."

Joe plucked a long stem of brown grass and gripped it with his teeth. "Beautiful country."

"Come on. There's Indians. And outlaws."

Joe said, "Didn't see too many outlaws."

"I saw a few," Johnny said. "None of 'em were much to write home about."

Thad ignored Johnny and focused on Joe. "What are the Indians like?"

Matt said, "I thought you fought a bunch of them. Called them *red devils*, as I recall."

"That was just talk. Those boys wanted to be entertained, and I did the entertaining. Sometimes you have to give the people what they want."

"At least you have to appear to, especially if you're going to run for office," Matt said.

Thad ignored him, too. He focused on Joe. "What were they like? The Indians?"

Joe shrugged his shoulders. He was wearing his buckskin jacket and his wide, floppy hat. He hadn't shaved in weeks, and his beard was back.

He said, "Indians are people, that's all. From a different way of life, so they don't talk the same or have the same customs. But people are people. They laugh and they cry and they love and they fight. I think people are people, the world over."

Thad looked to Johnny. Thad said, "All right. You really think you can out shoot me? I've been practicing all summer. Show me what you can do."

Johnny hadn't shot his guns since before he had come home. But when he faced the cans, it felt like he had last shot them just yesterday. It seemed a natural thing to him, as natural as breathing.

He pulled the right-hand gun, cocking it as he did so, and brought his arm to full extension. All in less than a second. He squeezed the trigger and a can flew into the air."

"Wow!" Luke shouted. "Incredible!"

Joe said quietly, "The stuff legends are made of."

Johnny hooked his finger into the trigger guard, spun the gun and slapped it back into his holster. "Pick a can."

Eleven cans still stood on the fence. Matt said, "Second from the left."

Johnny's gun leaped into his hand and he fired, and the second can from the left went flying into the air.

Johnny said, "Here's an old trick I used to do, when I was practicing as a kid. Let's see if I can still do it."

Johnny shot a third can from the fence, and then he fired another shot at it. This shot missed, however, and the can fell to the grass.

He said, "When I was a kid and practicing all the time,

I used to be able to shoot a can in the air and then keep it in the air until my gun was empty. I'm a little rusty at it, now. Powder and bullets are expensive, out West. You don't want to waste any of 'em target practicing."

Thad said, "Too much showing off is not good for the soul."

Johnny found his ire rising, maybe because Thad shouldn't be one to make comments like that.

Johnny said, "I'm not done, yet."

He fired again, catching the can near where it touched the ground and made it spring up into the air again. And he fired another shot through it before it could begin its return trip downward. The can went spinning away and landed fifty feet behind the fence.

"Now, that's what I call shootin'!" Luke said.

"It ain't showing off," Johnny said, "if all you're doing is showing the people what you can do."

Johnny was smiling, Matt realized. Truly smiling. He didn't think Johnny had truly smiled since coming home. He might have grinned once or twice, but nothing like this.

Thad said, "I heard Becky Drummond's getting married."

Matt looked at him with disbelief. It was a crappy thing to say. Johnny was showing up Thad, and Thad couldn't be a man about it so he tried to throw a dagger at him.

Johnny said, "That she is. To a good man, too."

"That doesn't gall you at all?"

Johnny shook his head. "Nope. I encouraged it. Becky and I are good friends and always will be. Trip Hawley's a good man."

Matt decided it was time to change the subject or he was going to drive a fist into their cousin's face. Matt said to Johnny, "Let's see that border shift we've heard so much about."

Johnny popped the cylinder out of his gun and pulled a fresh one from a jacket pocket.

"All right," Johnny said. "A border shift."

With a fresh cylinder in place, he began firing. One after another, so close together they were almost a continuous roar. The cans leaped off the fence. When the right-hand gun was empty, Johnny pulled the left one, then tossed both into the air, catching the left-hand gun with his right and continued shooting before the roar of his previous shot had fully faded. He slid the empty gun into his left holster while he plucked five more cans from the fence.

He stood with the empty gun in his hand, a cloud of powder smoke enveloping him like land fog.

Thad was staring at the fence, then he looked at Johnny. "You ought to come west with me. Shooting like that, you're just wasting your talent behind a plow."

Johnny slid the gun into his holster. He looked to Matt, and Matt gave a little shrug. He looked to Joe, who still had the strand of grass in his teeth and was looking off toward the distance.

Thad said, "What?"

Matt slapped his shoulder. "Sometimes, Thad my boy, what's not being said is something not meant for your ears."

The next few weeks, Thomas McCabe and his sons harvested the land, taking bushels of corn and potatoes. They grew potatoes as a sort of secondary crop. Not good to put all your eggs in one basket, he had said.

The crops were sold, and the money went to paying off all the people Pa owed. Such is the way of the farmer, Johnny thought. Always had been, and probably always would be. They borrow throughout the year against their crops so they can obtain supplies for the farm. Even when the farmer goes into town for a haircut, he does so on credit. Then come harvest time, he sells his crops and pays off the loans. For a short time, money exchanges hands throughout town. And then the whole process begins again.

Some might have wondered why a farmer lived a life that would seem to be filled with constant frustration. Breaking even but seldom getting ahead. But Johnny understood. A farmer didn't plant seed and coax his crops along through droughts and floods in hopes of profits. He did so to be close to the land, to bring life from it. The sale of a farmer's produce simply paid his debts and kept his family's needs paid for and allowed him to continue this lifestyle for another year. It wasn't much different for cattle ranchers out in Texas.

Come late October, the leaves of the maple, birch, ash and alder covering the hills behind the house were turning red and gold and falling to the ground. Soon the mornings would bring a frost.

Pa and the boys began heading out into the woods by day to bring in more firewood. Logs would be cut into four-foot lengths and left to age over the winter and then burned the following winter.

On days they weren't working on the firewood, Johnny practiced with his pistols. After a time, he found he could once again keep a tin can aloft for a volley of three shots, but the fourth would always miss.

Amazing, he thought, how his trick shooting had seemed to be at its best when he was fifteen.

Joe began practicing with him. Joe could match him in accuracy, but he couldn't shoot as fast.

Throughout it all, Johnny's mind kept returning to the thought of going west. The idea had been fully planted the evening he had spent with Becky Drummond, and it wouldn't leave him be.

One night, Johnny was sitting in the parlor with Joe and Matt. The night was turning off chilly and a fire was crackling away in the hearth. Ma and Pa had turned in and so had Luke.

The only light in the room came from the fireplace, creating an orange glow that flickered along the walls. It was quiet, except for the crackle and snap of the fire. The wind outside picked up, sounding cold, and rattled the window pane.

Then Joe spoke. "I'm going West with Thad in the spring."

Matt and Johnny looked at him.

"Isn't that kind of sudden?" Matt said.

"I been thinkin' on it quite a while. Even before Thad said anything about it."

"Just like that? Have you thought about how Ma and Pa are going to feel? We've been gone for three whole years, and now you're heading back? Just like that?"

"It ain't *just like that*. It's something I been thinking about long and hard. I just don't belong here anymore. I'm out of place. We been back here more'n four months, but I'm as much an outsider now as I was when we first rode in."

Matt said, "Joe, I know how you feel. Believe me. There's still a part of me that will always long for the sea. But this is our home. Think about what it will do to Ma and Pa."

Matt looked to Johnny. "Talk to him, will you?"

Johnny was staring into the fire. He said, "I can't.

Because I'm going with him."

Matt gave his brother a long look, like he hadn't been expecting Johnny to say what he did.

Johnny got up from his chair and went over to the fire. He took a wrought iron poker and shifted the wood around a little.

He said, "You know how I feel. We've talked about it enough. You can't think after all that talk I'd be staying."

He set the poker down and looked at Matt. "If I was staying, then I'd be with Becky."

Matt nodded. "I guess I knew that. It's just now that decisions are being made, I'm thinking about Ma and Pa."

"You think I'm not? If not for them, I would have ridden out the day after that dance."

"The dance you never actually showed up at."

"Yeah, that one."

Joe grinned.

Johnny went back to his chair. A high-backed chair with old, beaten-down velvet upholstery.

Matt said, "So, when do you leave?"

Joe rubbed his fingers through his beard. "Thad says he's leavin' after Christmas."

Johnny said, "I don't know if I'd really want to travel with him. He's too confident in the things he doesn't really know. He could get a man killed."

"We should wait a little ways after Christmas. Let the snow melt a little and the trails open up."

"So," Matt said. "I guess that's it. You've made your decisions."

Joe shrugged. "Guess so."

Johnny said, "Becky and Trip are going to be married in the spring. I'd like to be long gone by then."

Joe nodded. He said to Matt, "What about you? Are you staying?"

Matt looked like he was about to say *yes*. But he hesitated. He let his gaze drift from Joe to the fire.

He said, "I don't know."

They sat in silence for a while. The fire crackled, and the wind outside blew.

Matt said, "Well, that gives us a few months at least to figure out how to tell Ma and Pa."

23

THE STORE WAS closed, and Hector Drummond was finishing a cup of coffee before he headed home. The coffee had gone cold, but he didn't mind.

Actually, he didn't really care about the coffee, but wanted some time alone. Time to think. He had a lot on his mind.

He sat at his desk in the store room, with the cup of cold coffee in front of him. A lot had gone on this summer and he was trying to digest it all.

Johnny McCabe had come back into his daughter's life, and Hector thought that after Johnny's three-year absence, things could now be as they should be. Becky and Johnny had always seemed so incredibly linked together, from their early school years on. If Johnny was down at the stream with a fishing pole, Becky was usually with him. If there was a church picnic, you could almost bet money they would be at each other's side. When Thomas McCabe and his sons went hunting and brought home some deer, Becky was right there in the kitchen with Mrs. McCabe, cutting up the venison.

And then when the kids got into their teens and were not so much kids anymore, a true romance blossomed. Hand-holding. Stealing kisses on the front porch. Becky and Johnny thought the old man didn't know about that, but there wasn't much that went on in his house or with his family he didn't know about.

And Hector knew there had been intimate times, too. Becky and Johnny were discreet, but Hector knew his daughter. A look in her eye, a certain bounce in her step. A certain proprietary way a man and a woman have toward each other once they have been intimate.

Of course, no man wants anyone touching his daughter. It makes your hackles rise. And society had a serious taboo about anyone consummating before marriage, even though a lot more consummating went on than people wanted to admit. But Hector had at least the comfort of knowing it was Johnny. A good boy, who came from good stock. Hector had always assumed Johnny would be the father of his grandchildren.

Then Johnny and his brothers had gone off to join the military, on the advice of their father. See a little bit of the world.

The expectation was Johnny would return once his enlistment was up, and he and Becky would marry. But Johnny somehow returned a different man. Hector could see it. He figured everyone could. He knew Becky could. Johnny's brothers were different, too. Josiah, especially. Whatever happened was not being talked about, but people were speculating. Lots of wild stories. The most popular theory was they had deserted from the military and become outlaws. Their father and their uncle Jake had a wild streak when they were younger, Jake especially, and people were thinking these boys had it, too.

Johnny hadn't written to Becky, except for once shortly after he had left. Hector always wondered why. Becky tried to wait for him, but as one month blended into another, Becky started to wonder if Johnny would ever be coming back. Hector did, too.

Then Trip Hawley started showing interest in Becky. Hector wasn't surprised other boys were showing interest in her. Becky was pretty as all get-out, just like her mother. Trip Hawley was a good boy. Rock solid, and also came from good stock. Hector was not disappointed with the idea of his daughter marrying him.

But then Johnny returned. The night of the dance, Johnny had been her escort, not Trip. And Johnny and Becky hadn't arrived at the dance. Hector knew the way of folks—he knew Becky and Johnny weren't playing checkers.

Then, a few days after the dance, Becky announced she was marrying Trip. If Trip was the man she wanted, then Hector would be supportive. But he would feel better about the whole thing if Johnny and his brothers would leave again. And this time, not come back. He didn't think his daughter could ever fully focus on Trip with Johnny around.

Hector decided to head home. As he walked across the store to the door, a couple floorboards creaking underfoot, he thought about how he had built this store. Not only built the business, but built the actual building. It had been an empty lot before he started. He had nailed every board in place. Becky was his only child, and one day it would go to her. Her and Trip.

They would run it, and the thought pleased him. Trip had a strong work ethic, and Becky had a good head for business. Trip had been talking about the old Wheeler place, but Hector was working at convincing Becky to let go of that idea and take the store. It would be much steadier income over the years.

He blew the lamp out behind the counter, locked up and started down the street. His and Mavis's house was just outside of the small business section of Sheffield. It was dark, and he walked along. After being on his feet at the store all day, it felt kind of good to step along and stretch his legs a little. He was hungry, and he knew Mavis had been preparing a roast. There was nothing like her roast.

He crossed the street. The hotel ahead was active, with light in the windows. As he walked, he decided to check the time. He had told Mavis he would be home by eight. He figured he would be able to see the face of his watch in the light from the hotel.

He reached into his pocket for his watch, but the watch wasn't there. *Oh, that's right*, he thought. He had pulled it out when he was at his desk, finishing that cup of cold coffee. He wanted to see if he had time for one more cup before heading out. He had left the watch on his desk.

Getting absent-minded in his old age, he thought with a chuckle. Even though he wasn't that old. Forty-nine.

He turned and crossed back over the street. As he approached the store, he noticed a lighted window.

Had he left a lamp burning, too? Must be really getting absent-minded. He cursed himself. No excuse for carelessness. He was always saying that to Becky, when she was growing up. Take care of business. Keep everything in order.

He unlocked the front door and stepped in. The light was coming from a kerosene lamp mounted on the wall behind the counter. He was sure he had blown that lamp out before he left, but there it was. Still burning. He stepped around the counter to blow it out. This time he would be sure he did.

And he noticed the cash register drawer was hanging open. It was empty. He usually left ten dollars in the drawer in ones and coins, to make change with the following day. He fully remembered doing that before he sat down at his desk, to finish his coffee.

Then a man stepped into the room, through the door leading to the storeroom. He wasn't much older than Johnny or Trip. He wore a battered bowler over his head and a tattered jacket. His face was boyishly smooth, with only some fine fur at the chin, and his eyes were wide and scared. A short-barreled revolver was in one hand.

The face was familiar. Where had Hector seen him before? Then he remembered. In the store earlier in the week. The boy had drifted in while Hector was assisting other customers. The boy had milled about for a few minutes, then drifted back out.

He aimed the pistol at Drummond, and Drummond noticed the hammer was cocked. The barrel of the pistol was shaking a little.

The boy said, "Where do you keep the money? There was only ten dollars in that there register."

Hector Drummond should have been afraid. He realized he was probably going to die.

He had never been in battle before. He had never joined the Army or gone to war. He didn't really know how you were supposed to feel in a situation like this. He figured maybe he should be terrified and start begging for his life. But what he felt was a strange calmness. Like he was somehow removed from the scene and was watching it like a spectator.

"That's all there is," Hector said. "I took the day's take down to the bank a half hour before I left."

"You lie." There was the sound of desperation in the boy's voice. He was the one who was scared. How odd, Hector thought.

Hector shook his head. "It's the truth. I don't leave the day's take just laying around in the store. There was more than fifty dollars there. More than most men make in a full week. We had a good day. I'm not going to just leave that laying around."

"You gotta have something. A safe. Somewhere to keep extra cash."

"No need to. The bank's just down the street. I drop all the money there. I start each day with only ten dollars."

The boy said nothing. His eyes were wide, and a drop of sweat rolled down his forehead and into his eye. He reached up to wipe it away.

"How'd you get in here?" Hector said. "Did you break in the back door?"

"You hesh up," the boy said. "You just hesh up while I think."

Hector held out his hand. "You don't want to do this. Why don't you give me the gun?"

The gun went off, and the bullet caught Hector in the chest.

The shot slammed him back a few steps, like being hit with a hammer. But he stayed on his feet, and he found the strange calmness was still there. He opened his jacket and looked down at his white shirt. A hole had been ripped into it just above where his vest was buttoned, and it was already starting to soak with blood.

"You shot me," Drummond said.

The boy stared at the gun wide-eyed, like he was surprised. Like he hadn't meant to fire it.

He took a step backward. Then another. His heel caught against the toe of his other foot, and he fell and landed on his butt. He sat and stared at the man he had just shot.

Hector turned toward the counter. What were you supposed to do if you were shot? The doctor, he supposed. Go fetch the doctor. There was no one here to do it, so he would have to do it himself. The doctor's office was just across the street, and the doctor and his wife lived on the second floor above it.

Drummond was starting to feel a little light headed. He looked down at his shirt again and saw the entire front was now soaking in red. But he didn't think about dying. He thought that Mavis was going to have to find some way to get all that blood out. That was, if she could patch the bullet hole effectively.

Then his knees buckled. He was losing strength and he was finding it hard to breathe. He grabbed hold of the counter to try and hold himself upright, and then he went down to the floor.

24

THE MORNING AIR WAS brisk. A thin layer of frost caused strands of grass near the barn door to take on an ice-like quality. Johnny could see a cloud of white when he exhaled.

He hitched the team to the buckboard. By the time he was finished, Pa and his brothers were coming out of the house.

They were all heading out to the woods. In the back of the buckboard were axes and two cross-cut saws. By evening, Johnny expected they would be returning with a wagon full of four-foot lengths. Pa had seen a couple of oaks he wanted to bring down. Oak was good for burning because it burned slow and hot.

They headed out. Pa had the reins, but Johnny and his brothers walked. They didn't want the cold to start biting into their toes like it might if they sat in the wagon.

They followed a logging trail Pa and Luke had cut over the past three years. After a half mile, Pa pulled the reins and brought the team to a stop.

Pa said, "Only a little ways in there," indicating with a nod of his head the woods to the right of the trail.

"Lead the way," Matt said.

Johnny walked with a double-edged axe over his shoulder. Joe carried an axe the same way, and Matt carried one of the long crosscut saws. Luke carried a kettle of steaming coffee and a stack of tin coffee cups.

They followed Pa along and came to the trees. Two giants, now almost leafless, reaching their bony fingers to the sky. What few leaves remained were brown and curled.

Johnny had always been amazed by the different character these hills would take on, as the seasons changed. In the summer, the woods had seemed thick and closed-in. Now, with the leaves gone, they seemed open. He could see a low hill a few hundred feet away, but he doubted the hill would be visible from this spot in summer.

"There they are, boys," Pa said. "Let's bring 'em down."

Johnny pulled off his jacket and dropped it to the ground, and leaving his gray hat in place to keep some of the cold away from his head, he began to have at one of the oaks with the axe. Joe did the same.

First Johnny cut a wedge in the front of the tree. The idea was to make the tree fall in the direction of the front wedge. Then Johnny and Joe both stood behind the tree, Johnny at one side and Joe at the other, and they went to work on it.

The sound of the axes rang out. Wood chips flew. Pa lit his pipe and Matt had poured himself a cup of coffee. Once the tree was down, Pa, Matt and Luke would limb it, then start with the crosscut, reducing the tree to four-foot lengths, while Joe and Johnny attacked the second oak.

Joe stopped at one point and straightened up to stretch his back muscles a little.

He said, "It's almost a shame in a way to take down this big old oak. Been here a lot of years. The Cheyenne believe every living thing has a spirit, even plants and trees. And by taking a tree down, you're killing it."

Pa said, "Well, them Cheyennes, or whoever, can have their beliefs, but I've gotta keep my family warm at winter."

Luke said, "What do the Indians use for firewood?"

"They take wood from deadfalls," Joe said. "Or they break off low-hanging branches that have died. In the mountains out West, there's some hardwood in the lower valleys, but along the slopes and ridges it's mostly pine."

"Different land," Pa said. "Different people, different ways."

Johnny wondered what Pa would say if he knew Joe had lived among them and adopted many of their ways and even almost married one.

Matt said, "There was a time when the entire east coast was covered by a grand pine forest, probably not much different than the one Joe is talking about in the mountains out West. It is said there was little underbrush because the ground itself was usually covered in shade, and a man could ride a horse through."

Pa chuckled. "That's what they say, but it was a long time ago."

Johnny's shoulders and back felt warm from swinging the axe. He liked using his muscles and seeing the result of his work. He found himself smiling as he and Joe delivered their last strikes to the tree, and the giant old oak began to fall.

It started going over slowly, then picked up speed and hit the ground with a crashing sound, actually bouncing a little. Leaves flew up, and the branches waved wildly for a moment.

Pa said, "Well done, boys."

Joe said nothing. He just looked at the tree a moment. Johnny figured Joe was thinking about how something they had done so often and taken pride in when they were growing up was now something he didn't entirely approve of.

Joe didn't say much, but if you spent enough time with him and were observant, you could figure him out.

Joe's hair was getting longish again. The haircut he had gotten from Fred Whipple a couple days after they first arrived was now growing out. The tops of his ears were covered, and hair was once again touching his collar in back. Pa would ask Joe when he was getting another haircut, and Joe would characteristically shrug but say nothing.

Johnny and Joe hadn't yet told Ma and Pa of their plans to go west. Matt had been pestering Johnny and Joe to tell them, and sooner would be better. Give them time to get used to the idea of two of their sons being gone again.

Pa, Luke and Matt used axes to limb the tree, then set to work with the crosscut, and Johnny and Joe took their axes to the second oak.

Johnny's hair was now soaking with sweat, so he tossed his sombrero to the leaves and then raised his axe to drive it into the tree.

After a time, they took a break. Johnny poured two cups of coffee and handed one to Joe.

Pa wiped some sweat from his forehead with the back of his hand. "This work sure does go faster when there are five of us."

The boy ran. He had lost his tattered bowler somewhere during the night, when he had run out of the store, down the dark street and off into the farmland surrounding the town. Now he was in a thick patch of woods.

His old coat was hanging open, and he still clutched the revolver in his hand. In his coat was the ten dollars he had taken from the general store register.

He was running almost in a blind panic. Not watching where he was going. One foot caught an exposed root, and he went sprawling onto the wet leaves on the ground.

The pistol's hammer still rested in front of the empty chamber from when he had fired at the store keeper. Otherwise the gun might have gone off when he fell, and he might have shot himself.

He pushed himself to his feet. He was exhausted from running, but he was too filled with fear to stop. He had shot a man.

He was hungry, too. He had stored some food. He just had to get to it without getting caught. Then he would eat, and figure what to do next.

He started running again.

Johnny finished off his coffee and dropped the cup to the ground by the fire. The coffee had been made by Ma. It wasn't the coffee he had grown used to during his years in Texas, but it was hot.

Johnny felt a chill along his back. He had worked up a sweat while cutting the tree, and now the sweat was catching the cold morning air. Time to go back to work.

The sound of footsteps crunching on dried leaves caught his ear. It came from the direction of the hill yonder.

Johnny caught sight of a man come running up and over the soft, rounded crest. He wore an old, battered coat and had something in his hand. He looked like he was about Johnny's age. Johnny noticed the youthful face. The peach fuzz on the chin. And then he realized the something in the boy's hand was a gun.

The boy ran with a look of fear in his eyes, and he was running straight toward Johnny and the others. Johnny didn't think the boy saw them. He ran with his head a little to one side and his mouth hanging on, like he had been running forever and was near the breaking point.

"Hey!" Pa called to the boy. "You, there!"

The boy came to a stop, sliding a couple feet on the frosty leaves. He seemed to notice Johnny and Pa and the others for the first time.

His eyes darted off to the side, then back to Pa. He glanced over his shoulder, then back to Pa again. The boy was now maybe a hundred feet away.

"Who are you?" Matt said. "Do you need help?"

The sound of Matt's voice seemed to bring the boy out of his trance. His eyes darted to Matt with a look of confusion.

Pa said, "Are you all right? Who are you?"

The boy then raised his gun, hauling back the hammer, and he fired directly at Pa. The crack of the gunshot echoed through the woods.

"No!" Johnny roared.

He reached for his own guns, but they weren't there. He had left them in his room at the farmhouse. The only time he wore them anymore was when he and the boys were target practicing.

Pa was lying on the ground on his back.

"Pa!" Luke cried out, his voice breaking. "Pa!"

Johnny started toward the man at a dead run, his axe in his hand. Johnny knew guns. If he could cross that hundred feet before the gun could be cocked for another shot, he had a chance to take the man down with his axe. Johnny was no farmer. He was a gunfighter, and the man with the gun had picked the wrong people to shoot at.

But the man got the gun cocked again and fired. A bullet creased Johnny's temple. Not badly, but enough to make him stop running. He felt disoriented for a second, and realized he had fallen to his knees. He reached up his temple, and he found his hair was wet with warm blood.

His vision steadied, and he and the gunman stared at each other.

The boy aimed the gun at Johnny again. He fired. But Johnny had been shot at a lot and had caught lead more than once. He was able to estimate the trajectory of the bullet and began twisting away from it as the gun was being fired. The bullet ripped away the sleeve at the shoulder, but didn't cut into him.

The boy then turned and ran, back the way he had come.

Johnny, still on his knees, called out, "I'm coming after you! Nothing will stop me!"

He watched as the boy ran up over another low hill and was gone from sight. His crunching footsteps faded into the distance.

Johnny got to his feet, a little unsteady at first. He kept one hand pressed to his temple. His hair was wet, but there wasn't a whole lot of blood. He knew he wasn't hurt bad. He hurried back to Pa and his brothers.

Pa was still on his back, in the leaves. The front of his shirt was all ripped up from the bullet, but there was little blood. Not a good thing, Johnny knew. Dead men don't bleed.

Matt kneeled over Pa and pressed his head to his chest.

Tears were streaming down Luke's face. "Pa. No. Pa."

Johnny looked to Joe. "Get Luke out of here."

Joe grabbed Luke's arms and pulled him away, toward where the buckboard waited. Luke was calling out, "No! Pa!"

Johnny pulled a bandana from his pocket and pressed it to his temple, and he knelt beside Matt. Pa's eyes were staring toward the sky, no life in them.

"He was dead before he hit the ground," Matt said.

Johnny stared at Pa. He felt like the bottom had dropped out of him.

"Hey," Matt said. "You've been hit, too."

Johnny shook his head. "It's nothing. I've been shot worse. I'll be all right."

Matt decided not to pursue it further, at least for the moment. "Did you get a good look at him?"

Johnny nodded. "Saw his face real good."

"Is he anyone we know?"

"Nope. Never saw him before. But he'll be seeing me again. That's a promise."

Matt lowered a hand to Pa's face, and shut Pa's eyes.

25

THE REVEREND WILSON WAS tall and willowy, and his age was impossible to guess. He had been the Baptist minister in town for as far back as Johnny could remember, and he had always seemed old.

He shut his Bible and said, "Amen."

A chorus of murmured *amen*s rose from the crowd gathered around.

Behind the preacher was an open grave, and in the grave was a rectangular pine box.

A wind picked up and bare tree limbs clattered like noisy skeletons. A brown leaf, one of the last stragglers, blew past Ma. She reached up to wipe a tear from her face.

Johnny stood at Ma's side. He was in his gray suit again, and his sombrero was in one hand. The doctor in town had washed out the gash on Johnny's temple and then stitched it shut. The doctor had wanted to tie a bandage around Johnny's head, but Johnny had said no. Said he wouldn't need it.

To Ma's other side was Matt, in the suit he had brought with him when he came home. Standing nearby were Joe and Luke. Joe had one hand across Luke's shoulders.

Luke stared at the grave and was doing his best not to cry.

"I'm not gonna cry," he said. "You never see a real man cry."

"Ain't true," Joe said.

The preacher walked over and said a few hushed words to Ma. Johnny wasn't really listening. His own gaze was fixed on the grave, too.

Then the preacher moved on, first to Matt and then to Johnny. The preacher shook Johnny's hand, placed a hand on his shoulder, and said something preacherly. Johnny still wasn't really listening. Then the preacher moved on to Joe.

The crowd began to break up, each person going their own way. A couple of men who picked up extra money maintaining the cemetery would cover up the casket.

Matt fetched the wagon. He was going to take Ma and Luke home, but Johnny intended to stay until the grave was fully covered over. Just something he felt he had to do. Joe was going to stay with him.

Becky Drummond and Trip Hawley were still there,

and they walked over. Becky's father had been buried the day before.

Becky gave Johnny a hug but said nothing. There were no words for a moment like this.

Trip tried anyway. He shook hands with first Johnny and then Joe, and said, "I'm so sorry. Both of you."

"Are you all right?" Becky said to Johnny.

He nodded. "I will be. How about you?"

She took a deep breath and let it out slowly. "I don't know if I ever will be."

Johnny said, "What's going to happen with the store? Have you put any thought into it yet?"

She nodded. "Trip and I are going to run it, and Mama's going to live with us. We decided against the Wheeler farm. We're going to push the wedding up, to just after Christmas. Not the usual time for a wedding, maybe, but this whole business makes me feel I want to start building. Growing something. Bringing a child into the world. I don't want to wait anymore."

"I understand."

"Oh, Johnny." A tear streamed down her cheek. "The whole world can fall apart so fast. So incredibly fast."

He nodded. "Sometimes."

Trip and Becky left, and Johnny and Joe stood and watched as the cemetery workers grabbed their shovels and started scooping up earth and dropping it into the grave.

The wind picked up a little. It brought a chill. Winter was coming.

26

THEY ALL SAT in their usual places at the table. Except for Pa, who would never be there again. His chair at the head of the table was empty.

Nothing was being said. The clinking of silverware seemed extra loud.

Ma just looked at her plate while she ate. Luke did the same. Joe seemed more distant than ever. And Johnny seemed to have a fire simmering inside him.

Matt realized more than he ever had since they came home that his brother was really no longer a farmer. Johnny was a gunfighter. Like Joe had said, the stuff of legend. He knew Johnny intended to get his hands on the man who had killed Pa, and Matt thought, *God help that man when Johnny does.*

Johnny had taken to wearing his guns again, and no one said anything. Ma may not have even noticed. She spent much of her time in her rocker in the parlor, looking into the fire. But everyone else saw it.

It was Luke who said, "Johnny, why are you wearing them things?"

Johnny said nothing, but Joe said, "Because if we had our guns with us, that man wouldn't have shot Pa."

Joe was wearing his buckskin shirt again, with the belt tied around the middle and his own revolver tucked into the front. Matt had looped his belt through a sheath, and was wearing his Persian knife at one side

But somehow, it was Johnny's guns that got the attention. Maybe because there was something menacing in the way he wore them. So naturally, like they were a part of him. Like he somehow wasn't complete without them.

What Johnny had become over the years was made real clear to Matt the night of the shooting, when Johnny had refused a bandage for the wound on his head.

"Won't need it," he had told the doctor.

The doctor was an older man with a kind eye and wispy white hair. He had said, "You'll need to keep infection out of it."

Johnny shook his head. "Won't need it."

The doctor decided not to argue. Maybe it was the look in Johnny's eye.

After the doc had left, Johnny asked Matt to come out

to the barn with him. Johnny then dug a flask out of his saddle bags.

"Corn squeezin's," Johnny said.

Matt remembered what Johnny had told him about pouring raw home-made whiskey into a wound.

Matt said, "You're not serious."

Johnny pulled the cork and handed the flask to him. Johnny then sat on a sawhorse and leaned his head to one side.

He said, "Pour a couple ounces of it over the wound."

Matt looked at him with disbelief.

Johnny said, "Do it."

Matt did. Johnny sat, his fists tight and his teeth clenched together, but he made no sound.

When Matt was done, Johnny said, "There. Won't be no infection now."

Matt stood speechless as Johnny left the barn and walked back to the house.

27

SIX DAYS HAD PASSED since Tom McCabe and Hector Drummond were shot. Six days, and the killer was still not caught.

Johnny and his brothers had offered to go along with the search party the constable assembled.

"No," officer Dugas had said, speaking with a voice heavy with authority and the weight of responsibility. He had a thick white mustache, and eyes that looked tired. "You boys belong here with your ma. She needs you here, not traipsing across the countryside. We'll find him."

Six days. Nothing.

Johnny stood beside the hearth, leaning with one hand against the mantel. Joe paced back and forth in the shadows at the far side of the room. Firelight danced in a haunting way against the walls.

Johnny was not wearing his guns at the moment. His gunbelt was in the kitchen, slung over the back of a chair.

They heard the wagon outside. That would be Matt, returning with Ma. They had been at Uncle Jake's house for dinner. It was good to get Ma out, the boys thought. Here at the house, she tended to just sit and stare at the fire, her needlepoint in her hand but not being worked on. At Uncle Jake's house, she would find herself working alongside Aunt Sara, and keeping busy.

"It's the waiting that's killing me," Johnny said to Joe. "I'm used to being a man of action. Getting things done. Not sitting and waiting for someone else to do it for me."

Joe nodded. "Me too."

Coffee was boiling away on the stove in the kitchen. Johnny went out and filled two cups, and brought them back to the parlor. He handed one to Joe. This wasn't the thinner stuff Ma and Aunt Sara made. This was the real thing. Thick and strong. Trail coffee.

Joe said, "Wonder what's going on? Matt's probably tending to the team, but why isn't Ma coming in?"

After a time, Matt came in. Alone. He shook off the cold and shouldered out of his coat.

He said, "Aunt Sara invited Ma to stay the night. I thought it might be a good idea. Where's Luke?"

"Upstairs," Johnny said. "He was exhausted. This is taking a lot out of him."

"It's taking a lot out of all of us."

Johnny nodded. "Coffee's on. I brewed it good and strong. Grab a cup."

Matt opened a cupboard door, took a cup and filled it from the kettle. He took a sip and nodded. His seal of approval. He brought the coffee into the parlor.

Johnny grabbed the iron poker and gave the fire a little stirring, then stood back and took a sip of coffee.

Joe ceased pacing and lowered himself into an armchair. It had always been Pa's chair. An ash tray and one of Pa's pipes was still on a small table by the chair.

"So, how is she?" Joe said.

Matt said, "The same. To be expected, I guess."

She seemed drastically aged since the morning Pa had been shot. There were lines on her forehead and under her chin that Johnny had never noticed before. Her eyes, which were normally fiery and filled with humor, were now distant. Drained. Old.

"I can't believe they can't find him," Johnny said, slapping the mantel with one hand.

Matt shrugged, "Would they be able to find one of us, if we didn't want to be found?"

"That's different."

"How?"

"Joe and I spent three years in the West. Hunting and tracking men. We know the ways of doing it. And we know these woods. And even though you've been at sea, you know these woods, too."

Joe said, without looking up, "If I didn't want to be found, ain't a man alive who could find me. I learned from the best there is."

Johnny said, "But some farmer from back east, here? I've got nothing against farming. I have a world of respect for it. But farming doesn't prepare you for a manhunt. A farmer, running through these woods on foot. He should have been found within hours. A day maybe, tops."

Matt took a sip of coffee. He got a mouthful of grounds. To be expected with coffee like this. He took another sip to wash them down. "Who's to say he's a farmer?"

"Well, what else would he be?"

Joe said, "A coal miner? Not much difference, in that it

don't prepare you for running from the law."

Matt said, "Three years ago, we were just farmers. Now look at us. A gunfighter—no offense..."

Johnny shook his head. No offense taken. He was what he was.

Matt said, "...a mountain man and scout, and a man of the sea. We're all much different than we were before going out into the world. Who's to say this man is just one thing or another? We don't know who he is, or what his background is."

There was a creak on the stairs. Subtle. Easy to overlook, if your mind wasn't tuned to notice the slightest sound that shouldn't be there. Johnny and Joe both looked toward the stairs and Matt followed their gaze.

Luke was standing at the base of the stairs. He was in a night shirt and had pulled on a flannel robe.

"Luke," Matt said. "Why aren't you in bed?"

Luke said, "I heard you all talking down here. I wanted to hear. This all involves me, too. I'm Pa's son as much as any of you."

Johnny nodded. "I guess you're old enough to know when you're ready for bed. Come on in."

Luke came in and stood by the fire. It was a little cold upstairs.

Johnny looked to Matt. "Six days. I know Dugas told us to wait, but I say we've waited long enough. I say we go after him."

Matt was about to say something, then hesitated. Johnny knew Matt was tossing it all over in his mind.

Matt finally said, "You know what Dugas said. He wants us out of the search, for obvious reasons. We're too closely involved. We wouldn't be thinking objectively."

"And," Joe said, "Dugas wants the man brought back alive. With us along, there's no guarantee that would happen."

Johnny said, "We've given Dugas six days to find him. He couldn't do the job. I say it's our turn, now."

Joe said, "I'm with you."

"All right," Matt said. "All right. If we were to do this, if we were to start our own search, where could we possibly look that Dugas and his men haven't already looked themselves?"

The brothers were silent. Where, indeed?

Johnny said, "Dugas and his men have combed these woods. They lost his trail maybe a half mile from where Pa was shot."

Matt picked up the narrative. "The killer happened upon the stream cutting through Pa's property, the stream we made coffee by that time last summer. He ran along through the water. They couldn't find where he exited the stream. They sent men in groups through the woods, trying to find any sign of tracks or a campfire. They positioned men on all the roads leading to and from Sheffield."

Joe said, "They looked through every barn and chicken house in the area, and sent wires to the towns all around Sheffield to watch for this man, based on the description Johnny gave."

Johnny let all of that settle for a moment. Then he said, "You don't just disappear in the woods. Especially if you have only the clothes on your back."

"On top of that," Luke said, "he'd have wet feet. He ran through the stream for maybe miles. I remember how cold it was that day. You'd freeze out there."

"Unless you knew where you were going. Unless you knew these woods."

Joe looked up, the light of an idea in his eyes. He said, "Pirates Cave."

Johnny looked at Joe. Pirates Cave, was the name they had given to a little opening in some bedrock at the side of a hill. It wasn't more than five feet deep and three feet high, and it was hidden behind a stand of fir trees. The three boys had played there as children, pretending they were pirates, carrying sticks for swords and hiding pretend treasure in the cave.

Luke knew of the place, too. He said, "I've never been to Pirate's Cave, but from what you boys say, it's a long way's off. More'n two miles south of where we all were when Pa was shot. Would the killer have gone that far out of his way?"

Joe looked at his little brother. "How far would you go out of your way to avoid being caught. Remember, he's facin' a noose for two murders."

Johnny said, "I don't think Dugas and his men searched the woods that far out."

Matt was pacing. "It might make more sense to assume the killer would be trying to get to one of the surrounding towns. Danbury. Cartersville. Pine Grove."

Joe said, "That's assuming he's a farmer or a coal miner, running for his life. Running blind, not knowing what to do. But running to another town is not what one of us would do."

"What would you do?" Luke said.

"Find a place to hole up. Wait it out. Let the trail grow cold. Give the search party a little while to grow tired and give up."

"How long would you wait?"

"A few days."

Matt shook his head. He said, "And you think he might have stumbled on to Pirate's Cave?"

Joe said, "He might not have just stumbled on it. He might somehow know the area."

"How? How could he? We've never seen him before."

Johnny said, "There are a lot of people in town we've never seen before. We've been gone a long time."

"All right," Matt said. "In the morning, I've got to go to Uncle Jake's to get Ma. But you boys can go into town and find Dugas, and tell him about Pirate's Cave."

Johnny shook his head. "In the morning, I'm riding out to Pirate's Cave myself."

Joe said. "And I'll be with you."

Matt sighed wearily. "All right. In the morning, *we'll* go out to Pirate's Cave. Luke, you'll have to go and get Ma yourself."

"Not me," Luke said. "I'm going with you."

"No, Luke."

"I'm coming along. He was my father, too."

Johnny looked to Matt. "He's right. I know I wouldn't want to be left behind."

"Besides," Luke said, "I'll just follow you anyway."

Matt threw his hands up in defeat. "All right. But he doesn't carry a gun."

"Agreed," Johnny said.

All four brothers were awake before the eastern sky began to show a hint of morning light.

Johnny said to Luke, "Go get the eggs. I'll start some bacon frying."

Luke said, "Eggs? How can you think about breakfast on a morning like this?"

"Always eat whenever you can," Joe said. "Especially

on a day like this."

They ate in silence. Until the silence was broken by Luke saying, "What do we do when we catch him?"

Matt said, "We take him into town, to Constable Dugas."

Johnny glanced at Joe. Joe met his gaze, but said nothing. In saying nothing, he said everything.

After they ate, Johnny buckled on his gunbelt. He shouldered into a charcoal gray jacket that fell to his belt only. Something he had picked up in Mexico. By being waist-length, it gave him plenty of freedom of motion for grabbing his guns. He was in his riding boots, and his gray hat was in place.

Joe wore his floppy hat and his buckskin shirt. His gun was tucked into his belt, and a sheath at his right side held a twelve-inch long bowie knife.

Matt said, "That looks like something you'd scalp someone with."

"Done it before," was all Joe said.

"I hope you're kidding."

Joe said nothing.

Johnny didn't even glance at Joe. He had seen rough men do some savage things, and scalping a man wasn't nearly the least of it.

Johnny said, "Come on. Let's get going. The sun's almost up and we got a lot of ground to cover."

The three horses were saddled, and Johnny swung up and onto the back of Bravo. It felt good to be in the saddle, he thought. Joe mounted his horse and pulled Luke up behind him. Matt was riding the old mare.

Johnny said, "Let's ride."

28

THE SUN CLIMBED climbed into the sky, and the morning warmed a bit. A silvery frost had coated the brown leaves on the ground when the boys first rode out, but the frost soon faded and Johnny found he had to unbutton his jacket.

They were riding along a logging road, single file. Johnny was first in line, and Matt was next, bouncing along in the saddle. Then came Joe and Luke behind them.

Johnny kept Bravo to a walk. Johnny held the reins in his left hand and kept his right at his side and within easy reach of his right-hand gun.

They turned off the logging road and guided their horses through a field where a neighboring farmer was growing hay. Then they were back in the woods. They ducked their heads below some low hanging birch branches, and they found a trail that took them on past the woods and toward a grassy hill. At the foot of the hill was a farmhouse with a peaceful strand of smoke rising from the chimney.

They passed a few dozen acres of brown, broken corn stalks. All that remained of a harvest. Dead soldiers laying down, Johnny thought.

After the cornfield was another logging road that took them into another section of woods. After a time, Johnny reined up.

"This is where we go in on foot," he said. "The woods will be too thick for the horses."

Johnny swung out of the saddle and pulled his Colt rifle. Joe had an Enfield rifle in his hands.

Johnny handed his rifle to Luke.

"Johnny," Matt said. "I thought we agreed Luke wouldn't carry a gun."

"I've been doing some thinking about that. If the killer is at the cave, I don't expect he'll give up without a fight. He's killed twice already, so there is no reason to believe he won't kill again."

Johnny said to Luke, "Pa taught you how to shoot."
Luke nodded.

Johnny said, "This ain't much different than Pa's rifle, except it's a repeater. You cock and shoot, just like Pa's, but then you can cock and shoot again. You have seven shots."

They started into the woods. Johnny took the lead. He had been told he fell into the role of leader naturally, but he wasn't thinking much about it at the moment. He was just doing what needed to be done.

Johnny stepped along, the leather soles of his boots landing quietly on the leaves. When an autumn morning warms up a little and the frost fades, sometimes the leaves covering the ground are a little damp and don't crunch underfoot like they do when they're dry.

Johnny reached to his right-hand gun and kept it loose in the holster. His left gun was tucked down a little tighter. Wouldn't do for it to fall out if he had to run, but he wanted the right gun ready in case he needed it in a hurry.

Matt fell into place behind him and was followed by Luke. Behind them was Joe, walking with his rifle ready. Joe was in buckskin boots and had a second knife tucked into one of them.

Johnny stopped after a moment and heard one more footstep behind him.

He looked back to Matt and said, "When I stop, you stop."

Matt said, "I did stop."

"You took one more step."

Joe said, "When the man up front stops, you all stop dead in your tracks. Not one more step."

Matt said, "Did you see something?"

"If I did, with all this talking, it wouldn't matter. Sometimes you just have to stop and listen. Look around you. See what might be there."

Johnny started forward again, and the others fell into place behind him.

It had actually been a lot more than three years since Johnny had seen this section of woods. He and his brothers hadn't been to Pirates Cave since Johnny was twelve. The woods had changed a lot. A stand of pine was taller now. An old pine had fallen and three young birches were growing about it. He stopped a moment to gain his bearings. It wouldn't do to have come all this way and not be able to find the place.

An old oak should be within sight, he thought, but it was not. Then he spied a long lump covered with leaves and realized it must be the oak, fallen and returning to the earth.

He stopped at the base of a hill. Toward the top, bedrock was visible. The brothers broke formation and gathered beside him.

"There it is," Matt said.

Luke said, "Where? Up there?"

Johnny said, "Keep your voices down."

Matt said, keeping to barely more than a whisper, "See that line of cedars up there? Just beyond that ledge? Right behind the cedars, that's where the cave is."

"If he's there now," Johnny said, "he's going to have a clear field of fire at us as we climb the hill."

"So," Luke said, "what are we going to do?"

"You're going to wait here."

Luke was going to protest, but Johnny cut him off. "This is serious business, boy. You don't have any experience at this, and if worse comes to worse, I want at least one of Ma's boys left alive."

"What do you want us to do?" Matt said.

"We'll spread out, maybe fifty feet apart, and then climb the hill. Keep your gun's ready."

Johnny drew his right-hand gun. Matt's Navy Colt was in his belt, and he drew it and moved away a little further along the base of the hill. Joe held his rifle with both hands and got into position.

Johnny nodded to them both and started up the hill. It wasn't steep, about the same slope as a flight of stairs. Johnny's boots slipped a couple of times on dried, damp leaves, but Joe's buckskin boots did just fine.

There was no gunfire. Matt and Joe met Johnny at the top of the hill, at the line of cedars.

Johnny said, "Let's go in. We'll rush him. If he's there and shoots back, we cut him to pieces."

Matt nodded.

Joe said, "Let's go."

They charged through. Johnny came to a stop beyond the cedars, his revolver out at arm's length and the hammer cocked. Matt held his revolver the same way, and Joe had his rifle up to his shoulder.

The man they were looking for wasn't there.

The cave looked much like it had. Except it struck Johnny as looking somehow smaller. Maybe because he had grown a lot since the last time he was here.

In front of the cave were the ashen remains of a campfire. Scattered around on the ground were empty cans of beans.

"He's been here," Joe said.

"We don't know who it was," Matt said. "Let's not jump to conclusions. It could have been anyone up here."

Johnny said, "How many people do you know who come all the way up here to camp? Whoever was up here, he was here for a few days."

Joe shook his head. "He was here the whole time Dugas and his posse were hunting him."

"Been here and gone. Those ashes are at least a day old. Maybe two."

Matt went to the edge of the hill and waved Luke up while Johnny and Joe went to cut for sign. But they found nothing. It had rained the night before, and the entire day before that.

"Any trail he left," Johnny said, "has been washed clean away."

"That's just it?" Joe said. "He's got clean away?"

Johnny shook his head. "We'll find him."

"So, where do we go next?"

Matt said, "Town. We tell Constable Dugas what we found."

Johnny and Matt found Dugas sitting at his desk.

"What are you doing here?" Johnny said. "Why aren't you out with your men?"

Matt said, "We figured you would be out with the search parties. We had planned on leaving you a note."

Dugas held up his hands in a gesture of helplessness. "I had to call off the search, boys."

"You called it off?" Johnny's voice could roar when he wanted it to, just like Pa's. Ma's temper, Pa's voice. This was one of those times.

Matt laid a hand on his shoulder. "Easy, Johnny."

"Boys," Dugas said, rising to his feet, "I've been searching for six days. I asked around town, and some folks remember a boy meeting the description you gave. They remember seeing him here and there in town a couple of days before the shooting. No one knew who he was or had ever seen him before. Since then, it's like he dropped off the face of the Earth. But constables on both sides of the state line have his description. He's bound to turn up."

Matt said, "We have something that may be of use to you."

He told Dugas about the cave, and the remains of the

campfire, and the old, empty cans.

Dugas said, "You think he was there?"

Johnny said, "I know it."

Dugas nodded. "All right. I'll go check it out."

"Check it out?"

"It sounds like it's over in the next county. I'll ride out there and talk to the sheriff."

Johnny's hands were on his hips, and he shook his head and looked away.

Dugas said, "What would you have me do?"

"The whole time you and your men were searching for him, he was hiding almost right under your noses."

"What else could I have done?"

"You should have let us join the search. We would have had him by now. Maybe it's time we went and did your job for you."

Johnny turned and started for the door.

Dugas pointed his finger at Johnny's back. "Don't you go doing anything foolish. You go home and keep your nose out of this investigation, or I'll run you in for interfering with the law."

Johnny slammed the door behind him.

Johnny got as far as the saloon. He was leaning both elbows on the bar with a glass in front of him when Matt walked in.

Matt said to the bartender, "I'll take one of those, too."

The man set a glass in front of Matt and poured a splash of scotch into it.

"Come on," Matt said. "Be generous."

The bartender complied.

Johnny said, "Leave the bottle."

Matt took a gulp of scotch.

He said, "I had a little talk with Dugas after you left. He's not angry with you. He told me if it had been his father who was shot, he would feel the same way. But he meant what he said. If any of us interferes with the investigation, he'll lock us up."

"I meant what I said, too. I'm going after the man who killed Pa."

Johnny drained the glass, then grabbed the bottle and refilled it.

"All right," Matt said. "But tell me this. How do you

know for sure the man we're after was the one out at the cave? Sure, it looks like it probably was. But that's what they call circumstantial evidence. How do you know for sure?"

"Gut feeling. Pa said sometimes that's all you have. He said trust your gut because it's the only thing you can really count on. Your eyes can be deceived, and you can talk yourself out of a good idea if you try hard enough. But your gut will never lie to you."

Matt nodded. "Pa did say that, didn't he."

"More'n once."

Matt took another sip of scotch, and then stood the glass on the bar.

He took a few moments, tossing it all around in his head. Then he said, "All right. I guess that's good enough for me."

Johnny stood his glass on the bar. He said, "How many cans did you count on the ground, out at the cave?"

Matt shrugged his shoulders. "Eight. Maybe ten."

Johnny nodded. "The day he shot Pa, I got a real good look at him. He didn't have any pack with him. Just the clothes on his back and the gun in his hand. So where did those cans come from?"

Matt nodded his head. "All right. Let's say you're right. He set up camp there at the cave, then went into town. He was planning on a robbery. Do you think he knows the area, or he just happened onto the cave by accident?"

"That cave's too far out of the way for a stranger scouting the town to have found it by accident. He either knows the area, or knows someone who does."

Matt brought his glass up for a drink, but then held it in front of him while he thought.

"Let's think about this logically. If you had just shot a man, and then you went out to the cave and laid low a few days, where do you go from there?"

"He had provisions with him that he left at the cave. He must have had access to more. He might know someone in the area."

"Or he could just break into another store and steal some."

"He's prepared. As scared as he looked, he seems not to be making stupid mistakes. Maybe he was panicking when we saw him, but then he pulled himself together. If I was in his place, I would assume every constable in the nearby towns would be watching for me. What I'd do is go west. Stay to the woods and the fields. Travel by night. Get to Ohio. Find a horse and start using a different name. Beyond that's Indiana and eventually Missouri. Some wide open country there, and a lot of remote areas."

"So, what are you going to do?"

"Ride in the direction I think he would probably go. Stop at every farm on the way. Every town. Ask about him. Someone's bound to have seen him."

"He got only ten dollars from Mister Drummond's cash register, and sooner or later any supply of provisions he might have is bound to wear out. We should ask about any robberies. Any stores that were robbed, or farmhouses that were broken into. He's going to need food."

"So are you saying you're coming around to my way of thinking?"

Matt shrugged. "At least your ideas are better than searching blind, like Dugas was doing. And I can't let you ride off alone. If you're right, and you do find him, you might need help."

"We'll find him," Johnny said.

"And I have a feeling we won't be bringing him back to stand trial."

Johnny looked at Matt. "Do you really want to bring him back for trial? I know you feel we should, and maybe that's what the law says. But is that what you really want?"

Matt found himself saying, "No."

29

THAD STAYED over for supper. After Ma had turned in for the night, the boys sat in front of the fire in the parlor.

Johnny stood, leaning with one hand against the mantel. Matt and Luke were on the sofa, and Thad had taken the rocking chair. Joe was pacing about.

Johnny hadn't thought much about it over the years, but as he had listened to Thad throughout dinner telling stories of his Army escapades or expounding on his political positions, Johnny realized he didn't like his cousin very much.

Uncle Jake had never been one to say more than needed, often preferring silence to filling the air with pointless words. Much like the men of the West Johnny had met. But Thad, somehow, didn't take after his father much.

"Unbelievable tragedies," Thad was saying as he sat in the rocker. "The loss of two great pillars to this community. I don't think the lives of any of us in Sheffield or the surrounding area will ever be the same."

Johnny said, "The time for words has passed."

Matt nodded his head. "I agree."

Thad looked from Johnny to Matt. He had no idea what they were talking about.

Johnny said, "We're going to go find him."

Thad said, "But where will you look?"

Johnny wasn't really in the mood for talking, and Joe was even more silent than usual this evening. Johnny figured it was a combination of losing Pa and the annoyance of having to spend an evening listening to Thad. So it fell to Matt to explain Johnny's idea.

"Were going to ride west, checking every town and farm we happen upon. Ohio. Indiana, if we don't find him in Ohio. Illinois, if we have to go that far. All the way to Missouri, if it comes to that. But I don't think it will."

"But," Thad said, "what'll you do if you find him?"

Time for Johnny to speak. He said, "Whatever it takes."

Thad said, "You're all going?"

Matt nodded. "We leave at sun-up."

Thad was silent for a moment. Then he said, "Your father was my uncle. My father's brother. Count me in."

Well, Johnny thought. *Maybe the boy has some substance, after all.*

Luke was hearing most of this for the first time. He said, "I'm coming, too."

Johnny shook his head. "No, Luke. Like it or not, you're too young."

"I'm only three years younger than you were when you rode off to join the Army," he said.

Johnny nodded. "But those are three big years."

Matt said, "Somebody has to stay behind with Ma. We can't leave her alone."

Joe spoke. First time tonight, as far as Johnny could remember. He said, "We've all been through this kind of thing. You haven't."

Luke said, "I can learn."

"You can. But not this time. This won't be a time for learnin'. This is a time for doin'."

Matt said, "Stay behind with Ma. Take care of her. We're counting on you."

Luke looked away. Johnny figured Luke was caught between the boy's pride of being told he was not man enough for a job, and the man's understanding that they were right.

"So it's settled," Johnny said, looking from Matt to Joe to Thad. "We leave at first light."

Johnny, Joe and Luke headed upstairs, and Thad went home. Matt sat a while longer in the parlor, watching the fire dwindle down. Then he climbed the stairs.

Ma spoke from her bedroom door. "Matthew?"

He stepped into her doorway. "Ma?"

She was sitting up on the edge of her bed.

She said, "Thank you for not letting Luke go with you."

"You heard? We thought you were up here asleep."

"It's a mother's job to know what's going on in her household."

"We were going to tell you in the morning, before we left."

She said, "I knew sooner or later you three would leave to find the man. You are all too much like your father. Even you, who tries so hard to think first and act second. Your father was a man who faced a problem head-on. In your place, he would be doing the same thing you're going to do."

She got to her feet. Matt had noticed how much the

past week had taken out of her. It was like she had aged ten years. She walked toward him, taking each step carefully. Like an older person might do.

She said, "I knew John and Josiah would be leaving to go back West, anyway. And you would probably go back to sea. I could see it in you. A restlessness that hadn't been there, before. You had gone out and seen different parts of the world, and those places took ahold of your heart."

It struck Matt that he and his brothers were being selfish.

He said, "Maybe we shouldn't be leaving, Ma. With Pa barely gone, you'll need us here."

"Don't you worry about me. I'm going to miss your father whether you are here or not. And I have my faith to get me through. I want you three to do what you need to do. Go try to find that man. And when you're done, then go to sea if you need to. I want John and Josiah to go West, if that's where they feel they need to be. I want you all to build the lives you need to."

"You'll be okay?"

She nodded. "I'm a survivor. My grandparents survived the famine in Ireland. My parents came here to build a life, and they survived drought and other hardships. You're from hardy stock, on both sides. And I'll have Luke here. He's almost a man, and we'll put in a crop next spring. Right on schedule."

Matt had always been filled with pride over his McCabe heritage. But he realized there was a lot to be proud of on his mother's side, too. The O'Briens.

"Promise me one thing," Ma said. "You have the calmest head of the three of you. If you should find the man you are searching for, don't kill him unless you have to in self-defense. And don't let your brothers kill him. If all your father believed in and what he and I taught you is to mean anything, then that man has to be brought here and he has to stand trial. It can't be any other way."

"I understand, Ma. I promise."

"And promise me one other thing. When you get where you're going, write to your ma."

He smiled. "I will."

"Now, give me a hug and get to bed. Sunrise will come early, tomorrow."

30

WHEN JOHNNY WOKE up, it was still dark outside, and Matt was asleep across the room.

Johnny had never seemed to need anyone to wake him. He knew when he needed to be awake, and he seemed to wake up on schedule.

Downstairs, the grandfather clock chimed four times. About time to be getting up, he figured. And he realized he could smell bacon and coffee.

He climbed out of bed and pulled on his pants and grabbed his shirt. When his boots were in place and his gunbelt was buckled on, he went over to Matt's bed and touched Matt's shoulder.

Matt woke with a start. Johnny said, "Come on. It's four o'clock. Time to get moving."

The bed springs creaked as Matt sat up and swung his feet to the floor. "What's that I smell?"

"Smells like Ma's cooking."

"What's she doing up?"

Johnny shrugged, though he knew Matt probably couldn't see it because the room was mostly dark. Johnny said, "I have no idea. You know, I've been a little concerned about how things would go this morning. I don't want for us to just ride out, and she wakes up and finds us gone. But leaving a note doesn't seem enough."

Matt was running his hands over his face, trying to rub the sleepiness away. He said, "She talked with me last night. She was awake. Somehow, she knew of our plans."

"This is something we've gotta do. We can't just let the guy who shot Pa ride off free."

Matt nodded. "I know."

"But I so hate the idea of leaving her and Luke here alone. We could be gone for weeks."

"What about the spring? You and Joe riding off with Thad for the West. Are you still planning on doing that?"

Johnny shrugged again. "I don't know."

Johnny left Matt and stepped into the doorway of the room Joe and Luke shared. Joe was already up, tying together the strips of rawhide at the front of his shirt. It was still dark outside, but a lamp burned low on a bed stand. Johnny could see the second bed in the room was empty.

"Where's Luke?" Johnny said.

Joe said, "Ma came and got him a while ago. Don't know what for."

Johnny went downstairs and found Ma in the kitchen.

"Ma?" he said. "What're you doing up? It's four in the morning."

She was at the stove, with bacon sizzling in the skillet and coffee brewing. Muffins and bread were in the oven.

"I'm not going to let you boys leave with empty stomachs. I know you want to be leaving early, so you can eat your breakfast on the trail. The muffins and bread will give you some lunch."

"Matt said you talked with him last night."

She nodded.

Johnny said, "I hate just riding out like this."

"You're doing what has to be done. Someone takes a stab at the McCabe family, and we stab back. Had it been your Pa and Uncle Jake in your position, they would be doing the same thing."

"But will you be all right here?"

"I've sat and looked at the fire long enough. It's time to live. There's work to do."

She stopped fussing with the bacon in the pan and looked at him. "I loved your Pa dearly. I always will. And someday I'll join him, when God calls me home. But now is not the time for dying, or sitting by the fire and thinking of what was. Now is the time for living. For doing."

"Where's Luke?"

"He's out fixing packs for the three of you, and saddling your horses."

"The thing is, we don't know when we'll be back. It could be weeks."

"Could be longer." She went back to the stove. The bacon was popping away and had to be flipped over so it wouldn't burn. "You boys have a big job ahead of you, and it's something that probably can't be done in just a few days. And if you don't come back at all, if the land out West keeps calling to you so much that you can't resist it, that's all right, too. I know how the West has taken hold of your heartstrings, and how it has with Josiah."

He looked at her with a little surprise.

She said, "Don't think I don't know that you've been looking west ever since you've been home. A mother knows what's in her son's heart."

"But Ma, I hate the idea of you being here alone."

She waved off the notion, waving a hand like she was swatting at a fly, and went back to the stove. Bacon was sizzling away with a passion. She started scooping some of it out onto a plate.

She said, "I'll be fine. Life goes on, for all of us. Luke is almost a man, now. Come spring, Luke and I'll put in the crop. We'll run this place."

She looked at him again. "We all have to live our lives, and that means you boys, too. You can't just turn away from what you need out of guilt. My life is here, and I'll be fine. Luke's life is here too, for the moment. When he's grown, maybe he'll stay here and maybe he won't. Time will tell. But promise me two things. Find a good woman to bring children into the world with, and build a good home for them. And like I asked Matthew last night, write to your ma, once you get settled."

Johnny said, "You're one of a kind, you know that?"

She grinned. "I've been told that a time or two. Now grab a plate and sit down. Breakfast is almost ready."

When Johnny stepped out of the house, the stars were gone and the eastern sky was a steel gray.

Bravo was waiting for him. The saddle was in place, and his Colt rifle was in the scabbard. His bedroll was in place on the back, and his saddle bags were full. All thanks to Luke.

Johnny had been a little concerned that Bravo would have given Luke some problems. But Luke had apparently handled it. He was indeed becoming a man.

Not just a man, Johnny thought. A McCabe.

Joe's horse was beside Johnny's. Johnny didn't know if Joe had given a name to the animal. And beside Joe's horse was the old family horse Matt was going to ride.

The door opened and they stepped out behind him. Matt and Joe. Ma was with them, and so was Luke.

Ma was saying, "Don't you boys worry about Luke and me. We'll be fine."

Matt said to Luke, "I know you wanted to come with us."

Luke shook his head. "I did, but I've been thinking about it. It's like you said. My responsibility is here. This is where I need to be. Ma and I'll run the farm. You boys go and catch that killer."

Johnny said, "Luke, I've been thinking you're almost a man. But I was wrong. I realize now, you *are* a man."

Luke was giving a wide grin. Johnny extended a hand, and when Luke took the hand, it was with a man's grip.

Johnny said, "And you're every bit a McCabe."

Johnny could hear a horse coming up to the house. It was Thad.

"Morning everyone," Thad said. He tipped his hat and said, "Aunt Elizabeth."

"Morning, Thaddeus," Ma said. "I've said this to the boys, so I'll say it to you. Take care of yourself, out there on the trail."

He nodded. "I will, ma'am."

The dog came running up. He had been out chasing rabbits, or whatever a dog did in the morning.

Johnny knelt down and rubbed the dog's neck and the top of his head. "You take care of things, Jeb."

Johnny swung into the saddle. Joe did the same. Matt climbed up onto the old mare, but there was nothing graceful about it. Johnny grinned.

They started out, turning their horses toward the hill out beyond the house. The hill they had rode down when they first came home, all those months ago.

Ma stood on the porch waving at them, and Luke stood tall and strong beside her. Old Jeb ran alongside them until they were partway up the hill, then the dog stopped and stood looking at them. Then he turned back for the house. A dog's way of seeing them off, Johnny supposed.

Johnny wanted to rein up at the top of the hill and take a long look at the place. When he had ridden out three years ago, he didn't have such feelings. He had been a kid, not much older than Luke, riding off on a grand adventure. But now, he was aware that he might never see the old farm again.

After all he had seen and done and especially after Pa's death, he was feeling more world-weary than he thought a man of not quite twenty-one should feel. And as much as the West was calling to him, he knew this old farm would always be tugging at a piece of his heart.

He decided not to give himself the long last look he wanted, because if Ma and Luke were watching, they might think something was wrong. But as Johnny topped the hill, he glanced back over his shoulder. Bravo felt the motion and slowed down his pace.

The house stood as it always had. The porch, the white clapboards. The upstairs window to his and Matt's room. The brick chimney rising from the center of the roof. The old oak standing tall out front.

Matt said, "So ends our return home."

Johnny nodded. "Maybe it's like you said. A man can never really return home."

The horses continued on, and they rounded the crest of the hill and the farm was gone from view.

"Let's ride," Johnny said. "We got us a killer to catch."

PART THREE

The Outlaw Trail

31

Montana, 1881

BREE SAID, "So that's how you left Pennsylvania?"

Johnny nodded. "It was a fool's quest, I know. But at the time, we were young and angry. Angry at the man who had shot our father, and angry at the constable who we felt was not doing his job."

Dusty said, "So, at least we know where Josh got his temper."

"Hey," Josh said. "I don't have a temper."

Temperance giggled and Ginny smiled.

Bree said, "You don't ever really mention your cousin Thad. I think I've maybe heard the name only once."

Johnny nodded. "There's a reason for that, and I'll get to it."

"Did you ever see the old farm again?"

Johnny shook his head. "No, Punkin. I always wanted to, but we never went back. I never saw Ma again. Your grandmother. We exchanged letters. Lots of them. It sometimes took months for her to get our letters, or for us to get hers. Especially from here."

"Grandma died when I was fourteen. I remember when you got the letter."

Johnny nodded. "And now Luke runs the old farm. Him and his wife, and their kids. But my memories of the old farm live on in this house, in a way. The reason I built it the way I did. It's shaped a lot like the old farmhouse."

Jack said, "I got to visit the place a few times when I was back East, in school."

"So," Josh said, "what happened when you started hunting down Grandpa's killer?"

Bree said, "Did you ever catch him?"

"One step at a time, Punkin," Johnny said. "The search led us through Pennsylvania, and then on to Ohio."

And Johnny continued the story.

32

Ohio, 1856

THEY STOPPED in taverns and restaurants and the offices of constables. They gave a description of the man they were hunting and asked if anyone had seen him. They stopped at farms and stagecoach way stations.

A farmer in Ohio, in the loft of his barn and with a pitchfork in his hands, said he had seen a man who looked like that.

"Come through maybe two weeks ago," he said. "Thought it was kind of strange. He was riding a horse without no saddle. Asked if he could split wood in exchange for some supper. I ain't about to turn away a stranger in need, so I let him fill the wood box, and then we gave him some supper. He slept here in the barn and then moved on."

Matt said, "Did he say anything about where he was going?"

The farmer shook his head. "Not that I remember. Didn't say much, really."

"Thank you kindly," Matt said, and they continued on.

"That horse was probably stolen," Thad said.

Johnny nodded. "Come on. Let's ride."

The winter winds were strong and there were patches of snow on the ground. Johnny pulled his jacket tight as they rode along.

Matt had his thick, woolen pea coat, and Joe had a buckskin coat that kept out the cold and a coonskin cap he had made himself. But Johnny had come home with only his waist-length jacket.

Ma had apparently thought of this, because when he checked the saddle bags after they left home, he found Luke had packed Pa's old coat in there. He was thinking it might be nigh onto time to put the old coat on, even though the coat fell almost to his knees and didn't allow for easy access to his guns.

A town was just a few miles ahead. A farming town, just on the other side of a small stream that was covered with a wooden bridge. They figured the rider would have had to pass through here.

They asked at the constable's office and at the lone saloon they found in town. No one remembered seeing him.

They slept the night beside a livery barn. They built a fire, and the barn blocked them from the cold wind. But it was still winter.

Johnny stood by the fire, a cup of coffee in one hand. The coffee was warming him from the inside out, and he had finally dug out Pa's coat and was wearing it. It was made of tan leather, with a sheepskin lining. He wouldn't be able to get to his guns, but at least it would keep him warm.

Matt walked up beside him and poured a cup. Matt said, "What're you thinking?"

"I'm thinking, what if we don't ever catch up to him?"

Matt gave him a look of surprise. "It's not like you to be pessimistic."

"Just being realistic. We've been gone six weeks, now. We spent Thanksgiving with canned beans, out in the cold night with only a campfire for heat. But we don't seem to be getting any closer. That farmer today saw him, but that's the first person we've found in over a week who's seen him."

Matt nodded. "We'll find him. It's just a matter of time."

But Johnny wasn't so sure. He had been on manhunts before, with the Rangers. He had seen a man ride off into the open land and just seem to disappear.

In the morning they rode on. Down the trail to the next town and other farms.

They came to a fork in the road. One branch bent to the southwest, and the other went directly west. The only other choice was to go back the way they came.

"Now, this is a real pickle," Thad said.

Johnny looked off toward the sky, like he often did. It was gray and overcast. The wind was bitter cold, and he thought he felt snow in the air. The scientists will say you can't feel when it's going to snow, but Johnny had always thought the wind had a different feel to it when there was snow in the clouds.

Matt said, "Is there really any way to know which way he would go? What would you do?"

The question was directed at Johnny, but it was Thad who answered. "West. I'd go west. With a murder charge hanging on my head, I'd put as much distance between me and the State of Pennsylvania as I could."

Johnny was silent, letting what Thad said settle in and deciding what he thought about it. While he was thinking, he glanced at the clouds again and the snow he thought the clouds held.

He said, "I'd take the southern branch. If I was in his place, I'd be figuring there's probably no one behind me, and if there were, I'd have a six-day lead on 'em. We're this deep into Ohio, and we'll probably be in Indiana by tomorrow or the next day. Dugas said he wired all the nearby towns with the man's description, but we're way beyond that area, now. I think I'd figure, in that man's place, the biggest concern now is staying warm. Winter's upon us and the worst of it's yet to come. Those clouds up there are going to bring snow. I think I'd be heading south."

Joe nodded.

Thad shrugged. "All right. If you say so."

Johnny was about to say, *It don't matter what you think, Thad.* But he caught himself.

Matt said, "I'm convinced."

Johnny turned Bravo toward the road that went south and said, "Let's ride."

33

OHIO WAS now long behind them, and they weren't finding anyone who had seen the man. But Johnny's main concern at the moment was the weather.

Snow was coming down hard, and when they came to a way station, they decided they could go no further that day. They split wood and filled the wood box in exchange for their supper, and they slept on the floor in the kitchen, in front of the woodstove.

The hostler at the way station was a man with a deeply lined face and white hair. He hadn't seen any riders come through that met the description Johnny gave.

"Did have a horse stolen, though. Almost two weeks ago. Took a saddle, too."

"Could have been him," Johnny said to Matt. "No way of knowing."

The boys continued on the next morning.

They followed roads that skirted along the southern end of Indiana, and then into Illinois.

The weather turned warmer and they slept in a clearing off the trail. A stand of pines blocked most of the wind, and Johnny shot two rabbits for their supper.

Just across the Illinois border, they found a farmer who remembered seeing a rider come through.

"He might'a been about the age of you boys," he said.

He himself was a man about Pa's age, with a face that was hard and weathered. The kind of face a man sometimes gets from years of working in the sun and wind.

Johnny told him the boy had hair that was a little wavy, and he described the face. Prominent cheekbones. A jaw that was a little narrow. Scared-looking eyes.

The farmer shrugged. "Could be. He was wearing a wide hat, so I didn't get a look at his hair. Eyes that looked like eyes. I don't remember him looking all that scared. I don't really remember his cheekbones or jaw or anything like that. Just come in and did some work around the farm for a place to sleep for a couple of nights. I let him sleep on the kitchen floor. Too cold this time a'year to sleep in the barn. I do remember he had two horses. One he rode and one he led."

The boys rode on past the farm a little ways, then

reined up.

Matt said, "Could be the one. I mean, who else would it be?"

"I don't know," Thad said. "Why would he need two horses?"

Johnny said, "So he could switch horses when one got tired. You cover more ground that way."

Joe piped up. "Indians'll do that, sometimes."

Thad pulled off his hat and rubbed one hand through his hair. "We really got no way of knowing. It could be him, or maybe not. Maybe we took the wrong road, back at that fork."

"What would you have us do?" Joe said. "Turn around and go back to that fork, just on a guess?"

Matt said, "We can't go on second-guessing ourselves. At this point, going back to the fork makes no sense. It's over a week behind us. We go back, and even if he did take the western road, he'll have increased his lead on us by a week. And if he didn't, then we'll never catch him."

Joe said, "We committed to this direction. We're either right or we're wrong. We'll never know until we catch him."

"Or we don't," Thad said.

Johnny stood listening to the banter. He had talked them into the trail that bent southwestward. He had been so sure, at the time. But now he was thinking that a lot had depended on his guess.

What he said was, "Let's keep riding."

Bravo sensed it was time to start moving again, and he began his way along the road at a walk. The others fell into place behind him.

34

CHRISTMAS WAS always Ma's favorite time of the year. Johnny had thought of her every Christmas when he was in Texas. He thought of her now, on Christmas eve, as the boys were huddled around a fire at the edge of a small patch of thin woods in southern Illinois.

Johnny filled a tin cup with hot coffee, then he gripped the cup with both hands so the coffee would warm his fingers.

He looked up at the night sky. It was clear, the way a night sky can be in the winter.

The stars filled the sky. One in particular was a little brighter than the rest, off near the northern horizon.

Matt stood beside him.

"The North Star," he said. "Some call it Polaris. It's the star we use to guide by, out at sea. It doesn't change position, you see. The night sky seems to revolve around it, for whatever reason. No matter what time of night it might be, you see that star and you know you're facing north."

Johnny said, "I sometimes think about that night, all those years ago. Wise men, following a bright star. About to see the newborn child that would change the world."

Thad stood nearby, trying to stomp life into his freezing toes. "You boys believe all that? I mean, I would never say anything back home. People would think too bad of me. But out here, just between us, you boys really believe?"

Joe was sitting near the fire, stirring some beans in the skillet.

He said, "Ma has strong beliefs in it. Pa always did. Them two ain't no fools."

Johnny nodded. It was all that needed to be said.

Johnny turned back to the sky, and the North Star, and he wondered what it might have been like, all those years ago.

Thad said, "You know, we're almost out of food and money."

There were only two cans of beans left. They had pooled their cash together, and had only a dollar and twelve cents.

Johnny said, "Joe and I usually shoot our supper. The beans are only for the times we can't."

"That's not the point."

"Then what is?"

"The point is, it's been two weeks since we found anyone who's seen anyone who even looks like the man we're chasing. So my question is, what's next?"

"What's next?" Johnny said. "Missouri. That's what's next. We're probably a day from the state line."

Matt said to Thad, "You can turn back if you want to. We're not."

Thad shrugged. "I'm with you boys all the way. Missouri, it is."

When the beans were ready, they sat and ate and then climbed into their blankets. All except Johnny. He put some more wood on the fire, and then he poured another cup of hot coffee and went to stand and look at the night sky again.

The farm was now a long ride away in one direction, and Texas just as far in the other. No matter which place he thought of as home, he felt a long way from it.

He took a sip of coffee and he thought of Ma. And he thought about Pa, the man who had stood so strong and been such a rock in his life when he was growing up. But then a gun had been fired and Pa was gone. Just like that.

He thought of Luke, who had been but a boy when Johnny rode out to join the Army three years ago, but was now a man.

And he thought about Becky Drummond and wondered if he was the biggest fool who ever lived.

35

THEY WERE surrounded with mile upon mile of low, rolling hills covered with brown grass. Occasionally there might be a small stand of trees by a riverbank, but any deep woods were now behind them. Here and there were patches of snow.

Johnny figured it was time to rest the horses a little. He seemed to be the one they turned to for leadership, so he reined up and so did the others.

They swung out of the saddle and loosened the cinches. The horses poked their noses into the brown winter grass underfoot.

Johnny was still in Pa's coat, though it was much warmer than it had been back in Ohio. Though *warm* is a relative thing, he thought, at the risk of sounding like Matt. He sure wouldn't have minded a tight cabin and a hot stove to sit by. He brought his hands to his mouth to warm them.

"Look at this countryside," Matt said. "It goes on like this for as far as the eye can see."

Joe said, "Some think this was all woods once, and the Indians set it all to burning to start the game running. They'll still start grass fires for just that reason. But I don't see how any woods could have ever grown here. It's too dry."

They were in Missouri. They decided St. Louis was simply too big a city to search thoroughly, but they had visited the constable's office and told him about the man they were looking for.

Outside the constable's office, they stood and watched the traffic moving up and down the street. Wagons, a stagecoach. Riders. One closed-top carriage went by with a driver sitting in an open seat up front. He was in a black suit and a top hat.

Some of the people glanced to the McCabes, and they gave the boys a wary look.

"We look a sight," Thad said. "These city folks don't usually see people who look like they just crawled out of the woods."

"We'll never find him here," Johnny said, "unless luck is with us."

"Don't seem luck is," Joe said, "if you look at the way things have gone the past couple of months."

Matt scratched the scraggly whiskers covering his

chin.

He said, "We look like outlaws, and we haven't had a bath since the last time we got rained on."

"And it was sure a cold rain," Joe said.

"We got no money for a hotel or a bath."

Johnny was getting a little impatient. "All right. So we look like outlaws."

"My point is, so would he, by now. He'd be in about the same shape as we are. He can't have much money, if any at all. It would be impossible for someone looking as rough as we do right now to get very far in this city."

"So, you don't think he's here?"

"There's no way to know, for sure. But I would say no. If a man is on the run, he doesn't want to be in an area where he's going to stand out."

Thad made a scoffing, huffing sound. "There's no way to know if he came this way at all. I still think he went west, back at that fork in the road we came too, back in Ohio. He's probably all the way to Nebraska Territory, by now."

Johnny ignored him, but Joe said, "He'd freeze to death there. Ain't prepared for the kind of winter they get in that land. You think winters in Pennsylvania are hard, you ain't seen nothing like the winters in Nebraska Territory."

Johnny said to Matt, "So, where do you think he is?"

Matt shrugged. "There are small towns, up and down the river, right?"

Johnny gave a nodding shrug. "From what I understand. I never spent much time in Missouri."

"I say we meander along. Check farms, and towns. Any place we come to. Just like we've been doing."

Joe said, "Do we follow the river north, or south?"

Thad shook his head. "Here we go again."

Matt said, "There seems to be more population north, doesn't there?"

They had seen a map on the wall in the constable's office, and took a few moments to study it.

Johnny said, "Seemed like there were more towns north along the river."

And so they took to wandering their way north from St. Louis. They didn't ride in a straight line, but instead explored side roads as they saw them. They found themselves sometimes as much as twenty miles away from the Mississippi River, and at other times riding alongside the river.

They stopped at every place they could find to ask about the man they were searching for. Constables offices, saloons, farms, way stations, trading posts.

Occasionally they would find a home where they could do some odd chores in exchange for a meal. One hostler at a way station let them sleep on the kitchen floor.

A man who ran a hotel in Hannibal, a bustling town along the Missouri, had just paid for three cords of wood and needed it cut. He hired the boys and actually paid cash. It was enough for them to pay for a hotel room for the night, and to get a bath, a haircut and a shave. Except for Joe. He partook of the bath, only. His hair was nearly as long as it had been when he first met Johnny on the trail months ago, and his beard was thicker than ever.

There was enough money left over to buy some more cans of beans and a couple sacks of coffee.

They left Hannibal behind and continued their way along. When Hannibal was a week behind them, they decided to turn inland and work their way south. Maybe hit the Missouri River, where it cuts across the state from west to east to join the Mississippi. The man they were hunting might very well have ridden along that river looking for work.

They continued as they had, asking about the man they were hunting. They rode up to a farm, where a man was cutting wood. He shook his head no. Hadn't seen anyone like that riding through.

The nights were cold, leaving a frost behind in the early morning. But the days warmed up enough to be comfortable. One night they slept in a barn, and when they woke up there was an inch of snow on the ground. By noon, the snow had melted away.

As they rode along one morning, Johnny reined up and the others did the same.

"Let's rest the horses for a bit," he said. "We've been pushing 'em pretty hard the past couple of months. If one of 'em goes down, then we're going to be in trouble."

They were surrounded by old corn fields that had been harvested months ago. The land was flat and stretched for as far as the eye could see.

Thad said, "We've got to admit it, boys. The trail has gone cold. We haven't found anyone who's seen him since we left Illinois."

Matt said, "So, what would you have us do?"

"Head back. If we ride hard, we might make it in time for spring planting."

"I thought you were all intent on heading West. Finding gold."

Thad shook his head. "I've had enough of sleeping on the cold ground, for a while."

Johnny said nothing, and he wandered off a bit to stand and look off at the short, brown remains of the corn stalks.

Matt walked out to him and said, "So, what do you think?"

Johnny drew a breath and let it out slowly.

He said, "I don't know. On one hand, Thad might have a point, as much as I hate to admit it."

"No one wants to admit that."

"It's easy to lose track of the days, when one day is pretty much like another, but I figure it's probably near the end of February."

Matt nodded. "Seems about right. The calendar in the constable's office in Hannibal indicated it was the ninth, and that was about two weeks ago."

"If we leave now, we should be able to get back in time to help with the spring planting."

"Is that what you really want? To farm?"

Johnny shook his head. "No. If that was what I wanted, I wouldn't have told Becky to marry Trip Hawley."

"If they went through with their wedding plans like Becky said, then they've been married nigh onto two months now."

Johnny said, "And then there's Texas. Just calling to me from the distance. And I don't think Ma's really expecting us back, anyway. Or, at least, she's not expecting Joe and me to come back."

Joe had wandered out, too. Johnny hadn't heard him because Joe walked so quietly in his buckskin boots.

Joe said to Matt, "What about you? Do you want to farm in Pennsylvania? Ma'll probably leave the farm to you, if you go back. Or to both you and Luke."

Johnny said, "Or is the sea calling to you like Texas is to me?"

Matt said, "I don't know. I guess I feel torn between what I want and what I think I should do."

Thad had wandered out, too. He was holding back a bit, as the brothers were talking. He was showing a little discretion—Johnny thought, *Will wonders never cease?*

But now Thad said, "Well, we gotta figure out something. I'm hungry and cold and there's a town up ahead a ways. I don't want to spend the night out on these cold plains. It's gonna be freezing tonight."

Matt said, "We're down to our last eight cents."

"Maybe we can find some odd jobs. Split some wood, or something. Like what we did in Hannibal."

Matt looked to Johnny and Johnny nodded.

Johnny said, "He's got a point. We don't have to make any decisions about home right now. Let's go to that town and get some food into us and warm up a bit, and then we'll figure things out."

The town was Mansfield, and it was just after noon when the boys rode down the center street.

They found Mansfield to be a small farming town. Smaller even than Sheffield.

The center street had a sleepy, closed-up quality to it. A few leafless trees stood in front of boardwalks, and a wagon with a bored-looking horse was waiting in front of a feed store.

A man was standing in front of a mercantile with a broom in his hand. An apron was tied on over his pants, and a thick white mustache decorated his face.

The boys reined up.

They looked to Johnny for leadership, but when it came to speaking to strangers, Johnny passed the reins to Matt.

Matt said to the man with the broom, "Excuse me, sir. We're just passing through, but we were hoping maybe there might be an odd job, or a chore that might need doing. Something we can do to pay for some supper."

The man said, "The best thing you hooligans could do is ride on. We don't want your kind around here."

He turned away from them and stormed back into the store.

Thad said, "Well, that ain't too friendly."

Johnny looked at Matt and then at Joe and Thad. Their faces were covered with trail dust and a little campfire soot. Matt's jaw and chin were covered with a thin beard half an inch long, and Thad was in about the same condition. Joe's beard was thick and bushy, and his hair was now approaching his shoulders. Johnny figured he looked as rough as the rest of them.

He said, "We do look like a bunch of desperados. Outlaws from Texas or the Nations sometimes ride up this far north, trying to avoid the law. It doesn't happen much, but enough that these folks might not be too friendly toward anyone looking like we do."

Thad said, "Folks were a lot more friendly in Hannibal."

"We're a considerable distance further south than Hannibal."

Matt said, "Understandable. And especially with all of the violence we've been hearing about in Kansas and Missouri as of late. John Brown and such."

"I don't care about none of that," Thad said. "That man has canned goods inside that store. There's no reason he couldn't give us a little work in exchange for some of them."

"Nothing we can do about it now," Johnny said.

Up ahead and on the other side of the street was a sign that read, SALOON. Johnny had seen some towns where the buildings were barely more than shanties and the signs were hand-painted. But this one looked like it had been professionally painted. The letters had the look of what you normally saw in a newspaper.

"A saloon is a good place for information," he said. "Maybe we can find out if anyone's hiring."

Matt said, "On a ship, it can get downright cold sometimes, and there's nothing like a pull of rum to warm the insides. I'd bet a belt of tequila would have about the same effect."

"For eight cents, I think the best any of us can count on in that saloon is information."

They found the door locked. No surprise, considering it was a Tuesday, just before noon.

They decided to leave their horses in front of the saloon and split up to look for work individually. Maybe someone needed some wood split. Maybe the livery attendant needed some horses tended to.

It was late in the afternoon when they were back together, in front of the saloon. They had found no work. Johnny had checked the livery, and a man there had threatened to call the constable if he didn't leave. Thad had gotten the same reception at a boarding house.

"I will admit," Matt said, "I'm not looking forward to another night in the open. The last two nights have been downright cold. I would be satisfied with just a barn."

Two men came walking toward them from the other side of the street. One was the man from the general store. The other wore a thick coat that was hanging open, and Johnny could see a badge pinned to his vest. He was cradling a shotgun in the crook of one arm.

He opened by saying, "You boys have got to ride on."

"We don't want trouble," Matt said. "My name's Matthew McCabe. These are my brothers John and Josiah, and our cousin Thaddeus. We're not looking for any kind of trouble. We're just passing through, and we're looking for any odd jobs we can find that might help us pay for our supper. And maybe a barn to spend the night in."

"Don't care what you're looking for. You're not gonna find it here. Ride on."

"It's mighty cold out there," Johnny said. "It's gonna be even colder tonight."

"Don't rightly care. Whatever trouble you're bringing, we don't want it here."

Thad said to the man with him, "Ain't you from the general store? You went and got the constable?"

The man reared up with a defensive sort of pride. "We don't want your kind here in this town."

Thad was about to spout off at the man, but Johnny pushed a hand into Thad's chest, as if to say, *slow down.*

Johnny gave a long look to the man from the general store, then said, "All right. We want no trouble. Let's ride."

36

A SMALL DEER STOOD shoulder deep in some tall junipers, and Johnny sat in the saddle and sighted in with his Colt rifle.

"That's a long shot from here," Matt said.

"I don't care. I'm hungry and it's almost nightfall."

"But even if you can make the shot, there's not enough wood around here for a campfire. And it's gonna be mighty cold out here tonight with no shelter."

"Quiet, Matt. I'm drawing a bead."

Bravo held still. He often did when Johnny was about to make a shot. Bravo had a way of knowing what Johnny needed him to do. A sort of cooperative relationship a rider can develop with a good horse.

Johnny pulled the trigger, but the deer moved at the last moment and the bullet missed. The deer exploded away in a full sprint.

Johnny cocked the gun and brought it back it to his shoulder, but it was useless. The deer was zig-zagging from right to left as it ran, and then it was over the crest of a small, grassy hill and was gone from sight.

Johnny knew he wouldn't get off a second shot, but had tried against the odds because he was too hungry not to.

They found a small, abandoned farm a few miles outside of town. The house was small, not much bigger than a tool shed. The walls were made of sod, and the roof was falling in. But the barn was in better shape. The boards were aging and had dry rot in places, and portions of the roof were missing. But at least it was shelter.

They decided to risk a fire, in a section of the barn where there was no longer any roof. They broke off some boards from what was left of the sod hut's roof and used them to burn.

It grew dark, and the almost spring-like warmth of the day was long gone.

Joe sat cross-legged by the fire and wrapped his blankets around himself. Thad was pacing about with a load of impatience, blowing on his fingers and trying to stamp life into his feet.

Johnny filled his coffee kettle from his canteen and started fixing some coffee. His canteen was now empty, but he had seen a small stream out beyond the farm.

Matt was pacing about, too. He said, "What I wouldn't give for a mug of rum, right now."

Johnny said, "Coffee will have to do."

Thad said to Joe, "How do the Injuns do it? How do they keep warm on nights like this?"

Johnny thought there was more than impatience in Thad's voice. Sounded like he was working himself toward anger.

But Joe was as calm as ever. He said, "Cain't speak for all Indians, but the Cheyenne wouldn't let themselves get caught in this kind of situation. They wouldn't be out riding around in weather like this. But if they had to, they'd be a lot better prepared. They'd have bearskins and smoked meat. Pouches full of nuts and dried berries."

He shook his head, "Mm-boy, you spread a bear skin on the ground and sleep on it, with two more draped over you, and you're toasty warm."

"They wouldn't be out riding around in the winter?" Thad was downright angry, and Johnny heard a challenge in Thad's voice. "What if they were in our situation. Having to chase a murderer? And then lost his trail like we did?"

But Joe was unflappable. He said, "They wouldn't be in our situation because they wouldn't have been out in the woods without their weapons, like we were. A man took a shot at their father, and he wouldn't have lived long."

Johnny nodded. He agreed. He said, "If we had our guns that day, he wouldn't even have gotten a shot off. I would have plugged him as soon as his gun came up. Pa would still be alive, and we wouldn't be out here freezing."

Thad turned on Johnny. "Oh, you think you're so danged flashy with them guns. I'd like to see you in action. See how good you'd be with another gun actually aiming at you."

Johnny stood up and looked him dead in the eye. "No you wouldn't."

Thad took a step toward him. "I don't think you're all that danged good. I don't believe those stories. What do you think of that? I know how stories get made up just so you can sound good when you're bragging to people."

"I'm not like you."

"What's that supposed to mean. You think I'm a liar?"

"Everyone thinks you're a liar."

Thad took one more step toward him. "Take that back, or I'm gonna make you."

Matt pushed his way in front of Thad and said, "Stop this now, before someone gets hurt."

Joe was still sitting by the fire. He said, "This keeps up, someone's gonna get killed. And it ain't gonna be Johnny."

Thad said, "Oh, you don't think so?"

Matt gave Thad a shove backward. Not a hard one, but firmly, moving Thad back and away from Johnny.

Matt said, "We all have to stop this right now. Fighting amongst ourselves will only make things worse."

Thad looked at Matt with fury in his eyes, then he turned to Joe. He found Joe wasn't even looking at him. Joe was looking into the fire, or beyond the fire, in the distant way of his.

Thad turned away, maybe seeing the common sense in not challenging a gunfighter, or a mountain man who had lived among Indians.

Thad said, "Well, we can't just stand around and starve and freeze to death."

Matt said, "What would you have us do?"

Thad turned back to him. "Well, for one thing, if I was leading us, we wouldn't be out here starving and freezing while that store back there in town is full of food."

"He wouldn't do business with us. He called the constable on us."

"Don't matter. That food back there is just waiting for the taking."

Now Joe looked at him. "You talkin' about stealin'?"

"No. I ain't talking about stealing. I'm talking about borrowing."

Matt gave a look to Johnny. Johnny shook his head and went back to making coffee.

Thad said, "We take only what we need. We keep an inventory of it. Once we're working, or back East or wherever we're going, we save up some money and send it to him."

Johnny said, "It's still stealing."

"And just who appointed you leader, anyway? Matt's the oldest among us."

Johnny shrugged. The coffee grounds were in the water, and he pushed the kettle into the flames.

He said, "We're gonna need more wood for the fire."

Joe nodded. "We keep burnin' wood at this rate, the boards from the house will be gone, and we'll have to start usin' boards from the barn. Then there won't be any barn left for shelter."

Thad said, "I say following you hasn't done us a whole lot of good. I say we follow me, now."

Matt shook his head. "It's like Johnny said. Borrowing without permission is the same as stealing."

"These are desperate times, Matt. We'll pay him back. We're not thieves. We don't steal just for the sake of stealing. We only borrow without permission as a last resort."

He glanced about at the remains of the old barn. "And this looks pretty desperate to me."

Matt said, "Think about the irony of it. More than three months ago, Pa and Hector Drummond were both shot and killed by a man who broke into a mercantile. Now we're considering doing the same thing."

"I don't care anything about irony," Thad said. "What I care about is eating. And maybe getting some more warm blankets."

Joe said, "I can't believe we're even considerin' this."

Johnny looked from him to Matt. Matt said nothing, but Johnny could tell by the look in his eye that he reluctantly agreed with Thad. Cold and hunger can make a man do things he never would do otherwise.

Johnny knew it was wrong. But he knew they were going to do it. They were going to rob a store tonight.

37

MATT SAID, "So, what would you have us do? Kick in the front door and go in with guns out and bandanas over our faces, like desperadoes?"

Thad shook his head. "Nothing so outrageous. Just ride into town quiet-like. By the time we get there, it'll be nigh onto midnight. That little farming town will be sound asleep. We just go in through a back door. Shouldn't be all that hard to break the lock. Or we go in through a window. Then we help ourselves, but only to what we need. Then we're gone. By the time the old coot opens up tomorrow and realizes some merchandise is gone, we'll be miles away."

"They'll know it was us," Matt said.

Thad shook his head. "They might suspect us, but they won't have any real evidence of any kind."

Joe said, "What if someone sees us?"

"Won't nobody see us. Everyone in that little town will be asleep by the time we get there. We'll move quiet. Break in quiet, take only what we need, and then we'll be back out and on our horses and we'll be away into the night."

And so, with Thad in the lead, they headed back to the little farming town of Mansfield.

They rode in single file. Since Thad had campaigned for a leadership role and this whole thing was his idea, he was first in line. Matt was following. Then came Johnny, with Joe riding drag.

A quarter moon was in the sky, giving them enough light to ride by, as long as they held to the trail.

Johnny had a bad feeling about this whole venture. It seemed to him that stealing was stealing. He wondered what Pa would have thought about it.

He was starting to think maybe they should have left Thad back in Pennsylvania. And yet, as bad an idea as Johnny thought this venture was, he and Joe and Matt had agreed to it. Made them all as guilty as Thad.

They found what they had expected. The town of Mansfield had closed up for the night. The winter wind rattled window panes and door knobs.

The boys reined up behind the general store.

Johnny said, "If we're gonna do this, let's at least be smart about it."

He swung out of the saddle and led Bravo into a dark alley. The other boys followed.

"I like it," Thad said. "Keeps the horses out of the cold wind, and it's harder to see them."

"All right," Johnny said. "You're the leader of this robbery, so go ahead and lead."

"It's not a robbery," Thad said.

Johnny wasn't about to start arguing semantics. But the longer they stood and argued, the more likely it was someone could hear them. The people of the town were most likely inside, asleep in warm beds and safe from the cold, winter winds. But Johnny had chased enough outlaws when he rode for the Rangers to know most of them got themselves caught because of mistakes. Rash actions they did without thinking things through, or assumptions they shouldn't have made.

Johnny said, "We should leave one of us behind with the horses."

"I thought I was in charge," Thad said.

"Just offering advice."

Joe said, "I'll stay with the horses. I ain't in favor of this whole thing, anyway."

"None of us is," Matt said.

Thad tried the back door of the general store. It was locked. He then began trying windows. All were shut tight.

"Gonna have to break in," Thad said. "Maybe find a rock or something to break through a window."

Johnny shook his head. "You're gonna get us all thrown in jail, you know that?"

"Well, what do you suggest?"

Johnny wrapped a bandana around his fist, and then made a light punch at the glass. The window didn't budge. Then he hit a little harder. Then harder. The glass cracked, then one pane fell through. There was a tinkling sound as the glass shattered on the floor inside, but it was much quieter than breaking the window with a rock would have been.

The window was the kind that slid up rather than swung open. Johnny reached a hand through the broken glass and turned the lock, then he slid the sash up.

He looked to Thad and said, "You first. You're the leader."

Thad pushed his upper body through the window, until only his butt and legs were visible. Then with his feet kicking, he went the rest of the way in and landed on the floor. Sounded to Johnny like Thad attempted a head-first roll but landed harder than he had wanted to.

Matt was next, and then Johnny.

Matt said, "We need to find a light."

Johnny looked out the window and to some buildings at the other side of the street. The feed store was directly across from the general store, and there was a second floor. Probably living quarters.

He said, "Any light in here will be visible from across the street."

"No one's awake at this hour," Thad said.

"If we're gonna do this, we have to go ahead like people are out there. Be extra careful."

Matt said, "Err on the side of caution."

"All right." Thad started across the floor.

Matt said, "Be careful."

As soon as he said it, Thad bumped into something in the darkness and glass shattered on the floor.

Johnny shook his head. He didn't know if he was more embarrassed about being part of an operation like this, or being part of it with Thad.

Thad said, "We've got to risk a light."

He pulled down the window shades, and then Johnny reluctantly struck a match.

A kerosene lamp was on the counter, so Johnny lifted the glass and applied the match to the wick. Soon a pale glow was coming from the lamp. Johnny kept it low, because he had never seen a shade fully cover a window. If he was to turn the lamp up enough, then small cracks of light would be visible from outside.

"All right," he said. "Let's get this over with."

Johnny could see a brown bottle on the floor, the bottle now in pieces. The neck was still intact and the cork was in place. It was what Thad had knocked over. Looked to be some kind of liniment.

Matt followed his gaze and said, "That bottle is more merchandise for which we're going to have to reimburse the owner."

Johnny said to Thad, "You're the leader. So, lead."

"All right," Thad said. "Let's organize this a little. Matt, see if you can find some blankets. The rest of us will grab the canned goods. Maybe find an old sack and fill it."

"What about someone to watch the door?"

Thad rolled his eyes. "No one is up and about at this hour."

Matt said, "Remember, err on the side of caution."

Thad was getting a little exasperated. "All right. I'll watch the door. Johnny, grab the canned goods."

Johnny found an empty grain sack and started grabbing cans from a shelf. He focused on food that would be easy to cook in a skillet over a campfire. Beans, mainly.

He heard Matt say, "Found some blankets. Thick, wool ones. I'll grab one for each of us."

Joe was at the back window. He said in a loud whisper, "Hurry up. How long you gonna be?"

"Just a few more minutes," Johnny said.

He was focusing on the canned goods. He was paying no attention to what Thad was doing, until Thad said, "How do you get this thing open? It's locked."

Johnny found Thad not watching the door, but standing behind the cash register.

"Thad," Johnny said. "We didn't say anything about taking any money."

"If it's here, there's no reason for us not to take some. We can reimburse the old goat later. Maybe we can ride back to St. Louis, rent ourselves a room and get a hot bath."

Johnny said to Matt, "I think he's enjoying this too much."

"Come on," Joe said from the window. "Let's get out of here."

Matt had a bundle of blankets in his arms, and he went to the window and handed them out to Joe.

Matt said, "Roll these up and tie them to the back of our saddles."

Johnny found some canned peas and string beans. Not the easiest things to cook without a pot, but Ma had always said you need your greens. He grabbed six cans of each and tossed them into the sack.

A gun went off behind them. Johnny turned, his right hand darting down for his own gun but instead brushing against the long coat that was in the way.

Thad was still by the register, and now had a pistol in his hand. Smoke was drifting from the barrel of the gun.

He slid out the register drawer. "Got it open."

Johnny said, "Thad, are you crazy? That gunshot will

wake up this whole town."

Thad looked at Johnny with disbelief in his eyes. "Are you really afraid of these people? They're just a bunch of sheep. Holier-than-thou hypocrites. They could have given us work. They asked for this. And that old marshal. He couldn't stand up to any of us. If you're even half as tough as you seem to want people to believe, you wouldn't be afraid."

"I'm not afraid. I just know right from wrong."

Matt went to the front door and pushed the shade aside to look out.

"Someone's coming," he said.

Matt ran across the store to the counter and turned out the lamp, and then ducked down. Johnny crouched behind a display of cookware.

Thad was stuffing his coat pocket with cash. He didn't duck until a key was pushed into the door.

A man stepped in, his shotgun in both hands. Twin barrels of what Johnny figured was probably buckshot.

Johnny could see the man's outline in what little light made its way in from the moon outside, and he knew it was the constable.

The man said, "Don't move, boys. I know who you are. I seen your horses and one of your men in the alley."

Thad's gun was still in his hand. He rose up from behind the counter and cocked the hammer back.

The constable looked over at the sound and swung his shotgun around. But he was no gunman and hadn't cocked either barrel.

Johnny called out, "No!" But it was too late.

Thad fired, and the lawman staggered back a step. Thad fired again, and the constable took another step backward and the shotgun fell to the floor.

Thad fired a third time. The constable's knees folded and he went down.

"Thad," Matt said. "Are you out of your mind?"

Thad said, "I'm not going to any jail."

Johnny ran over to the constable. The man was on his back, Johnny put an ear down to the man's chest.

"He's not breathing."

Thad called out, "Come on! Let's get out of here!"

He went through the window much faster than he had the first time.

"He's right," Matt said. "The whole town's going to

come running."

Johnny snatched up the sack of canned goods.

Joe was at the window again. "What in tarnation is goin' on in there?"

Johnny handed the sack out to him, and then climbed out the window. Matt was next.

"Where's Thad?" Matt said.

"He ran to the alley and jumped on his horse."

"Always thinking of himself first," Johnny said.

He looked back at the store through the window, but it was too dark in there to see the constable's body through the window.

It shouldn't have happened this way, he thought. He and his brothers never should have agreed with Thad's harebrained idea. The townsfolk had been afraid of them, thinking they were some sort of outlaws, and now they had proven the townsfolk right.

The horses were waiting for them, all except Thad's. A blanket was now tied to the back of each saddle.

Johnny tied the sack to his saddle horn, and they all mounted up.

Johnny said, "We gotta ride, fast and hard."

They rode a mile with the horses at a gallop, and by the end of the mile, they caught up with Thad. He had reined up to wait for them.

At the sight of him, Johnny pulled up and the others did so, too.

"Come on," Thad said. "We've got to ride."

Johnny said, "We keep this pace up and we'll kill the horses. A lot of good it'll do for us to be on foot."

"So, what next?" Joe said. "Ride back to that old barn?"

Johnny shook his head. "We rest the horses, then we keep on going."

"Not me," Thad said. "I'm cold, and I'm hungry, and we've got ourselves a whole sack full of food."

"We killed a man back there."

Matt said, "If I remember right, it was *Thad* that killed a man."

Johnny shook his head. "It was *us* who was there. We'll be blamed."

Thad looked at Johnny like he thought Johnny was an

idiot. "The only one who could point a finger at us is the constable back there, and I put three bullets in him. He ain't talking to no one."

Matt looked at Johnny. "Are you sure he was dead?"

Johnny said, "I don't think he was breathing. But it was hard to tell with his coat on."

Thad said, "Sure he's dead. And it's a good thing. Otherwise, we'd be facing a noose."

"Thad," Johnny said. "It's never a good thing to have to kill a man."

Matt said, "And you didn't have to kill him. If you hadn't fired that gun to break open the register, we might have gotten out of there with no one hurt."

"Firing the gun had nothing to do with it," Thad said. "He had already seen our horses. The man had to be shot."

Johnny shook his head. He didn't know what to say.

Matt, however, who was seldom at a loss for words, said, "I can't believe we've sunk this low."

Thad said, "We haven't sunk anywhere. We're doing what we have to do to survive. That's all. There's no one back there to identify us. All we have to do is rest these horses a little while and then keep riding."

Johnny stepped out of the saddle to rest Bravo, and he took the opportunity to better tie the sack to the saddle horn. Then he walked off away from them all, to stand alone a few yards out on the dried, winter grass.

Thad shook his head, like he couldn't believe his cousin's limited view on this. Thad walked away too, in the other direction, and reached inside his coat to his vest to pull out some fixings, and he rolled himself a cigarette.

Joe said to Matt, "Stay with the horses," and walked out to where Johnny was standing.

Johnny said to him, "There was a man back there in town. Across the street from the general store. I saw him when we were riding out. I don't know who he was, but he had to have gotten a look at us."

Joe nodded. "I seen him too."

The man on the boardwalk was the bartender from the saloon. He lived in a small room above the grain store. He had been woken up by the gunshot and hurried down a flight of wooden steps along the side of the building.

He had been standing on the boardwalk in front of the

grain store when three more shots were fired, and they came from the general store. In the moonlight, he could see the front door to the store was open.

He watched one rider charge out of the alley and down the street, and then three more that followed. He thought it looked like the wild boys from earlier in the day. The ones that looked like a cross between saddle bums and outlaws. They had looked like what the newspapers were starting to call *border ruffians*, and apparently that's what they were. One of them had asked him for a job, earlier in the day. What had they said their name was? He wasn't so good with names.

He ran across the street.

Milt Evans ran the general store and lived upstairs. By the time the bartender had crossed the street and was in through the front door, Evans was already kneeling by the constable.

The bartender said, "Milt, what happened?"

Milt looked up at him. "The store was robbed. They shot Eb."

But Eb the constable wasn't quite dead.

Milt said, "Get a doctor."

But Eb shook his head. He got out the words, "Won't do no good."

"Did you see who done it?"

Eb nodded.

The bartender said, "It was those hooligans from earlier."

Eb nodded again.

The bartender said, "I forget their names."

"McCabe," Milt said. "I remember their names. Their first names are from the Bible. Matt, John, Josiah. The fourth one was...I forget."

Eb got the word out, barely more than a whisper. "Thaddeus."

Milt said, "That's it."

Eb then sucked in a rasping breath, and his eyes closed.

Milt looked over at the bartender. "He's dead, Walt."

Walt the bartender said, "In the morning, we'll send a wire for the federal marshal. Those boys won't get far."

38

THEY RODE most of the night. Patches of snow almost glowed in the moonlight, but mostly the open grassland and occasional patches of trees looked like dark emptiness.

After a time, Johnny saw the stars beginning to disappear toward the northwest. He knew this meant a cloud cover was coming in.

Joe had seen it, too. When they stopped to rest the horses, Joe said, "We've got some weather comin' in. Maybe snow."

By daylight, the entire sky was covered with a grayish white overcast, and a cold wind was coming from the north.

Johnny thought it might be best to turn away from the trail. There was a creek that seemed to meander its way along, and small patches of woods surrounded it. Looked like mostly alder and ash.

Thad said, "I thought I was in charge, now. I say we keep riding."

Matt shook his head. "You were in charge last night, and look where it got us."

"None of that was my fault. Things just went wrong. It could have happened to anyone."

Matt looked at Johnny with disbelief, then said to Thad, "It was *all* your fault."

Joe said, "Fightin' amongst ourselves won't get us anywhere."

Joe looked at Johnny, as if waiting for instructions.

Johnny said, "We're turning off the trail. Find us a good place to hole up for a bit. Rest the horses, and start a small fire. Grab something to eat."

Thad said, "No one's gonna find us. No one knows it was us, last night."

"Like Matt said," Johnny looked to Matt, "how'd you put it?"

Matt said, "Err on the side of caution."

"That's it. Joe, want to lead the way?"

When it came to working their way through a patch of woods, he figured Joe had the most experience.

Joe turned his horse off the trail, keeping it to a slow walk. Matt followed. Johnny said to Thad, "Come along or keep on riding. Don't matter much to me."

And he turned Bravo off the trail to follow Joe and Matt.

Thad shook his head. "You boys are too much to believe. You know that?"

He sat in the saddle and watched the three moving through the trees.

"Oh, all right," he said, and turned his horse to follow them.

Once a fire was burning, Johnny set to making coffee. Matt dumped a can of beans into Johnny's skillet and set it in the fire.

Thad held his hands out to the flames to warm them.

He said, "I hope the smoke from your fire isn't seen from the road. Then these hordes of lawmen you seem to think will be coming after us might see it."

Joe was standing off a bit. He had stripped the saddle from his horse and spread a blanket over its back.

He said, "Fire from this kind of wood shouldn't throw off too much smoke. And it won't stand out at a distance because it's about the same color as the sky."

Thad gave a snort of disgust and said, "More Injun wisdom?"

Johnny said, "Your pa is a good man, Thad. But somehow, he never managed to teach you it's sometimes best to just keep your mouth quiet."

"Why? Afraid the Injun-boy over there'll take my scalp?"

Johnny shook his head. Johnny had to admit to himself he didn't quite know what Joe was capable of. Johnny wasn't afraid of him, but thought it was downright foolish of Thad to try and goad him.

But Joe said, "Your scalp wouldn't be worth the effort."

And he turned and walked away.

Johnny looked at Matt and they shared a grin.

Thad said, "You all blame me, is that it? Since it was my idea, things went wrong and so you blame me."

Johnny said, "Things didn't go wrong, Thad. You brought them on by firing that gun."

"Well, I couldn't get into the cash drawer, otherwise."

Matt said, "We didn't say anything about taking money. We were there to take only what we needed."

Thad looked at Matt like he thought Matt was stupid.

"Well, we need money, don't we? Whether we turn back to home or we keep on going, I'm not sleeping out in the cold, anymore."

"Thad," Johnny said. "You killed a man."

"I had to. How's it different from all of them men you claim to have killed out in Texas? Five Comanches with five shots, and all of that. Sounds really grand when you're bragging to a bunch of hick farmers. But now that we're out here in the real world and you have to put your money where your mouth is, it's a whole different thing, ain't it?"

"Thad," Matt said. "You don't know what you're dealing with. Don't go challenging him."

Johnny said, "I've never shot a man that didn't need it. You want to add yourself to the list of the ones who needed it?"

Thad said, "I thought we were family."

"Then start acting like it."

Matt said, "Back off, Thad."

Thad turned and walked away, into the trees.

Johnny said to Matt, "There's going to be lawmen on our trail. Maybe a posse coming after us."

"How can you be sure?"

Johnny told Matt what he and Joe had seen. A man standing on the boardwalk across from the general store as they rode away.

"Are you sure?" Matt said.

Johnny nodded.

Matt said, "Could you see who it was, in the darkness? Any of the men we had seen in town, that day?"

"No. It was too dark."

"Then, maybe he couldn't see us clearly enough to recognize us."

"Who else would it be? Four riders driven out of town because they were afraid we were outlaws. Then four riders break into the general store and shoot their constable."

Matt nodded. "And even though it was Thad who killed the constable, we'll all be looked at as murderers. Guilt by association."

Matt went back to tending the beans, and Johnny stood a while, waiting for the coffee to boil up. And he thought about this predicament and how he had let himself get caught up in it.

A snowflake came down. It was small and thin and

came shooting down and past them on the wind. Then came more.

"Sleet," Matt said.

Johnny nodded.

After a time, Thad came back. "Are those beans ready? I'm starved."

"Just about," Matt said.

Thad reached into his coat pocket and pulled out a wad of cash. Mostly ones, but a couple of fives.

"There's fifty dollars here, in paper money. Should last us a long time. I didn't have the time to grab coins."

Fifty dollars was a lot to have in a cash drawer, Johnny thought. He had been around the Drummond store enough as a kid to know Mr. Drummond kept much less.

"Just think," Thad said. "If we had done things my way, we'd be riding on to the nearest town. Maybe take a week in a boarding house just to rest up. But now we're doing things your way," he glanced at Johnny, "and we're standing out here in the sleet that's coming down, waiting to share a can of beans."

Johnny said, "You want to ride on and find a boarding house, you go ahead and do it. But you'll be in a jail cell before the day's through."

Thad shook his head and smiled in his disbelief.

Johnny said, "Someone saw us, Thad. Back in town. There was a man standing in front of the saloon when we rode out."

"I didn't see anyone."

"I did. And so did Joe."

"And you left him just standing there? You didn't put a bullet in him?"

Johnny didn't know what to say to that.

Thad turned his back to them and threw his arms in the air in frustration. "I can't believe you boys. It's like you're asking to be caught."

Joe came back and said nothing to Thad, and Thad said nothing to him.

Once the beans were gone, Joe said, "I seen a silo standing in the distance, out beyond the trees. Let's put this fire out and ride on over. Maybe we can wait out this snow in the barn."

"Sounds like it could be dangerous," Matt said.

Johnny nodded. "But maybe not so dangerous as it

would be in a town. You've got to figure, the town officials in Mansfield are probably sending wires out with our descriptions. But a farm this far out may not have word, yet. Might be worth the risk."

"What if we get the same reception we did in town?" Thad said. "You willing to make the hard decision and do what has to be done?"

"We're not shooting anyone. No more killing. I mean it."

They rode single file, with Joe leading the way and Matt and then Thad following. Johnny was last, and as they rode, he would throw occasional glances back over his shoulder to see if there was any sign of riders behind them.

The sleet tapped against the brim of Johnny's hat and created a small layer of ice along the brim. He watched Thad hunching his shoulders against the cold and the sleet. And he thought about the look in Thad's eye back at the fire, talking about doing what had to be done.

Johnny had always thought Thad was something of a wind bag, but now he had seen something he found even more disturbing in Thad's eye. Thad seemed to feel no remorse because of last night's killing. Even worse, Johnny thought Thad might have enjoyed it.

39

THE FARMHOUSE WAS two-floors high, with white clapboards and a front porch. Common in Pennsylvania, but not so much out here in Missouri. Some farmhouses were nothing more than sod huts.

When the boys reined up in front of the farmhouse, the sleet was coming down so thick they could scarcely see the silo standing out behind the barn.

Matt climbed down from the saddle, then stood a moment with the reins in his hand like he didn't know quite what to do with them. Even after three months on the trail, he was still more of a seaman than a horseman. Finally he handed them to Joe and stepped up onto the porch.

Johnny handed the reins of Bravo to Joe, also.

Johnny said to Joe and Thad, but more to Thad, "Wait here."

Matt knocked on the door. A man spoke from behind them.

"What can I do for yuh?"

Johnny saw a man carrying a heavy-looking bucket in each hand. Johnny squinted against the sleet, which was now blowing sideways. He couldn't make the man out all that well, but he figured the man had been in the barn milking the cows. A cow's need to be milked didn't change with the weather.

Matt left the door and stepped toward him. Johnny heard Matt over the wind. "My name's Matthew McCabe, and I'm here with my brothers John and Josiah, and our cousin Thaddeus. We're just passing through, and would appreciate the chance to wait out the storm in your barn."

"I've gotta get these buckets in the house," the man said.

"Let me help you." Matt took one bucket, and Johnny took the other.

They followed the farmer to the door, and Johnny glanced to Joe and Thad. Joe sat tall in the saddle, regardless of the sleet. Thad sat hunched over.

Johnny and Matt followed the farmer around to a side door and into what was a small kitchen. An iron stove was burning away, and Johnny thought it felt almighty good.

A woman was at the stove. She was a bit heavyset, in

the matronly way Johnny had seen so many women take on as the years passed. Especially after children.

The farmer appeared to be about forty, but it was hard to tell. A lifetime of hard work can make a man sometimes seem older than he was. He had a beard that was dark at the chin but white at the sides, and lines trailed away from his eyes.

The farmer held out a hand and said, "My name's Cobb."

Matt shook it, and then Johnny.

Matt said, "We must look a wreck. But we've been on the trail a lot of days."

The door opened behind Johnny and he heard feet shuffling. Two sets of them. He had asked Joe and Thad to stay out with the horses. Somehow, Johnny figured it was Thad's idea to come on in.

Cobb said, "I've got to be honest with you boys. There's been a lot of rough-looking riders here in Missouri in recent years. Lots of bad doings. Shootings and such. You've heard about John Brown, last year."

Matt nodded. "We surely have."

"You have to understand, I've gotta be careful."

His wife said, "Henry, we've never turned away strangers. Especially in weather like this."

Thad pushed forward, pulling his pistol from under his coat and aiming it at Cobb.

He said, "Now you listen here, old man. We ain't asking."

Matt took a step back from Thad. He said, "What are you doing?"

"This old man's gonna turn us away. Are we gonna let him?"

The woman's eyes were wide open. Her eyes were darting from Thad to Henry and back again. She said, "Henry?"

Johnny said to Thad, "Put down the gun."

"You ain't in charge anymore. You ain't got the backbone to do what's gotta be done."

Johnny thought about that old Chinaman he had known in Texas. Some of the tricks the man had shown him. How to bend a man's hand in a way that's contrary to the way a wrist wants to bend. How you can use that trick to take a knife right out of a man's grip, and it doesn't matter how strong the man is. You just had to be fast and sure. Two things Johnny had always been.

He thought the trick would work on a gun, too. Especially since Thad hadn't been smart enough to cock the gun first. Thad's gun was a Colt .44 Dragoon, what they called a single-action. It had to be cocked before it could fired.

Johnny grabbed at the gun with one hand and pulled it toward himself, then he got the other hand on it. He turned the gun to Thad's left, making Thad's wrist bend inward in a way that weakened the grip, then Johnny pushed the gun toward Thad, which slid it away from his fingers. All in a second and a half.

Thad was left staring at him, caught between anger and disbelief that Johnny had actually just pulled the gun out of his hand.

Johnny glanced at Matt. Matt seemed to somehow know what Johnny was thinking, and he nodded.

Johnny aimed the gun at Thad, and he didn't forget to cock it.

Johnny said. "Give me that money from your pocket."

Thad reached into his pocket and pulled out the fistful of cash. It was no longer rolled neatly but in a crumpled mess. Johnny held out his left hand and Thad pushed the money into it.

"Now, ride. I don't care where you go. Just go."

Thad said, "You ain't sending me out into that storm?"

"I don't care where you go, as long as it's not here."

Thad looked to Matt and said, "Matt?"

Matt was looking at him sadly. "Just go."

Thad gave Johnny a long, hard look. Thad said, "What about the food we took? And one fourth of that's mine. One fourth of that money is, too."

Johnny said, "You take what's on your horse and nothing else, and you ride."

"You ain't got the nerve to pull that trigger."

Henry Cobb's wife had her hand over her mouth.

Thad stood there looking at Johnny. Maybe actually seeing the steel in Johnny's eye for the first time. Thad apparently decided maybe it wasn't so smart to test Johnny after all, so he turned toward the door.

He found himself face-to-face with Joe.

Joe said, "Don't let me ever see you again."

Thad stepped around Joe and out into the cold.
Joe said, "We never should have let that sum'bitch ride along with us."
Johnny eased back the hammer on the pistol, and said, "Now, don't go speaking ill of Aunt Sara."
"Didn't mean to."

40

HENRY COBB SAID, "You boys are in a bit of trouble, ain't you?"

Johnny nodded. "You could say that."

"And let me guess. That boy that just left is the main cause."

Matt shook his head. "We didn't have to go along with him. The fault is partly ours."

Cobb nodded. "I know how the world works."

"Henry," Mrs. Cobb said. "We can't turn these boys out in cold like this. They need a hot meal."

He nodded. "A hot meal, then you can bed down in the barn."

The hot meal was a breakfast of bacon and eggs and biscuits, and then they settled into the barn. The horses got a good rubdown. Johnny thought Joe's idea of putting a blanket over his horse was a good idea, so he did the same with Bravo.

There was an upright chair in the barn, old and dusty. Matt brushed it off and gave the chair a try. It creaked a bit, but held up.

"That had to be one of the best meals I've ever tasted," he said.

He glanced at the walls of the barn and at the roof. There were bales of hay stacked against one wall.

"Funny how it feels so warm in here, even though there's not a stove burning."

"It's the hay," Joe said. He was sitting cross-legged on a blanket on the floor. "It helps keep out the cold."

"Hay keeps you cool in the summer, and warm in the winter."

Johnny set Thad's pistol on an old table. "He didn't have a rifle in his saddle. As far as I know, this is the only gun he had."

Joe said, "Unless he had one tucked away in his saddle bags."

Matt took off his hat and rubbed his hair back. "I can't believe it's come to this."

Henry Cobb came in with a kettle and four cups. "Thought you boys might like some more coffee."

He poured, then he said, "At sunrise, maybe an hour

before you boys rode in, a deputy constable rode out from town. Told us about a robbery and a killin' in Mansfield last night. Was that you boys?"

Matt nodded, a cross between sheepish and sad.

"It was that boy you run off, wasn't it? It was him what done the shooting."

Matt nodded again.

Johnny said, "We grew up with him and thought we knew him."

Henry stood there a moment, looking off at a wall. But somehow Johnny didn't think it was the wall Henry was seeing, but another time, long ago.

Henry said, "Got myself into some trouble once. Running with the wrong boys."

Johnny took a sip of the coffee. Considering he still felt half-frozen from the all-night ride in the winter wind, this coffee struck him as some of the best he had ever tasted.

Henry said, "You boys are gonna have to ride. Put as much distance between here and yourselves as you can."

"Where?" Matt said.

"Texas."

Johnny nodded. Something about the way he did and maybe the look in his eye caught Henry's attention.

Henry said, "You know Texas?"

Johnny nodded. "Rode with the Texas Rangers for a while."

"Then go there. Take different names. Keep yourselves out of trouble. This should all blow over after a while."

When the coffee was finished, Henry went back to the house. Johnny pulled a bale of hay down to sit on, and he wrapped one of the new blankets around his shoulders.

He said, "I can't believe what we let ourselves get talked into. What'll we ever tell Ma?"

They all sat in silence a while. Johnny was weary right down to his bones. He decided to pull down some more bales of hay and make a bed for himself.

He took off his gunbelt and stretched his arms out. It felt good to have the gunbelt off, but he was keeping it within reach.

Joe said, "You don't like them guns too far away from you, do you?"

Johnny shook his head.

He stretched out with the blanket over him, and felt

sleep coming on. The last thing he remembered was Joe sitting like an Indian on the barn floor, striking a match to light his long, wooden pipe.

    Joe touched his shoulder to wake him. Joe said, "We got riders."
    Johnny blinked a moment. He had been in such a deep sleep, it took him a moment to remember where he was. Such a thing could have gotten him killed when he was sleeping out under the Texas sky, he knew. A brief moment of disorientation was all a Comanche needed to come up on you with a knife in his hand.
    Matt was lying on the floor, wrapped up in his bedroll. Johnny decided to leave him where he was. Johnny's gunbelt was still where he had dropped it. He slid one pistol from it and gave the cylinder a spin, checking to make sure the percussion caps were all in place.
    He went to the barn door. It was actually a double door that swung out, so he opened it just a crack to see through. Joe had pulled his own pistol and walked over to a window.
    Four riders were pulling up at the front porch. One of them was wearing a long coat that fell almost to his shoes. Johnny had seen coats like that before. Not so many down Texas way, but men from Kansas or Missouri sometimes wore them.
    Henry came out onto the porch, and they talked. The man in the coat gave Henry a description of four riders, and he was clearly talking about Johnny and his brothers, and Thad.
    Henry shook his head. "Nope. Ain't seen 'em. I'll watch out for 'em, though."
    The rider stood and chatted a moment. Henry called him Bob. Henry asked about Bob's wife and kids, and Bob asked about Henry's wife. And then the riders were off.
    Johnny said to Joe, "How long was I asleep?"
    "Maybe four hours. It's about noon."
    He nodded. "As soon as it's dark, we've got to be riding on. The longer we stay here, the more trouble we'll bring to Henry. I don't want that."

    Come nightfall, they were saddled up. The sleet had fully stopped, and the clouds had blown off. The sky was alive with stars.

Johnny still had Thad's revolver, and he handed it to Joe. Joe tucked it into his belt, along with his own pistol.

Henry's wife—Johnny had heard Henry call her Marnie—handed up a basket to Matt. She said, "These are hot biscuits, just out of the oven. They'll give you boys something warm for your stomachs."

Henry handed Johnny up a sack of potatoes. "Take these, too. Them cans of beans you have will do you good, but you need potatoes."

"Thank you kindly," Johnny said. "But we don't have a pot to cook 'em in. Only a skillet."

Marnie held up one finger, as if to say *wait a minute*, and she ran into the house and came back with a pot.

"Mrs. Cobb," Matt said. "We can't take your cookware."

"You will, and you'll use it." She handed him the pot.

He stuffed it into one saddle bag. "I don't really know what to say."

Johnny said, "Will you take some money for your troubles? Ten dollars?"

Henry shook his head. "No, sir. You don't be neighborly for payment. You just do it because it's the right thing to do. When I was young and in trouble, I'd prob'ly be dead if a kindly soul hadn't given me some help."

Johnny reached down and shook Henry's hand. "We're mighty beholdin' to you."

Henry said, "It should be a good night to ride. The moon'll be up in a while. There's a warm front coming in, and it shouldn't be as cold as last night. The snow and ice we got will melt fast. By tomorrow morning it should feel like spring.

"Like I say, if I was you boys I'd be heading to Texas. But be careful going through Injun territory. There's some mighty bad men down there. Lots of outlaws from Texas hide out there, and some hard cases from Kansas and Missouri ride down there. Texas cattlemen drive their herds north through there, and the Injuns ain't too happy about it, from what I hear."

They started out, riding abreast of one another. Johnny held the sack of potatoes in his right arm and the reins with his left. He wouldn't be able to get to a gun if he needed to because of the potatoes, but he wouldn't have been able to wearing Pa's long coat, anyway.

Matt said, "So, where to?"

Johnny let the question roll through his mind for a moment. In a way, home would seem mighty good. His old warm bed, and Ma's cooking. But he knew his destiny didn't lie in Pennsylvania. Ma had seemed to know it, too.

He said, "I think Mister Cobb had the right idea. Texas."

Matt nodded. "What about those Indians he mentioned? And those outlaws?"

"We'll avoid 'em. We'll take the Shawnee Trail, which is how I came north."

Joe said, "You know the area. Lead the way."

PART FOUR

Texas

41

Montana, 1881

BREE SAID, "I remember you said once that you had a price on your head for a time."

Johnny nodded. "It was in Mansfield, Missouri that it happened. As a result, we had to avoid towns and farms all the way down to Texas."

Joe said, "That was my first time in Texas. Never been there until then."

"I knew of a trail called the Shawnee Trail," Johnny said. "I've heard it called the Sedalia Trail. Or the Texas Trail. Sometimes the Texas Road. Back then, it was one of the main routes for drovers to take cattle to Saint Louis or other spots on or near the Missouri, like the town of Sedalia. This was before the railheads.

"We didn't follow the trail directly, because we didn't want to be seen, but we followed in the general direction. We kept to within a mile or two of the trail. We camped by creeks as we found them, and we shot our supper when we could."

"A rough way to live," Dusty said.

Johnny nodded his head. He knew his son was speaking from experience.

Johnny said, "We were hoping, once we got to Texas, we could find jobs using an assumed name. Maybe settle in. But it was rough going, especially since it was winter. Like Mister Cobb said, the weather was warming up and the days were like spring. But the nights were still chilly, even with a campfire. We were taking a risk to have a fire, because a fire can be seen from quite a distance in a land as flat as the land is from Missouri down into northern Texas. But the nights were too cold to go without one."

Johnny took a sip of coffee. "Eventually, we made it to Texas. And let me tell you, the Red River was sure a welcome sight."

42

The Red River, Texas, 1857

JOE McCABE EMERGED from the water with a roar. He stood chest-deep in the Red River, and he shook his head and sprayed water from his long hair and beard.

"Gol dang, but that feels good!" he called out.

Matt was watching with a little disbelief. He had a cup of coffee in one hand. He said, "You look like a grizzly bear."

"You ever seen one before?"

Matt shook his head. "No. But if I did, it would probably look like you. Look how hairy you are. You could almost comb your chest."

"My Cheyenne name is *Nahkhoe*. Means bear."

"I'm not surprised."

Johnny was walking on the bank of the river with his Colt rifle in both hands. The bank was sandy with patches of grass. Behind him was a stand of trees that had leafed out. A sure sign spring was coming.

The river was wide. Partway across it was a small, narrow island of mostly sand but with a few short trees growing.

At the other side of the river, the bank was a lot like this one, and there were more trees beyond it.

As Johnny walked, he would scan the other side of the bank for any sign of movement and then shift his gaze to the tree line behind him. Watching for riders.

Johnny had been the first in the water, and Joe had patrolled along the bank. Johnny didn't feel quite as clean as he would have from a hot bath, but the water was high in minerals and did a fair enough job. He surely felt better than he had after all those weeks since they left Hannibal.

Johnny and his brothers had camped the night before in a small clearing of trees within walking distance of the river. Where water had been scarce on their way south from Missouri, it was now plentiful. He heated a kettle full and shaved. His hair was still a little longish, but he felt like he no longer looked quite like a hooligan or a highwayman.

"That water looks cold," Matt said.

"It *is* cold," Joe said. "Feels great!"

He was rubbing his hands through his hair, then he submerged himself again and came back up with another roar that sounded something like, "Yee-hah!"

Johnny looked over at Matt. "Sure wakes you up."

"Your turn next," Joe said.

Matt shook his head. "That water doesn't strike me as all that inviting."

"Don't matter. By the smell of you, if you don't jump in, Johnny and I are gonna throw you in."

Once Joe was out and used a blanket to wipe himself dry, he pulled on his union suit and his pants. Matt had now peeled off the clothes he had been wearing since they left Hannibal, Missouri, and was sticking a tentative toe in the cold water.

Joe rushed at him and gave him a push, and with a yelp, Matt went face-first into the water.

Johnny was laughing, but he didn't forget to keep his attention on the banks of the river. Wouldn't do for riders to come up on them by surprise.

Joe was pulling on his buckskin shirt. He said, "So, what can we expect ahead of us?"

Johnny thought about it for a moment. He had swung them east from the trail as they approached the river, and now they were about forty miles from the trail. He had wanted to camp at a remote section of the river.

He said, "There's the town of Clarkston, maybe twenty miles thataway," Johnny nodded his head toward the southwest. "We probably ought to avoid it, though. Just in case there's reward posters issued on us. But there's a pretty large cattle ranch thirty or so miles directly south. Maybe we should try to find work there."

Matt was now chest-deep in the water. "You know, this isn't so bad, once you're in here."

Joe said, "I ain't never done any cowboy work."

Matt shook his head. His hair was now wet and flattened down to his head. "Neither have I."

Johnny said, "You'll learn. I've done a little. You catch on real quick."

43

THERE WAS no need to ride hard. They were in Texas and would either find work at a local ranch, or continue on to Mexico. It would depend on if word of the shooting in Missouri had made its way this far south.

They took no chances with trails, though. They rode directly south from the Red River.

"I prefer to travel overland," Johnny said. "Less chances of highwaymen, and you get to really see the land this way."

Matt was riding beside him and Joe was a little behind them. They were keeping the horses to a casual walk. Considering all of the miles they had logged over the past few months, the horses didn't seem to mind.

"The old mare seems to be holding up quite well," Matt said.

Johnny grinned. "She looks healthier than she did back in Pennsylvania. I think life on the road agrees with her. Maybe getting out and moving was what she needed."

"I don't know how you do it," Matt said, standing in the saddle a little. "Three months on the back of a horse, and I still can't seem to take to it like I did the deck of a ship. I still bounce along. I've got bruises all over my backside."

"You're tryin' too hard," Joe said. "You gotta just let yourself and the horse be as one."

Matt shook his head. "You make it sound easy."

The hills about them were long and low, and were covered with green, springtime grass. A few wildflowers were bobbing their heads to the wind.

The day was spring-time warm. Johnny had rolled both his jacket and Pa's coat into his bedroll. Matt's pea coat was tied to the back of his saddle. Joe's coonskin cap was something he said mountain men often wore in the winter. But he had tucked his into his saddle bags and was once again in the floppy wide-brimmed hat he had been wearing when Johnny first found him on the trail, last summer.

The wind was constant and strong. Matt had to grab his cap a couple of times to keep it from being lifted from his head. Johnny and Joe pulled their hats down tight about their temples, and the wind made their hat brims shake. The grass would ripple in the wind like the waves of a great, green ocean.

"See there," Johnny said, pointing to such a wave. "That's what I was telling you about."

Matt nodded. "It is beautiful, out here. And in some ways, not unlike the sea. The great openness. The wildness. Being in a part of the world that is as God created it, with no buildings or settlements made by man."

"Right nice," Joe said.

The hills were long and almost flat, barely hills at all. But when the boys topped one they could see for a few miles in any direction.

As they topped one hill, on toward noon, they saw riders ahead.

Johnny's first thought was, *dang! They're coming for us.* But then he noticed they weren't riding toward him and his brothers. They were riding directly west.

One seemed to be up front, and there were six more maybe a quarter mile back but riding hard.

"What do you make of that?" Matt said.

"I'm not quite sure."

The day was bright and he squinted his eyes, trying to see just who the riders might be. Not that he thought he might recognize them, but often you could tell what kind of riders they were by their outfit. Cowhands or lawmen. Or banditos.

"They seem to be chasin' that first rider," Joe said.

Johnny nodded. "Looks that way, doesn't it?"

Matt said, "I think that first rider's a girl."

Johnny said, "Now, what would a girl be doing this far out from anywhere? We have to be ten miles from that ranch I told you about and even further from the nearest town."

But then the rider's hat tumbled away, and long dark hair fell free.

Joe said, "Danged if you ain't right. It's a girl."

Johnny knew the look of a tired horse, and hers had the look. Trying to keep up a hard, driving gait but just didn't have the strength. The six riders bearing down on her looked to have fresh mounts.

"Come on, boys," Johnny said. "Something ain't right here."

Old Bravo had been kept at nothing more than a walk all morning and was fully rested. He had a way of stretching his legs into a long run, and that's what he did now.

Joe's horse was a mountain-bred mustang. Barely fourteen hands and a strong runner, but didn't have the speed of Bravo. And the old mare was a good enough horse but wasn't built for galloping at full speed over the Texas prairie. Bravo pulled ahead of them right from the start.

Johnny thought the riders ahead of him were Mexicans. They were in flat-brimmed sombreros and short, waist-length jackets. Two of them wore what he had heard called California pants, which buttoned down along the side of both legs and the buttons were usually framed with long patches of embroidery.

Johnny could see the girl snapping her quirt at her horse's hip to try to inspire it to run faster. But there's nothing you can do when your horse just doesn't have any wind left.

The girl's black hair flowed something furious-like in the wind as she stood in the stirrups and leaned forward to create less wind resistance.

One rider caught up and rode alongside her, on her left. She transferred the quirt to her left hand and began to strike at him with it. One swipe missed and the other landed on the shoulder of his jacket but didn't seem to do much harm. A third swipe caught the brim of his sombrero and knocked it from his head. The chin strap pulled at his neck and the hat bounced against his back like a thing alive.

A second man was at her right side, and he reached to the bridle and began to pull her horse to a stop.

She swung the quirt once more at the hatless man, but he caught her by the wrist.

The other four reined up in a circle surrounding her.

The hatless man smiled. He said something Johnny couldn't hear because, even though Bravo was going at full steam, they were still too far away.

Johnny didn't know what was going on, but Pa had taught him how to treat a lady, and these boys weren't doing it right.

He pulled his right-hand gun. He had always been good at firing from a running horse, and Bravo held a good steady gait even on the uneven footing of the sod.

Bravo could somehow sense that Johnny had pulled a gun and actually slowed down a might to let Johnny have a steadier aim. Some would argue a horse is a dumb animal. Johnny knew horses, and they were anything but dumb.

He hauled the hammer back on his gun, allowed for distance and the constant Texas wind, and pulled the trigger.

It didn't hit anyone, but it caught the dirt in front of one of the horses. The horse reared up and the rider had all he could do to hold to the saddle.

Johnny fired a second shot and then a third one. Horses were now spinning around, and one rider got dumped to the grass.

They began firing back. Johnny felt the wind of one bullet as it passed within inches of his head.

He heard a yelp from behind him and looked over his shoulder to see Joe falling and rolling to the grass, and his mustang tumbling head-first, hooves flying wild in the air.

A bullet must have hit Joe's horse, Johnny figured. He hoped Joe would be all right.

Matt was behind Joe, so Johnny had to trust Matt would tend to Joe while Johnny focused on the girl.

Johnny fired a fourth time, and the bullet caught a rider. The man lurched when the bullet hit him, but he managed to stay in the saddle.

Johnny fired again and the bullet kicked up dirt near the rider who had been the first one to reach the girl. The man's horse reared up and he tried to hold to the saddle. Another horse was turning about in circles, in the confusion.

The girl kicked her horse into a gallop. Never let a good opportunity go to waste, Johnny thought.

The rider Johnny had shot fell from the saddle. Three of them were trying to steady their horses and one of them was on the ground, trying to grab his horse's reins. The horse was rearing up and the man was trying to grab the reins but also avoid the front hooves.

The first rider started after the girl.

The rider pulled a pistol and shot at her. The horse lurched beneath her. The bullet hit the front shoulder, Johnny thought. The horse continued on for another few galloping strides, but then began a forward tumble. The girl leaped free of the saddle and landed, tumbling on the ground.

Johnny was still five hundred feet away, but Bravo was showing no sign of fatigue. Johnny's gun was empty but he didn't dare try something fancy like a border shift while on the back of a galloping horse, so he just slid his right-hand gun back into the holster. His reins were in his left hand, so he reached around with his right and grabbed his left-side gun.

The girl sat up in the grass as the Mexican reined up in front of her. She looked a little shaken by the fall and staggered to her feet in an attempt to run. The rider reached down with one arm, wrapped it around her waist and pulled her from her feet.

Johnny reined up fifty feet from them. The Mexican pulled the girl around so she was perched in front of him, and he wrapped one arm around her neck and put his pistol to her temple.

"Throw down your guns! Both of you!" The man called to them. Definitely Mexican, Johnny thought.

Both of you? Johnny heard hoofbeats behind him. He looked over his shoulder to see Matt closing in.

Matt said, "Joe's horse is down. Joe has a banged-up leg, but otherwise he's all right. He sent me ahead in case you needed help."

The Mexican said, "Throw down those guns or the lady gets a bullet in her head!"

Matt said, "Johnny, we'd better do as he says."

Johnny cocked his revolver and aimed toward the man.

"Johnny," Matt said. "I think he means it."

Johnny said, "Quiet, Matt. I'm drawing a bead."

"Don't be foolish, gringo," the rider said. "Even if you get lucky and hit me and not the girl, my gun will still go off and she'll be dead."

"Johnny," Matt said. "There's nothing we can do."

Johnny said, "Senorita, could you lean your head a little to your left?"

She did.

He fired.

The bullet tore into the man's elbow. His hand was whipped forward by the force of the bullet, and his gun went off like he said it would, but the bullet went into the sod. The man howled.

The girl pulled away from him and dove from the horse. The man was now alone in the saddle, with his gun hand hanging in the air, most of his elbow torn away.

The rider managed to turn his horse and kicked it into a trot. Trying to get away, Johnny thought. But blood was rolling down his right arm and hitting the ground like a pouring rain.

"He won't get far," Johnny said.

Matt said, "How did you possibly do that?"

Johnny holstered his gun and nudged the horse toward the girl. "Are you all right?"

"I've had better days, but I'll be fine." She spoke with a gentle Spanish flair.

Her hair was flying wild, and the buttons of her shirt had been ripped enough to give Johnny a view of her camisole beneath it.

He said, "That's two head-first tumbles from a horse, today."

She cocked a brow. "I'm tougher than I look."

He couldn't help but grin a little. "I have no doubt."

She returned the grin.

Her gaze lingered on him. He felt the breath catch in his chest, the way a man feels when he looks at a truly beautiful woman and she's looking at him as though she likes what she sees.

She struck him as picturesque—Matt threw words like that around lightly, but Johnny did not. Elegant cheekbones, like something out of a painting. Eyes that were a deep brown. Lips that made a man want to kiss them.

She walked over to her horse, which was lying on its side in the grass. It was still breathing, but the breathing was labored.

She knelt by the horse and cradled its head. "Poor Bonito," she said.

Johnny swung out of the saddle and handed Bravo's reins to Matt.

He said, "Your horse took a bullet to the shoulder. Looks like it might have broken a leg in the fall."

She nodded. "I know what has to be done. I just need a moment, because Bonito and I have been through a lot together."

Johnny waited while she gently rubbed the horse's nose and head and spoke to it in a cooing voice. The words were too soft for Johnny to hear.

Then she rose to her feet and said, "Lend me your gun."

Johnny pulled his left-hand gun. It still had four shots left. He gave it to her.

She cocked the gun and brought the muzzle to within

a couple of inches of a place just behind the horse's ear. Johnny could tell by the way she handled the gun that she was no stranger to it.

"Buena suerte, mi amigo," she said, and pulled the trigger.

She then handed the gun back to Johnny.

"I'm sorry," Johnny said. "I know how much a good horse means to a good rider."

"My name is Maria Carerra Grant," she said.

Johnny touched the brim of his hat. "I'm Johnny..." He thought for a quick moment. "Johnny O'Brien. This is my brother Matt."

"I am very pleased to make your acquaintance." She extended a gloved hand toward him, and he took it. "I wish it were under better circumstances."

Johnny said, "Do you want to save the saddle?"

"I'll send a rider for it later."

Johnny's brows raised a little at that. Apparently she was a lady of prominence.

He said, "May we give you a ride somewhere?"

"My husband's ranch. It's about ten miles south of here."

Johnny blinked with surprise. Husband? He hadn't expected that word out of her, considering the way she was looking at him.

He said, "We're heading there, anyway. Looking for work. You might as well ride with us."

She nodded.

Johnny leaped back onto Bravo, then held his hand and helped Maria up and onto the horse behind him.

Matt turned his horse back the way they had come. "I'd better go get Joe."

Maria looked at Johnny. "I think I might have hurt my shoulder a little when I fell."

"Well, I'm sure there's a doctor in Clarksville that can tend to it."

"Could you see if it's broken?"

He wasn't so sure about this. After all, she had said she was married. But he turned in the saddle as much as he could. He gently took her shoulder and rubbed first one spot, then another.

"I don't think it's broken," he said.

"Maybe I'm just a little shaken up."

He tried to give a reassuring smile. "You have reason to be."

"So, Mister O'Brien," she said, giving him a smile. "Will I be safe in your company on our ride back to my husband's ranch?"

"Yes'm, that you will." He was about to say he wouldn't let any harm come to her. But then he realized there might have been a double meaning in what she said.

She had said she was married, but she let her smile linger on him a little longer than he was comfortable with.

They rode back to where Joe had fallen.

"They got my horse," he said. "Dang. That was a good horse. Twisted my leg when I fell."

The woman said, "Come back to the ranch. I'll send a rider for your saddle and belongings."

Joe got situated behind Matt on the old mare, and they started riding.

Joe said, "I've gotta say, that's maybe the best shot I've ever seen anyone make."

"It was quite incredible," Maria said. "You must be what they call a gun wizard."

Johnny shook his head with a grin. "No, ma'am. Just a lucky shot."

"I know a lucky shot when I see it. And I know skill."

The land was wide open, like it had been since they left the Red. The grass was spring-time green, but the ground was dry and the horses kicked up a little dust as they stepped along.

Johnny could see for miles in any direction. After they had ridden a short while, he saw a small dust cloud off to the west, and he knew it was more riders.

"Look alive, boys," Johnny said. "We ain't out of trouble, yet."

He reached for his rifle.

44

SOON, THE RIDERS WERE visible. Seven of them. Johnny gave Bravo's reins a little tug and the horse stopped. Joe and Matt reined up, too.

"It's all right," Maria said. "They are my husband's men."

The riders bore down on them, and they surrounded Johnny and his brothers.

Some of them had worn, wide-brimmed hats, others sombreros. Some had longish hair and thick mustaches. One had hair that was graying and a bushy white beard. The brim of his hat was flipped up in front, like he had ridden into the wind too long.

They all had pistols. Some were holstered at the hip, and some wore their guns in front and turned backward for a cross-draw. None of the guns were drawn, but they looked like men who could draw their guns fast enough.

One was clean-shaven and a few years older than Johnny. He wore a sombrero pulled tightly to his brow. A bandana was tied about his neck, and he was in a waist-length jacket like Johnny's. His pistol was worn for a cross-draw.

"Senora Grant," he said. "Are you all right?"

She nodded. "I am fine, Goullie."

"Mister Grant worried when you were gone so long."

"There was trouble, and these men helped me."

"I am glad they did." He gave Johnny a level look. "For their sake."

"They are looking for work," she said. "I was hoping they could find some on our ranch."

He shrugged. "That remains to be seen. We'll ride back with you. And," he looked at Johnny again, "it might be better if you hand over your guns."

Johnny said, "I've never handed over my guns. I'm not gonna start now."

"Goullie," she said. "It's all right. These men can be trusted."

The one she called Goullie gave Johnny a long look, then he turned his gaze to Joe. Goullie didn't seem so sure, but he finally said, "All right. Follow us."

But only Goullie rode ahead of them. His men

remained at either side, and two rode behind them. Apparently Goullie's trust of them involved keeping them on a short leash. Johnny would have done the same in his place.

They stopped after a couple of miles to rest their horses. Joe rolled a cigarette. The man with the white beard was smoking a pipe. Johnny decided to slide his rifle back into the scabbard.

Johnny said to him, "So, this ranch is the Broken Spur, am I right?"

Goullie nodded. He had chaw in his mouth, and spit some brown juice to the grass.

"How much further till we get there?"

"You're on Broken Spur land, now."

Johnny said, "Owned by Breaker Grant."

Goullie looked at him. "You don't sound like you're from Texas."

"Not *from* here. But I rode with the Rangers, further south. Haven't spent much time this far north. These here are my brothers."

"My name's Gould. They call me Goullie."

Johnny said, "Our name's O'Brien. I'm Johnny. This is Joe, and Matt."

Goullie extended a callused hand, and Johnny shook it.

Johnny gave a short account of how they had met Maria. She had drifted over while he was talking, and she said, "His shot was the best I have ever seen."

Johnny said nothing.

"Well," Goullie said, "I'm sure Mister Grant will want to hear all about it. We've been here long enough. Let's ride."

They mounted up, and Maria now rode behind Goullie. Johnny left his rifle where it was. As they rode along, with Goullie and Maria ahead of Johnny, he tried to think about all he had heard about Breaker Grant.

An old man, if he remembered right. At least Pa's age, if not older. But tough as rawhide. Had built the ranch himself, and some said the ranch was even bigger than the King Ranch, more than four hundred miles south of here.

Johnny had found guessing a woman's age was one of the more difficult things in life, but if Maria was older than he was, it wasn't by much. Clearly young enough to be old man Grant's daughter, and yet she had claimed to be his wife. To complicate matters, she had given Johnny a look earlier that was the kind a man wants from a woman who looked like she did.

Johnny figured it would do no good to ponder questions he had no answers for, so he just rode along. He would find his answers soon enough.

45

JOHNNY FIGURED they had covered four miles when they rode up a grassy hill that was higher and steeper than the others. From the top, he could see a collection of buildings maybe a quarter mile in the distance. One stood two floors high and was made of white adobe that gleamed in the sunlight. A front porch was shaded by a roof held up by a row of white pillars.

Far to the right of the building were more structures, and from this distance, they looked like they were made of sun-bleached wood. Stables, Johnny figured, and a barn. Maybe one was a bunkhouse.

Cattle were scattered about the low, grassy hills beyond the ranch. Maybe two or three hundred head. He saw a rider out there, moving through the cows.

Matt said, "Is that herd just roaming free? Where are the fences?"

The man with the white beard was riding beside him. He grinned. "You ain't from around here, are you?"

Matt shook his head.

Johnny said, "It's not like back East, where pastures are fenced-off. Out here, a cow can roam for miles and not get lost."

"You call them cows. Aren't there any bulls out there? Or steers?"

Johnny was grinning, too. "You'll learn."

Goullie reined up in front of the porch and with one hand eased Maria down to the ground, then swung out of the saddle himself and handed the reins to a Mexican man with a stocky build and wide shoulders.

Goullie said, "Take care of my horse, Ciego."

"Yes sir, boss."

Maria was already up the steps and going through the front door. Goullie said to Johnny and his brothers, "Follow me."

They did. Up the steps and through the door. Johnny noticed it was made of oak, and looked to be engraved with what looked like laurel leaves at the corners. At the center of the door was a big brass knocker.

This was no door that had been hammered together out of scrap wood, like the doors to a lot of cabins and sod huts Johnny had seen in Texas. This was store-bought, probably shipped in to Corpus Christi from somewhere back East, or maybe even Europe. Probably cost more than a cowhand's yearly pay. If anyone had doubted that Breaker Grant had money, that doubt would be gone when they got a look at this place.

The entryway was facing a stairway that went to the second floor. Johnny got a glimpse of Maria at the top of the stairs as she scurried away into a room.

The man called Goullie said, "Wait here."

He went up the stairway, his dusty spurs jingling.

The walls of the entryway were made of adobe, and two wooden framed arched doorways opened to other rooms. At least one was probably a parlor, Johnny figured, but the doors were closed.

An armchair with green, velvet upholstery was at one side of the entryway, and a matching one was at the other. Overhead was a chandelier with dozens of crystal prisms. In the middle of the chandelier was a candle. The ceiling was twelve feet high, and Johnny had to wonder if you had to use a ladder to light the candle.

In the corner by one of the chairs was a potted fern, and by the other chair was a small tree that was also potted. Johnny wasn't educated enough in the finer things of life to know what kind of tree it was.

Johnny had little interest in the finer things in life, anyway. He thought, *Give me a good cabin that's built tight, with a roaring fire and a good cup of coffee, and I'd be content. Give me a good woman and a brood of children to share the cabin with, and I'd be the happiest man on Earth.*

Joe sat in one of the chairs, to take weight off his leg. He stretched it out on the floor.

"How's that leg?" Johnny said.

"I think I twisted my knee. Seems to be swelling a little. I don't think anything's broken, though."

Matt said, "I would say this Breaker Grant is not hurting for cash."

Johnny shook his head. "I've never seen this place, but I've heard talk of him clear to the Mexican border. They say he has one of the biggest ranches in Texas. Maybe *the* biggest."

Joe said, "What do they say about the man, himself?"

"Not much. He rode with the Rangers back in the War

with Mexico. He built this ranch with his own two hands out of the Texas grasslands."

"Sounds like a man I'd like."

Johnny nodded. He had to admit, he agreed with Joe. And yet he wondered about Maria, and the way she had looked at him. The way Johnny and his brothers had been raised, a married woman should have eyes only for her husband.

"You know," Matt said. "If anyone had any doubt about your ability with a gun, they wouldn't if they had seen that piece of shooting you did."

Joe said, "The legend grows."

Johnny shook his head and turned away. "I hate talk like that."

Joe grinned. "That's partly why we do it."

Johnny said, "Don't neither of you go saying anything about the Gunman of the Rio Grande. They'll connect that to my real name, and they'll know who we are."

"Don't think it'll matter," Joe said. "Word gets out about that piece of shootin' you done today, they'll be talking about it from the Mexican border all the way to the trading posts in Cheyenne country. Maybe all the way out to California."

"Then maybe it's best we don't mention it to anyone."

Matt shook his head. "She'll be telling her husband. And you know once she starts talking about it, word will spread among the men here at the ranch."

Joe said, "That's how legends grow."

"I'm not a legend," Johnny said. "I'm just a man."

Matt nodded. "I'm sure Daniel Boone said the same thing. And Sam Houston."

Joe was grinning. "One day your bronzed baby shoes will be in a museum."

Johnny said, "I don't want to hear any more talk like that."

Matt said, "In all seriousness, though, you did save her life. There's no way I could have made that shot."

Joe said, "I could have shot him, but his gun would have gone off and she'd be dead, too. To shoot the man's arm in a way that it would swing the gun out away from her is like nothing I've ever heard of being done before."

"They can talk about this without having to embellish it at all."

"I have to admit," Joe said. "That woman has to be one of the prettiest I ever did see."

Johnny had to agree with him on that.

Matt glanced about first, to make sure they were alone in the entryway, then he said, "I saw how she was looking at you back there. Like she wanted to eat you up."

Johnny said, "There's something strange going on around here. I was thinking we should try to find work on this ranch, but now I'm wondering if maybe we should just ride on."

After a time, a man stepped onto the second floor balcony. He had a white beard, and long white hair fell to his shoulders. He was in a Spanish-style waist-length jacket and a string tie.

"Gentlemen," he called down to them. He had a voice that sounded like he enjoyed cigars and whiskey. "Come on up. I'd like to meet you all."

Joe found he could now put little weight on his injured leg, so he slung one arm around Matt's shoulders and the other around Johnny's. They lifted, and he bounced along on his toe up the stairs.

Once they were on the second floor, the old man said, "Allow me to introduce myself. I am Breaker Grant, owner of the Broken Spur. The woman you rescued today is my lovely wife, Maria Carrera Grant."

"I hope she's all right," Johnny said. "She took two hard spills from a horse."

The old man nodded. "She's off to the bath, and I've sent to town for the doctor. She seems to have injured a shoulder."

Grant looked at Joe. "You're injured, too."

Joe nodded. "Yes, sir. Them men what were after your wife, they shot my horse out from under me. Hurt my leg when I fell."

"When the doctor gets here, we'll have him check that leg out too, then."

"Much obliged."

They followed Grant into his office. Another man was pacing about by the desk. He was maybe thirty, with dark curly hair and dark eyes. He was in a bolo tie and a gray, Mexican jacket. The buttons caught Johnny's attention. They were brass, with a pattern on them that Johnny thought was called a fleur de lis. French, which struck Johnny a little odd.

You didn't see many French symbols in Texas.

Grant said, "This here's my son, Coleman."

Coleman shook hands with the men. He said, "Maria told us what you did. We will be forever grateful."

"You boys must be hungry," Grant said. "I insist you stay for supper. The cook's preparing a real feast."

Coleman looked at his father, as if to say, *are you serious?* But the look was gone in a moment. If Johnny had blinked, he would have missed it.

Coleman said, "Yes. We won't take no for an answer."

"Well," Johnny said, and looked at his brothers.

He had that feeling that something was wrong here more than ever. He wanted to just be riding on. But he didn't know how to say no to Breaker Grant's gracious hospitality. Matt looked at Johnny and shrugged his shoulders.

Grant said, "It's done, then."

Coleman gave an apologetic smile. "What my father wants, he gets."

"My lovely wife says you boys are looking for work."

"Well," Johnny started, again.

"You're all hired, starting today. Top pay."

Coleman looked at his father again, and he tried to repress that *are you serious* look again. This time it got away from him.

"Coleman, show these men to the bunkhouse."

Coleman shrugged and said, "Follow me."

Grant isolated his gaze on Johnny. "I'd like a word with you, first. If you don't mind."

Matt looked at Johnny and shrugged again, and he and Joe followed Coleman from the room. Joe had his arm around Matt's shoulders and was hopping along.

Grant said, "Do you like a good cigar?"

Johnny hadn't had a cigar since his last poker game in a cantina south of the border, nearly a year ago.

He said, "I'd never turn down a good cigar."

Grant went to a box on his desk and flipped open the lid. "I got these all the way from Cuba. The best cigars in the world."

He held out the box to Johnny, and Johnny took one. Johnny didn't want to bite off the end. It seemed like it would be uncivilized, in a house like this. While he tried to figure out what to do, Grant took a cigar cutter that looked like an ornamental pair of scissors and clipped off the end for him.

Then Grant struck a match and Johnny held the cigar to the flame and puffed it to life.

Grant brought his own cigar to life, and said, "My Maria, lovely girl that she is, described an impossible shot you made with a pistol, today. Maria is not taken to exaggeration."

Johnny said nothing.

"She said you seemed to be aiming the pistol. In my experience, gunmen don't actually aim a pistol, the way you would a rifle. They just point and shoot. Kind of an intuitive thing."

"Yessir," Johnny said. "That's usually the way. But for a shot like that, where the shot had to be exactly perfect, I've found I can aim the gun using the sight. My left-hand gun pulls a little to the right, where my right-hand gun is nigh onto perfect. I have to make sure which gun is in which holster."

Grant shook his head. "I don't think I've ever met anyone with quite that kind of ability. How can you tell them apart, to know which one is in which holster?"

"There's a scratch on the handle of my left-hand gun."

"There aren't many with your kind of shooting skills. I don't think I could even name five."

Johnny didn't like the direction this was going. He decided to say no more, and drew in some smoke and let it out slowly.

Grant smiled, "It is a good cigar, isn't it?"

Johnny said, "I've never tasted one like this before."

"With all due respect to the tobacco plantations in Virginia and the Carolinas, the finest cigars in the world come out of Cuba."

"I can easily believe it." Johnny took in another puff on the cigar.

"Goullie mentioned that you had ridden with the Texas Rangers."

Johnny nodded. "A couple of years."

Grant said, "Those pistols at your belt look to be Ranger-issue."

"Yes, sir."

Grant stood and said, "Let me show you something."

Johnny followed him to a gun rack standing in one corner on a bureau. The rack had glass doors, and Grant opened one and reached into the rack. He came out with a revolver.

He said, "Ever seen one of these before?"

He handed it to Johnny.

"Yes, sir," Johnny said. "A Paterson Colt."

Johnny did like Uncle Jake had told him to do with a gun. Check to see that it was loaded. Every chamber of this gun had to be loaded manually with powder and a ball, and a percussion cap would be placed at the breech of each chamber. He pulled the hammer partway back and gave the trigger a little squeeze, which freed-up the cylinder, and he then turned it one notch at a time to make sure there were no percussion caps in place.

Grant said, "Those guns were standard issue during the War."

"I had a set of my own, once. My uncle was a Ranger during the war, and he gave me his guns," Johnny said. Then he realized he needed to guard against saying too much.

Grant said, "Can't say I knew a Ranger named O'Brien. But there were a lot of Rangers. A man couldn't know all of them."

Grant walked back to his desk and his gaze fell on a decanter.

He said to Johnny, "Do you like bourbon?"

Johnny nodded. "I wouldn't turn one down."

Grant filled two glasses and handed one to Johnny.

Grant said, "My wife is a lot younger than I am."

Johnny shrugged. "It's really none of my business, Mister Grant."

"She's my entire world. She comes from a wealthy family that has a ranch down in Victoria County. I met her four years ago when I was down there on a business trip. We fell in love and married, and I brought her here. Those outlaws would have demanded a hardy ransom, from both me and her family."

Johnny said, "They had the look of Mexican border raiders. I chased border raiders when I was with the Rangers, but we're a long way from the Mexican border."

Grant nodded. "Five hundred miles, more or less."

Grant poured the bourbon and handed Johnny a glass.

Grant said, "Those outlaws are indeed Mexican. Or at least some of them are. They have apparently taken to hiding in some mountains, up in the Nations. Indian Territory. A range they call the Oachita Mountains, about forty miles northeast of here. We've chased them into those mountains, and lost them. They've been taking cattle from us. Started a stampede and then took some head. I don't know if they're selling beeves to the Indian tribes, the Cherokee or whoever, or what they're doing."

"What about the law?"

Grant gave a bitter chuckle. "In this remote part of Texas, we *are* the law. I've written to the governor about sending in some Texas Rangers. He's written back that resources are limited but he'll do what he can. That's political double-speak for we're not a big enough problem for him to bother with. When we had Jim Henderson in office, he would have done something about it. A good southern Democrat, he was. But this man Pease, he's a glorified Whig."

Johnny knew little about politics, and so decided to say nothing.

Grant took a draw on his cigar. "This is the first time those outlaws have done something as bold as attacking by daylight. To think what would have happened if they had gotten their hands on my Maria. I owe you much, son."

"Think nothing of it, sir."

Grant shook his head. "Just the opposite. I think *everything* of it."

He took another puff on his cigar and said, "Maria is not just my life, but she's also my future. I'm an old man, O'Brien. I need an heir. I am hoping Maria can provide me with one."

Now Johnny was a little confused. "But you introduced Coleman as your son."

Grant nodded. "Yes. Quite right. He was an orphan boy I adopted, and I consider him my own. Coleman has been a good son over the years, but he's not a leader. I need a son who can be a leader, a son I can trust with the running of this ranch after I'm gone. This ranch is my life's blood. I built it out of nothing. I don't want a stranger running it, some businessman hired by the family. I love Coleman like my own, but he's not the man to run this place." He held up his glass of bourbon and looked into it, "And I'm afraid I might be running out of time."

Grant sat in a chair behind his desk.

He said, "You see, O'Brien, I have built something of an empire. It began as a few wild cattle I rounded up back in the twenties, and I used this land as what you might call today *open range*. I'm one of the original Texians. Moved here shortly after Mexico began allowing people in. Came down the Santa Fe trail with a wagon train of freight, and I stayed here. Learned cattle, and I built this ranch."

He took another puff of the cigar. Clearly he was enjoying it as much as Johnny was his own.

Grant said, "Over the years, I invested in shipping. Then in a couple of gold claims in California. When I use the word *empire*, I don't use it lightly. I own the tobacco plantation in Cuba where these cigars come from. I own a shipping company in Corpus Christi and another out in San Francisco. I was one of the major contributors to the election campaign of Peter Bell for governor, back in forty-nine, and Thomas Rusk for re-election to the Senate last year. He's a good Southern Democrat, too."

"Sounds like you've done right well with your life," Johnny said.

"I have. I've been blessed," Grant said. "O'Brien, what do you want out of life?"

Johnny shrugged. The cigar was smoldering away in one hand, so he drew some more smoke.

He said, "I was raised on a small farm in Pennsylvania, by good, God-fearing folk. I came West three years ago, and now this land has ahold of my heart. I suppose what I want is to build a small ranch somewhere and find a good woman and raise a family."

Grant nodded with a smile. "I felt the same way, many long years ago. This ranch just grew and grew, and now I'm afraid it owns me as much as I own it."

Johnny nodded. He supposed he could understand.

Grant said, "I want you to know I am deeply grateful for what you did for my wife. I thought she would be safe if she remained within five miles of the ranch."

"If you don't mind my saying, sir, she was a good deal more than five miles from the ranch."

Grant nodded and raised his brows in a sort of defeated gesture. "Maria is headstrong. She's going to have her way. I'm just grateful you boys were there. I feel I owe you something more than just a job. Cash? Cattle? Horses? You name it."

Johnny shook his head. "With all due respect, you owe us nothing. Our father taught us that sometimes you have to do the right thing just because it's the right thing to do. We just did what any decent men would have."

"True. Any decent men. And you're proving you have even more honor and chivalry by refusing to accept any reward."

Johnny didn't know what to say. Pa had always said if you have nothing to say, it's best to remain silent rather than fill the air with nonsense. Johnny decided to take Pa's advice, and took another draft of smoke from his cigar.

Grant said, "Where are you and your brothers bound for?"

Johnny didn't like the way this conversation was going. He decided to be as vague as possible. "We were just riding. Looking for work."

Not totally a lie.

Grant said, "I'm serious about that job offer I made you. Men as resourceful as you, and with your capabilities, I want on my payroll. All three of you. I can offer you eighteen dollars a month plus meals and a bunk. Those are the best wages in this part of Texas, and the Broken Spur has the cleanest bunkhouse. No lice or rats. Men like you would be an asset to this ranch, especially if your brothers can shoot even half as well as you."

Johnny shook his head. "Sorry, Mister Grant. I sympathize with the problem you're having with those raiders from the Nations, and I can't speak for my brothers, but my gun is not for hire."

Grant lowered his foot to the floor and sat forward in his chair. "You misunderstand me. I'm not hiring gunhands, I'm hiring *cow*hands. But I expect all of my men to be willing to fight for the ranch if need be. And you all demonstrated you are first-class fighting men, and more important, men of honor."

"I'll need to discuss it with my brothers."

"Fair enough."

As Johnny went down the stairs to the entryway, he found Maria waiting for him. She was now in a dress with a lacy neckline that fell off the shoulder, and her black hair was piled all up on the top of her head.

She gave a smile to Johnny, the kind of smile that can warm a man clean through and get him thinking all sorts of thoughts that could lead to trouble.

She said, "Mister O'Brien. I wanted to thank you again. You and your brothers saved me from a horrible fate."

He nodded. "Just glad we came along when we did, ma'am."

"Now, don't you call me *ma'am*. For you, I am forever Maria."

Johnny was becoming more uncomfortable by the moment. "If you'll excuse me, ma'am—Maria—I've got some things to tend to."

"Well, of course, Mister O'Brien. Johnny."

"I hope we'll be seeing you at dinner," she said.

He gave a smile, hoping it looked more polite than nervous. He touched the brim of his hat to her and was out the door.

He stopped a moment on the front porch and let his gaze wander over the ranch yard. The long bunkhouse. A barn twice the size of the one at the farm back in Pennsylvania. Three small stables further out. A corral where a couple of horses frolicked about. The low-rising grassy hill out beyond where cows grazed.

It didn't feel right, the way this woman looked at him. She was about his age and more than just a little pretty, but she was married. Being with a married woman was a line he refused to cross.

He liked Breaker Grant. He felt a sort of kinship in the old man's attitude. But Grant's young wife was trouble. No way around it.

He decided he was going to present Grant's job offer to Matt and Joe. They could decide for themselves what they wanted to do, but Johnny had already made up his own mind. There was a lot he could learn from a man like Breaker Grant, but come sunrise, Johnny would be riding on.

46

THE RANCH HAD a bath house for the men to use. It contained five tubs. The water was heated on an iron stove outside the bath house and hauled inside in buckets.

One of the drawbacks was that you had to heat your own bathwater. A small price to pay, Johnny thought. Johnny and his brothers got a fire going in the stove, and then he worked an iron pump to bring water up from a well.

Johnny and his brothers each took a tub. Their first hot bath since Hannibal, Missouri. They wanted to be presentable for dinner with Breaker Grant.

The other tubs were empty.

Johnny held a mirror in one hand and lathered his face with shaving cream.

Matt was sitting back with his eyes shut. "Now, this beats that cold river of yours, any day."

Joe said, "I have to admit, it *is* right nice."

Johnny began scraping away at his chin with the razor.

Matt said, "Didn't you shave just this morning?"

"Yeah. But you can't get as clean a shave using river water for a mirror."

Joe was grinning. "He just wants to look his best for Miss Maria."

Johnny shot him a scowl. "She's married. Remember?"

"Don't mean she ain't pretty."

Matt looked at Joe. "So, are you going to shave that fur you have growing on your face?"

Joe shook his head. "Not a chance."

The doctor had arrived and had a look at Joe's knee. Like Joe had thought, it wasn't broken. But it was sprained, and the doctor had said for him to stay off it entirely for a couple of weeks. After the doctor had left, Breaker Grant told them that Joe would still receive full pay while his knee healed.

Matt glanced at the door to see it was closed. Even still, he didn't want anyone outside to hear him, so he kept his voice down. "We have to make a decision. Do we stay, or continue on?"

Joe said, "I've never seen a place like this. A bath house. This ranch has three stables."

Matt settled back in the hot water and closed his eyes again. "It would be awfully easy to become lulled into complacency."

Joe gave him a frown. "Is that English you're speakin'?"

Matt grinned. "What I mean is, we can't let the luxuries of this place make our decision for us."

Johnny said, "I've made my own decision. I'm riding on in the morning. I hate to, in a way. But I can't be here with that woman looking at me that way. It just ain't right."

Matt and Joe were looking at him but saying nothing.

Johnny said, "You think I'm seeing something that's not there?"

"No," Matt said. "We've seen it."

"I just don't want to stay here with her looking at me that way. I feel like I'd somehow be betraying the old man just by being here."

"What are the other options?"

Johnny shrugged. "We keep riding."

"How far?"

"Far as we have to," Joe said.

Johnny said, "Mexico, if it comes to that. We'd be safe there. We're probably six days away, if we make good time. Maybe seven. Or maybe we could go further west. California. But traveling means going back to living like we were."

"Living on the run. Washing in rivers, and even then not on a regular basis. Sleeping on the open ground."

Joe said, "Maybe we should stay for a little while. Let ourselves rest up a bit from all of the traveling."

"I don't know about resting," Johnny said. "Ranch work is anything but easy."

"Maybe it's hard, but it'll be a different kind of hard. Let us earn some honest money for a while. We can keep going by the name of O'Brien. Maybe there's a chance we could settle in here. But if not, then we ride on."

Johnny nodded. He had to admit, Breaker Grant had some great-tasting cigars. And the pay Grant was offering was better than most cowhands ever saw.

Matt said, "And you can always avoid Mrs. Grant. After all, we'll be sleeping in the bunkhouse. And by day, we'll be working. I doubt any of us will be at the main house all that much."

"Let's give it a try," Joe said. "Stay a few weeks. A

couple of months, maybe. Then we can move on."

Johnny said, "If I ride out, there's no reason you boys can't take the job offers."

Matt shook his head. "I think we should stick together. At least for now. I'm totally new to the west, and with potentially a price on our heads," he glanced to the door again to make sure no one was there, "I'd like to have someone with me who knows their way around."

"Me too," Joe said. "I know the mountains good enough up north of Laramie. But I've never been to Texas before."

Johnny was silent a moment, weighing one option with the other. "All right, then. I've got a bad feeling about this, but we stay. For now. At dinner tonight, we tell Mister Grant that he's hired himself three cowhands."

47

JOHNNY HAD never been to a shindig of this quality, and he hoped he didn't look as out of place as he felt. The steak was from a steer butchered only hours ago and was probably the best he had ever tasted. But before the steak they had been served salad. Johnny had never heard of a meal served in sections, but it seemed to be what was happening.

He reached for a fork—for some reason there were two of them at each setting. Matt made eye contact and shook his head, and he indicated the fork on the outside. Johnny had grabbed the one on the inside. The one with the longer tines.

Then it came time for the wine. Johnny expected the butler to come on in with a couple of bottles and then pull the cork and start pouring up. But that's not what happened. The butler stood empty-handed by Breaker Grant, and Grant said, "Would one of you boys like to select the wine tonight?"

Johnny didn't know anything about wine. He didn't know you selected it. He thought you just drank it.

He looked at Matt, who said, "I think a hearty pinot noir might go well with tonight's fare."

Grant nodded with a smile. "My thoughts exactly."

Grant looked at the butler, a Mexican man with a little girth and some gray hair. He was in a string tie and jacket.

Grant said, "Alfredo. Bring us two bottles of pinot noir."

"We have some of the thirty-two vintage in the cellar."

"That would be great."

Alfredo left to get the wine.

1832 vintage, Johnny thought. It sounded like this wine was older than he was.

The table was made of raw oak but sanded smooth. It was covered with a cloth that Johnny thought might be pure silk. Not that he knew fabrics. In the center was a candelabra, and hanging overhead was a chandelier of what had to be maybe a hundred small crystals. Kind of like the one in the entryway.

Grant was at one end of the table and Maria at the other. Johnny was sitting beside Joe and across from them were Matt and Grant's son Coleman.

Maria was in a gown that was a sort of canary yellow with a lacy neckline that fell gently off the shoulder. Not the same dress she had been wearing earlier. Rich folks must change their clothes a lot, Johnny figured. Her hair was done up all fancy-like and a yellow rose was in it.

Alfredo came back with a bottle of wine, and a boy maybe Luke's age stood behind him holding another bottle. Alfredo pulled the cork and then with a white towel over one arm, he handed the cork to Grant.

Johnny had no idea what was going on. He glanced at Matt, but Matt didn't seem the slightest bit puzzled, so Johnny decided to sit tight.

Grant gave the cork a sniff, and he then nodded to Alfredo. The butler poured some into a goblet, but he didn't pour enough to even be called a shot.

Everyone was sitting and waiting patiently. Johnny glanced at Matt again, then he looked over at Joe. Joe shrugged and gave him a look that said, *I ain't got no idea what's going on.*

Grant lifted the goblet to his nose and twirled the wine around while he gave it another sniff. These rich folks seemed to sniff their wine a lot.

Grant then looked at Alfredo and nodded again, and Alfredo took the bottle and went to Maria and filled her glass, then filled the glass of each guest, then Coleman's and finally he returned to Grant. A bottle of wine has only four or five glasses worth of wine in it, so while Alfredo was pouring wine, the boy was pulling the cork on the second bottle. Grant gave that wine the sniffing test too, while the other glasses were being filled.

The second bottle was now half-full, and it was left on the table.

Eventually, the steak was served. It was porterhouse, served with vegetables dumped over the top of it. Among the vegetables were tiny tomatoes. Looked like a mess to Johnny, but Grant seemed all pleased with it.

When Johnny and Grant had talked earlier up in Grant's office, the old man had seemed to Johnny like a cattleman with maybe a little touch of gunfighter mixed in, who was missing the old days of living on the range and sleeping under God's open sky. But as Johnny sat at the table, he had the notion that maybe Grant was even more removed from campfire living than he realized.

After dinner, they retired to the parlor. Joe was on a pair of wooden crutches on loan from Grant, and strapped to his knee was a wooden split the doctor had given him.

Grant had Alfredo serve bourbon, and cigars were offered.

Maria said, "If you don't mind, my love, I think I'll retire for the night. I have the feeling the talk in this room is going to become downright masculine. Horse flesh and cattle prices."

Grant chuckled. "I should apologize."

"Nonsense. I've had a very trying day and need some sleep."

She gave him a peck on the cheek and swept away in her gown toward the door.

"That's a good woman," Grant said to the boys. "A man is lucky to find just one good woman like that in his life. I was already on the other side of middle age when I met her, but she was well worth the wait."

Johnny had a glass of bourbon in one hand. With the other, he leaned against a wooden timber that was the mantelpiece to a hearth made of stones. He held a smoldering cigar between two fingers.

He was thinking about what Mr. Grant had asked him earlier in the day. What did he want out of life? And he was thinking about his answer.

For the first time in a while, he thought of Becky Drummond. He wondered if she and Trip Hawley were happy. And Johnny wondered if he had made the right decision. If he could have settled down on a farm outside of Sheffield or at the family store with Becky. If he could have done this without looking off to the western sky at night and wondering *what if*, like she said. But when he saw the Red River, and all that grass blowing in the wind and the springtime flowers, and felt the Texas wind on his face, he knew he had made the right decision. Maybe not the easy one, but ultimately the right one.

His gaze drifted to the hearth. He thought, if and when he someday built the ranch house he wanted, he would want a fireplace like this one.

There was a Queen Anne chair upholstered in cowhide and placed at an angle to the fireplace. Matt had been offered it, and he sat with his legs crossed. He took a deep draw of a cigar.

He said, "It's mighty nice to sit on something other than a saddle. I'd almost forgotten what a good chair felt like."

Grant said, "I take it you're not a cattleman?"

Matt grinned and shook his head. "I'm a man of the sea. But it looks like my life is going in a different direction."

The talk then drifted to cattle prices in Chicago. A problem was the trail between Texas and Chicago was long, and it took a lot out of a herd. You could make some money selling a few head here and there in Missouri and Kansas, or to the Army, but if you wanted what Grant called *real money,* you had to be able to deliver a herd all the way to Chicago. There was talk of the railroad running across Kansas Territory and eventually reaching to the west coast. It would make taking a herd to market much easier.

"That is," Grant said, "if war doesn't break out between the states."

Matt said, "Do you think that's likely, sir?"

Grant shrugged. "You never know, with those crazy politicians back east. There was talk of the south breaking away about seven years ago. In fact, there was talk of it more than thirty years ago, too. Both times, that senator from Kentucky, Henry Clay, stepped in. He came up with plans both sides could live with. But now he's gone, and I don't know if there's anyone in Washington with the common sense needed to keep this country together."

Grant took a draw from his cigar. "Not that I'm all that in favor of keeping the Union together. The states in the north seem to be moving further and further away from the Constitution. Maybe it's time for the states here in the south to form our own union. But what I object to is any war that might come of it would delay the building of the railroad."

Matt said, "But do you think war will definitely develop if the southern states pull away from the Union?"

"I hope not, son. But I've met some of those senators and congressmen from the north. Seems to me they want war and are looking for an excuse."

Johnny noticed as the talk went on, Coleman Grant stayed off to the side. He had a cigar in one hand but was saying nothing.

After a time, Joe decided it might be best to head to the bunkhouse and rest his leg. Matt said, "I'll walk down with you. Make sure you don't fall on your face using those crutches."

Johnny said, "I'll be right along. I want to finish this

cigar, first."

Then Coleman said, "I have some things to attend to," and left the room.

This left Johnny and Grant as the only two remaining.

A fire was crackling low in the hearth. Not enough to warm the room, because the night wasn't cool and no fire was really needed. Grant had asked Alfredo to start a small fire because sometimes he just liked to have a fire burning.

Johnny understood how he felt. Sometimes it was nice to just sit by a fire with a good cup of coffee. It somehow eased the mind.

Grant stood in front of the fire with his feet apart, like he was prepared for a fight or whatever life might throw at him. He had one fist on his hip and in the other hand he held a cigar.

He said, "A lot of the young men I see today strike me as soft. Good enough men, I suppose, but they couldn't hold a candle to the original generation of Texians I rode with when I was a young man. I took Coleman in as a young pup. I think he means well and has good business sense to a point, but he wouldn't have been able to last five minutes in the Texas I knew when I was his age. I swear, those Texians could lasso a twister and pull it down."

Grant took a pull from his cigar. "O'Brien, you remind me of those men. You have a backbone. You can look trouble in the face and not blink. You have what it takes to do what has to be done. I built this ranch out of nothing, and I think you have what it would have taken to stand beside me."

"Thank you, sir. Coming from a man like you, that means a lot."

Grant looked to the guns at Johnny's hips. Grant said, "Even if Maria hadn't told me about that shot you made today, I can tell by the way you wear those guns that you know how to use 'em. And I can tell by the look in your eye that you have had to use your guns more than once."

Johnny looked at him. "I suppose I've done what had to be done, over the years."

Grant nodded. "That's what I mean. You have the spirit of Texas in you, boy."

Johnny took another draw on his cigar. It was almost down to a nub.

Grant said, "Toss that away. Take a fresh one."

Johnny flipped the butt into the fire. A box of cigars

was on an end table, so Johnny took another. He bit the end off and tossed it into the fire, and then struck a match to light the cigar.

Grant said, "Think about the future, boy. Think about what you want. And think long."

Johnny wasn't sure he knew what Grant was talking about, but he said, "Yes, sir."

"I'm heading upstairs. It's late. Stay as long as you want and enjoy that cigar."

Grant left the room, and Johnny stood alone in front of the fire.

48

BUNKHOUSES WERE seldom hospitable places, and cowhands weren't known to be great housekeepers. Some bunkhouses were so louse-ridden that the cowhands preferred to sleep outside. But not this one, Johnny noticed. The floor was swept, and the mattresses were fresh like they were aired out regularly. He decided if he ever owned a ranch big enough to require a bunkhouse, he would keep it like this one.

Wearing only his long-handled union suit, he spread his bedroll out on the mattress of the bunk assigned to him and climbed in.

He decided to keep his gunbelt rolled up beside him, so his guns would be within reach.

On the bunk overhead, Matt was snoring away. Other bunks were filled and there was snoring going on, creating a staccato sort of rhythm. One man was muttering in his sleep. "Aw, but darlin'..."

Johnny was so worn out, it actually hurt. It had been one long danged day. But he found as his head rested on the pillow that his mind was too filled with thoughts for him to sleep. He found himself thinking about what Breaker Grant had said. *Think about the future, boy. Think about what you want.*

Johnny was thinking more and more that what he wanted was what he had been thinking about back in front of the hearth. A small ranch, a good woman and a passel of children.

He wondered if when Breaker Grant had first started building this ranch, he had ever thought it would grow to the size it now was.

Johnny didn't think he would want an operation this big. A smaller place, he thought, with a house more like the one he had grown up in. But with a big stone hearth.

He decided to get out of bed. Maybe a walk would help him settle his mind so he could get to sleep.

He pulled back on his jeans and his boots. He moved as quietly as he could. He didn't want to wake anyone up. These were hard-working men and needed their sleep.

On the bunk across from Johnny's, Joe was sleeping. On the top bunk, a man called Clancy was sleeping on his stomach and one arm was hanging down. His rifle was leaning on the wall beside the bed.

Johnny tended to notice guns. The rifle was a Hawken, an old mountain rifle. There weren't a lot of them left. Johnny had seen only one before. This gun was a .50 caliber. A muzzle-loader, but it was said a Hawken was well-balanced and durable. Johnny had heard a buffalo could be taken down at two hundred yards with one.

Once Johnny's feet were in his boots, he reached for his gunbelt and buckled it on. He intended to go nowhere without his pistols.

He stepped out into the night.

The stars overhead were bright, and they seemed so close you could almost reach up and pluck one down. Johnny loved the Texas sky at night.

The wind that was so constant and strong during the day had died down a little. It always seemed to at night.

The barn and the bath house were a little ways off and looked dark. But the adobe walls of the main house were almost glowing in the moonlight.

Johnny let himself walk aimlessly for a bit, while he wondered about his future.

He found himself hankering for another one of Mr. Grant's cigars. Funny, he thought, how quick you get used to the finer things in life.

Johnny's wanderings took him to the side of the barn, and he caught what he thought was a touch of cigar smoke on the breeze. He looked toward the main house and saw a small red glow from off to the side. Someone was out there drawing smoke from a cigar.

He then heard a woman giving a quick giggle.

Johnny decided to see what was going on. Probably nothing, he thought, and it probably wasn't his business. But men who looked like banditos had tried to kidnap Breaker Grant's wife earlier in the day and there was talk of cattle rustling. Grant had guards posted at the outer reaches of the ranch yard, but Johnny thought he still should see who was outside the main house at this late hour.

Though moonlight was touching the front of the house, the side of the barn where Johnny stood was lost in shadows. He moved along, holding to those shadows. Then he crossed through a lighted section of ranch yard, but he figured the only way he would be seen from the house was if someone was standing in front of the porch, not off to the side.

He was in riding boots, and the hard leather soles tended to make a crunching sound on the gravel of the ranch yard when he walked along with a normal gait. So he stepped down gently with the heel and then rolled off to another step.

A row of white ash trees stood to one side of the house, and another stood to the right. Must have been planted early on, Johnny thought, because they stood nearly fifteen feet high. They also provided some cover for a man who wanted to advance toward the house without being seen.

Johnny took advantage of the trees, and of the dark shade they provided from the moonlight.

He was closer to the house now, and he heard the girl giggle again. He could also hear a man's voice but couldn't make out the words.

From one tree, he moved with careful steps to the next. After a time, only two trees remained between him and a small yard at the side of the house.

Moonlight fell to the yard, and Johnny could see a woman with dark hair. Had to be Miss Maria, he thought. And a man was there.

They were standing close together, like they were hugging. But then Johnny saw the woman's robe slide down on one side, and the moonlight caught her shoulder. The man's face was on her neck and working down toward the shoulder.

She said, "Oh, Coleman. We can't. Not here. What if someone saw us?"

He laughed. He had one arm wrapped around her back pulling her toward him, and he held the other hand away. In that hand was the cigar, Johnny figured.

Coleman said, "Why not here? Where's your sense of adventure?"

She pulled back from him and slid the robe back up over her shoulder. Johnny could now see she was in a night robe or house coat. He wondered if she had anything on under it. By the look of the shoulder, he didn't think so.

She said, "Oh, I have a sense of adventure. I thought I had already proved that to you."

He gave a snicker.

She said, "But we can't let ourselves grow careless. There's too much at stake."

"The old man is sound asleep upstairs. I checked before I came out here."

"Breaker posted guards tonight, because of the raiders who attacked me today."

He sighed and gave a reluctant nod of his head. "You're right. It's just that it's been so long."

"Some day, Coleman, I will be yours. Every day and every night. But we have to be patient."

"Will you really be mine?"

"Now, what's that supposed to mean?"

He turned away and paced a bit. He said, "I saw the way you were looking at that gunman today. The one who calls himself O'Brien."

"And how was I looking at him?"

"Like you wanted him."

She laughed. "Oh, please, Coleman. Your jealousy isn't necessary."

"I'm not jealous."

"Oh, sure you are."

He grinned. "Well, maybe a little."

"I can't help but be a little impressed. He did rescue me today. He and his brothers. And the shot he made with his pistol was astounding."

"I'm sure it wasn't the impossible shot you describe. You were frightened. You may not be remembering it clearly."

"Coleman, I'm not some dimwitted fragile girl who faints at the thought of danger. I know how to shoot. And I'm a Carrera. The daughter of Vincente Carrera. That means something."

"It does in terms of wealth, yes."

Her hands were on her hips. She was getting a little miffed. "My father carved his ranchero out of the Texas wilderness just like Breaker Grant did. With his own two hands. He is a man of courage and honor, and as his daughter, I will not shame him. I know what I saw today. Mister O'Brien and his brothers came riding practically out of nowhere, like knights out of some childhood fable.

"One of those banditos had a gun to my head, and Mister O'Brien shot him in the arm, in a way that wouldn't cause the bandito's gun to harm me when it went off. I've never seen such a thing."

Coleman waved off the suggestion with the hand holding his cigar, then he took another draw of smoke and the end of the cigar lit up with a red glow in the night.

Coleman said, "He and his brothers are two-bit gunfighters. As soon as my father's fascination with them ends, they'll be gone from here. I'll see to it. I'm the ramrod of this place, and as soon as my father gives the word, I'll be firing all three of them."

She said, "You're jealous."

"Of two-bit gunfighers? Saddle bums?"

She said, "There's nothing to be jealous of. I assure you."

She laid one hand gently along the side of his face. He said nothing.

She said, "I should be getting inside. The longer I'm out here, the better the chance of being seen."

She stepped away along the side of the house. Johnny heard a door open and then shut. A side door, apparently.

Coleman Grant stepped up and onto the front porch and walked along until he stood in front of the main door. He then looked out toward the ranch yard. He had a fist on one hip, and with the other he brought the cigar to his mouth and took a long draw of smoke.

He then turned and walked through the front door, and Johnny heard the door shut.

So, Johnny thought. *Coleman plans to not only inherit the ranch, but he's working on the woman, too.*

When Johnny was certain no one was coming out of the house, he left the stand of trees and headed back to the bunkhouse.

He found Matt standing outside, leaning against one wall. Matt had a tin cup in one hand.

"I didn't expect to find you awake. You were sawin' 'em off in there, like working the woodpile back at the farm."

Matt chuckled. "I woke up and saw you were gone."

"That coffee must be cold by now."

Matt nodded. "Just felt like having a taste. So, what have you been doing, wandering about the ranch at this time of night?"

Johnny told him what he had seen and overheard.

Matt shook his head, and took a sip of the cold coffee.

He said, "We can't go getting ourselves caught up in these types of complexities. It's already quite clear that Coleman has little use for us."

"As soon as Joe's leg is ready to ride, I think that's

what we should do. Ride. Clear out of here."

"Agreed. But in the meantime, we need to lay low. Not draw any attention to ourselves. Work as cowhands and earn a little money."

Johnny nodded. He stood in silence for a moment, and let his gaze drift back toward the house.

Then he said, "It's going to be a hard thing, not saying anything to Mister Grant about all of this."

"You like the old man, don't you? Does he seem to remind you of Pa a little?"

Johnny nodded. "Maybe. And maybe I'm seeing a little of what I might be like when I'm older. Except for sniffing wine corks. I don't know if I can bring myself to do that."

Matt laughed.

Then he said, "So, when you're older, you want a place like this?"

Johnny allowed himself to pace a bit, as he thought about it. "A ranch, maybe, but not one like this. A ranch this size operates almost like a small country. But I mean the man, himself. I kind of wonder if when he was our age, he was a man I could have ridden alongside. A man I could have understood. I met a few of them when I rode with the Rangers."

"Well, we can't say anything to him about it. We can't cause any trouble at all. None of this is our business, and if we interfere, all it'll do is draw attention to ourselves."

Johnny nodded. He knew Matt was right.

Johnny said, "I'm gonna turn in. The day starts early on a ranch."

"It does on a ship, too."

Johnny grinned. "Well, tomorrow, your education as a cowhand is going to begin."

49

THE DAYS PASSED, and Joe no longer needed crutches. The swelling around his knee was gone, but he found he still had to favor his left leg. It made climbing up and into the saddle difficult.

Joe hobbled his way outside the bunkhouse. He stood with his weight on his good leg, and leaned his back against the wall. He began to roll a cigarette.

Joe said, "I hope I can be in the saddle soon. This loafing around ain't in my blood."

Johnny was outside with him, with a tin cup filled with hot trail coffee. The sky above was a gunmetal gray, and nightfall was not far off.

Johnny said, "We've been putting long days in the saddle. We could sure use an extra hand."

"Maybe if I can wait another couple of days, you and Matt'll have all them strays rounded up."

Johnny grinned. "You'd like that, wouldn't you?"

Joe returned the grin. "No. Not really. Pa taught us boys not to be afraid of work. How's Matt doing out there? He ain't the most natural on horseback."

Johnny took a sip of the coffee. "He's doing fine. Riding a cutting horse during roundup is different than just riding down a trail. He's learning to move with the horse and not bounce in the saddle so much. Goullie told him to let his legs act as springs, and Matt's making it work for him."

Joe nodded. "We'll make a cowhand out of him yet."

"Not here, we won't. Payday is in a couple of weeks, then I say we ride out."

Joe said, "I won't mind. I'm not cut out to be a cowhand. I long for the mountains."

Johnny nodded, but said, "I think I'll kind of miss this place. If things had been different, I might have been able to settle in on this ranch."

Goullie came riding in, covered with dust.

He reined up in front of the bunkhouse. "You boys working hard?"

Johnny said, "Hardly working."

"That's what I thought."

It was an old joke. Johnny had heard his father and other farmers using it, and he had heard it in Texas. He figured it had been around as long as there had been working men.

Goullie swung out of the saddle and called for Ciego, who came and got the horse.

Goullie said, "Any of that coffee left?"

Johnny nodded. "A whole pot of it."

Goullie went into the bunkhouse and came back out with a cup.

Soon Matt wandered over. He had washed the dust and sweat off from a day of rounding up strays, and he had a book in one hand.

Two other cowhands joined them. One was tall and walked with a bowlegged swagger, and Johnny knew him as Williams. The other was young, not much older than Luke. He had a freckled nose and a jaw covered with fine, wispy whiskers. He went by the name Tompkins.

Williams said, "Another couple or three days in the saddle ought to do the job."

Tomkins shook his head. "I sure do hate a stampede. We're lucky no one got hurt."

Three nights ago, something had started two hundred head running on a section of range a half mile east of the ranch house.

Tompkins said, "An odd thing, that stampede was. I've seen a thunderclap spook a herd, but there weren't a thunderhead in the sky."

He looked at Goullie and said, "You think maybe it was a wolf or a coyote?"

Goullie said, "It was a coyote, all right. But the kind that walks on two legs."

"You think it might have been those men what attacked Miss Maria?"

Goullie said nothing, and began rolling a cigarette.

Tompkins said, "What do you think Mister Grant is gonna do about it? Call in the Texas Rangers?"

Goullie shrugged.

Johnny hadn't been aware Coleman Grant was approaching, until Coleman said, "We'll handle this ourselves."

Coleman was in a white shirt, a black string tie, and a brown corduroy blazer. He was wearing what Johnny thought of as a *gentleman's hat*. It was a light gray in color, with a stiffly blocked brim that curved slightly at the sides.

Coleman said to Matt, "Did I see you at the main house a little while ago?"

Matt nodded. "Yes, sir. Mister Grant has an extensive library. He said he doesn't make much use of it himself, but he told me to help myself. He has a Shakespeare collection and an edition of Plutarch."

"It's apparent we're not keeping you busy enough."

Coleman didn't look like he was in a good mood. Johnny and his brothers had been here nearly two weeks, and Johnny didn't think he had ever seen Coleman in a good mood.

Coleman said, "We're going to ride night herd tonight. But we're gonna do it different than we have been. We're not just gonna protect the herd. We're gonna see if we can catch these raiders in the act, and maybe bring one of 'em back. I want to question them."

"Not a bad idea," Johnny said.

Coleman looked at him. "Oh, really? And did I ask for your opinion?"

Johnny decided it was best to say nothing. As soon as pay day arrived, he and his brothers would be riding on.

Coleman said, "Since you're so full of opinions, you won't mind riding night herd tonight, will you?"

Goullie said, "With all due respect, Mister Grant, O'Brien rode night herd last night, too. And he put in a long day yesterday and today rounding up the strays."

"Did I ask you, Goullie?"

"No sir."

"But since you're so concerned, you can go along with him."

Coleman turned his attention to Joe. "How much longer before you'll be ready to ride?"

Joe shrugged. "Soon, I hope."

"I hope so, too. We're paying you to do nothing but wait around the bunkhouse."

Johnny didn't like the way this was going. You didn't accuse him or one of his brothers of milking an injury to avoid work. Johnny's gaze met Coleman's, and for a moment Johnny thought Coleman was going to challenge him. Coleman would learn his lesson fast, Johnny thought.

But Coleman looked away and said, "All right. Eat your supper and then saddle up."

Coleman strode away, back to the main house.

Joe said, "For a moment there, I thought you were gonna give him a thrashin'."

"The thought crossed my mind." Then Johnny said to Goullie, "For a ramrod, you don't see him getting dirty all that much, do you?"

Goullie snorted a chuckle and said, "Come on. Let's grab a plate of beans, and get going."

50

HAD TO BE PAST midnight, Johnny figured, looking up at the moon. Maybe close to one o'clock.

He was kneeling on the downside of a small grassy hill. Ahead of him was a small creek that was now running half-dry. Beyond the creek were dozens of dark shapes. Cows, most of them were down for the night.

He could hear a harmonica going from a ways out. One of the men riding night herd had a harmonica. Calm and easy music soothed the herd.

These cows had been rounded up from the last stampede. Johnny estimated there to be about two hundred head, and bunched up the way they were, if they got spooked then they could start running again.

A fire burned low nearby, and a kettle of coffee was being kept warm. Johnny had a tin cup in one hand. He had lost count of the number of cupfuls he had put away tonight. He had managed only about two hours of sleep over the past two days.

Coleman Grant was running him and Matt ragged. Night herd two nights in a row, and two full days of rounding up strays. If Coleman wanted them to ride on, then he was making it plain. Johnny didn't intend to disappoint him. As soon as they had their pay.

Johnny's horse Bravo was on the hill behind him, standing in a sleepy kind of way with his head hanging. Johnny had loosened the cinch. The *girth*, they called it here in Texas.

A man came striding over. It was Goullie. The night had turned off a little cool and he was in a coat. He had leather leggings strapped onto his pants. He called them *chaps*. Vacqueros had used them for years, and now white cowhands were starting to wear them.

"Gotta get yourself some chaps," he said. "Riding through the brush is a good way to get your pants all torn up."

"Maybe with my first paycheck."

"You ain't gonna go into town and whup it up with the boys?"

Johnny shook his head. "Nope. My brothers and I are gonna be riding on."

"I hate to see that. You're proving yourself to be a top hand, and Matt's learning fast."

"Well, it's plain Coleman doesn't want us here."

"Don't let him bother you, none. It's old man Grant who gets the final say in the running of this place."

Johnny took a sip of coffee. "You know, I have to wonder about what Coleman's thinking. If any raiders turn up to cause trouble, he wants them taken alive. Does he have any idea how hard that's gonna be?"

Goullie said, "Just betwixt you and me, I don't think he has any idea about much. He's the ramrod because the old man took him in as a whelp and made him his son. But Coleman don't know squat about cattle or horses. I've never seen a ramrod lead from an office at the main house before. Every other ramrod I've ever worked for works alongside the men."

"He might be Mister Grant's son, but from what I've seen it takes more than just a family connection to lead. You have to be able to hold the respect of the men."

Goullie shrugged. "He doesn't get much respect. He doesn't earn it. But a lot of the men are afraid of him. He's really good with his fists. I've never seen anyone as good. He beat a man unconscious last year in town. The man challenged him and Coleman took him down. He killed another man last winter."

Johnny got to his feet to stretch out his knees a little. They were cramping up from where he was kneeling in the grass.

He said, "You don't strike me as the kind of man who's afraid of much."

Goullie shook his head. "Cautious, maybe, but I can't think of any man I'm afraid of."

"Then why do you stay on at the ranch?"

"Respect for the old man. I've been with him nearly ten years, now. But if Coleman ever gets too far out of hand, I can always ride out."

"Ten years."

Goullie nodded. "I was younger than you when I first signed on with him. Mister Grant ran the ranch himself, back then. Coleman was just a snot-nosed kid."

"You should be ramrod."

"That's what I was hoping for. We had a ramrod a few years ago who was a good man. He got married and headed west. New Mexico Territory has a lot of wild cattle. Longhorns that drifted away from herds and multiplied. They're there for the taking, if you've got what it takes to do the work. There's also Apaches that don't take too kindly to white men. Our old ramrod left with a couple of the men to round up some of that wild cattle, and then with his new wife, they've set up a small ranch outside of Santa Fe. Thought sure I was gonna be the ramrod here, but the old man gave the job to Coleman."

Goullie left for the fire, poured himself a cup of coffee and then came back.

He said, "Just betwixt you and me, Coleman's got a mean streak, and he's not someone to turn your back on. Not someone you can trust."

"Mister Grant must be aware of that."

Goullie shrugged again and then blew on the coffee to cool it a bit before taking a sip.

He said, "Mister Grant's an old man. Maybe he's hoping Coleman is a better man than he seems. Maybe he's hoping the job will make a better man of him. I know he's been wanting an heir who can actually run this place, and marrying Miss Maria doesn't seem to have helped any. Coleman might be all he's gonna have."

Once the coffee was gone, Goullie thought he might saddle up and take a ride out among the herd.

Johnny decided to take a walk to where Matt was stationed. He also decided to bring along his rifle.

He found Matt standing behind a small poplar growing beside the creek. Matt was leaning one elbow against the trunk and looking out toward the herd.

"It's all I can do to stay awake," Matt said.

Johnny nodded. "This isn't doing anyone any good. If we're too tired to see straight, we're of no use out here."

Matt nodded in agreement and was about to say something, but a gun fired from somewhere out at the edge of the herd.

Johnny stepped away from the tree to get a better look. Matt was with him.

A gun fired again. Then four more times. Some of the cows were moaning and bawling, and they were getting to their feet.

"They're trying to get the herd running," Matt said.

Johnny cocked the rifle and took aim at where he had

seen the gun flashes. It was a shot in the dark—literally—but he felt he had to do something.

He estimated the distance at close to a thousand feet. He allowed for the distance, aiming a little high. The problem wouldn't be hitting the target, as he had hit targets before at that distance. Target shooting he had done with the Rangers. The problem was the man who did the shooting might have moved.

The cows were already starting to run, so he wasn't concerned about his own shots spooking them.

Johnny pulled the trigger and the rifle bucked against his shoulder. He then cocked and aimed to a point a few yards to one side of where the shots had been fired, and pulled the trigger again. Then he got off a third shot in the other direction.

The herd was in a full stampede, and the ground was rumbling. Dust often seems to settle more at night, but even still, the cows' hooves were stirring up a cloud of it.

Johnny caught a glimpse of one rider trying to keep up with the herd. Might have been Goullie. Then the herd and the night riders were off into the distance.

"Come on," Johnny said. "No need to bother saddling up. We won't catch up with 'em, anyway."

"Where are we going?"

"To see if I hit anyone."

There were two shots remaining in his rifle, so he tossed it aside and pulled his right-hand gun.

Johnny and Matt each took the small stream with a running leap, and they charged out into the open where the herd had been bedded down. Matt stepped into a fresh cow chip and slid a bit but kept his footing and continued on behind Johnny.

They found a man lying in the grass. Johnny knelt down and placed a hand on the man's chest. He wasn't breathing.

In the moonlight, Johnny had a look at him and thought he was a Mexican. He was young, not much older than Johnny. He was in a shirt that looked gray in the moonlight and pants with buttons down the sides. He had a pistol still in his hand, and it looked like one of Johnny's shots had caught him in the chest.

"Unbelievable," Matt said. "You shot into the darkness, at where you figured he had to be by the flash of his gun, and you got him."

The man hadn't been alone. Johnny realized this when he saw another one of them standing a few yards off, bringing a rifle to his shoulder.

Matt fired, and the man went down.

"That's two," Matt said.

"There could be more."

Johnny faced in one direction and Matt the other, each protecting the other's back. But there were no more rustlers. They were alone in the night.

In the distance, the rumbling of the herd had stopped. Then they heard some shots, sounding hollow in the distance. Three, four. Then a scattering more.

"That's coming from more than one gun," Johnny said.

"You think they found more outlaws?"

Johnny shrugged.

Matt said, "Should we go after them to try to help?"

Johnny shook his head. "By the time we get there…"

The gunshots had stopped.

Johnny finished his thought, "…it would be too late to help."

They went to confirm the man Matt shot was dead. Then Matt said, "Now what?"

"We wait for Goullie and the others." Even though there seemed to be no more rustlers, Johnny kept his gun ready.

Matt said, "We just killed two men."

Johnny nodded. "Had to be done."

"Yet we don't seem too shaken up about it."

"I suppose not. I've had to kill before. So have you." Johnny started walking toward the campfire. "Come on. Let's get some more coffee."

Matt fell into place beside him. "I wonder what Ma would say."

"I hope she never finds out. Joe says they're talking about me in saloons and cattle camps, but I hope he's exaggerating."

"From what I've seen lately, I doubt he is. The shot tonight, getting a man in the dark when you couldn't even see him. And the way you shot that raider in a way so that Miss Maria wouldn't get hurt."

"It wasn't that great a shot."

"Johnny, it was probably the most fantastic thing I've

ever seen. How did you even think to do that?"

Johnny stopped walking. "There's this strange thing about me, Matt. I never mentioned it back home. But when the bullets are flying and death is all around me, I just get this strange calmness about me. A strange sort of quiet inside. Like I'm doing just what I need to be doing, and I'm where I'm supposed to be. Like I'm focused and have a sense of purpose. I never feel quite that way any other time."

"Weren't you afraid, any of those times? Like the story you tell, about shooting those five Comanches?"

Johnny shook his head. "They were riding down on Zack Johnson and me. Ten of 'em. First Zack caught an arrow in his leg, and then his horse went down. I jumped out of the saddle and stood at his side. I wasn't going to leave him behind. That was a sort of code of honor we had in that particular band of Rangers. We didn't leave a man behind, no matter what.

"So I just drew my gun and faced those riders. Ten of 'em, bearing down on me. They were about a thousand feet away and coming fast. I just drew my gun and this strange calm came over me. It occurred to me it was no different than shooting cans off a fence. I just started firing. Five shots—five riders.

"I did a border shift so I'd have a fresh gun in my hand, but the remaining five wheeled their horses around and rode off."

"Just like that."

"Just like that. It was over almost before it started. Zack saw it and couldn't stop talking about it back at the fort. But I never felt a twang of fear. And it was the same when that raider had a gun to Miss Maria's head. I got that strange calmness again. I just knew what kind of shot I had to make and that I could make it."

They started walking again.

Johnny said, "I don't know. Maybe something's wrong with me."

"If there is," Matt said, "it is with me, too. When pirates were boarding our ship one time, I didn't feel any fear at all. It was just me and the sword in my hand, and I knew what I could do. It turns out I'm rather good with a sword. I slashed and parried and ducked when others were slashing."

"That old scout I mentioned. Apache Jim. He calls men like us *gunhawks*."

"Well, I can't use a gun like you. Not even close."

"Doesn't matter. I don't think he was talking about guns. I think he was talking about something inside a man. Even with that sword in your hand, facing those pirates, you were a gunhawk."

They poured more coffee.

Matt said, "Including that rustler back there, and the four pirates I killed that day, as well as others, I've killed twelve men."

Johnny was quiet a moment. Then he said, "Like I said before, I lost count a long time ago. I got two men on my first foray down into Mexico. We chased a bunch of border raiders. There was a fight and I plugged two of them. Then those five Comanches. One time there was a gunfight with a group of highwaymen who had robbed a stagecoach. Six men. It was Zack and me and one other man by the name of Scott Hansen. We were behind rocks and guns were going off. In the end, all six were dead, but I had no way of knowing how many I had actually gotten. From there on, there was just no way to count. Border raiders. Comanches. Five different gunfights in those border towns I talk about. One, like I said earlier, I shot the gun out of his hand. But the other four I killed. Then those raiders who were going after Miss Maria. I got two of them, counting the one I shot in the arm. That was a bad wound. I can't imagine he lived."

Johnny grabbed his rifle from where he had dropped it. Two shots remained in the cylinder. Once they were back at the bunkhouse, he would reload it.

"What I'd really like is a Spencer," he said. "It takes metal cartridges. You just push 'em in. It loads through the back of the stock. Then you jack the trigger guard to chamber a new cartridge. Zack Johnson used one."

"Where'd you get this Colt rifle?"

"Ranger issue. I could never seem to save up enough money to buy a Spencer. I suppose I like tequila too much."

After a time, two riders came back. Goullie, and a man they called Frenchie. He gave his name as Pierre D'Arnot and he claimed he was from Quebec, but Johnny didn't think he heard much of an accent. Frenchie had dark hair and dark scraggly whiskers. His nose was long and he had long teeth.

"You boys all right?" Goullie said.

Johnny said, "Yeah. You?"

Goullie swung out of the saddle and loosened the

girth.

He said, "They got maybe forty head. Hard to tell in the darkness. They were waitin' when the stampede started and headed 'em off. We traded shots with 'em."

Johnny nodded. "We could hear the gunfire from here."

"They got Williams."

"Anyone else hurt?"

Goullie shook his head.

Frenchie said, "Wheeler and Gates and Tompkins stayed with the herd. We rode back here to see what the situation was."

Goullie glanced to the cup in Johnny's hand, and said, "Got any of that coffee left?"

Matt said, "Maybe enough for another cup. We can put a new pot on."

Goullie nodded. "The herd is scattered again. All that work of rounding 'em up, gone."

Matt fetched the pot and filled a tin cup for Goullie.

Matt said, "We got two of 'em."

"Rustlers?" Frenchie said.

Johnny nodded. "The bodies are back yonder, a ways."

Matt said, "One fired a bunch of shots to get the herd going. Johnny shot him, firing at the flash of his gun from way back beyond the fire. That has to be the second greatest shot I've ever seen. I got the other."

Goullie shook his head. "Coleman ain't gonna like it. He wants us to bring back at least one of 'em so he can get some answers."

"We'll get some answers anyway," Johnny said.

All eyes were on him, now.

Johnny said, "I say, come morning, we find their trail and start following it back to where they started from."

Matt grinned. "I do like the way you think."

"I don't know," Goullie said. "Coleman won't like it. He'll want us to ride back to the ranch and let him decide what to do. Besides, Coleman led a bunch of us into those mountains two months ago. We lost their trail."

Johnny said, "There's more than one way to flush out vermin. I've done this kind of thing before."

"The thing is," Goullie said, "we're cowhands. We've never tracked a group of outlaws, like you did with the Rangers."

Matt smiled. "We'll be all right. We're gunhawks."

51

JOE COULD WALK with a hobble. His left knee still couldn't tolerate a lot of weight, and getting up and onto the back of a horse wouldn't be easy. Once he was there, though, he was sure he would be able to ride.

One of the men had gone back and gotten his saddle, and it was now on the floor beside his bunk. But, dang, he would miss the horse those raiders had shot out from under him. A Cheyenne pony he had broken himself.

These cowhands could learn a thing or two from the Cheyenne about breaking a horse, Joe thought.

He was sitting on a wooden upright chair he had hauled out from the bunkhouse. Sitting and watching the activities of the ranch go on around him. The ringing of a blacksmith's hammer from down by the barn. A rider coming in and swinging out of the saddle in front of the big house. Someone from town, maybe.

It was mid-morning. Joe didn't really think in terms of what the exact time was. Nine o'clock, or whatever. He now thought of that as *white-man time*, irrelevant to the Earth and the creatures upon it. And irrelevant by the thinking of the Cheyenne. So much of the way he looked at life had been reshaped by his time with them. It was the middle part of the morning—that was all that mattered.

Johnny and Matt weren't back yet. They had ridden out the night before with Goullie and three other cowhands. Frenchie, Wheeler, Gates. They were to ride night herd, and if the raiders struck again, to try and bring one of them back alive. A tall order, Joe had thought at the time. Not practical.

What concerned him the most was they should have been back near sunrise, but they had not been heard from.

Coleman Grant had another shift of riders ready to go out and spell them. Guard the herd during the daylight hours. When the night riders didn't come back, Coleman sent the morning shift out anyway.

Joe sat in front of the bunkhouse, thinking about how good a taste of tobacco from his Cheyenne pipe might be. But he understood that smoking an Indian pipe might seem odd to the cowhands, and the goal was for Joe and his brothers to not draw attention to themselves, so he left the pipe in his saddle bags.

From where he sat, he could see a low grassy rise out beyond the stables and corrals. He could see motion on that rise. A rider.

Joe had learned to identify a rider by the way he sits a saddle. The way he moves with the horse. Every rider had his own way of doing it. As distinctive as the way a person walks. He knew who this was. Shelby, the lead rider of the morning shift. Five had ridden out, and one was coming back.

A man called out, "Shelby's back!" and went running for the main house.

Shelby came in. He had a wide-brimmed hat that stood tall at the crown and a thick mustache that almost covered his mouth. He wore a gun at his belt for a cross-draw, and he had a heavy-looking leather vest that was buttoned from top to bottom.

He skirted around the stables and then rode past the bunkhouse and up to the barn.

Joe decided to hobble over and see what was going on.

The front door of the main house swung open with a bang and Coleman came striding out. Not running, but as near as you could get to it without actually doing it. He was driving his heels into the dirt of the ranch yard and kicking up a little dust with each step.

He was at the barn before Joe could limp his way over, but Joe was close enough to hear.

Coleman said, "What're you doing back?"

Shelby had swung out of the saddle, and he said to him, "The herd stampeded in the night. Raiders. We found Gates and Martin and Frenchie out there waiting for us, but the other three are gone. Two raiders were shot and killed. The O'Brien boys and Goullie went to back trail the stolen cattle."

"I didn't order them to do that."

Shelby shrugged. "They done it anyway."

"When they get back, they're fired. Goullie, too."

Ciego handled the stable and did the blacksmith work, and he had the shoulders and arms of a man who looked like he could bend a fireplace poker with his bare hands.

He said, "Goullie, too? He's been on this ranch a long time."

Coleman said, "You want to join him?"

Ciego said nothing.

Joe was now standing beside Coleman. He was in his

gray, Mexican jacket with the stylish buttons and a string tie. A foreman who never got his hands dirty, Joe thought.

Coleman said to him, "And you're gone, too. I don't care if you don't have a horse or can't walk. Once you're brothers get back, or once their bodies are hauled in, I want you gone."

Joe said, "You've hated us from the start. Why?"

Coleman stepped closer to him, and reared up in a challenging way. Joe didn't find Coleman threatening. Joe found him amusing. Joe had left his revolver back at the bunkhouse, but on his belt was the long knife he had been wearing when he first returned to Pennsylvania. Even with his bum knee, he could drive that knife into Coleman and gut him like a pig before Coleman could even react. So Joe didn't feel threatened by him at all.

But the plan was not to draw attention to themselves. Gutting a blow-hard like Coleman was the kind of thing the cowhands might tend to remember.

Coleman said, "I know what you three are. You're saddle bums. Your brother got off a lucky shot and saved Miss Maria and my father felt obliged to give you all jobs. Jobs that weren't needed. The payroll was already full. And now your brothers think that gives them license to go off on their own. Well, it doesn't. I run this place. It's time you all learned it."

Joe said nothing.

Coleman gave a triumphant smirk, apparently mistaking Joe's silence for fear. Coleman turned on his heel and started back for the ranch.

Shelby called after him, "Mister Grant."

Coleman turned back. He looked like he liked the sound of the name *Mister Grant* being applied to him.

Shelby said, "What about Goullie and the O'Brien boys? Do we ride after 'em?"

Coleman shook his head. "If they're dead, they're dead. If they come back, they're fired. I don't want to expend any more manpower. Ride back out to the herd and start rounding 'em up."

"What about Frenchie and Gates and Wheeler? They been out there all night."

Coleman thought for a second. "Can you and your boys handle it?"

"Yes, sir."

"Then send the other three back. Let them get their rest."

"Yes, sir."

Coleman continued on toward the house.

Joe waited until Coleman was all the way inside and the door shut.

"Why do you all put up with him?" Joe said.

Apparently Shelby had been waiting too, because as soon as the door was shut, he let go a sigh and relaxed a little.

He said, "He's Mister Grant's son. Mister Grant wants him to be the ramrod, so he's the ramrod. I ride for the brand."

Joe nodded. "I understand that. Ridin' for the brand. But Coleman would be a much better ramrod if he wasn't struttin' around here like a peacock. Sometimes a man has to be taught the hard way."

"Ain't a man alive who can stand up to him. He's the best man with his fists I've ever seen. One of the hands challenged him last summer. Coleman beat him unconscious. In town last year, some drifter accused Coleman of cheating at cards, and Coleman killed him with his fists. The county sheriff decided to call it self-defense."

"Was it?"

Shelby shrugged and looked at Ciego.

Ciego said, "Mister Grant is one of the most powerful men in the county. Maybe this side of Texas. No one is going to accuse his son of murder."

Joe nodded and said, "The fact is, there's not a man alive who can stand up to my brother. I've seen tougher men than Coleman, and I don't think any of them could stand up to Johnny."

Shelby shook his head. "It would be your brother's funeral. That is, if your brother is still alive."

Joe decided maybe it was time to ignore Coleman Grant, as well as the pain in his own knee, and find a horse and go after Johnny and Matt.

52

JOE STOOD on the front porch and rapped his knuckles against the oak door. He waited. There was no answer.

Maybe no one heard me in there, he thought. It was a big house, after all.

Maybe he should use the big brass door knocker. Back in Pennsylvania, the farmhouses Joe had known when he was growing up didn't have door knockers. The farmers were just regular folks and had regular doors, and if you were visiting someone you just knocked on the door. And among the Cheyenne, if the doorway flap to a tipi was down, you tapped on the outside framework.

But this wasn't Pennsylvania farming country or a Cheyenne village. The brass knocker was there, so Joe used it. Three taps with it, good and loud.

He waited, and after maybe thirty seconds, the door opened. It was Alfredo.

Joe took off his hat. He said, "I need to see Mister Grant."

"Which one?" Alfredo asked, looking bored and maybe a little annoyed at the interruption from his household duties.

"*Breaker* Grant."

"I'll see if he's available."

"Tell him it's Joe O'Brien." Joe had to be careful. He almost said Joe *McCabe*. "Tell him it's one of the men who saved Miss Maria a couple of weeks ago. I need to talk with him."

Alfredo made a visible attempt at trying not to roll his eyes. "The master knows who you are. Wait in the entryway."

Joe sat in one of the Queen Anne chairs and waited. Alfredo climbed the stairs, making a point not to hurry.

Joe wondered if Coleman was going to come downstairs and tell him to leave. Joe decided the time of trying not to draw attention to himself had ended. If Coleman tried to force Joe out of the house, Joe was going to give him an instruction in manners. Cheyenne style. In the process, Coleman might lose some hair.

It wasn't long before Alfredo was coming back downstairs.

He said, "Mister Grant will see you. Upstairs, second

door on the right."

Joe nodded. He knew where Grant's office was.

Now, to climb the stairs. His knee wasn't going to like it. Joe grabbed hold of the railing for support and took the steps one at a time.

Once he was up there, he waited a moment to make sure his knee was going to support his weight. Climbing the stairs was the biggest workout his knee had faced since the injury happened. He then hobbled his way down the hall to his right and to the second door.

The doorway was open. Breaker Grant was standing in front of his desk.

"O'Brien," he said. "Come on in."

Joe came in, stepping gingerly.

Grant said, "How's that knee coming along?"

"Slow," Joe said. "But much better'n it was a couple weeks ago."

Breaker Grant was in a white shirt, a string tie, and a burgundy colored smoking jacket. He had a cigar going.

He said, "Would you like a cigar?"

Joe had never really taken to cigars. He preferred his Cheyenne pipe. He said, "No, but thank you."

"Please, sit. Take a load off that bad knee."

Joe took one of the chairs in front of the desk.

Grant said, "What can I do for you, young man?"

Joe explained the situation. Johnny and Matt had gone out with the men the night before to defend the herd against the raiders who had been striking lately, with orders to bring one back for questioning.

Grant gave him a little frown of surprise. "Who gave that order?"

"Your son, sir."

He nodded. "Coleman. I should have known. An order like that would be almost impossible to carry out. Most of my men are cowhands, not fighters. Even though your brother rode with the Texas Rangers, he's still just one man."

"That one man is better than any other three men," Joe said.

Grant nodded agreement.

Joe said, "But they ain't come back. Word has it they're trying to backtrack the raiders."

Grant nodded again. "Good men."

"Sir," Joe said, "Coleman has told me I'm fired, along

with my brothers if they return. But I want to go after them."

Grant said, "You're not fired. But how can you go after them with that bum leg?"

"I can still ride."

Grant gave him a long look. He took a slow draw on his cigar and let out a cloud of smoke that made spiraling shapes as it spread out along the ceiling.

He said, "Am I mistaken, or have you spent some time among the Indians?"

"Cheyenne, sir."

He nodded. "You have a way about you. Also, that sheath on your belt. I thought it was plains Indian, but it didn't look quite Comanche or Kiowa."

"I want to ride after them and find them."

"By yourself?"

Joe nodded. "I'll be all right."

"I think you probably will be. Men like you have a way of being all right. Go pick the best horse in the corral. Tell Ciego I told you to do so. And bring those men back."

"Yes, sir."

Joe headed out to the hallway. He had seen a long-legged bay in the corral and thought that was the one he wanted. But at the moment, his mind was on getting down the stairs with his bad knee. He was hoping downhill would be better than uphill.

He took it the way he had on the way up. First one step and then another, with one hand firmly hanging onto the railing.

When he got to the bottom floor, Coleman came from the parlor. He was almost steaming with anger.

"What are you doing in here, bothering my father?" he said. "You're not only fired, I want you off this ranch right now. This very moment. Or I'll throw you off myself."

Joe's knife came out of the sheath in one smooth motion and the long blade was under Coleman's chin before the man could even react. Joe let the tip, which was honed to a fine point, jab a bit into the soft flesh under Coleman's jawbone. Coleman went up onto his toes.

Joe said, "You back off, before I wind up wearin' your scalp on my belt."

A thrust of maybe eight inches and then a sideways slice, and the management problems on this ranch would be ended.

Coleman said nothing. His anger seemed to be gone like blowing out a lamp, and he was staring down at Joe wide-eyed.

"I'm gonna get a horse," Joe said, "and I'm goin' after my brothers and Goullie. Mister Grant has given the say-so. I want no fuss from you."

Coleman said nothing. Joe figured Coleman was too a-feared to.

Joe let the knife down, and Coleman took a couple of steps backward.

Joe turned and strode out of the house, or as close to striding as his knee would allow.

Breaker Grant was at the balcony at the top of the stairs, leaning on the rail with a cigar smoldering in one hand. He couldn't help but smile.

Joe told Ciego what Mister Grant had said. Ciego went to the bunkhouse and hefted Joe's saddle up on his shoulder and headed to the corral. Joe preferred to saddle his own horse, but carrying that saddle with his bad knee would have been impossible.

He got his rifle. It was an Enfield. A little longer than most mountain rifles, but it took a .577 caliber minie ball and had saved his life more than once. One time, a grizzly had been bearing down on him and Joe put a ball right between the bear's eyes. Joe had gotten the rifle in trade at Fort Laramie. It cost him a whole pile of furs, but it was worth it.

Joe tucked his Colt revolver into the front of his belt and then hobbled his way to the corral. The bay was saddled and waiting for him.

Ciego was still there, waiting for him.

Ciego said, "I sure hope you know what you're doing."

Joe nodded. "Me too."

He slid the rifle into the saddle boot. Because of the length of the rifle, Joe had made the saddle boot himself out of buckskin, and the rifle slid into place with ease.

The next trick was to get into the saddle with a left leg that wouldn't support much of his weight. You can't mount a horse from the right side without the horse getting all squirrely on you. Joe could have with the horse he had broken himself, using Cheyenne methods, but he doubted this one would stand for it.

Here goes, Joe thought.

He grabbed the saddle horn with his left hand and the saddle's cantle with his right, then he lifted his left leg and pushed the toe into the stirrup. Then he took three bouncing steps off his right.

The horse looked at him and rolled its eyes the way a horse will, like it thought Joe was crazy.

Then Joe was pulling himself up and he managed to swing his right leg over the cantle. His bedroll was tied behind the cantle and he had to push his leg up and over it, but he managed to succeed and slid it down to the other side.

Made it, he thought. His left knee felt a little numb.

"Be safe," Ciego said.

Joe nodded. He turned the horse away, and he started toward the low, grassy hill out beyond the ranch yard.

Forty head of cattle make a trail that even the most untrained eye couldn't miss. Johnny, Matt and Goullie followed it directly to the Red. They crossed at a point maybe a mile below where the brothers had camped the night before the rescue of Miss Maria.

However, there was no trail on the other side.

"This was where we lost 'em," Goullie said. "They took 'em either in one direction or the other for a while. Probably driving the beeves in water shallow enough that they can get through it without having to swim, but deep enough that the current will fill in the tracks."

Johnny looked at him like he wasn't quite sure what he was hearing. "Mister Grant told me you boys lost the trail in the mountains."

Goullie nodded, and he had the look of a man who was about to say something he didn't want to say. "That's what Coleman said he was gonna tell the old man. And he told us we were to say nothin' different if we wanted to keep our jobs."

Matt said, "We could ride up and down the river. We can find where they left the water and trail 'em from there."

Johnny nodded. "You can't move all that fast when cows are with you. We'd probably catch 'em. But I want more than that. I want to find their camp. Put a stop to all of this, once and for all."

Johnny looked at Goullie. "What do you know about the mountains? The old man called them the Ouachitas."

Goullie nodded. "Been through there a couple of

times."

"Well, when we're done, you'll be able to say you've been through there three times."

53

"THESE MOUNTAINS AREN'T unlike our own, back in Pennsylvania," Johnny said.

About them were ridges that rose and then dropped down, and then rose up again. They looked to be mostly covered with hardwoods. Maples, oaks, maybe some hickory.

"I don't see how you have any hopes of finding them in all of this," Matt said.

Ahead of them was a small stream. Johnny reined up by the water. The stream was a couple of feet wide, and a stand of oaks grew alongside it.

Johnny swung out of the saddle and loosened the girth. Matt and Goullie did the same.

Matt said, "We didn't trail the cattle. We just rode directly for the mountains."

Johnny nodded. "That's what we did, all right."

"You haven't answered my question," Matt said.

Johnny shrugged. "Haven't heard a question. Just a lot of complainin'."

Goullie was grinning.

Johnny said, "All right. I'll explain it all. But in the morning."

"The morning?"

The sun was trailing low.

Johnny said, "We don't have much daylight left. We're gonna be spending the night in the mountains."

"Spending the night? We didn't bring any supplies with us. Our bedrolls are back at the bunkhouse. Are you planning on shooting our supper?"

Johnny shook his head. "A gunshot might be heard for miles, the way sound tends to echo in the mountains. I have some jerky in my vest."

Goullie said, "And I have a can of beans in my saddle bags."

"There's dinner," Johnny said. "And breakfast."

Matt said, "You can't be serious."

"So," Goullie said. "Make camp here for the night?"

Johnny shook his head. "No. It's too open."

They found a spot at the base of a hill, a mile east of the stream. There were short pines growing about a small depression. Looked like when it rained, the depression might fill up and form a little pool.

"Here," Johnny said.

Matt swung out of the saddle and peeled the saddle from his horse.

He said, "Aren't you concerned this little hollow might fill up if it rains?"

"It's not gonna rain," Johnny said. "The sky's clear and the breeze is easy."

"And I don't mean to complain, but I'm not looking forward to a dinner of cold beans."

"Won't bother me none," Goullie said. He slid his saddle from the back of his horse. "I'm hungry enough to eat the whole thing myself, tin can and all."

"The beans'll be heated," Johnny said. "We're going to have a fire."

"A fire?" Matt said. "I figured you wouldn't want a fire. The light might be seen from a distance."

"Let me show you something."

With his knife, he began to dig a hole in the washed out basin.

He said, "The dirt is soft, here. Easy digging."

Goullie grinned. "You're digging yourself a fire pit."

By dark, the hole was two feet deep and Johnny had built a small fire in it. The can of beans was open and standing by the flames.

"The trick," Johnny said, "is to keep the fire from rising above the top of the hole. It'll still be visible from maybe a half mile off, but no more. And these pines will help block the firelight."

Johnny found a dead piece of pine and whittled it flat, and it served as a spoon. They took turns handing the beans around until the can was empty.

Then they bedded down for the night near the fire pit. They each used a saddle as a pillow, with a saddle blanket spread over them.

Johnny expected to hear some complaining from Matt, but there was none. Johnny looked over at Matt, and he found his brother had fallen to sleep as soon as the blanket was over him.

Johnny grinned. Dog tired, he figured. Coleman had allowed them little sleep over the past couple of days. Now was the time to catch up on sleep. Come morning, they would be finding the rustlers, and Johnny doubted it would go easy. He had never before seen such a thing go easy. He wanted all three of them well rested, with their reflexes sharp.

Johnny tossed a glance at Bravo, and the horse was standing lazily and letting his head trail down.

Then the horse looked up and off into the night. Johnny rolled over, kicked off the saddle blanket and grabbed a pistol.

Goullie was still awake. "What is it?"

"Something out there, in the night."

Then Johnny heard the call. "Hello, the fire!"

The same voice he had heard nearly a year ago at a campfire in Kansas Territory.

He grinned. "Come on in!"

Joe was on foot, still favoring his bad leg a little. In one hand were the reins of his horse, and he walked the animal into the camp.

Johnny slid his pistol back into his holster. He said, "What brings you all the way out here?"

"Come lookin' for you three. Followed your trail."

Goullie said, "You bring anything to eat?"

Joe shook his head. "Ate cold beans along the trail."

He stripped off his saddle and gave his horse a rub down.

Then he said to Johnny, "So, what've you got planned for tomorrow?"

"Tomorrow we find their camp."

Joe grinned. "That's what I figured."

"Did you manage to keep your powder dry when you crossed the Red?"

Joe nodded, and he started unrolling his bedding. "Figured I'd need dry powder when we find them rustlers."

Goullie said, "Don't you mean *if?*"

Joe said, "Nope."

54

BY SUNRISE, THEY WERE in the saddle.

Matt said to Joe, "I can't believe you have your bedroll with you."

"When Ciego saddled my horse, he made sure my bedroll was on my saddle. Good man."

"So where are we going?" Matt said.

Johnny pointed to a ridge that was maybe ten miles in the distance. "See that there ridge? We're going to the very top."

Trees grew close together in places and there was thick underbrush, and the men had to go afoot and lead the horses through. In other areas, trees grew further apart, and the men could ride through.

There were groves of pine, and groves of hardwood. At one point, halfway up the ridge, a deer broke away and darted off.

The thought of venison made Johnny's mouth water. There had been no breakfast but jerky this morning. But now was not the time for hunting.

They topped the ridge and looked for an open area, from which they could have a look at the mountains.

The morning air was still a little brisk, and the sun had been in the sky not quite two hours.

Joe said, "We made good time climbing this here ridge."

Johnny nodded.

Goullie said, "I still don't know what we're looking for."

Ahead of them was a view of the next ridge over and then another one beyond that. As they rolled away into the distance, they looked like they were made of green velvet.

Johnny pointed to the northwest, and said, "There."

A small tendril of smoke was rising into the morning sky.

"Careless of 'em," Joe said.

Johnny gave his head half a shake in disagreement. "Not really. They've got no reason to think anyone would be out here looking for them. Coleman and the men lost their trail at the Red, last time they tried to trail them."

"Prob'ly was grateful to lose the trail. Prob'ly scared to death at the thought of actually finding them."

Goullie gave a look that said, *I don't know about that.* He said, "I really doubt there's any man alive Coleman Grant is scared of."

Joe said, "He's not scared of men he thinks he can beat. But it's not the same if the odds are a little more even. I almost gave him a shave with my bowie knife yesterday. He almost wet his pants."

They were all looking at him, but Joe said no more. Johnny knew Joe wouldn't until he was ready.

Matt looked off at the thin line of smoke. It was coming from somewhere beyond the ridge that was further out.

"How far away do you think that is?"

"Ten miles," Joe said. "Maybe fifteen."

"It'll take most of the day to get there."

"Let it," Johnny said. "It's important that we get there without letting them know we're here. We've gotta move slow and quiet."

They rode in single file, with Joe first and Johnny bringing up the rear. Matt was second in line, and the going was slow. They stopped at one point while Joe explored further ahead. Then he came back and waved them on.

They climbed one ridge, making a diagonal line so the traveling would be easier on the horses. Then they started down the other side of the ridge

In one ravine between ridges, they found a spring. They stopped to let the horses drink, and then they refilled the canteens and continued on.

Matt found himself growing drowsy. He had been without much sleep for the previous two days, and last night he hadn't slept well. A saddle for a pillow and a stiff old saddle blanket to keep him warm.

Joe had brought his bedroll along. But the rest of them weren't as prepared.

Matt found himself nodding off once in the saddle. He shook himself awake. Then his head started drifting downward again, and for a moment, he was back on the ship at sea.

He was standing beside the wheel. The pilot had a scarf wrapped around his head and a heavy dark blue pea coat, and his hands were on the wheel. The captain was a man with a short, white beard and a black Greek cap on his head. He was looking off to one side of the ship with a spyglass.

"Steady as she goes," the captain said.

"Steady as she goes," Matt repeated the order to the pilot.

Then he heard Joe say, "We better go in on foot from here."

Matt was brought back to consciousness and realized his horse had stopped. Goullie and Johnny were stepping out of the saddle. They had been climbing a ridge and were now surrounded by tall pines. The sun was low in the sky, and the shadows were stretching long through the woods.

Joe was keeping his voice down. "It's about three or four hundred feet that-a-way," indicating with his left hand off toward their left. "It's bigger than a gully but not quite a canyon. Boxed in at one end."

"Goullie," Johnny said, keeping as quiet as he could. "Stay here with the horses. They'll probably be all right, but if something happened to them, it would be a long walk home."

Then Johnny said to Joe, "Lead on."

Three hundred feet ahead, the land rose up a bit and then dropped off in front of them. Like Joe had said, it was more than a gully but not quite a canyon. It was shallow at their end, but at the far end was twenty feet deep.

Smoke was drifting from a fire at the far end. Matt could see two men stirring about down there, and he could hear the bawling of some cows.

"Pay dirt," Johnny said.

Matt nodded. "So, now what do we do?"

"We wait for dark," Johnny said. "And then we go on in."

55

ONCE IT WAS dark, they picketed their horses near the opening of the small canyon. Then they began working their way down.

"The wind won't reach much down there," Johnny said. "But there might be a little breeze drifting in from the entrance. There's a chance the horses are gonna catch our scent."

"What'll happen then?" Matt said.

"That's when the lead could start flying."

Once they were on the canyon floor, they began forward on their hands and knees. They moved carefully, slowly. No need for a careless move to let the raiders at the far end of the canyon know what was going on.

A small chunk of bedrock rose from the dirt, and Johnny worked his way toward it. The rock was big enough to give him cover.

Once he was behind the rock, he estimated he was about a hundred feet from the campfire. Two men were stretched out on unrolled blankets, and another was at the fire filling a cup from a kettle. A fourth was cleaning his rifle.

They were talking. One said, "Rafe and Harley should'a been back by now. Something must have gone wrong."

"We hang tight," another said. "If they ain't back by mornin', then maybe I'll contact the boss. See what he wants us to do."

There were some cows off past the fire, at the other end of the canyon. Johnny could hear an occasional bawl. A string of horses was back there, too.

Matt came up beside Johnny. Goullie had taken up a place behind a juniper that was in a small depression near the cattle. Joe had disappeared into the darkness at the other side of the camp.

One of the men lying down said, "I'd feel better if this boss of your'n was paying us in cash. Not in cows."

"Cows is as good as cash in this country. You know that."

"I ain't no cowboy. I'd feel better with cash-in-hand."

The man kneeling by the fire set the kettle back down and said, "He's got a point."

A horse stirred, and another nickered.

The man by the fire said, "Hold it. Something's out there."

"Now," Johnny glanced to Matt, then he called out, "You're surrounded! Don't anybody move!"

The ones lying down sprang to their feet and were all drawing guns.

Goullie fired, catching one of the men squarely in the forehead. Joe's Enfield barked from off in the darkness at the other side of camp, and a man's head snapped to one side and the man went down.

Johnny rose up from behind the rock and shot at the man by the fire. The bullet took the man's hat off, and he returned fire. Johnny dove to one side, his hat falling away, and he fired again.

Matt went on his belly beside the rock and propped himself up on his elbows, and he cut loose with two shots.

The man who had been by the fire had a rifle and was jacking in a cartridge. Goullie got him.

The last man standing fired toward Johnny but his shot was wide, and Johnny put a bullet into the man's chest. The man took a couple of steps backward and then fell.

And it was over. The men by the fire were on the ground. The horses were panicking and pulling against their hobbles. The cows were on their feet but in running from the gunfire, they came right quick to the canyon wall and could go no further.

Johnny stepped into the camp. Gun smoke was drifting overhead in a small cloud, and the noise of the gunfire was ringing in his ears.

He looked over to Matt, who was on his feet and coming in. Goullie stood up, holding onto his arm. Joe was walking into the camp. His rifle reloaded and ready to fire if any of the rustlers was playing possum.

"You hit?" Johnny said.

Goullie nodded. "Not bad, though. I think it just grazed me."

One of the men wasn't dead, though. He lifted his head and his gun, and Johnny didn't realize it until he heard the man cock his gun.

Joe swung the Enfield around and fired. The man rolled over and was done.

Johnny had switched guns so he was holding one that was fully loaded, and he held it ready. Matt had popped a freshly loaded cylinder into his own gun, and he stood by Johnny.

"So now," Matt said, "we still have two questions."

Johnny said, "Just who is it they're working for."

"And are there any more of them outside the canyon?"

Johnny and Goullie did a quick count, and they found there were fifty-two steers in the canyon, all of them bearing the Broken Spur brand.

Goullie said, "I don't really know what to make of it all."

They brought their horses in, and Matt had stretched out by the fire with his head on the saddle and his saddle blanket over him, and he and was out cold.

Goullie said, "We should get these cows back to the ranch. And these bodies. See what Coleman thinks about all of it."

Johnny nodded. "That should be the first order of business. But it's not."

He looked to Joe and said, "Do you mind standing guard up at the top of this little canyon? In case there are any more raiders out there who might be returning to camp?"

Joe shook his head. "I don't mind at all."

"One of us will come up and spell you in a couple of hours."

Goullie said, "I'll do it. Coleman has been riding you and Matt hard for the past few days. You both need more sleep than what you got last night."

Joe turned, and with his rifle in one hand, he started away for the edge of the canyon.

56

JOHNNY AND JOE WERE on horseback, descending the long, low grassy hill behind the ranch yard, and Johnny heard a man call out, "Riders comin'!"

Behind them came the herd. It didn't take many men to handle fifty-two beeves. Matt and Goullie had it under control. Matt had learned a lot about handling cattle in just two weeks. Goullie had wrapped a bandana around the scrape on his arm that he had gotten from a bullet.

Johnny was leading a small string of horses. Joe had another. Four of the horses were saddled, and the dead bodies of the outlaws were slung across them.

Johnny could see men running across the ranch yard to watch them coming in.

"Look at all the fuss they're makin'," Joe said.

"That's what you get when you do what we did," Johnny said.

There was no corral at the ranch large enough to hold fifty-two longhorns, but there was no need to. The range out beyond the ranch headquarters was open. Johnny looked back over his shoulder and called out, "Leave the herd out here!"

Goullie nodded, and he and Matt headed them off and scattered them.

Eight men had climbed the corral fences for a better view. Johnny saw Shelby and Chancey were there. Frenchie and Gates. Ciego came walking up, a heavy leather smithy apron tied around his middle. He had a big smile.

Johnny and Joe led the horses down the low hill and into the ranch yard, and the men let out whoops and cheers. Shelby was waving his hat in the air.

Ciego nodded and said, "Welcome home."

Johnny nodded back. "Good to be here."

Coleman was striding out from the main house, and he didn't look happy.

"O'Brien!" he called out.

Matt and Johnny both were answering to that name, but Johnny figured Coleman meant him.

Johnny reined up and said, "We've been in the saddle most of the day. Had a hard last couple of days."

"I don't care. You disobeyed orders and it's time you

learned who's boss around here. Get down from that horse."

Johnny handed the reins over to Joe, and swung out of the saddle.

The men were gathering around. Shelby was standing beside Joe's horse, and looked at him.

Joe said, "Watch this."

Shelby shook his head. He was clearly worried, but Joe had no doubt about how this fight was going to turn out. Joe figured Shelby would have a new way of looking at Coleman once Johnny was done with him.

Goullie and Matt came riding in.

Goullie said, "Mister Coleman, what's going on?"

"You're all fired. All four of you. After I get done with him."

Coleman was wearing a gun. Johnny's Colts were at his hips, and they were fully loaded.

Johnny said, "How do you want it? With guns, or fists?"

Coleman unbuckled his gunbelt and handed it to one of the men. "I'm gonna give you a beating you'll never forget."

He glanced about the men, then looked back at the house. Maria was standing on a second floor balcony.

"You sure you want her watching?" Johnny said.

"Might be good for her to see just what kind of man you are."

"Johnny," Matt said. "Are you sure you should be doing this?"

"Coleman has been asking for this." Johnny began to unbuckle his gunbelt.

But then something caught Johnny's attention off toward the main house. He said, "Mister Grant's coming."

The crowd parted to let Breaker Grant through. He was in a gray vaquero jacket and black pants. As always, a string tie was in place.

Grant was giving a wide smile, and he said, "Welcome back, men."

He extended his hand and Johnny grasped it.

Grant said, "You did good work, O'Brien. Did you get them all?"

"As near we can tell, sir."

Johnny's focus was on Grant, but he could see Coleman off to one side. It looked like Coleman was caught between being so angry he could bust and feeling a little embarrassed.

Johnny had little pity for Coleman, but Grant had actually made Coleman look small in front of the men. A man can't be a leader if he's made to look small. Johnny wondered if Grant realized what he had done.

Grant said, "Come on in to my office. I want you to tell me all about it."

Johnny looked down at his pants and his range shirt. They were covered with dust.

"Well, sir, we're just in from the trail."

"No matter. Come on."

Grant looked at his son. "Coleman, check those bodies for any kind of identification. See if the men recognize any of them. Then send a rider into town for the sheriff."

Grant and Johnny started for the house.

Coleman stood for a moment and said nothing, looking at the men. Then he said, "All right. Enough standing around. You all have work to do."

Matt and Joe were still in the saddle. As the men began dispersing, Coleman didn't go to the bodies draped over the saddles but instead strode away. Off toward the barn. Matt didn't know where he was going. Maybe Coleman needed to walk off his anger.

Matt said, "So, I don't know if this means we're still fired, or not."

Joe shrugged. "Either way, the old man kicked Coleman's legs right out from under him in front of the men. Don't know if he meant to do that or not, but life for us could get a whole lot harder if we stay on the payroll."

Matt nodded. "I don't think there's much that old man does without meaning to."

57

JOHNNY TOOK ONE of the chairs in front of Grant's desk, and he dropped his hat into a chair beside it.

"I hate to be the cause of trouble," Johnny said. "Your son Coleman ain't very happy with my brothers and me. Or Goullie. He's fired all four of us."

Grant was pouring a bourbon for himself and one for Johnny.

Grant said, "Nonsense. Coleman gets himself fired up sometimes, but you boys aren't fired. Not after what you did for my wife and then stopping those raiders. And Goullie's not fired, either. He's been here so long, he's almost a part of the ranch."

Grant held out one glass of bourbon, and Johnny reached forward to take it.

"When I was your age, I did things your way," Grant said. He sat back in the chair behind his desk. "I wasn't like you are with a gun. I haven't really known any who are. But I would have ridden after those raiders, just like you did. You're a man's man, O'Brien. The kind of man I would have ridden with, back in the old days."

Grant's eyes were alive with wonder. He said, "Tell me about it. The whole thing."

Johnny began with the two men he and Matt shot, and carried the story all the way to the small canyon up in the Nations and the shootout by the campfire.

Grant was nodding and grinning the whole time. "Just like the old days. Now, I don't so much own this ranch as it seems to own me. But back in the old days, I was like you and your brothers. On the back of a horse, doing the job that needed to be done. By any means necessary. There were others like me, back then. Nathan Shannon, for one, a little further south. Richard King. Charles Goodnight. Most of 'em are gone now. Or old men like me who sit behind a desk and think about times gone by."

"I've got to admit," Johnny said, "the size of this place still seems a little overwhelming to me. And this house."

Grant grinned. "A little more than what you expect from a ranch house, isn't it?"

Johnny nodded.

Grant said, "There's money to be made in cattle. It's

like gold. It just has to be delivered to the customer. Back twenty years ago, I was taking herds up the Shawnee Trail and then on to New Orleans, or St. Louis. Even brought a herd all the way to Chicago, once. That was a journey, let me tell you. But most of the money is made by delivering herds to the ports along the Gulf. Ship 'em by sea to cities along the east coast. Bought me a shipping line, that way I get more of the profit. I ship everything, not just cattle."

Johnny nodded. "And you've mentioned a couple of gold mines, and that tobacco plantation in Cuba."

Grant smiled. "There's a word. Diversify. That's what I've been doing. I guess it could be said I have something of a head for business. And yet, I was never happier than when I was a small-time rancher with a small herd. The first two years I was here, I didn't even have a house. Slept under the stars, or under a buckboard when it rained. Which it doesn't do much in this part of Texas."

Grant reached for the cigar box on his desk. "I'm in the mood for a cigar. You want one, O'Brien?"

"I sure wouldn't say no."

Once Johnny's cigar was smoldering in one hand, he said, "There's something I've got to tell you. Something we overheard those outlaws talking about, before the shooting started. We haven't told any of the men. We all agreed I should talk to you about it, first."

"I'm listening."

"They were referring to a man they were waiting for. A man they called their boss. Apparently he was paying them in Broken Spur cattle rather than cash, and they weren't happy about it. We waited there for a day after the shootout, but no one showed up."

"So," Grant said, holding his cigar in his hand and letting what Johnny was saying settle in. "You're saying a man here is working with them?"

Johnny shrugged. "I'm not really saying anything. I'm just telling you what we heard."

"Sounds pretty clear what they were saying, though, doesn't it?"

Johnny nodded. "It does seem to."

"We have a turncoat here."

"I don't see any other way. We all talked about it before we came back."

"What does Goullie think?"

"He said it has to be someone working here. But none of us can figure out who or even why. The cattle they stole, they can sell. There's ranching and farming going on in the Nations. Indians who are taking up the white-man ways. If any of them aren't too particular about the brands of the cattle, then there are small markets here and there. But nothing worth all of the risk that would come with stampeding a herd and trying to steal some cows. It just seems like a lot of risk for what wouldn't be a whole lot of money."

Grant took a draw from his cigar. His brow was furrowed with thought.

He said, "Do you think they were connected to the ones who tried to kidnap Maria?"

"No way of knowing. One of 'em was killed, and the others rode off. The one I shot in the arm rode away too, but I can't imagine he lived long. His arm was all torn up and he was bleeding bad."

Grant nodded and took another draw on his cigar. Johnny waited while Grant mulled it all over.

"All right," Grant said. "I'm open to suggestions."

"So far, except for you, only my brothers and me and Goullie know about it. Maybe we should keep it that way for a while."

"All right. Let's see if we can figure this out using the process of elimination. I know it's not you or your brothers behind it, because if it was, when you rescued Maria you would have been shooting up your own men."

Johnny nodded. "And I'm sure it's not Goullie, because he killed some of the men at that canyon. And he seemed as surprised as the rest of us."

"That means it's someone else. But I can't imagine who. Some of these men have been with me a long time. Shelby. Clancy. Ciego. And there's newer ones like Frenchie and Gates and Wheeler. A few others. I just can't imagine one of them turning on me."

"I'd rule Ciego out because of lack of opportunity."

Grant nodded.

Johnny said, "Matt's idea, and I agree, is we should just not say anything. Not let anyone else among the men know what's going on. Just keep watch. See if there are any more stampedes or any other kind of trouble. If there isn't, then we know the four we got in the canyon were the last of 'em. But watch for anything that doesn't seem right."

Grant nodded. "You and your brothers and Goullie can do that because you'll be right there among the men."

Johnny held one hand up in a stopping motion. "Goullie can do that. He's loyal to you all the way. But my brothers and I'll be riding on, as soon as we're paid."

Grant said, "I'd like you all to stay."

"Well," Johnny wasn't sure how much he should say. "There are reasons we have to be moving on."

Grant got to his feet and paced a bit, then he stopped in front of the window and looked down at the ranch yard below. "You and your brothers will be safe here. I guarantee it."

Johnny said nothing.

Grant turned to look at him. "I've got a confession. I know who you boys are. I did from the start. I rode with a Jake McCabe back in the Texas Rebellion, and I remember him well. Is he your father?"

Johnny was silent a moment. Grant knew. Johnny realized he shouldn't be surprised. He had the feeling there was little that got past this man.

Johnny said, "He's our uncle. Gave me my first brace of pistols. Taught me how to shoot."

Grant grinned and nodded. "I knew it. You have his look. I think your brother Joe would too, if he shaved off that wild-looking beard."

Johnny nodded. "Matt looks more like our ma's side. That's where we get the name O'Brien from."

Grant said, "I know about Missouri. There's a reward poster for you in town. But your secret's safe with me. All three of you will be safe here. I'd like it if this place could be a home to the three of you, for as long as you like."

"Well, that's very generous, Mister Grant."

Johnny was about to say he would talk it over with his brothers, but Grant cut him off.

Grant said, "I know you've been here only a short time, but you have shown real leadership. And the men fall into place behind you. They accept you as a leader as though it was the most natural thing on Earth. You're a man not unlike myself. I like to think I know people."

Grant drew some more smoke, and said, "I would like to offer you the job of ramrod."

Johnny's mouth fell open. He said, "I don't know quite

what to say."

"Then, say yes."

Johnny said, "What about Coleman?"

"I've raised Coleman as my son, and there'll always be a place for him. He knows business, but he doesn't know cattle or horses, or men. I've shown him all I can, but there's a certain aspect of leadership that you have to be born with. I believe you were.

"We've talked about the other operations I own, other than cattle. I've been trying to manage all of that while Coleman ran the ranch itself. I'm instead going to put Coleman in charge of the other businesses, but the cattle part of the operation will be yours to run. Then maybe what I'll do is retire. Take long rides during the day with my lovely Maria. What do you say?"

"Well, I do have to talk it over with my brothers. We had been planning on riding on."

"When can you give me your answer?"

"Maybe a couple hours."

"How about tonight, over dinner?"

Word on a ranch traveled fast. Faster than Johnny would have thought possible. Johnny was walking from the house back to the bunkhouse, intending to talk with Matt and Joe about Grant's offer, and he saw Ciego leading a horse from the corral to his anvil.

Ciego called out, "I just heard. That's great news."

As Johnny stepped into the bunkhouse, Frenchie was there and slapped him on the back and said, "I guess we gotta start callin' you Boss."

Goullie was pouring a cup of coffee. He said, "We all just heard. I can't think of a better man for the job."

Johnny said, "But you've been here so much longer. It seems like the job should go to you."

Goullie shook his head. "It's going to the right man. O'Brien, after what you showed out there on the range, I'd follow you anywhere."

58

JOHNNY HAD SAT for a while in a hot bath and had shaved, and now he stood in the doorway of Breaker Grant's office in a clean shirt and canvas pants.

"You're a little early for dinner," Grant said. "But come on in."

Johnny said, "My brothers will be here in a while. I just wanted to talk to you myself, first."

Grant motioned for Johnny to take one of the chairs in front of the desk.

Grant said, "Have you had a chance to talk with your brothers about my offer?"

Johnny nodded. "I have. And I'd like to accept. If you're really sure you want me."

"Absolutely, McCabe. You're the best choice for the job. I'll have to make a serious effort not to call you that, though. I'll have to remember it's O'Brien."

"Why don't you just call me Johnny?"

"Johnny it is, then. Tell you what. Now that you're here, how about we share a glass of bourbon?"

"One question," Johnny said, as Grant placed two glasses on his desk and filled them each with a couple of fingers of bourbon from a decanter. "What about Coleman? Does he know?"

Grant nodded. "I had a talk with him. Explained things to him."

"How'd he take it?"

Grant handed a glass to Johnny. "He wasn't happy. But he'll be all right. Sometimes, when running a business, you have to make a hard decision. I did. I'm sure he'll respect it."

Johnny had his doubts.

As they sat at the table and enjoyed a dinner of porterhouse steaks, frijoles and red wine, Coleman said little. When a joke was made, he would grin half-heartedly.

Maria was elegant in a green gown with a wide, lacy neckline, and her hair was all done up in some fancy fashion. It looked to Johnny like it was just all piled together on the top of her head, but knowing women, she had probably spent hours on it.

She was laughing and a couple of times raised her glass to Grant and called him, "My love." But there were times her eye would catch Johnny's and linger longer than Johnny was comfortable with.

After dinner they all moved to the parlor. A fire was burning low, even though it was mid-spring and Johnny didn't find the night cool enough to require a fire.

Maria was holding a glass of white wine in a way that struck Johnny as regal. Breaker Grant had a glass of bourbon and so did Johnny and Joe. Grant had offered brandy, which Matt had accepted. Even though Matt's suit and tie had been left behind in Pennsylvania, he managed to look somehow dapper in his range shirt. The top button was fastened, and his hair was neatly combed and he had shaved. He stood erect with one hand behind his back and a brandy snifter in the other hand, and he spoke in a way that made every word sound like it was weighted with thought.

Joe's beard was now so thick and long you couldn't even see the top button on his shirt. His hair was covering his collar in back and on the sides. He held to the edge of the small crowd, sipping his bourbon.

Joe was saying nothing, but Johnny thought Joe also missed nothing.

Coleman was also silent. Standing off to one side, he had a brandy snifter in one hand, and he seemed to be brooding.

Johnny had a cigar in one hand, and he set his drink on the mantel. He had left his guns at the bunkhouse. He thought they might be out of place at a fancy dinner like the ones served in this household. He had put on a clean shirt and shaved, and he buttoned his top button.

Grant started talking about cattle prices. He said, "Johnny, we're going to need a hundred head pushed on to Jefferson next week."

"I'll take care of it, sir."

Grant grinned. "I have no doubt."

Talk of cattle prices led to talk of politics, and Matt made a joke about northern Democrats that got Grant laughing.

Coleman strolled over to Johnny and said, keeping his voice low so only Johnny could hear, "You might think you've won, O'Brien. But you haven't. I guarantee you that."

Then Coleman walked away.

After dinner, when their guests had left and the house had quieted, Maria stepped out of her room. She was in slippers that were soft and quiet on the floorboards. Her gown had been replaced by a satin robe.

Breaker was sleeping quietly in their bed. She shut the door gently and started down the corridor.

The house had two sets of stairs. The grand staircase that began at the entryway and a back stairway that led down to the kitchen. It was the second set that she took.

She found Coleman in the kitchen. His jacket and tie were gone and his collar was unbuttoned. His vest was hanging open.

He said, "You're going to him, aren't you?"

"What I am doing is none of your business."

"I knew it. As soon as Mister Grant fired me as ramrod, you would no longer be in my arms."

"You always call him *Mister Grant*. You are his son. Why do you not call him *father*? I have always wondered."

Coleman turned away. "He's not my father. Yes, he adopted me, but I'm not his blood."

"I don't think that makes a difference to him."

Coleman began pacing. "Of course it does. A young orphan. My parents were killed by Comanches in a wagon train. I wasn't his. How could it not make a difference?"

She said, "Breaker has said more than once it's not blood that makes a family, but love. I believe him."

Coleman's pacing had taken him to an island in the center of the kitchen floor. A work station, with a wooden chopping block. The cook had left a butcher knife there, and he wrapped his fingers around the hilt and lifted it.

He said, "Well, it makes a difference to me."

He drove the knife down into the chopping block.

She said, "Maybe it shouldn't."

He shrugged.

"Breaker didn't fire you. He promoted you. You'll be overseeing the shipping business and the plantation. The gold mines out west, too. All Johnny will be overseeing is the cattle business."

Coleman looked over his shoulder at her. "*Johnny*, is it now?"

"You know as well as I that those other businesses account for easily three-quarters of the family income.

Breaker has been handling it, but now he is handing it to you. He is giving you quite a responsibility. But handling all of that with the cattle is just too much for one man."

Coleman shook his head. "He handled all of it at one time. *I* should be handling all of it. Not some wandering saddlebum gunfighter who made a lucky shot when you were stupid enough to let yourself be captured by banditos."

"That was no lucky shot. I have been around guns all of my life. He sighted in like he was fully confident in what he was doing. He sighted in with his pistol the way you do with a rifle. I had never seen such a thing before."

He walked toward her. He grabbed her by the chin, harder than she liked, and said, "And now you go to him instead of me?"

She pulled back, away from him. He let her go and said, "What's to keep me from telling the old man? He finds out, and you'll be out the door."

"If he finds out, I'll also tell him about you. Sampling the goods behind Breaker's back. You'll be out the door, too."

Coleman gave a sigh that left him looking a little deflated. She had made her point.

He said, "Go to him, if that's what you feel you have to do. But remember," he pushed past her and started for the stairway. "This place will be mine, one day. All of it. I have a plan."

"And what do you mean by that?"

He stopped at the foot of the stairs and looked back at her. "I have always had a plan, and that plan is in motion. With or without you."

She stood looking at him, waiting for more explanation. He smiled, apparently liking the look of uncertainty on her face.

He said, "Good night, Maria. Go enjoy your nighttime repast."

He turned and started up the stairs.

59

MATT AND JOE CLIMBED into their bunks. Grant had given Johnny a cigar for later, and Johnny thought he might smoke it now. He was bone-weary but somehow not sleepy. Too much on his mind, he supposed.

He buckled on his guns. It felt good to have them back in place. Then he stepped outside and lit the cigar.

One of his concerns was about Coleman Grant. The man was going to be trouble, and Johnny wanted as little trouble as possible. He wanted nothing that would draw attention to him and his brothers.

As long as only Breaker knew the truth, then Johnny wasn't concerned. Johnny thought Breaker was a man of his word. But if it became known that Johnny and his brothers were wanted men, Johnny doubted Breaker could protect them from the law. Breaker had a lot of money, and with money comes power, but even Breaker wasn't that powerful.

Another concern was Maria. All through the evening, she had given Johnny little smiles. She was discrete about it, but that didn't make it any less unsettling.

Riding out of here as soon as they were paid made sense. Yet, Breaker Grant had ridden a trail similar to Johnny's, and Johnny thought there was a lot he could learn from him.

Johnny strolled a bit while he let all of this roll around in his mind. He held the cigar in his left hand, so his right could be near his right-hand gun.

He thought about Ma and Luke. He hoped they were well. He figured they would probably be starting the spring planting soon. Luke still a boy but was stepping into the role of a man.

Johnny and his brothers had set out to find Pa's killer. They had been so determined. Or, at least, Johnny and Joe had been. Matt hadn't been sure they were doing the right thing. Now, all these months later, they had a price on their head. He wondered what Ma would think about what had happened back in Missouri. Would she be ashamed of her boys?

And he thought about Becky Drummond. Married to Trip by now. Maybe on their way to having their first child. Running the family store.

You never heard of something as drastic as murder in the little town of Sheffield, Pennsylvania. In the entire time Johnny had grown up on the farm, the only crime he had ever remembered hearing about was a cow that got stolen once.

Murder was fairly common in the south Texas border towns Johnny had been frequenting a year ago, though. In some of those towns, it wasn't unusual on a Saturday night to find a man face-down in an alley with a knife wound in his back. Johnny thought he had been leaving that behind when he returned home.

What was the word Matt had used for Sheffield? *Tranquil.* Another time he had called it *placid.* And yet a man with a gun had shot both Hector Drummond and Pa, and he had gotten away. There would be no trial. No conviction. No one even knew the name of the killer. Just like in those border towns.

Johnny's strolling brought him toward the barn, and he became aware of a touch of perfume on the night air. The breeze was working its way from the side of the barn toward him. He looked in that direction and saw Maria standing in the moonlight.

Her dress had been replaced by a robe that fell to her slippers. The robe looked gray but might have been a sky blue by day. Hard to tell in the moonlight.

"Miss Maria," Johnny said. "Didn't expect to find you out and about this time of night."

She walked toward him. "Or, is it that you didn't expect to find me alone this time of night?"

He didn't know what she was talking about, so he said nothing.

She said, "I know you saw us, that night. I know you saw Coleman and me outside, by the kitchen door. He didn't see you there, but I did."

Johnny hadn't realized either one of them had seen him. Now he felt a little embarrassed.

She said, "Coleman is no longer a factor."

She reached up and touched the side of his face. He had to admit, he liked her touch. She seemed to radiate sensuality, and Johnny figured a man could easily get lost in it.

But she was married.

He said, "How can you do this to Mister Grant?"

She let her hand slide away.

She said, "Breaker is an old man. Yes, he provides a beautiful home for me. But he is old and a time will come when he's no longer here. Probably quite soon. Where I am a young woman and have my whole life to live."

"So, you see a relationship with Coleman as a way of providing for your future."

"It sounds so cold when you say it that way." She turned and faced away, not in anger but as though she was turning away from the distaste of what he had said.

"How would you put it?"

She shrugged. "I suppose you have me on that."

She turned back to face him. "Breaker has long wanted a son to run this place when he's gone. He took Coleman in as an orphan and adopted him. But Coleman is not a strong man. Not the kind of man Breaker would feel comfortable running the family business. It's a sizable estate, you know. Much more than what you see here."

Johnny nodded. "He's talked to me of it."

"I am no fool. Breaker talks of love, but part of what he and I have is a thing of circumstance. He will leave part of the estate to Coleman, but he wants an heir to run the place. I come from good stock. My father runs a large ranch down in Victoria County. Vincente Carrera. But a child has not come."

Johnny didn't really know what to say. Matt could pull words out of the air and wax poetical about practically anything. But when Johnny didn't know what to say, he decided to follow Joe's way and just say nothing. He took another draw on his cigar and waited for Maria to continue.

She started walking a bit, and looked up at the night sky.

She said, "You are very quickly becoming like a son to Breaker. The son he wanted but never had. If you play your cards right, you can wind up inheriting part of this place. And running all of it."

Johnny blinked with surprise. He saw himself as nothing more than a former farm boy from Pennsylvania, who was too good with a gun and became a bit of a hell-raiser along the southern border. A young man who drank a little too much tequila and cavorted a little too much with border-town senoritas. Now Maria was talking about him as a future owner of a huge estate like this.

He had to admit, things were happening fast and making his head spin a little.

He didn't know what to say. But then he thought of what Pa had taught him. *Always speak honest and from the heart.* So that's what Johnny decided to do.

He said, "I'm not playing cards. I took the job Mister Grant offered because he seems to be a man something like myself. I think there's a lot I can learn from him. I have no hidden motives."

She said, "So much like Breaker. Like the way he probably was when he was younger. And like he still is, in so many ways."

She took a step toward him. "It's not that I don't love Breaker. I do. But just not in the way a woman is supposed to love her husband. He is so much older than I am. Almost old enough to be my grandfather. I am a young woman, and I want to love the way a young woman does."

She placed a hand alongside Johnny's face again. "And when he is gone, I will still be here. And so will you, if you want to be. We can raise children together right here. I am the sole heir of my father's ranch. Breaker will likely leave controlling interest in this place to you. That will make us one of the most powerful couples in all of Texas. The children we raise will be leaders of society. A governor. A senator. Who knows, maybe even a president."

Her hand felt good and her lips looked inviting. A lifetime of kissing his way down her neck every night was not something to turn away from lightly.

But his Pa had taught him that the journey is as important as the destination. And while in this case the destination might be mighty danged desirable, he didn't think the journey was something he could live with.

He reached up to her hand and removed it from his face.

He said, "You're an intelligent woman, Maria. You sound educated."

She nodded. "I attended the finest boarding schools. One in New York. Another in Madrid."

"You probably understand business as well as Mister Grant. Maybe even better. You strike me as capable. You don't need to throw yourself at a man. You can build your own future, yourself. From what you've said, you'll inherit your father's ranch. Mister Grant will likely leave you part of the estate. Half, if I'm not involved. You can take all of that and build a sizable future for yourself."

"This is a man's world. A woman cannot succeed without the right man at her side."

He shook his head. "Don't marry because it seems like the right business move. Don't throw yourself at a man because you think he might fit into a certain plan for the future. You don't really need a man, Maria. I believe you're capable enough to build the future you want, yourself. You're a lot stronger than you know."

Then he said, "I don't know of many men who could take two head-first tumbles from a saddle as well as you did."

She smiled.

He said, "Marry because of love. Not because of opportunity. Don't marry because you feel you need a man. Marry only if and when you find the right man."

"But it has to be a man who can stand at my side."

He nodded. "A man worthy of your love will be worthy of standing at your side."

"You don't think you're worthy?"

He shrugged. "I don't know. My life seems to be filled with uncertainty. People are seeing things in me that I didn't see myself, and it's giving me something to think about. But the timing isn't right for us. You're married, to a man I greatly admire. Maybe the love isn't what you wanted, but marriage is an institution you have to take seriously. When the timing is right, you'll find the right man. Or he'll find you."

Johnny realized the mouthful he had just said.

He said, "I'm starting to sound like my brother Matt."

She gave a chuckle. He did, too.

She said, "I've never met a man like you before."

"Yes you have. You've said it yourself."

"Breaker."

"Maybe if the ages were right, he could have been the right man to stand at your side. You never know. But even with the ages not being right, you can still have a few years with him."

"You've given me a lot to think about, Johnny McCabe."

He blinked with surprise. Not the first time tonight. "You know?"

She smiled. "There's not much that goes on in this

household that I don't know about. But don't worry. Your secret is safe with me. Coleman will never know. I don't think even Breaker knows that I know."

Johnny said, "You have been with Coleman."

She cast her eyes downward. "Yes."

"Are you in love with him?"

She looked up at him again. "I thought I was. I'm young, I'm beginning to realize. Making foolish mistakes. He swept me off my feet. Maybe I knew what he was doing, and I let him. But I have been realizing more and more, in recent weeks, it isn't really love."

"Well, then your secret will be safe with me."

"Thank you. Breaker would never understand."

"I guess we both have a lot to think about."

She said, "I think it's time I went inside. I think I'm finding that I want to go be with my husband."

"You do that."

She turned and started away. Then she looked back at him and said, "Thank you."

He nodded.

She planted a light kiss on his cheek, and he watched her walk away.

He stood alone in the moonlight and took another draw from his cigar.

60

SPRINGTIME PASSED, and the full force of a Texas summer descended on the Broken Spur.

Early in the summer, Johnny led another small cattle drive to the town of Jefferson. Then he took another two hundred head to Fort Belknap. Later in the summer, he put Goullie in charge of taking fifty head to a small Army post by the name of Camp Colorado, within riding distance of the Colorado River.

The trick to business, Johnny was learning, was to keep the cost of doing business low. Breaker Grant called it *low overhead*. If the cost of doing business is low, then even if the prices aren't high, there will be at least moderate profit. When it came to cattle, this meant delivering a herd that wasn't too thin or distressed from trail conditions.

Breaker Grant talked, and Johnny listened. Often in the evening, with a cigar in one hand and a glass of bourbon in front of him, Breaker would ramble on about various cattle drives he had conducted over the years. Once he had taken a thousand head to New Orleans. And he talked about the cattle drive to Chicago. He drove smaller herds to Sedalia, and he sold a lot of cattle to various army posts.

Breaker would talk cattle. Raising them. What was good grass and what wasn't. He would talk how to find water in Texas in the spring and how to find it in the fall, which is not necessarily the same thing. He talked about what would happen when it rained hard and the Red flooded. Apparently it could become a mile wide if it flooded enough.

Johnny also listened when Goullie talked. Shelby and Clancy had experience with cattle, too. Not all of them agreed on the best methods, but he listened to it all and then used his common sense to decide which way he thought was best.

Johnny found part of the cattle business was negotiating the right price. If you started a little high, the buyer would start low, and you'd settle somewhere in the middle, which was the place both parties were shooting for in the first place. Not much different than Pa dickering over the price of his crop, back in the old days.

Coleman was hardly seen all summer, and Johnny found Coleman's absence quite pleasant.

A few days after Johnny's talk with Maria out by the

barn, Coleman hopped a stern-wheeler that took him down the Red to Jefferson. Somewhere during the summer, he took a few weeks to visit the tobacco plantation in Cuba.

Coleman had also talked Breaker into letting him buy into a shipping outfit based in Corpus Christi. It was showing that Coleman had a head for business, and Johnny thought he saw pride in Breaker's eyes when the old man talked about it.

Johnny had dinner with Breaker and Maria a few times, and he found the atmosphere about the house much more relaxed without Coleman there.

Maria no longer slipped discreet smiles to Johnny. Her attention now seemed to be on Breaker. One time, as she and Breaker were sitting on the sofa in front of the fire, and Johnny was standing by the hearth and talking with Breaker about ranch business, Maria reached over and laid a hand across Breaker's hand and gave him a smile. Johnny found that right nice.

Then summer began to fade toward fall.

Fall roundup was a week away when Johnny and his brothers rode into Clarkston. Johnny knew roundup was going to be long, hard work, and he wanted the men to rest up a bit beforehand. He even moved payday up two weeks so they could have some jingle in their pockets while they rested.

Johnny now had a waist-length gaucho jacket. It was gray colored, because Johnny thought neutral colors would blend into the Texas countryside better. He might now be the ramrod of a Texas ranch, but he had been a Texas Ranger and had been shot at by Comanches and Kiowas and Mexican Border raiders more than once. He still found himself watching the terrain for snipers or riders, and the thought of wearing colors that were too light or dark, colors that would have stood out starkly against the Texas countryside, made him a little jittery.

He was in brown vaquero pants with silver conchos running down the side of each leg, and his Colt .44s were at his hips.

When Matt had first seen Johnny's vaquero pants, he had said, "Why, aren't you becoming the new face of Texas fashion."

Johnny had ignored him. He had seen pants like this worn in the border country and he thought they looked stylish. He was being paid thirty dollars a month now, more than twice what a cowhand could expect, so why not spend a little of it?

They swung out of the saddle in front of the saloon. Joe looked like he usually did. A dusty range shirt and canvas pants. He wore his buckskin sheath at his right side, and in the sheath was his big knife. His pistol was never holstered, but tucked into the front of his knife belt. Johnny had learned not to ask a man about the way he carries a gun or knife. Every man had his preference.

Johnny and Matt had trimmed their hair recently, and were freshly shaven for their night on the town. Joe hadn't cut his hair since Pennsylvania, and it was now touching his shoulders. His beard was long enough to touch his collar bone.

Matt said, "You look like a mountain man."

Joe said, "Then I guess I look like what I am."

Matt was in a white shirt and a black string tie. He had replaced his navy cap with a new black hat that had a flat crown and a flat, stiffly blocked brim. What they called a Boss of the Plains hat. He was wearing his Navy Colt in a holster he had bought from an old Mexican man. The belt and holster were engraved with lots of swirls and had a few conchos here and there. Matt had spent some of his money, too.

Matt no longer bounced in the saddle when he rode. He now moved like he and the horse were one. Maybe not quite as natural as Johnny and Joe looked on a horse, but he was getting there.

Once they were in the saloon, Joe bellied-up to the bar and ordered a bottle of beer. Miller, all the way from Milwaukee. The bartender was an older gent with no hair at the top of his head, and the hair at the sides was white and thick and bushy. He pulled the cork and handed the bottle to Joe.

Joe's knee had healed to the point that he no longer limped at all when he walked, and he could climb up into the saddle with ease.

Johnny said to the bartender, "Do you have tequila here?"

The bartender said, "Of course, boy. This is Texas."

Johnny grinned at Matt. "Then you know what I'll be having."

In one corner was a table, and a card game was in progress. Clancy and Shelby were there, and two other men Johnny didn't recognize. Cowhands, by the look of them.

Johnny had a glass of tequila in one hand. "I think I'll go join that game."

Matt nodded. He also had a glass of tequila. "I think I'll go find a quiet corner and maybe start writing a letter to Ma."

Johnny nodded. "When it comes to letter-writing, you're probably the one for the job."

Johnny stood by the table watching the game. Clancy and the two Johnny didn't know folded, and Shelby had increased his wealth by two dollars.

"Mind if I set in?" Johnny asked.

"Not at all, Boss," Shelby said. "Pull up a chair."

The two men Johnny didn't know were introduced as Caleb and Pike. Cowhands for a small ranch called the Bar 20. They were both about Goullie's age.

Johnny was handed the deck, and he began shuffling. "All right, men, the game is five card draw. Nothing wild. Ante up."

Pike said, "Is it true, what I heard? Coleman Grant is back in town?"

Clancy nodded, and looked to Johnny.

Johnny was dealing out the cards. He said, "I just found out this morning. He'll be staying for a few days and then he'll be going back to his office in Jefferson."

Clancy said, "Not a moment too soon, if you ask me."

Matt took an empty table in one corner. He reached into a vest pocket and brought out a small bottle of ink and a pen, and two sheets of paper folded together. He unfolded the paper on the table and opened the bottle of ink.

Now, how to begin? He and Johnny had talked about it on the ride into town. There was a lot to tell Ma and Luke about, but a lot they didn't want to tell them, as well. Words usually came easy to Matt, but not this time.

Dear Ma and Luke,

That part was easy. Now for the rest of it. He took a belt of tequila.

He glanced at the card game. One man shook his head and folded. Shelby said, "I'll raise you fifty cents."

Matt put the pen to the paper again.

How are you both? I hope you are fine.

Johnny, Joe and I are in Texas. We long ago lost the

trail we were following, and we settled in to work on the Broken Spur ranch seven months ago. We're becoming real cowboys. I am becoming more accustomed to the bouncing and rolling motion of a horse, and I am becoming quite handy with a lariat. Some of the men joke that they are going to introduce me to bronco busting, but I have not yet worked up the courage or the foolishness to try it.

Matt stopped and took another belt of tequila.

Johnny had taken the first pot, and Shelby was now shuffling the deck.

We all seem to be well-liked here, especially Johnny. The natural leadership qualities he has always seemed to possess are manifesting themselves even more here. He has been given the job of ramrod, which means he's the boss. He has a natural way with men, who seem to want to follow him without even being asked to. Some people simply have the gift. I think Pa did, and Johnny does, too.

Matt grabbed his glass and walked across the room to Joe.

"How's the letter-writin' goin'?" Joe said.

Matt shook his head. The bartender was down at the other end of the bar, so Matt felt free to talk. "There's so much I want to say, but there's so much we can't say. Like Missouri. And that Thad rode on and we have no idea where he is. Or that it was Thad who killed that marshal. What would Ma think? What would Uncle Jake and Aunt Sara think?"

"I wonder where Thad is now?"

Matt shook his head. "As long as he's not here, I'll be happy."

"Just thought of another problem, too."

"What's that?"

"How do we give them a return address? If you use the name O'Brien on the letter, then you'll have to explain why. And you cain't use our real names."

Matt placed his elbows on the bar and hung his head. "I hadn't thought of that."

There were cheers from the card table. Joe looked over his shoulder at them, and Joe said, "Looks like Johnny just won another pot. There's a small crowd gatherin' around the table."

Matt looked over. Five men were standing with bottles of beer in their hands, watching the game.

More cowhands were coming in. Mostly men from the Broken Spur. They had been paid early and were determined to burn up that money before spring roundup began.

Matt went back to his table. The ink had dried on the letter so he folded up the two sheets of paper and tucked them into one vest pocket, and then he tucked the bottle of ink and the pen in another. He would work on writing the letter later.

He went over to the card game to watch.

Johnny had just won seventeen dollars. More than most cowhands made in a month.

"Hey, Matt," Shelby said. "Want to join the game?"

Matt shook his head. "Thank you kindly, but chess has always been my game."

It was Clancy's turn to shuffle. He was grinning at Johnny as he split the deck. "No one can be that lucky twice in a row."

"What'd he have?" Matt said to one of the men watching the game. A man called Tanner.

Tanner said, "A full house."

Matt shook his head. "Johnny always was lucky."

"I'm not lucky," Johnny said from the table. "Just good."

"Yeah, yeah," Shelby said. "Let's see just how good you can be two times in a row."

Matt worked his way around so he was standing behind Johnny and could see his cards.

"If I lose this time, I'll be out of the game," Clancy said. "I'm going to have to save *some* cash to get me through to the next payday."

Johnny grinned. "I'll try to go easy on you."

Shelby said, "You can't draw a full house two times in a row."

"A good poker player doesn't need luck to win."

Matt grinned. He understood poker wasn't just about how well you played a poor hand, it was how well you played a good hand. A metaphor for life, he thought.

Matt's problem with poker was he had a terrible poker face. It took nerves of steel to draw something like a full house and not flinch or in any way react like you had just drawn a hand that couldn't be beat.

Clancy dealt the cards. "All right, gentlemen. Five card draw. Nothing wild."

Johnny picked up his hand and Matt was able to catch a glimpse. The eight of diamonds and four deuces. *Four.*

Matt took a gulp of the tequila in an attempt not to let his eyes pop open at the sight of the four deuces. He had seen a little poker played aboard ship and in seaport saloons and had played some himself. He had played countless rounds of gin rummy with Ma and Aunt Sara over the years. He had never seen anyone ever draw four deuces.

Johnny didn't flinch. Didn't react. Just looked at the cards. He glanced at the other players. Clancy was rubbing his chin with a motion that said, *Okay, now what do I do?* Pike was shaking his head. Shelby was looking at his cards and scratching his head. Caleb didn't react.

The only way Johnny would make any money with this hand would be if he could keep the betting going for a while.

"I'm out," Shelby said, and slapped his cards on the table, face down.

Johnny started the betting, keeping it low. Five cents. The price of a beer. Clancy matched it. Pike and Caleb did, too.

Clancy drew two cards. Pike and Caleb folded. Johnny tossed down the eight of diamonds.

Clancy looked at him long and hard. Matt knew what Clancy had to be thinking. *Is your hand really that good, or are you bluffing?*

Clancy put down a silver dollar and called. Johnny put down a dollar and then raised another dollar. Clancy matched the dollar and called, and Johnny put down a dollar and raised one more.

"I've gotta see what's in your hand," Clancy said. "But if I do, then I won't have anything left until next payday."

Shelby said, "Don't do it, Clancy. Ain't worth it."

Johnny said, "What about that rifle of yours? That Hawken?"

"My old rifle?"

"Sure."

Shelby said, "Clancy..."

"All right," Clancy said. "I'll wager the rifle and what I've put in this pot against your hand. I'm thinking about getting a new rifle, anyway."

"All right," Johnny said.

Matt had never known Johnny to have much of a flair

for the dramatic, but Johnny had some tequila in him and didn't want to waste an opportunity.

He laid down one deuce. No one said anything. He laid down a second one.

Pike said, "We folded for a pair of deuces?"

Clancy shook his head. "I gave my rifle away for that?"

Johnny set down the third deuce. A load of whoops went up. Matt looked around to see there were now close to twenty men watching the game. The stage driver was there, a couple of drifters, and the rest were cowhands.

"Brace yourself," Johnny said to Clancy and set the fourth one down.

There were gasps. Then cheers and whoops and Johnny was getting slapped on the back. Cries of, "Four deuces!" and "Never seen such a thing!"

Clancy smiled. "Well, I would hate to think I gave up that rifle for two deuces."

"You can keep the rifle," Johnny said.

Clancy shook his head. "No, sir. A bet's a bet."

Pike said, "I've never seen such a run of luck."

"Neither have I."

Matt looked over at the man who had spoken. It was Coleman Grant, leaning his back against the bar. Matt hadn't seen him come into the saloon.

The group of men stepped away, giving Johnny a clear view of Coleman.

Johnny said, "What's that supposed to mean?"

"You know what that means. No man can have two hands like that without helping it along some."

"Are you calling me a cheat?" Johnny said.

"What are you, stupid?"

"Just wanted to clarify." Johnny rose to his feet. "I wanted to make sure, before I drive those words back down your throat."

Coleman stepped away from the bar. "Better men than you have tried, and failed."

Clancy said, "Careful, Johnny. He killed a man with his fists last year."

"He's not going to kill anyone tonight."

Joe was still at the bar. He said, "Don't do it, Coleman. My brother is a wildcat. I don't believe there's a man alive what can take him down with his fists."

"Your brother is about to be a dead man. I'm going to

beat him until there's no more life in him. He has it coming, for more than one reason."

Matt didn't like this. He knew Ma would want him to try to stop it. But one thing Matt had learned about living in the West-a man had to have his honor, or he was worth nothing. If a man's accused of dishonesty and doesn't answer the charge, then his honor is as good as gone.

Joe took his beer and stepped to the end of the bar.

The bartender said, "I'll put five dollars on Coleman Grant."

Joe shook his head. "It wouldn't be fair. I'd feel like I was stealing your money."

Johnny said to Coleman, "With or without guns. How do you want to go down?"

"It'll be you going down, O'Brien. But it'll be my game. Fists."

Johnny grinned. He unbuckled his gunbelt and handed it to Matt. Coleman was wearing a gun, and he drew it and placed it on the bar. Coleman was wearing his gray jacket with the odd French buttons, and he shouldered out of the jacket and dropped it onto the bar with his guns.

This is not good, Matt thought. This could get bloody. Matt knew by Johnny's grin that he was as mad as all get-out. Johnny had Ma's temper. Ma always had a way of grinning right before she exploded.

A man stepped into the saloon, with a badge pinned to his vest. His hair was white and he had a thick, white mustache. Matt had seen older men who were still tough as nails, and this man had the look about him. Must be Harris Newcomb, the county sheriff. Matt had heard the sheriff and Breaker Grant were old friends.

Matt figured the sheriff was going to stop the fight, but instead the sheriff folded his arms and leaned one shoulder against the door jamb.

Coleman and Johnny began circling each other, like two wild animals looking for an opening.

61

COLEMAN CAME IN fast, swinging with his left. Johnny ducked, and he sidestepped so Coleman's momentum brought him a little past him.

Johnny then drove a hard right up and into Coleman's floating ribs, and then he pulled away so he would be out of range should Coleman attempt a counter punch. Coleman grunted with the punch and hesitated a moment. Johnny's fist had found home, and he knew a punch to the floating ribs can hurt.

Johnny stepped around behind Coleman, so Coleman turned to face him.

Johnny had heard the stories of Coleman's previous fights. Johnny was seeing now, by Coleman's footwork, that he had picked up some fight training somewhere along the way. Apparently Coleman didn't win his previous brawls on brute strength alone. Even now, he was placing his feet like a boxer, with the left a little forward and the right a little back. Holding his fists up and his elbows in tight.

But Johnny knew something of boxing, too. His father had taught him and his brothers how to fight when they were growing up. Pa had hung a grain bag from a barn timber, a bag filled with a mixture of straw and sand. He showed them how to place their feet, and how to turn their body into a punch. Keep the elbows in close and the fists up.

It was said the first man in the family to come to the New World, a mysterious man by the name of Peter McCabe, had been a trained fighter of sorts. Much of the fighting skills Pa taught Johnny and his brothers had been passed down through the family.

And Johnny remembered what he had learned from the Chinese man he told Matt about.

Johnny remained loose on his feet, but he kept his feet side-by-side, a shoulder's width apart. Something he had learned from the Chinese man. Coleman's footwork set him up so he could move to the front or rear. Johnny would counter with side-to-side action.

Coleman attacked again, feigning with his right fist and then driving out his left in a hard jab.

But Johnny was stepping fast off to his left, and as he moved, he shot a right-hand jab at Coleman's right ear.

Coleman flinched. Johnny was sure that had to hurt.

After two failed attempts at attacking, Coleman had apparently learned his lesson. He began circling Johnny again, but this time holding back on the attacks.

Johnny's Pa had said always watch a man's eyes because his eyes will betray his move before he makes it. However, also be aware of what his feet are doing, because every move he makes begins with his feet.

Coleman jabbed and Johnny ducked. Johnny jabbed and Coleman raised a hand to deflect it.

Joe looked at the bartender and said, "Still want to make that bet?"

The bartender shook his head. "No one's ever lasted this long with Coleman."

The old Chinese man had said to Johnny, "Never fight with anger. If you are angry when you fight, then you give the advantage to your opponent."

Because of this, Johnny was trying to cool his anger and simply focus on defeating his opponent. Trying not to think about Coleman calling him a cheat and Coleman cheating on Breaker Grant with Grant's own wife. But it wouldn't hurt to try to get Coleman a little mad.

Coleman was already seething with anger. He felt Johnny was taking his place as the heir to the Broken Spur and its related businesses. But it wasn't enough.

Johnny said, "Come on, Cole-boy. Is that all you got?"

"Don't call me that," Coleman said, and lunged at him.

Johnny side-stepped again, and Coleman slammed into the bar. He caught himself with his arms and managed to avoid hitting his head.

Johnny stepped in fast and quick and sent an uppercutting punch into Coleman's floating ribs again. Pa had said your ribs just above your kidneys are some of the most sensitive areas to strike.

Coleman grunted with pain and hesitated. Johnny could have ended the fight right there, but instead he stepped back.

Johnny had to admit, he was still feeling a little anger. He didn't want to just beat Coleman, he wanted to beat him in a way that sent him a message.

Coleman got to his feet. He staggered a moment then got his footing.

"Come on, Cole-boy," Johnny said. "You're nothing but

a pretender. You have the name Grant, but is it really yours? No one here thinks so."

Coleman lunged hard at Johnny. Harder and faster than Johnny would have thought possible, considering the punches Johnny had given him. Johnny realized maybe he had gone too far in taunting him.

Coleman launched a punch that Johnny was unable to duck. His fist caught Johnny on the cheekbone. Johnny's vision went dark for a moment, and his knees almost buckled.

Coleman's hands shot out and wrapped around Johnny's throat. For a man who managed from behind a desk and never seemed to do any actual physical work, he was strong.

Johnny remembered what the old Chinese man had taught him. Don't meet force with force. Meet force with emptiness.

Johnny stepped back and also turned his body, weakening Coleman's grip on him. Johnny then brought his hands upward through the loop in Coleman's arms, and the grip was broken.

Johnny bent his right arm and drove his elbow into Coleman's face. It caught Coleman on the nose, and Coleman staggered back, bringing his hands to his face. Blood streamed down over his mouth and chin.

Johnny then stepped in, his feet apart, and drove two uppercuts into Coleman's midsection, turning his body and grunting with each punch.

Coleman staggered back a couple of more steps. He was now bending over from the punches and had moved his hands away from his face. Blood was streaming from his chin down to his shirt.

Now that Coleman's face was open, Johnny shot a hard left jab to Coleman's right cheekbone and then a right cross that caught Coleman on the other cheekbone. Coleman's knees folded and he was down.

Johnny stood, waiting to see if Coleman was going to get back up. His own cheekbone was now numb from the punch he had taken. The right cross he had given Coleman had hurt his fist, and he was shaking his hand in the air, trying to shake off the pain.

There's a way to punch, Pa had said. Tighten the fist on impact, and make sure your finger joints don't make contact with your target. Also try to center the punch on your middle knuckles. But you can't always maintain proper form in the heat of a fight, and Johnny's smallest knuckle and finger had taken part of the contact with Coleman's face.

Coleman got to his knees, but then he fell back over. He was done.

The men in the saloon raised their voices in cheers and hoots.

The bartender said, "Well, I never thought I'd see it. The mighty Coleman Grant, beaten. Drinks on the house!"

Matt was still standing at the far end of the bar with Joe, and he watched Sheriff Newcomb give a little smile and step back out into the street.

62

BREAKER GRANT SAID, "You don't look too worse for wear."

Johnny had to admit, his neck was still a little sore from where Coleman had tried to choke him, and his fists were a little sore from the pounding they had taken against Coleman's face. A big bruise had risen on his cheekbone.

Johnny said, "I got lucky."

Grant shook his head. "From what I understand, it was pure skill."

Johnny's head was a little sore, too, but it wasn't from the fight. It was from too much tequila after the fight.

And now Clancy's Hawken rifle was on a couple of pegs in the wall by Johnny's bunk. Johnny had said again that Clancy could keep the rifle, but Clancy said, "No, I keep my word."

So Johnny gave Clancy the Colt revolving rifle. "A man doesn't need two rifles," Johnny had said.

Breaker Grant was at his desk, with a glass of bourbon in front of him. Johnny was in one of the chairs in front of the desk, and he had a glass in one hand.

Johnny didn't think it was going to be good, when Grant asked to see him. It was the morning after the fight, and Johnny was sure Grant wouldn't be pleased. But to Johnny's surprise, Grant offered him a drink.

Johnny said, "I feel a little bad about the fight. After all, Coleman *is* your son."

Grant nodded. "I appreciate that. But he had it coming."

Grant knocked back a belt of bourbon. "I adopted Coleman when he was young. Tried to treat him like he was my own. Trouble was, I never had a son before, and my own father wasn't much of a father. I take a lot of the responsibility for the way Coleman is. I know he's a bully and a braggart. I was hoping maybe serving as the ramrod of the ranch would be good for him. Teach him responsibility. But it didn't. He's had it in for you since you first arrived. I suppose I should have known it would come down to a fight."

"Why does he hate me?"

Grant said, "You're the man I've always wanted him to be. And you seem to do it without any effort."

Johnny shrugged. "Just being the man I was raised to

be, I suppose."

Johnny took a drink of bourbon. "So, how is Coleman doing this morning?"

"As well as can be expected. I've had the doctor out to see him. Coleman has a broken nose, and maybe some cracked ribs."

"I shouldn't have hurt him that bad."

Grant dismissed the notion with a shake of his head. "From what I've been told, he had his hands around your throat. He's already killed one man in a fight. You did what you had to do. What I would have done in your place. In fact, I might have gone even rougher on him."

Johnny nodded.

Grant said, "Coleman's gonna rest up here for a couple of days then catch a boat back to Jefferson. Nothing's changed. He's going to continue running the shipping and tobacco side of the family business and the gold mines, and you'll keep running the ranch."

Johnny gave a little grin. "And you'll keep enjoying your retirement. As it should be."

Grant returned the grin. "You couldn't be more right. This afternoon, I'm going riding with my lovely Maria. A leisurely ride around the ranch. We should be safe, since those banditos have been taken care of. Again, thanks to you."

Coleman was in his room, sitting in a rocker. But he wasn't doing much rocking, because the motion made his ribs hurt.

The doctor had wanted to put a heavy bandage on Coleman's nose and hold the bandage in place with a strip of torn bedsheet wrapped around his head. But Coleman would not have it. He figured he was already the laughing stock of the ranch. A ranch he had run with an iron fist. So his nose was unbandaged. But he couldn't breathe through it, and it was swollen and almost black. The bruising had spread to one eye, and both lids had gone nearly black.

He was in a smoking jacket and had not bothered with a tie this morning. In one hand was a glass of rye. His father preferred bourbon, and Coleman drank it when the old man offered. Another of Coleman's many attempts to win his approval. But on his own, he drank rye.

His door was shut. He didn't want visitors. He wanted

to be left alone. But regardless of his wishes, someone knocked.

"What?" he called out and then wished he hadn't. The vibrations of his voice made his nose hurt.

The door opened. It was Maria. She said, "I was just checking on you."

"So now you want to come back to me?"

She shook her head. She said, "No. Those days are long over. I was just checking to make sure you were all right."

"What do you care? Your man humiliated me last night. I'm sure you're laughing at me, just like everyone else is."

"From what I understand, you tried to kill him. And he's not my man."

Coleman tried to cock a brow at her in contempt and surprise, but the very motion hurt his nose.

He said, "You expect me to believe you're not with him?"

"I'm with my husband."

Coleman gave a scoffing chuckle and looked away. He took another drink of scotch.

He said, "You'll always need a man to cling to, Maria. You know why? You're weak. You always pick the strongest buck in the herd and throw yourself at him. I know you're with O'Brien. And you will be until someone stronger comes along. And one will. One always does, sooner or later."

She said, "You're pathetic."

He looked back at her. "That's rich. *You* calling someone pathetic. You might think O'Brien will inherit part of this ranch when the old man finally does the world a favor and kicks off. But O'Brien won't get one square foot of this ranch. I guarantee you that."

"What do you mean?"

Coleman decided he had already said too much. So he said, "Will you please just leave me alone? In two days I'll be back to Jefferson. Then I won't have to look at you or anyone else from this place."

She gave him a long look. He didn't know if she was feeling anger or pity or what, but he didn't really care.

She shut the door and was gone.

He shook his head with disgust at the very thought of her. It didn't occur to him for a moment that she wasn't bedding O'Brien behind the old man's back. And she was doing it because she thought O'Brien was successfully weaseling himself into the old man's will. But Coleman wasn't going to allow it. There was a plan in motion. In fact, it had been in motion before the O'Brien brothers even arrived.

The first version of the plan had been fool-proof. Maria was to be captured by the men camping in the canyon, off in the Oachita Mountains. The old man would have gone riding after her himself. And he would not have lived through it. Coleman had planned to attend to it personally, if need be. But then the O'Briens came along and Johnny made a trick shot with a pistol that saved Maria. And now he was weaseling his way into the old man's good graces and Maria's bed.

But Coleman was not giving up on his plan. He was now going to have to modify things a little, that was all.

But first he was going to have to do some investigating. Or at least, have someone do some investigating for him. One of the constables down in Jefferson had worked for the Texas Rangers at one point, and Coleman had become a drinking buddy of his. Coleman felt it made sense to become friendly with people in key positions. Not necessarily the obvious key positions, but ones he might have use for somewhere down the road.

It seemed to Coleman that if Johnny O'Brien had indeed made the shot Maria claimed he did when O'Brien rescued her, then he had uncommon skill with a pistol. Men with uncommon shooting skills tended to be known. Since Coleman had never heard the name Johnny O'Brien until the three brothers rode onto the ranch, he figured O'Brien was not their real name. He wondered if his former Texas Ranger friend could do a little investigating for him.

Coleman smiled, but found smiling hurt. He took another drink of scotch.

63

WINTER CAME ON, but it wasn't the same as winter in Pennsylvania. Johnny woke up to a dusting of snow a couple of times, but it was gone before the day was done. But that didn't mean the wind wasn't cold.

He was wearing Pa's coat one morning as he stepped from the bunkhouse. The sun hadn't been long in the sky, and the wind had a bite to it.

A thin layer of ice had formed over a water trough. He reached down with one hand and gave the ice a push, and the ice cracked and broke apart. Easier for horses to drink if they don't have to push their muzzles through ice.

It had been about a year since Pa had been killed, Johnny thought. A year that had seen a lot of change. Ma and Luke must have long since harvested the crop, and he hoped they got a good price. He imagined them hunkering down by the fireplace in the evening, with the cold winter winds blowing outside and the snow piling up.

And he thought of Becky Drummond. First time in a while. She was probably a mother now. He hoped she and Trip were happy.

A horse was saddled down by the main house, so Johnny walked on over. Breaker Grant came out.

"Ah, Johnny," he said. "A good morning to you."

Johnny said, "Going riding, sir?"

Grant nodded. "It's too cold for Maria to join me, but I find there's nothing like a crisp morning ride across the Texas prairie. Care to join me?"

Johnny shook his head. "I'd like to, but there's work to be done."

Grant swung into the saddle. "You're a good man, Johnny. Carry on."

"Yes, sir."

A good man, Johnny thought, as he stood and watched Grant ride away. Grant's praise meant much to him.

Johnny had been running the ranch for eight months, and he was learning about leadership. Learning you can't manage each man the same way and get good results. Some men needed to be barked at, and others need to be spoken to a little more kindly. You needed to ask them to do a job instead of outright telling them. And sometimes it was simply about staying out of the way and letting your crew do the job they knew how to do.

One thing that always bothered Johnny was he had been unable to figure out which man on the crew had been working with the raiders the previous spring. Assisting them in rustling steers and apparently in the kidnap attempt on Miss Maria. The attacks ended after the shootout in the canyon up in the Nations, so it all seemed to be forgotten. Or, at the very least, pushed aside for now.

Coleman Grant had gone on to Jefferson a couple of days after his fight with Johnny. The fight was starting to fade into the category of ancient history, too. Coleman was seldom mentioned, and the men didn't talk about the fight anymore.

Johnny decided to take a ride out to the far southern range. Eight hundred head were there. Winter grass wasn't as good as summer grass, and he wanted to check on them. They were checked on regularly—Shelby and Frenchie had gone out a few days ago. But Johnny was a hands-on ramrod and wanted to see the cows himself.

He headed for the stables to throw a saddle on Bravo.

By mid-morning, the winter chill had worn off, and Johnny had tied Pa's coat behind his saddle. He was wearing a vest where he kept his wallet and a couple of Mister Grant's cigars. Over his pants were strapped a pair of leather leggings that Ciego referred to as *Armitas*, but Goullie and the other cowhands called them *chaps*.

"Didn't have 'em when I was young," Breaker Grant had said. "The Texas brush would rip the dickens out of our pants. Then the vaqueros started wearing these chaps, and the idea caught on."

Johnny rode easily. Mister Grant was right—a leisurely ride across the Texas grass country was nice on a winter morning.

The sun was warm on his shoulders, but there was a solid mass of clouds off to the northwest. If it had been Pennsylvania, Johnny would have thought snow was coming tonight. But being Texas, Johnny figured it would be a cold winter rain. He intended to be back at the ranch before the rain struck, with the wood stove roaring and a cup of hot coffee in his hand.

But for now, he was going to ride.

He didn't know what it was that made him turn in the saddle. A sound, maybe. Or just a feeling that there was motion behind him.

He twisted around to see behind him, and he saw Joe, riding hard.

Joe reined up beside him.

"It's Mister Grant," Joe said. "He's been shot."

Johnny blinked with surprise. "Shot?"

Joe nodded. "His horse came back to the ranch without him. Goullie and Matt and I saddled up and rode out, back-tracking the horse. We found Mister Grant a couple of miles from the house, laying dead in the grass. Two bullets in him. One in his chest. Another in his head."

Johnny was staring at Joe, taking all of this in.

"Who did it?" Johnny said.

Joe shook his head. "No idea. Goullie sent me to get you."

Johnny had left Goullie in charge this morning.

Joe said, "Johnny, the one in Grant's head—it was at close range. You can tell by the powder burns around the wound. Someone shot him out of the saddle and then rode up and finished him off."

Joe stepped down from the saddle and loosened the cinch. He said, "You go and head back. I'll catch up. I have to rest this horse, first."

Johnny wheeled Bravo around and started back for the ranch.

64

JOHNNY FOUND Maria in the parlor. She was sitting in a Queen Anne chair that faced the hearth. Her eyes were glassy and her face was that sort of combination of red and flushed that you get from a lot of crying. She was staring at nowhere in particular and didn't react when Johnny stepped into the room.

A Mexican woman Johnny knew as Carlotta was standing in the doorway. Carlotta was one of the maids who lived here.

She said, "The senora hasn't moved since we got the news. Oh, Johnny, it's just so horrible."

Johnny took off his hat and went into the room. He said, "Miss Maria."

She didn't look up.

He said her name again. "Miss Maria."

He knelt beside her and touched the back of her hand. Then she looked at him, like she was realizing for the first time he was there.

She said, "Johnny? What am I going to do?"

"You're going to be strong. You're the daughter of your father, a man who built a ranch out of nothing. Just like Mister Grant did. My brothers and I will find the man who did this."

She nodded.

Johnny said, "What about Coleman? He's gotta be told."

She nodded. "I've sent a rider to Jefferson for him."

Good idea, Johnny thought. Sending a rider would be much faster than sending a letter.

Back east, there was a network of telegraph lines. Someday, the telegraph would probably be out west too, Johnny figured. But that day was not here, yet.

Maria looked at him and said, "You're the only man I've ever known who is as capable as Breaker was. And Breaker thought so highly of you. This man who shot him—I need you to get him, Johnny."

"We will. We won't let you down."

She nodded.

There was nothing left to say. Johnny strode from the room. He said, "Take care of her, Carlotta. Anything she needs."

"You know I will."

Johnny found Ciego at the stable.

Ciego said, "How is the senora?"

"Shaken," Johnny said. "I need a horse. Bravo has already covered a lot of miles, today."

Ciego wasn't the hostler, but he said, "I'll have one for you."

"And one for each of my brothers, too. We're going after the man who did this."

Matt and Joe were in front of the bunkhouse. Joe had just ridden in. Matt was leaning against the wall with his arms folded, and Joe was pacing about. Shelby was there, and Clancy. Goullie was smoking a cigarette.

When they saw Johnny coming, they circled around him.

Johnny said, "Joe, Matt. You're coming with me. We're going to get the man who did this."

"We're coming with you," Goullie said.

"No." Johnny placed a hand on Goullie's shoulder. "I know how you feel. But you're needed here. I don't know how long this will take. I need you in charge here while I'm gone."

Goullie nodded. "I'll take care of things."

"I have no doubt."

Johnny went into the bunkhouse and grabbed the Hawken. He had done a little target-shooting with it in the weeks since he had won it from Clancy. Shot right nice. Straight and accurate.

It wasn't loaded, so he loaded it now. Clancy had included a powder horn and a leather pouch of lead balls and greased patches. Johnny estimated two hundred grains of powder and poured it in, then he pushed in the lead ball on top of the greased patch. He then pulled the ramrod free and rammed the load in good and tight.

Ciego led three horses to the bunkhouse. Johnny went to the horse with his saddle and pushed his rifle into the scabbard. He also stuffed his slicker into his saddle bags, because of the rain that was coming in. Matt and Joe were doing the same. Matt had no rifle, but Joe had his Enfield in one hand.

"Ride careful, boys," Goullie said. "It's gonna rain, but it shouldn't be too hard a rain."

Matt nodded. "We'll be all right."

Johnny said, "Let's ride."

Joe and Matt led Johnny to where they had found Grant. Johnny saw the grass matted down where Grant's body had landed, and there was a dark patch of blood.

"He was here at least an hour, we figure," Matt said.

Johnny looked around. The sky was now fully overcast and the wind was growing cold. He looked at the land about him, figuring where he himself would have made the shot from, had he been a sniper lying in wait for a man.

He saw a small grassy knoll maybe five hundred feet to the south. He said, "There."

He rode toward the knoll, and Matt and Joe followed.

The grass was matted down in a mish-mash sort of pattern. Johnny handed his reins to Matt and stepped down.

He said, "One set of boot prints, but he was here a while. He paced back and forth."

Johnny knelt down and touched the grass. "He stood here. Watching off toward where he thought Mister Grant might be coming from."

He picked up the small remains of a cigarette. "He smoked a few of these while he waited."

"The fool," Matt said. "He could have started a grass fire with those."

"I've seen Shelby do it. He puts out the stub on the sole of his boot and then only drops it to the grass when it's cool enough to touch."

Joe said, "I've seen Wheeler do that, too."

Johnny said, "I hate to suspect anyone at the ranch. But we never did find out who was working with those rustlers. Where was everyone today?"

Matt thought about it for a moment. "Frenchie and Gates are off at the northwest line cabin."

Johnny nodded. "They've been there three weeks now. They'll be back on payday."

Joe said, "Ciego was in the smithy shop all mornin'. He was shoein' Miss Maria's horse and makin' roofin' nails."

"Shelby and Clancy were at the ranch all day," Matt said. "Goullie was there, too."

"What about Wheeler?"

"He rode out this morning," Matt said. "He said you told him to check on the grass out on the northern range. Winter grass sometimes isn't the best grazing."

Johnny said, "I gave no such order."

"That sum'bitch," Joe said.

Matt said, "Even still, none of that is concrete evidence. We need actual proof."

"I've got enough proof," Joe said.

Johnny shook his head. "Matt's right. We'll talk with Wheeler when we get back. Right now, let's follow this trail."

"I'd bet dollars to doughnuts it was Wheeler what done the shooting."

Johnny swung back up into the saddle. "We'll know soon enough. Let's ride and cover as much ground as we can. We're going to run out of daylight soon."

Johnny started down the knoll, following a trail made by one horse, and a line of grass that had been matted down as the horse stepped along. Matt and Joe fell into place behind him.

65

WHEN THE RAIN CAME DOWN, it came down harder than Goullie had thought it would. At first it was a light drizzle, but soon it was pounding down hard on Johnny's hat and soaking his shirt. He and his brothers pulled their slickers from their saddle bags.

Soon the rain was blasting its way in sheets across the open grassland. The wind picked up, and even though Johnny's hat was pulled down tight around his temples, he had to reach up and flatten a hand across the crown to keep the wind from lifting it clean off of his head.

"We can't stay out here like this!" Matt called to him.

Joe said, "There's a small cabin off east of here. A small dugout. Or what's left of one."

Johnny nodded. "I know of it. Let's go."

There was still some daylight left, but Johnny knew it would get dark early because of the cloud cover. He rode with his head leaning into the rain, so the brim of his hat would keep the rain from whipping against his face. He hoped the powder in his revolvers was staying dry. The scabbard carrying his rifle was made of buckskin—he had made it himself, with rawhide laces at the top that he could pull tight against the rain. It would keep most of the rain away, hopefully enough so the powder wouldn't get damp.

It was sometimes harder than you might think to find a location when traveling overland. They weren't using a map. They were riding by their knowledge of the Broken Spur range, and where they knew the remains of the old dugout to be. But things can look a little different when rain is slanting across in front of you, obscuring visibility.

They topped a low grassy rise, and Johnny thought it would be within sight, but it didn't seem to be.

Matt said, "I don't see it."

Johnny was looking from left to right.

Then Joe said, "Over there."

He was pointing off to their right. Johnny could see a small dark something that looked to be maybe a quarter mile off.

"Has to be it," he said.

They started for it.

Maria was still in the parlor, sitting and staring. Alfredo had started a fire in the hearth because it was going to be a cold night. *Not as cold as the emptiness in my heart*, though, Maria thought.

She was trying to accept the idea that Breaker was now gone. A man with so much personality, who seemed to fill a room with his presence just by walking through a doorway. It didn't seem natural that such a man should just be gone.

She also wondered what would become of her. She didn't think Breaker had changed the will to include Johnny. As far as she knew, the property and all of the businesses would be divided between herself and Coleman.

She heard the front door open, the wind and rain rushing into the entryway. And she heard Alfredo say, "Mister Coleman."

"Coleman?" she said with surprise and hurried to the parlor doorway.

The parlor opened onto the entryway, and she saw Coleman by the door, pulling a slicker over his head and handing it to Alfredo.

"Coleman," she said. "How did you get here so quickly?"

"As soon as that rider you sent told me what had happened," he said, "I chartered a private coach to bring me here."

She nodded. She certainly didn't feel relieved that he was here.

"So," he said, "let's get some hot coffee and you can fill me in on all the details."

The dugout was in the side of a hill that fell off a little more sharply than the rest. The hill had been dug out enough to create an opening half the size of the bunkhouse, and then a front wall was built. There were no windows, but there was a door. The dugout had served as a small tool shed, in the early days of the Broken Spur. Breaker Grant had built a small sod hut near the shed to serve as a ranch house. When the time came to build a larger house, Grant chose an area further away. The grass here was too good, he told Johnny once, to set up a large ranch headquarters. He wanted to keep the good grass for the cattle. The area of the current house and out buildings had originally been a flat expanse of gravel.

The old sod hut was now long gone. All that was left of the original ranch headquarters was the toolshed. The front wall still stood, but the door was long gone.

It was growing dark when Johnny stepped inside. He knew snakes tended to like dark places, so he struck a match.

The dugout was empty. Just an earthen floor, and an earthen roof with a few roots of grass hanging through.

"It'll have to do," he said.

There was enough room for the horses. Saddles were stripped off and the horses were rubbed down.

"It's going to be a cold night," Matt said, "but this place sure beats being out in the rain."

They hadn't brought bedrolls. They hadn't wanted to lose valuable daylight preparing them, when they could have been out following the trail of Grant's killer. Johnny was starting to think maybe they should have taken the time.

Matt slid his slicker off over his head and shook the water away. Then, with the wet side out, he sat on the floor against one wall and used the slicker as a blanket.

"Better than nothing," he said.

Johnny took off his slicker as well, and then pulled each pistol. He thought they seemed dry. He hoped they would fire if he needed them to. He then loosened the rawhide laces on his scabbard to open it, and he slid his rifle out. It was completely dry.

He said, "I don't anticipate any gunfire out here tonight, but there might be tomorrow if we catch up to the man."

"A single man it is," Joe said. "There was only one set of tracks."

"Doesn't mean he was working alone," Johnny said.

Matt said, "We have a lot of questions, but no answers."

Joe's pistol had taken some rain, so he popped out the cylinder and then took a dry one from his vest pocket. He checked to make sure the percussion caps were in place, then he placed the cylinder in the gun.

Johnny said, "We're going to have another problem. Coleman Grant. A rider was sent for him."

Matt looked at Johnny with a little surprise. "Do you think Coleman had anything to do with this?"

Johnny shook his head. "I wouldn't put anything past him. But even if he didn't, just having him around makes everything a whole lot harder."

Joe nodded. "That man's gonna have to be shot one of these days. Just sayin'."

It was Joe's turn for Matt to look at him. "What do you mean? Do you mean murder?"

"Just sayin'."

Johnny nodded at Joe. Matt hadn't been in the West long enough to know how things worked. Johnny thought about how to put it into imagery Matt would understand.

Johnny said, "You've told me something about that ship you served on as first mate. When you were out at deep sea, it sounds like whatever law you had was what was on the ship, and nothing else."

Matt nodded. "That's the way it was. And in some of the seaports where we docked there was often no more law than the gun you carried, or the knife."

Joe said, "Not much different out here."

Johnny paced a bit, putting his thoughts together. "What if Coleman served on your ship? A swabby, or whatever you called them? He's a trouble-maker, and no one you can trust."

Matt nodded slowly, as he thought this one over. "He'd wind up being keel-hauled. Or just plain pushed overboard. Or we'd find him in the morning with a knife in his back. I suppose I understand what you're saying."

Johnny went back to pacing. He started wondering if there was any way they could start a small fire.

Matt said, "So, what's next?"

"We wait out the rain here, then in the morning we see if there is anything left of that rider's trail."

Breaker Grant's body was in one of the guest bedrooms upstairs. It was on a bed and covered with a sheet. In the morning, once the rain stopped, it would be taken into the undertaker's office in Clarksville.

Coleman pulled the sheet back. The old man's eyes were shut and he could have been sleeping, if not for the bullet hole in his forehead. Coleman could see what looked like powder burns around the wound. The front of the old man's vaquero jacket and shirt were covered with a dark blood stain.

Coleman heard boot soles scuffing in the hallway, and he looked over to see Wheeler standing in the doorway.

Wheeler was in his early twenties. Hair that needed cutting, and scruff on his chin. He wore a gun at his right hip. Kind of nondescript. Not a man who would stand out in a crowd, but Coleman had found Wheeler was a man who wanted to play for the winning team. And Wheeler was good at identifying which team that was.

Wheeler said, "I heard you were back."

Coleman looked down at the body. "Looks like he was shot from a distance. A body shot that took him down. He laid there bleeding while the shooter rode up and then put one more in his head."

Wheeler nodded. "That's about what it looks like."

Coleman glanced to the doorway. It was empty. He said, "And there was no one else there?"

"No, sir."

"There was someone else there, though."

Wheeler was looking at him, a little confused.

Coleman said, "You were there, Wheeler. You rode out because you were concerned about my adopted father riding out there alone. He was an old man, and you were right to be concerned. And you saw the shooter. You heard the first gunshot, and as you got closer, you saw the shooter kneeling over the beloved Breaker Grant and putting the final bullet in him. But you were still too far off. By the time you could get to him, the shooter had mounted up and ridden off."

"Who did I see?"

"Why, Johnny O'Brien, of course."

Wheeler shook his head. "Beggin' your pardon, Boss, but ain't no one would believe that. Johnny's too well-liked here on the ranch."

"I know something about him that you don't. I had him investigated. It turns out that our O'Brien brothers might very well be the McCabe brothers. You ever hear of them?"

Wheeler shook his head.

"There's a reward poster at Sheriff Newcomb's office in town. I checked. They're wanted for murdering a town constable and robbing a general store in Missouri last winter."

"Do tell."

Coleman nodded. "Indeed."

"You and me, we talked once, about how I might make a good ramrod of this place."

"And indeed you shall, Wheeler. As soon as O'Brien is out of the way. Or McCabe, or whatever his name is. First thing in the morning, I want you to ride into town and get Sheriff Newcomb."

"Yes, sir."

"And also Harmon Jones."

"The family attorney?"

"The very one. I have something he will need to witness."

Maria came walking into the room.

Coleman said, "That'll be all, Wheeler."

Wheeler nodded and left.

"Coleman," she said. "I heard you telling Wheeler to get the sheriff."

He nodded. "Turns out there was a witness to the shooting, after all. Johnny O'Brien will probably get the noose for it. Or Johnny *McCabe*, as the case may be."

"You know?"

He smiled. "I suspected. But, of course, you knew. And you were more than willing to let my father harbor an outlaw, without him even being aware."

"Breaker Grant knew all about Johnny and his brothers."

Coleman gave a tired-looking grin. "I suppose I shouldn't be surprised. And I suppose there won't be a whole lot of people who will believe a man already wanted for murder would be incapable of murdering again."

"Johnny didn't shoot Breaker."

"Oh, but indeed he did. And whatever relationship you have been having behind the old man's back won't paint you in a very good light."

"I have no relationship with Johnny. He's a good friend, nothing more."

Coleman smiled. "You forget, Maria. I know what you're capable of."

He looked down at the body of Breaker Grant.

Coleman said, "Here's what we're going to do. You're coming back to me, and things will be like they were."

She shook her head. "I was young and foolish. Naïve. That doesn't excuse what I did, but I'll never let you touch me again."

"Then, if you're not here with me, you're not going to be here at all. You're going to sign your half of the ranch over to me. Harmon Jones will be coming out in the morning to witness it."

"I will do no such thing."

He looked at her. "Yes you will. Or I'll break your neck, and then the entire ranch will be mine, anyway."

He smiled. "You picked the wrong man, Maria. You chose Johnny O'Brien over me. Now you're going to regret it. Once you sign the paper tomorrow, I will want you off the ranch. Immediately and permanently."

66

THE RAIN LET UP sometime during the night. By daylight, the sky was covered with a blanket of gray clouds and the wind was cold, but at least it was dry.

Johnny and his brothers rode back to where they had left the trail. The tracks were gone.

"Not a trace of it," Matt said. "So, now what?"

"He had to have a place to wait out last night's storm," Johnny said.

Matt said, "There really aren't any, other than the three line cabins at the far reaches of Broken Spur range, and the dugout we were in last night. There are plenty of places to camp, but not in rain like last night."

Joe nodded. "That means he was at the ranch, itself."

Johnny returned the nod. "Let's head back."

They reined up at one of the stables and swung out of the saddle. Matt said, "As soon as we get these horses taken care of, I'm going to go sit by the bunkhouse fire and drink a cup of hot coffee."

"I'm with you on that," Joe said.

Johnny looked over at the main house. A buckboard was by the front porch, with some crates and a couple of trunks loaded on. He wondered what it was all about, but it wasn't foremost in his thoughts. He was focused on the unpleasant task that was waiting for him.

He said, "Before I go sit by a warm fire, I have to go tell Miss Maria that the killer got away. I told her we would find him, but we couldn't."

Matt said, "You want us to come with you?"

Johnny shook his head. "No. I have to do this myself."

He started on foot for the house. His spurs were jingling gently. He felt chilled to the bone as he walked along.

A year ago, Johnny and his brothers had left Pennsylvania to find the man who had killed their father and Hector Drummond. They had failed. Johnny felt they had not only failed Pa and Mr. Drummond, but Ma and Luke, and Becky Drummond and her mother. And they had failed themselves. Now they had failed Breaker Grant and Miss Maria.

Johnny went to knock on the door, but the door

opened. Shelby was stepping out with the handle of a carpet bag in each hand.

"Boss," he said.

"Shelby. You goin' somewhere?"

Maria stepped out behind him. She was in a hat and had a thick shawl about her shoulders.

"Johnny," she said. "We have to talk."

He nodded. He removed his hat and then reached up to flatten down any stray hair.

He said, "We failed, Miss Maria. He got away. We lost his trail in the rain."

She said, "Johnny, Coleman's here. He's claiming you and your brothers killed Breaker."

Johnny blinked with surprise.

She said, "Wheeler is working with him. Wheeler's claiming to have seen the whole thing, from a distance."

"But we didn't."

"I know that. We all do. But Coleman's word carries weight. The sheriff's in with Coleman now."

Johnny glanced back at the buckboard. Shelby was loading the carpet bags on.

He said, "What's that all about?"

She told him about Coleman taking the ranch from her.

"I signed the papers this morning."

"It's not right for a man to threaten a woman. I won't let this happen."

She placed a hand on his chest, as though to stop him. She said, "It's all right. I thought about this all night. I thought about what you said to me last summer. I was so young and foolish. I didn't know what I wanted, and Coleman took advantage of it. I can't believe I ever let a man like that touch me. But I let him take advantage of me, so I'm to blame too. I decided I don't want this place, considering the only way I could have it would be to be with him."

"But this was your home."

"I'll forever carry my memories of what Breaker and I had. And I'll carry the shame of how I betrayed him. But I'm going to be the woman you seem to think I am. I'm going back to my father's ranch. I'll run it alongside him. I'll use my knowledge of business and cattle. I'll make his ranch grow. You never know," she said with a smile. "One day it might rival this place."

"Are you sure it's what you want?"

She nodded. "It is. And I owe it all to you. You're the one who started getting me to believe in myself."

He returned the smile. "You can pay me back by making good. Make your father's ranch grow. If you marry again, marry well. Marry a good man, and marry him for love."

She nodded. "I will."

She placed a hand alongside his face, and said, "And now you have to run. Coleman is going to be placing a reward on your head. Along with the one that's already there. Run. Don't let them find you. Don't let them hang you for something you didn't do."

They walked to the buckboard. She said, "Shelby's going to drive me there. I also asked Ciego to come along. I'm going to see if Father can give them each a job."

Johnny glanced over toward the barn. Ciego had a horse saddled and was leading it toward them.

Shelby said, "Most of the men are riding on. They don't want to work for Coleman, especially now."

Johnny stood by while Shelby climbed up onto the wagon seat and took the reins. Ciego climbed into the saddle.

He said, "Be safe, Mi Amigo."

Johnny nodded.

Maria said, "Godspeed, Johnny McCabe."

He said, "And to you."

Shelby clicked the reins and gave a giddyap, and the wagon was off, with Ciego riding alongside them. Johnny stood and watched them make their way across the ranch yard and off to the trail, as Maria Carerra Grant headed off to her new life.

67

JOHNNY MET his brothers on their way to the bunkhouse. He said, "We gotta ride."

Matt nodded. "Ciego told us what's been going on. He saddled fresh horses for us before he saddled his own. We have to pack and be on our way."

They went into the bunkhouse and began fixing their bedrolls. There was no time to sit by a warm fire, now.

Then a man stepped in. Matt recognized him as the lawman who had watched the fight between Johnny and Coleman, all those weeks ago.

"Boys," he said. "I'm Harris Newcomb. County sheriff."

Johnny nodded. "Sheriff."

"I'll cut right to the chase," Newcomb said. "Coleman Grant has a witness that says you boys shot and killed Breaker Grant. Specifically," he looked at Johnny, "you."

Johnny nodded. "Miss Maria and Shelby told me."

"Here's the way it is. Money is power. It ain't fair, but it's the way it is. Coleman Grant might be a bully and a back-stabbing coward, but he's sole owner of the Grant estate and has all the power that money like that can buy."

Johnny nodded. "My brothers and I have little more than the money in our pockets."

"Look, I know you boys didn't do it. If I was to lay money on it, I'd say Coleman hisself was somehow involved."

Newcomb took a moment, composing his thoughts. He placed his hands on his hips and looked down at the floor. Johnny waited. He glanced at his brothers.

Matt was kneeling beside his bed and was in the process of rolling up his blankets when the sheriff walked in. Joe was standing by his bunk and had his hand on the hilt of his knife. Johnny shook his head *no*, and Joe took his hand away.

"Here's the way it is," Newcomb finally said, looking back at Johnny. "Breaker and I were old friends. I worked for him at one point, when his ranch headquarters were nothing more than a couple of sod huts he used as a ranch house and barn, and a dugout for a tack shed. That was a long time ago."

Johnny nodded.

Newcomb said, "I owed him my life a few times over,

and he owed me his. But among friends, you don't keep track. He thought highly of you, McCabe."

This caught Johnny by surprise.

Newcomb said, "Yes, I know who you are. So did Breaker. Coleman has done some digging, and has pretty much figured it out too. But Breaker told me you were all good boys and he trusted you. That was good enough for me.

"You see, boys," he began to pace. "I've been a lawman a long time, but there's two ways of looking at the law. There's the letter of the law, and the spirit of the law. The letter of the law—well, that means just enforcing the laws the way they're written on paper, whether they make sense or not. But the spirit of the law—that's harder to work with. It means understanding what the lawmakers wanted and making sure the letter of the law doesn't get you all tripped up and make you fall into some sort of injustice."

Johnny shrugged. "I'm not much into philosophy."

"Well, let's just say I'm a spirit-of-the-law kind of man. I believe in justice. But I know the Broken Spur brings a lot of money into the town of Clarksville and into Red River County. Coleman is now the single richest, most powerful man in the county. In this part of Texas. The county will appoint an attorney for you boys, but," he shrugged. "To have justice, you have to have equal parties involved."

He looked at Matt and Joe, then back to Johnny. "I'm a friend of Harmon Jones, the lawyer in town who's Breaker's attorney. The three of us shared many a glass of whiskey, and Harmon, well, he likes to go on about legal theory. Especially when he's had a little too much to drink. That's where I get all this *spirit of the law* type of thinking."

Newcomb rubbed his thick, white mustache. "What I'm getting at, boys, is for you to be railroaded by Grant money wouldn't be justice at all. And to extradite you to Missouri so you can be hanged there wouldn't do any good, either."

Johnny didn't know what to say to any of this. He glanced at Matt, who shook his head and shrugged at the same time.

Newcomb looked at Johnny and said, "The thing is, a warrant for your arrest is going to be issued this afternoon, and I'm going to have to enforce it. I'm going to have to come after you. First thing in the morning. I trust you three will be long gone by then."

Matt said, "If you beg my pardon, sir, this hardly

seems like justice."

"Son, sometimes you have to take justice as you find it. In this case, I'm afraid your brother not swinging from a rope is about the best you're going to get."

Newcomb turned toward the door, then looked back at them.

He said, "And one more thing. I know the judge issuing the warrant. He knows where the money flows from, but he also knew Breaker well, and he knows what Coleman is. The judge and I had a talk, and the warrant is going to be issued in the name of Johnny O'Brien."

Johnny said, "I appreciate that."

Newcomb nodded. "Ride safe, boys. Breaker Grant was a good judge of character. Don't prove him wrong."

"We won't, sir."

With their bedrolls tucked under their arms, they headed for the stable. Their horses were tethered in front of the stable. Johnny's saddle was on Bravo.

Clancy was leading a horse from the stable. The horse was saddled and a bedroll was tied to the cantle. Johnny's old Colt rifle was in Clancy's saddle.

Johnny said, "Are you quitting, too?"

Clancy nodded. "This place ain't home for me, anymore. And I'm riding out on my own horse. I don't want Coleman to claim I stole one from the ranch."

"Where will you go?" Matt said.

"Maybe the Carerra ranch. See if they need a cowhand"

Johnny said, "You tell Miss Maria that I asked her to hire you. Though I don't think you'll need to."

Clancy swung into the saddle. "So long. All three of you are welcome at my fire, anytime."

Johnny said, "I hope you know the same is true of you."

"Keep your powder dry," Joe said.

Clancy waved his hand and rode through the gate and down the trail.

When their bedrolls were in place, they mounted up. When they turned their horses away from the barn, they found the men walking toward them. Goullie, Frenchie and Gates. They all had their bedrolls with them.

Goullie said, "We're riding out. We can't ride for the

Broken Spur, anymore."

Johnny said, "Where will you all go?"

Goullie said, "I heard the Carerra ranch might be needing a ramrod."

Frenchie said, "There's a farm girl I've been seeing, outside of town. Maybe it's high time I asked her to marry me."

Gates said, "I'll find a job. I've done lots of things. Ridden shotgun for a stage company. Been a deputy sheriff once."

Johnny said, "It's been a pleasure working with you all. I've learned a lot here, at this ranch. Wherever I go, I'll take what I've learned with me. And I'll say this—you boys are all welcome at my side, anytime."

Johnny looked toward the gate that led to the trail out beyond the ranch yard. He didn't have to touch his spurs to Bravo. The horse seemed to know what he wanted and started forward. Joe and Matt fell into place behind him.

The gate to the Broken Spur was made of wrought iron and bore the name GRANT. Johnny looked at the name as they rode through. He thought of all he had learned from Breaker Grant in their months here.

Out beyond the gate, he was about to bring Bravo to a stop, but the horse stopped anyway.

"So," he said. "Where to from here?"

Matt shrugged. "You've been talking about those border towns. You've kind of gotten my curiosity up."

"I don't know if I want to go back there," Johnny said. "I poured down way too much tequila in those towns. Trucked with the kind of women Ma would never have approved of. Gotten into more than one gunfight."

Joe said, "I've always wondered about California."

Johnny looked at him. "California is a long ride from here."

Joe nodded. "Might be what we need."

Johnny looked to Matt.

Matt shrugged and said, "You're the ramrod."

Johnny grinned. "All right, then. California, it is."

PART FIVE

The Mountains

68
Montana, 1881

JOHNNY MCCABE GOT UP from the sofa and put two more chunks of wood onto the fire. It was going to be a long night, he realized. He had been telling the story of his early days, but the story was only partially told.

His joints hurt as he got up from the sofa. He had just been talking about his days at the Broken Spur ranch, in Texas. In those days, nothing hurt. He could sit in the saddle all day, and after a good night's sleep, get up and do it all again. Those days were long gone.

Gradually, as he had been telling the story, people had gone to bed. Joe was dozing. After all, life on a ranch began before sunrise, and even though there wasn't a whole lot of work to do in December, the habit of rising early persisted.

But Bree was wide awake and sitting on the floor in front of the sofa. Dusty and Haley were sitting on the edge of the hearth, and Josh and Temperance were on the sofa. Nina had gone to sleep, but Jack was standing by the fire, a glass of bourbon in hand.

Johnny settled back onto the sofa. At one point, when he was telling about the trouble he and his brothers had gotten into in Missouri, Ginny had gone to the kitchen and put on a pot of coffee. Johnny now had a cup of hot trail coffee standing on an end table, waiting for him.

Ginny also had poured herself another glass of wine, and she settled back into her rocker.

Johnny said, "Don't you want to go to sleep? Sam went to bed hours ago."

"Oh, no," she said. "I wouldn't miss this for the world. I've heard bits and pieces of this over the years, but never all at once."

Bree said, "What about Maria? Did you ever see her again?"

Johnny shook his head. "Never again. I heard she married well a few years later, and her ranch is the largest one in northern Texas."

Dusty said, "What about Becky Drummond? And your cousin Thad?"

"I'll get to all of that. One step at a time."

The wind outside picked up and rattled the windows. Had to be cold enough outside to freeze a glass of water in less than a minute, Johnny thought. And yet he loved these mountains. All they had to offer, their beauty and yet their harshness.

"All right, Pa," Bree said. "Tell us all about it. You and Uncle Matt and Uncle Joe had left the Broken Spur in Texas and were heading west."

Johnny began talking about where he and his brothers were in those first weeks after leaving the Broken Spur in Texas, back in the winter of 1857, and the long journey that eventually led him to this small valley in the Montana mountains.

"We rode through Texas much the way we rode into it. Avoiding ranches and towns. Texas had a lot of wide-open land back then, so it wasn't too hard. We had a choice. We could cut directly west through New Mexico Territory, or we could go northwest and into the mountains. I didn't know a lot about Apaches, and Joe knew nothing about them. But he knew a lot about the mountains, so that's the direction we chose.

"And so, in late winter, we found ourselves in Colorado, the foothills to the Rockies. Except they didn't call it Colorado back in those days. We were in the western end of what they called Kansas Territory..."

69

Western Kansas Territory
February, 1858

IT WAS dark. A campfire was crackling away, and the coffee kettle was boiling over.

"Coffee's ready," Matt said.

He knelt by the fire and grasped the kettle, using a bandana so he wouldn't burn himself on the handle. One thing Matt had learned during his time at the Broken Spur was the various uses for a bandana.

They were now at a higher elevation than they had been in Texas, and the winter nights were cold. Two inches of snow was on the ground. The country around them was hilly and they could see pines standing tall around them in the darkness.

Matt filled a tin cup with coffee and said, "Do either of you ever wonder about Thad?"

Johnny nodded. He had a cigar from Breaker Grant in his hand.

Joe said, "So, you gonna smoke that or just stand there and look at it?"

"Well," Johnny said, "it's the last one. I may not ever find another cigar that tastes quite like this one."

Joe nodded. "I know what you mean. I ran out of tobacco for my pipe. There's nothing like sitting by the fire in the early morning with a pipe full of tobacco."

Matt said, "Well?"

Johnny struck a match to light the cigar. "I think about Thad once in a while."

Matt rose to his feet and took a sip of the coffee. "Do you ever feel guilty about sending him away?"

Johnny shrugged. "A little, maybe. But I don't see what else we could have done."

Joe said, "I knew men like him in the Army. They're a danger to all the men around them. Sooner or later, one of us would've had to put him down."

"That seems to be your solution to a lot of things," Matt said.

Joe grinned. "Depends on the problem."

Matt returned the grin.

He said to Johnny, "How do we tell Uncle Jake and Aunt Sara that we sent their son off alone?"

Johnny shrugged again. "So far, we haven't had to tell anyone anything. We haven't written them, yet."

"Don't see how we can," Joe said.

Matt said, "It's partly our fault, you know. We let him talk us into robbing that store."

Johnny nodded. "But he didn't have to kill that constable. He did that all on his own."

Joe said, "If we had kept him with us, he just would've shot someone else. It's his nature. I've seen it before. Sooner or later, it would've come down to us or him."

The next morning, they rode deeper into the hills.

By noon, they were at the top of a ridge that was covered with pines. Down below was an area too small to call a valley, but more than a gulch. Pines stood tall and toward the center there was a small stream. From where they were, it looked like the water was running low and there was a thin ice cover, but Johnny figured by the look of the banks the water ran fast and deep in the spring.

Off toward the north, the sky was covered with clouds that looked to Johnny like a soft, cottony blanket. The wind was cold and coming directly from the north.

"That's snow," Joe said. "And a lot of it. We ain't gonna be getting very far."

"Well, what do we do?" Matt said. He was pulling his coat tight about his neck. Behind them were some tall pines, with boughs waving in the wind.

"We hunker down," Joe said. "We're better prepared for winter than we were last year."

"Winter?" Matt said. "It's almost spring."

Joe shook his head. "In these mountains, when you see clouds like that, it's still winter."

"But can we survive out here?"

"These hills ain't much different than the mountains I lived in when I was with the Cheyenne. We'll be all right."

"So, where do we make our camp?"

"Right here on this ridge." Joe swung out of the saddle. "Back in a ways. These trees are thick enough that they'll serve as a wind break."

Joe had bought a small hatchet while they were at the Broken Spur, and with it he cut some pine poles and used them as framework for a lean-to. He cut some pine boughs to use as thatching.

While he was working, Matt gathered as many fallen sticks and branches as he could for a fire.

Johnny went hunting. It was a great opportunity to try out his new rifle. This would be his first chance to use it in the field.

His pistols were buckled at his hips, and he thought about how heavy they were as he walked along through the woods.

It struck him as foolish to wear them out here in the mountains. There was no one to shoot at him. According to Joe, the Indians of these mountains were likely hunkered down for the winter. The nearest settlement would be in New Mexico Territory, probably a two-week ride from here.

Johnny was in his riding boots. The smooth soles slipped a little in some snow, and he almost fell. He knew Joe carried a pair of buckskin boots in his saddlebags. Johnny thought maybe he would have Joe show him how to make a pair for himself.

The cloud cover was now overhead, and the air had that certain almost undefinable feel it got before snow began falling. Johnny remembered the feeling well from his years in Pennsylvania.

Johnny stopped and looked up at the sky. He pulled off his hat and let the cold, mountain wind rush over him. The air was clean and he could catch a scent of balsam. Everything he loved about the mountains back in Pennsylvania was here, and so much more.

He put the hat back on his head and continued along. Ahead the woods opened to a field, but he waited by a tree and allowed himself a good long look at the field before he considered stepping out. Zack Johnson had said Johnny was overly cautious because of all the gun battles he had been in, but Johnny thought it was more like what Matt had said. Erring on the side of caution. Ma used to say, *it's better to be safe than sorry.* It seemed to Johnny to be the same kind of philosophy.

He then saw movement off toward the center of the field. Some brown stalks of weeds stood tall, and it was behind them that he thought he had seen some motion. Then he saw the motion again. Something dark was back there.

He waited. Best to be patient. Pa had said more than

once, *The hunter who hurries goes home hungry.*

He waited, and then he saw what was making the motion. A grizzly lumbered its way out from behind the dead weeds.

Kind of late in the season for a bear to be out and about, Johnny thought. But the last couple of days had been unseasonably warm.

Johnny stood and watched while the bear lumbered its way along. The most powerful critter in these mountains. He marveled at the strength in its paws. It could rip a man apart without working up a sweat.

Johnny wasn't afraid. The Hawken rifle could bring down a buffalo, and Johnny was fully confident in his ability to make a shot count. If he had to, he could stop this bear. But Johnny hoped he wouldn't have to. The bear was out here, in God's mountains, where life was as God had intended it to be. Unspoiled by the greed of people.

The bear stopped and looked at him. Maybe the critter had caught his scent, Johnny thought. The breeze was sort of drifting back and forth.

The bear watched him for a moment.

Johnny said out loud, "Keep on moving, big fella. I don't want any trouble."

The bear stared for a moment more, then it looked away and continued on its way.

Johnny watched while the bear disappeared into the trees, and he waited a few minutes more. He wanted the bear to be good and gone before he started moving.

Once he was sure the bear was no longer anywhere near, he started across the field, and that was when he saw tracks in the grass. A buck, he thought. He knelt for a closer look. The tracks were recent. The buck might have run through only moments before the bear had wandered out into the field.

He looked up at the sky and estimated he had a couple of hours of daylight left. Venison would sure go a long way to help him and his brothers get through some cold winter days in these mountains. And if the days grew cold enough, then the meat wouldn't spoil.

He decided to follow the trail for a bit. He stepped along carefully, trying to make as little sound as possible. Again he thought about the advantages of having a pair of deerskin boots like Joe's.

He didn't have to follow the trail long. He stepped out of the woods into another small glade, which the stream cut through. There, not even three hundred feet away, was the deer.

It was a mule deer, with antlers that rose to four sharp points. Different than the white-tailed deer of the Pennsylvania mountains, but not all that different. The buck was facing away from Johnny, and it was drinking from the stream.

The breeze had changed direction again and was coming from the deer toward Johnny, which meant the deer wouldn't catch Johnny's scent. However the deer would still be able to hear him, and cocking his rifle would make a little noise.

He brought the hammer back slowly, but there was still a *click* as the hammer locked in place.

The deer raised its head and looked back at Johnny. Any sudden motion might send the deer running.

Johnny had been hunting years ago in the woods behind the farm, and a deer had looked up at him when he cocked his rifle. Just like this deer had done. Johnny had raised the rifle as fast as he could but the deer took off running in a zig-zagging pattern and Johnny's shot missed.

So this time, Johnny didn't raise his rifle. He stood still, barely breathing. No motion at all. The deer looked directly at him, then looked at something in the woods off to Johnny's left. The deer then looked back at the stream but didn't drop its head just yet.

Johnny raised the rifle to his shoulder. A smooth, fluid motion. The rustling of the fabric of his coat was enough to get the deer's attention and it looked back at him again.

The deer turned to its left in a burst of speed.

Johnny fired, and the rifle kicked hard against his shoulder.

The deer went face forward and slid on the mossy shore of the river, and remained on the ground, kicking its hooves.

Johnny ran to the deer. He drew his right-hand revolver to finish it off but found he didn't have to. The deer was dead, kicking off its last remaining bits of energy in its death throes.

Johnny slid the pistol back into his holster. Then, before he went to work on the deer, he took the time to reload his rifle. Once you've been in a few gun battles, you don't walk around with a gun that's not loaded. He had the pouch of lead balls and greased patches in one coat pocket and the powder horn in another.

Once the rifle was again loaded, he drew his knife. He would gut the deer before he hauled it back to camp.

With the knife in one hand, he noticed a snowflake twirling its way down and landing on the carcass. Within seconds, a scattering of flakes were now falling.

He was about a half mile from camp. If he got to work now, he could have the deer back to camp before the snow started falling hard.

70

THE PINES STANDING between the lean-to and the edge of the ridge's summit would stop most of the wind but not all of it, so Joe built the lean-to to face toward the southeast. Joe knew from experience that most of the weather passing through these mountains would be from the west or the northwest.

The lean-to was thatched heavily. Wind still escaped into the shelter, and the shelter was not warm like the farmhouse had been on a cold winter night. But it was warm enough. Joe built another shelter for the horses nearby, and they seemed comfortable.

Matt hauled over a considerable amount of firewood. Enough to last a day.

By the time it got dark, a fire was burning strong and hot. Johnny stood in front of it with a cup of coffee and with his coat hanging open. His guns were still on his hips, and his rifle was leaning against his saddle in the lean-to.

Snow was falling fast and hard out beyond the two shelters. Johnny had rigged a spit over the fire, and a haunch of venison was roasting away. Snow would find its way into the fire and give off a hissing sound.

Joe sat cross-legged on the ground and had filled a cup with coffee. Matt was stretched out on his blankets in the lean-to, his head resting on his saddle.

"I sure hope that venison cooks up soon," he said. "I was already hungry, but something about the smell of venison cooking just makes your mouth water."

When it was finally cooked enough, Johnny hacked off some steaks and they commenced to eating. Johnny went to sit on the ground by his saddle, and he decided to sit the way Joe was. It was a better-balanced way of sitting when you were on the bare ground. Johnny used his skillet as a plate, and since he had no utensils, he speared the steak with his bowie knife and chewed off pieces of it. Joe was eating the same way.

Matt, who Johnny always called the more civilized of the three, had bought a knife and fork at a general store in Clarksville, and he was sitting with his steak on two flat pieces of bark he was using as an improvised plate.

"I've gotta say," Matt said. "This might be the best

steak of any kind I've ever eaten."

Joe nodded. "Cooking like this, outdoors and over an open fire, makes everything taste better. It's about the only way I ate for the last couple years, until we all went back home."

When the food was done, Joe tied the remaining venison to the end of a rope. Earlier, after he had finished the shelters, he had climbed high into a pine and draped the rope over a branch twenty feet off the ground, so both ends fell to the earth.

Matt had been too busy with the firewood to notice what Joe had been up to, but now he said, "What're you doing?"

"We'll store the meat high up off the ground."

"Why?"

"Wolves."

Matt didn't like the sound of that.

Joe said, "They prob'ly won't be out in a storm like this, but the smell of fresh deer meat might give 'em reason to."

He and Johnny pulled on the rope and slid the meat up the tree, and then he tied the rope off on a low branch.

"At least we won't have to worry about the meat going bad," Matt said. "It's cold enough out that it'll be like keeping it in an ice box."

Johnny woke up to the find the sky overhead a steel gray. Not quite sunrise, yet. A foot of snow was on the ground and covering the roof of the shelter.

He tramped through the snow to the horse's shelter, and they seemed well.

He started a fire and by the time coffee water was heating up, Joe and Matt were awake.

Matt said, "I'm amazed at how warm I slept last night. Much more so than last winter, when we were freezing to death in Illinois and Missouri."

"It helps when you're prepared."

Johnny stood by the fire, waiting for the water to boil.

He said, "Is this what it was like, living with the Cheyenne?"

Joe nodded. "Yeah, it was a lot like this."

Matt said, "I think I'm starting to see the appeal."

The coffee boiled over once. Johnny took it from the

fire. When the water had stopped boiling, he put the kettle back into the fire.

He said, "What'll we feed the horses?"

"These mountains ain't like back home," Joe said. "In a couple days it could feel like spring. Maybe even by this afternoon. We'll find plenty of grass for them."

Once the coffee was ready, Johnny took his cup and walked out beyond the lean-to, where he had a clear view of much of their little valley and the ridges beyond.

The ridges were covered with snow, and the rays of sunrise were coloring the far ridges a shade of scarlet. Overhead, the sky was blue. Johnny saw a bird circling about in the distance. Looked like an eagle.

He drew in a deep lungful of cold, mountain air.

There was something undefinable about Texas that he would probably always love. But here in the mountains, he had the strange feeling that he had somehow come home, even though he had never been here before. He now realized these mountains were where he wanted to one day build his home.

Maybe not yet, he thought. He still had miles to cross. Places to see and things to do. He had to gain experience. And he wanted to meet the right woman. Someone who touched his heart the way Becky Drummond had, and the way Maria Carrera might have, had the situation been different. But someone who could come to these mountains with him and live a life here.

By late morning, Johnny found Joe was right. The day was warming up. The ice in the stream had melted, and the snow was clearing away from the shore. Moss grew at the very edge of the stream, but a little further back were thick patches of grass. By noon much of the snow had melted away from the grass, so Johnny and Joe brought the horses down to graze.

Joe knew these mountains, so Johnny picked his brain. How far north do these mountains run? *Clear to the Canadian border and beyond.* How could a man make a living here? *They don't make much money in fur-trapping anymore, but there are wide spaces in places where grass grows. A man could run cattle there.*

"Why you askin'?" Joe said.

"I'm thinking I might one day want to come back to

these mountains. Spend my days, here."

Joe nodded. "They do have a way of grabbin' hold of your heart. I've thought about 'em every single day since I went home."

They heard the sound of someone walking up behind them. Sticks cracking and such. Johnny looked over his shoulder to see Matt.

Matt said, "I thought I'd come down here and join you."

He looked about. "My, it sure is beautiful here."

Johnny said, "You know, there really isn't any reason for us to hurry on our way to California. It's not like there's anyone here who could turn us over to the law."

Joe stroked his beard. "Prob'ly ain't anyone else within miles."

By midway through the next day, the little valley was clear of snow and the stream was rushing fast and deep with runoff. The horses grazed at the side of the stream. Matt sat with them while Joe and Johnny did some hunting. Joe had his Enfield, and Johnny carried his Hawken.

They worked their way up a ridge and were soon beyond the small valley. Joe was in his buckskin boots. They had both left their coats at the lean-to because the day was so warm.

Johnny said, "I need you to show me how to make a pair of moccasin boots like you have."

They stopped at a point where bedrock jutted out from the crest of the ridge. From here they had a view down the wooded slope and of the ridge beyond.

Johnny said, "You'd never know we had a blizzard just the night before last."

Joe said, "That's the way of these mountains. Not further north, though. You get there, and winter tends to hang on longer."

They moved on, and followed the slope down to a stream.

Joe said, "Likely the same stream that cuts through our little valley."

They followed it along for a bit. The shores of the stream were sandy in places, and in others there was mud or moss. Here and there were tracks. Johnny recognized some of the tracks as belonging to a mule deer. But there was another he didn't know.

"Elk," Joe said. "If we move along quiet enough, we might come onto one."

And they did. A half hour later, they saw an elk chewing on some grass. The land was fairly flat along this stretch, and Johnny estimated the elk to be more than five hundred feet away.

Joe indicated the elk with a nod of his head, and he gave a questioning look. A silent way of asking, *Can you make that shot?*

Johnny gave a nod of his head. Joe stepped back to give Johnny some room and because the roar of a gunshot doesn't hurt the ears as much if you're standing behind the one who's doing the shooting.

Johnny cocked his rifle. This gun had a double cock, so he pulled the hammer all the way back. The wind was blowing and the stream was rushing along with run-off from all of the snow that had melted. The elk didn't react to the cocking of the gun.

A Hawken was like many rifles of the time, with two triggers. Johnny squeezed the back trigger until he felt a little something release. This gave the front trigger a hair-trigger release. Johnny then sighted in on the elk. The breeze was blowing cross-ways, so he allowed a little for that. He gave a gentle exhale and a slight tug on the trigger, and the gun roared. It bucked against his shoulder and he lost sight of the elk for a moment in a cloud of gun smoke, then he saw the beast down on its side.

Joe shook his head. "That's mighty fine shooting."

The ball had caught the deer in the neck, but the animal was still breathing. Joe and Johnny walked over to it, and Johnny drew a pistol and finished it off.

He was about to reload the rifle, but Joe placed a hand on his arm to get his attention.

Two Indian men were walking toward them. One had jet black hair tied into two braids, and the other had his hair tied back in a long tail. They were both in buckskin shirts, leggings and breechcloths. They each had a bow in one hand and a quiver of arrows on their backs.

"Arapaho," Joe said. "I think."

They stopped on the other side of the elk.

"They're not wearing paint," Johnny said. "My only experience has been with the Kiowa and the Comanche, and then it was mostly fighting 'em. Do these Indians wear paint if they're looking for trouble?"

Joe nodded. "Every Indian tribe I know of does. I think they're hunting, not looking for a fight."

Joe raised a hand, and one of them did the same. Joe then began making some motions with his hands. The Indian did the same.

Johnny had seen this done before. Even though each tribe spoke a different language, sometimes as different from each other as the various languages of Europe, many of the tribes from Texas to Canada had a universal sign language.

Joe placed a hand to his chest and said, "Joe."

The Indian made the same motion and said, "Heete'i'eit."

Joe looked at Johnny and said, "Must be his name."

"What's it mean?"

"I have no idea. I don't speak Arapaho. I used sign language to tell him we shot the elk. He and his friend have been trailing the elk. They need it to feed their village."

"We don't really need it," Johnny said. "We still have a lot left from our last kill."

Johnny stepped forward. He aimed with one hand toward the elk, then he made a sweeping motion toward the Arapaho men.

"Take it," he said.

The Indians looked like they weren't sure what Johnny intended. He stepped back and made the motion again.

Johnny said, "How do I tell them the elk is theirs?"

Joe thought a moment. Then he said, "Point to the man, then make this sign."

Joe held his right fist in front of his chin, with the palm facing to the left, and he then made a downward sweeping gesture, his thumb aiming toward Johnny.

Johnny did as instructed, pointing to the man who had given Joe his name, and then made the sign.

The Indian then smiled and made another sign, raising both hands with the palms downward, and then he swept his hands out toward Johnny and then down.

Joe said, "He's saying thanks."

Johnny nodded to him.

Johnny and Joe left, to head back to the camp. Johnny looked back over his shoulder toward the Indians. They were kneeling over the carcass, and one had drawn a

knife and was beginning to work on it.
　　Joe said, "You did a good thing. I think you're going to do all right in these mountains."

71

EVEN THOUGH THE DAY HAD BEEN warm and most of the snow was now gone, the night was still downright cold. Matt had gathered some more firewood, and they had a fire blazing in front of their shelter. Johnny stood in front of the fire with a cup of coffee in one hand, and Joe was sitting Indian-style, letting the heat of the fire wash over him.

Matt was pacing about. He said, "I don't see why their hunger should come before ours."

Joe looked at Johnny. Johnny said, "From what I learned of the Kiowa and the Comanche, and I doubt it's much different with the Cheyenne, they think of the well-being of the whole village. When they go hunting, they get meat for the whole village. The women will divide it up by family, based on need."

Joe nodded. "If their village ain't too big, that elk will go a long way toward feeding them all for the night."

Matt scratched his head and said, "Really? That's how they do it?"

Joe said, "That's how the Cheyenne do it. And the Lakota and the Shoshone. From what I've heard, the Arapaho do it, too. From what we saw today, I'd say it's prob'ly their way."

Matt stopped his pacing and stood in front of the fire, and held his hands out to the warmth.

He said, "I don't understand that way, at all. A man has to make his own way in the world. Make his own life."

"Them people don't concern themselves with that," Joe said. "They're too busy just tryin' to survive."

The next day, the weather turned cold again. Johnny took the horses down to the stream and found there was a thin layer of ice near the shore. Nothing he couldn't break with a stick.

"Cold is good," Joe said. "This way, the meat we have left won't spoil."

The following morning, the brothers woke to find an inch of snow on the ground. It remained cold all day, and the snow didn't melt. It wasn't enough snow to keep the horses from grazing, but it was enough that an animal made a trail that was easy to read. Johnny was able to follow another mule deer as it wound its way through their little valley, and his Hawken barked and they had more venison.

They sat by the fire that night, and Joe told Johnny what he knew about Indians. Most of what he knew was Cheyenne. He talked about their religion and their ceremonies.

Matt listened and said, "Pastor Wilson back home wouldn't want to hear about any of this. He'd call them all heathens."

Johnny nodded and chuckled. "He probably would, at that."

Joe said, "I think whatever the religion is, they're all talkin' about the same God."

Matt nodded. "I do, too. I spent time with some islanders, in the South Pacific. They talked about their beliefs, and it occurred to me it was just another way of looking at the same thing."

Matt looked at Johnny and said, "You know what I'm having a sudden hankering for? Some of that Mexican liquor of yours."

"Tequila," Johnny said.

Joe stroked his beard. "As I recall, I didn't get a taste of any of that. You two drunk it all down while I was out workin' the fields with Pa and Luke."

"Well," Johnny said, "I've got a surprise for you."

He went to the shelter and came back with a bottle.

"Johnny," Matt said. "Why, bless you."

Johnny said, "I bought a bottle in Clarksville, a few weeks before we left. The bartender sold me one for cost after I threw out a rowdy drunk for him, one night. I was saving it for a special occasion."

"Well," Joe said, "this occasion feels right special."

Johnny pulled the cork and took a pull from the bottle. He said, "It's feeling more special by the moment."

They sat and handed the bottle around, and Joe talked of the Cheyenne. He talked of their myths, and he talked of warriors he had known. He told about the Sun Dance, which was a brutal method a warrior had of seeking a vision.

"If I had stayed," Joe said, "I would have wound up doing it. All warriors do."

Over the following days, Joe began teaching Johnny the sign language of the plains Indians. He also taught Johnny how to tan a deer hide and how to make from it a pair of boot-length moccasins.

Matt knew nothing about tracking, so Johnny and Joe

showed him how to recognize various tracks and how to tell how old the tracks were.

The snow had been on the ground for a week when the weather turned warm again, and by the end of the day, the snow was gone.

Matt and Joe stood on a ridge looking down at the little valley and off to the ridge beyond. They had both left their coats behind. Matt removed his hat and wiped away some sweat with a bandana.

Joe stood in silence, looking off at the distance. The sky was a clear blue.

Matt noticed in the far distance, three or four birds seemed to be circling. He said, "What kind of birds are those?"

Joe shrugged. "Hard to tell from here. Scavengers, most likely. Maybe buzzards. Something prob'ly died, and they're circling it. Won't be long before they're flying down and eating it."

Matt nodded. "Not unlike crows back home, just bigger."

Joe nodded.

Matt said, "Where's the nearest settlement from here?"

Joe thought for a moment. "There's Fort Laramie, maybe four hundred miles northeast of here. There's a couple of trading posts, down in New Mexico Territory. Couple hundred miles, at least. And the Mormons, out at the Salt Lake. Prob'ly four hundred miles, maybe a little more. There's Fort Bridger, a little closer. On the Green River. They call it a fort, but it's really nothing more than a trading post."

Matt looked off at the far ridge. "To look at this place, you'd think we three were the only people on the entire Earth. This is an unspoiled land, the way God meant for it to be."

Joe grinned. "You sure got a way with words. But I feel the same."

That night, Johnny stood off at the edge of the firelight. It was warm enough that they didn't need a large fire, but they kept a small one burning to keep wolves and coyotes away.

Joe was asleep, but Matt came strolling out of the lean-to.

Matt said, "You know, I think I could stay here

forever."

Johnny nodded. "I feel the same. I know we can't, though. We'll run out of supplies. The coffee's running low. And sooner or later, we'll thin out the game too much, so we'll have to move on."

"Are you still thinking California?"

Johnny shrugged. "I suppose. They have cattle there, and we can get jobs. They even have a seaport in San Francisco, or so I've heard. You could go back to sea if you want."

"I don't really know what I want. Do you?"

"I think I do. Or, at least, I know what I want eventually. A small ranch near mountains like these. A solid cabin to keep the cold out at night. And I want children. A family."

"But to do all that, you need the right woman."

Johnny nodded. "Ma said once that God will provide, in His own time. Pa said once that God can see the whole picture. We can't. We have to rely on His judgment."

"Do you believe all of that?"

Johnny shrugged. "No reason not to."

"I'll admit, over the years I've wondered about all of that. The *God* stuff. Is it real, or just a myth? The more I thought about it, the more it seemed not to make a whole lot of sense. But when I stood on deck and looked out at the open ocean, or I stand on a ridge here and look off at this land, you can feel God in your heart."

"Pa said once that a man can think himself out of a good idea and get himself all turned around, but he can feel in his heart what's right. That old scout I talk about, Apache Jim, said the same thing. Except he said *gut* and not *heart*. He said, always trust your gut. What's your gut telling you, now?"

"It's telling me I don't know nearly as much as I once thought I did."

Johnny looked off at the night, and at the stars overhead. "Maybe that's what education is really all about. Realizing you don't know as much as you thought you did."

Matt said, "Do you know what the date is?"

Johnny shook his head. "I couldn't even tell you what day of the week it is, now. When one day is pretty much like another, it's easy to lose track. I mentioned it to Joe yesterday, and he said none of that matters out here.

Marking time isn't as important to the Indians. They mark the seasons, but the exact day of the week is a *white man* concept that the Cheyenne often laugh at."

"I suppose I understand that. I wouldn't have, back in Pennsylvania or even in Texas, but now I think I do."

Johnny said, "I wonder what Ma and Luke are doing."

"Probably in bed, this time of night. They probably still have a foot of snow on the ground."

"You know, I think we missed Christmas. It was just before Thanksgiving when we left Texas."

Matt looked at Johnny. "I hadn't thought about that. We might have been somewhere on the trail between Texas and here. I've never missed a Christmas before. Even last winter on the trail, we knew when it was Christmas."

"Hold on." Johnny went to his saddle bags and came back with the bottle of tequila. It was still a third full. He took a swallow and handed it to Matt. "Merry belated Christmas."

Matt took a mouthful of it, and said, "And Merry Christmas to you."

Matt then said, "Do you suppose we're being sacrilegious?"

Johnny shrugged. "I suppose it's in how you look at it. The way I see it, if Christmas is alive in your heart, then it's Christmas."

"Is Christmas alive in your heart, or is it just the tequila talking?"

"You think about all that Christmas means. I would say, yeah, it's alive in my heart. Part of what Jesus was talking about, I think, is second chances. And here we are, standing in a land that could be called a paradise. Heading off to California, where maybe no one has heard the name McCabe. Maybe the wanted posters didn't make it that far west."

"I suppose you could call California a *third* chance, really. I had been kind of thinking of Texas as a second chance."

Johnny took another swig of tequila. "I'd like it if we act smarter, this time. Don't make enemies. Avoid the likes of Coleman Grant."

Johnny handed the bottle back to Matt. Matt raised the bottle to the night sky, and said, "Here's to second chances."

72

MATT TOOK a swig from the bottle and said, "Do you ever think of Maria Carerra?"

"Hard not to."

"The way she looked at you. Every man wants a woman like that to look at him that way."

Matt handed the bottle back to Johnny.

Matt said, "And then there's Becky Drummond, back home. I suppose her name's Becky Hawley, now. Married, and probably has a child."

"I suppose so."

"Any man would consider himself lucky to have the attention of even one woman like Becky or Maria in a lifetime. And yet, they're both behind you now. You're looking for the right woman to build a life with, and yet you rode away from both of them."

Johnny was silent a moment, looking up at the sky. The stars were so big and bright, up here in the mountains.

He said, "Pa said something once. He said for everything, there is the right time. With both Becky and Maria, the timing wasn't right. My gut feeling is I still have more living to do before I can settle down.

"Becky said she wanted to stay right where she was, to raise a family in Sheffield. She said if I could promise her not to be always looking off at the western horizon and wondering what might have been, then she would marry me. But I couldn't promise that.

"It's kind of the same thing with Maria. Her destiny seems to be to take her father's ranch and build it into something even greater. I suppose I could have found some happiness at her side, being the ramrod of that ranch. Maybe a lot of happiness. But I wouldn't have been content."

"So, you rode away from both of them because it didn't feel one hundred percent right."

Johnny nodded. "Something like that."

"But how can you be sure?"

Johnny shrugged his shoulders.

He said, "I suppose you're never one hundred percent sure. But it comes back to what Pa and Apache Jim said. Trust your gut."

They were silent for a while. Crickets chirped in the

darkness, out beyond the firelight. Further out, a coyote called out. Johnny glanced at the line of horses. They didn't seem bothered by it, so Johnny figured the coyote wasn't close enough to worry about.

Matt said, "I had a girl, once. In a seaport in Singapore. You ever hear of that place?"

Johnny said, "Can't say that I have."

"It's off in the South Seas. That's where I met her. She was from the Philippines."

Johnny grinned. "Can't say I've heard of that place, either."

"Filipino people look a little Chinese. But there's something exotic about them. At least, there was with this girl. Her name was *Ligaya*. It means *happiness* in her language. From the first moment I looked in her eyes, I was in love. Raven black hair. Skin that was a beautiful bronze and so smooth to the touch. Eyes that were a deep brown, almost black. And she had a smile that could light up my heart."

"So, what happened?"

"We were in port a few weeks. We had sustained some damage in a pirate attack."

Johnny took one more pull of the tequila, and he listened.

With words, Matt painted a picture of his ship sailing near the southern coast of India. Sails filling with the wind, and porpoises leaping and frolicking in the water off to one side.

They happened upon a ship that seemed to be hung up on a reef near the shore. The ship was listing a bit to its side, and when Matt looked through his spyglass, the ship looked to be abandoned.

Matt was the first mate. The captain, a man with a thick black beard and who wore a red sash tied about his middle and a revolver tucked into the front of the sash, asked Matt what he thought.

Matt was in a black Mediterranean cap, the one he had been wearing when he returned to Pennsylvania. He had no sash, but he tucked a gun into the front of his belt.

He said, "It's a frigate. Looks to be Portuguese."

"Should we take a look?"

Matt said to Johnny, "We weren't thieves, but we weren't going to let a cargo just set there unattended. If we didn't take it, someone else would come along and do so."

Johnny said, "You don't have to justify anything to me. I know our father didn't raise any thieves."

"It's just that the people back home might not have understood."

Matt told how they worked their way toward the ship.

"Quite an art, really," Matt said. "I'm no expert on sailing. I picked up a general knowledge of it while I was at sea. But every ship has a pilot. Ours was a Swede named Andersonn. We all called him Andy. Tall brute. He had a square jaw and features that looked like they were carved out of granite. He had a scar that ran from under one eye, across his nose, and down along the other cheekbone. It was said he got it in a swordfight. But he could sure pilot a ship. I'd swear he could put that ship anywhere he wanted. He could slide it between two rocks with but a foot to spare on either side."

Matt and the captain stood looking off at the derelict as Andy brought them in closer.

When they were about three cables' lengths from the derelict, the captain said, "I don't like the look of this, boys. I've got a bad feeling."

Andy said from the wheel, "Want me to turn us back, Cap'n?"

The captain shook his head. "No. McCabe's right. If there's a cargo here, it'd be a shame to just let it rot away or let someone else have it. But let's hold up here."

The second mate was an Irishman they called Blarney.

The captain said, "Blarney, go down and get my blunderbuss. And get McCabe's sword."

Johnny interrupted the story to ask what a *cable's length* was.

Matt said, "A nautical measurement. A way of measuring distance at sea. One cable's length would be about six hundred feet."

"So you were eighteen hundred feet from that ship."

Matt nodded. "Closer to two thousand, but I'm rounding down."

Johnny grinned.

Matt continued. "We wanted to see if there was cargo aboard. It wasn't a military ship, which meant it was either a cargo ship, or it had been seized by pirates. Either way, we had to check it out. But our captain was forever given to caution."

"Not a bad thing."

"No, indeed."

Blarney returned to the quarter deck with a double-barrel shotgun, which the captain referred to as his blunderbuss, and Matt's cutlass.

"McCabe," the captain said, looking off toward the derelict and squinting into the sun. "I want you to take a boat over there. But be careful. Something don't feel right about 'er."

Matt nodded to the captain. "I know what you mean, Cap'n."

The captain stroked his beard with two fingers while he thought. "Blarney, I want two guns trained on the derelict. Just in case."

Blarney said, "Aye, Cap'n."

Matt said to Johnny, "And of course, what he meant by *guns* was cannons."

"So," Johnny said. "When you took a boat over there, you found pirates?"

"Never got the chance. While we were lowering a boat over the side, one port was opened on the derelict and the muzzle of a cannon was pushed out. There was nothing we could do. Since we weren't anchored, the captain called out, *Hard to starboard!* But it was too late. The cannon fired, and our main mast was cut in two."

The captain gave the order for return fire. Andy swung the ship to the starboard side, and once they were broadside, a cannon boomed from the gun deck below. Matt's ship was rocked toward the side, and the cannon ball took out the quarter deck on the derelict. Boards splintered and flew into the air, but there were no casualties. No one standing there. Any men had apparently been hidden below decks.

Then a boat came around from behind the derelict. A single sail, and carrying men who were armed with swords and pistols.

Matt's ship fired at them, but missed. The cannon ball splashed into the water and the men on the boat were bathed with salt spray, but they kept on coming.

The wind was in their favor. The crew of Matt's ship fired again, but the shot went a little high. It missed the single sail by mere feet.

Then the boat was alongside the ship, and men were

climbing up and boarding. It was hand-to-hand.

Matt said, "I've never experienced anything like it. The rush. The excitement. I'm ashamed to admit, it was almost fun. That was the battle when I found myself face-to-face with the pirate captain, and that deadly calm we talked about overcame me."

"How long did the battle last?"

"It felt like hours, but when it was done I checked my pocket watch. Twelve minutes."

Johnny nodded. "That's the way it often is in a battle. Time seems to somehow slow down."

Matt said, "Blarney was killed. Andy took a blow to the head, and it was a day before he was ready to man the wheel again. But everyone who boarded us was killed. There were two men left on the derelict, on the gun deck. They surrendered and the captain shot them both. It sounds kind of cruel, but out there at sea, there is no law. There was no constable to turn them over to. The closest we had to law was our ship's captain."

"Not that much different in the West."

"The cargo was silks from China. And tea, and gunpowder."

"Sounds like quite a haul."

"Indeed. The captain took a quarter of it and gave me a quarter, and the men got to split the rest.

"The captain didn't want us to dally, though. He didn't want us to still be there if another ship came along, so we loaded the cargo quickly.

"We were a day out of Singapore, under normal conditions. But using the foremast and mizzenmast only, we figured it would take us three. We didn't want to sail by night because the area was given to reefs. But the following morning, we were underway. I was a capable enough pilot for smooth waters, which we had that day, and by the next day, Andy was back at the wheel."

Johnny said, "And it was in Singapore that you met the girl. What'd you say her name was?"

"Ligaya. Like I said, I fell in love the moment I first looked into those eyes. And she fell in love with me. For a few weeks, it was like heaven-on-Earth, and we found happiness together. Which I suppose was some sort of poetical justice, because that's what her name meant.

"She was an indentured servant, and I eventually used

most of my money from the pirate haul to buy her freedom."

"So, what happened?"

"She wanted to go home to the Philippines. They're a small group of islands a few days out of Singapore, if the wind's right. She wanted to build a life there. Her father ran a small farm. Her destiny was there, just like I suppose Becky's is back home and Maria's is at her father's ranch.

"Once the ship was repaired, I paid the captain a fee to transport her, and we brought her back to her home. I remember standing on the deck as we sailed out. She was on the shore, waving to me."

Matt was then silent for a bit.

Johnny said, "Do you think about her much?"

"Sometimes. But it's like you said. It wasn't entirely meant to be. Almost, but almost doesn't count."

Johnny had to say it. "Except in horseshoes."

Matt smiled, then he and Johnny stood in silence and looked at the fire, each thinking his own thoughts about what their lives might have been like had things been a little different.

73

ONE DAY BLENDED into another. Some days were warm and almost summer-like. Then would come freezing winter winds and snow would fall. At times Johnny would find himself knee-deep in snow, hunting for an elk or a mule deer. Other times, the weather would warm up and the snow would be gone. The stream cutting through their little valley would be rushing with current.

Joe made a trap to catch fish with, something he had learned from the Cheyenne, and more than once he brought back some trout.

Johnny continued to show Matt how to track an animal. Matt had no rifle, but using Joe's Enfield, he brought down an elk one day.

The following day, more snow fell, and the boys settled in for a cold patch that went on day after day.

They had wood, though. Matt had brought in enough from dead-falls.

The boys built a fire with flames that rose two feet into the air. Johnny put on some coffee, and they put some of Matt's elk on a spit to roast. Joe sat cross-legged on the ground, his blankets over his shoulders.

He chewed on a root he had dug by the stream a few days earlier. Tasted something like a carrot.

He said, "Boys, this is the life. I can see how them old fur-trappers were drawn to the mountains."

Johnny nodded. "Me too. With the right woman at his side, a man could build a cabin in these mountains and never have a care for the outside world."

After a week, the weather warmed a bit, and the ground lost some of its snow cover. Johnny and Joe decided to saddle up and have a look about.

Out beyond their valley, they descended a slope and came out of the pine forest and into a large, flat area that stretched on for a few miles. The ground was gravelly, and scattered here and there were junipers and occasional short, fat pines.

Johnny saw motion up ahead. Two riders. He was about to say something, but Joe saw them too.

They were Indian. As they drew closer, Joe said, "Are

they the two we saw before? The ones you gave the elk to?"

"I think so."

Johnny and Joe reined up. The two Arapahoes rode up to them.

Johnny sat while Joe and the two Arapaho warriors exchanged hand signals.

Joe said to Johnny, "They've been looking for us."

One man then looked at Johnny and held out a pair of deerskin boot-length moccasins. He said something that sounded to Johnny like, "Neeceenohoo."

Then he made the hand-sign that Johnny had learned meant *gift*.

Joe grinned. "He must've noticed your riding boots and figured you needed something better for these mountains. You gave their village an entire elk. The Indians I know tend to like to offer a gift in exchange for a gift."

Johnny looked at the warrior, and he nodded and said, "Thank you."

The warrior smiled. He and his partner then turned and rode back the way they had come.

When they got back to their camp, they told Matt what had happened.

Joe said, "So, what're you going to do with two pair of deerskin boots?"

Johnny dug into his saddlebags and pulled out the pair he had made himself, and he tossed them to Matt.

Matt said, "These won't fit me. You always had bigger feet."

"But you have a bigger head. It all evens out in the end."

Joe was grinning.

That night, they sat about the fire and ate the last of a mule deer Johnny had shot.

Johnny said, "We have to make a decision. Matt and I were talking a while back that if we stay too long, we're gonna start thinning out the game."

Joe nodded. "Been thinking about that, too."

"So, the question is," Matt said. "Where do we go from here? You still thinking about California?"

Johnny nodded his head.

On a morning with spring in the air, snow

disappearing from their little valley, and wildflowers growing in the clearing down by the stream, the brothers saddled up and tied their bedrolls and saddle bags to their saddles.

Johnny gave a last look to the lean-to. The pine boughs Joe had used for thatching had turned brown and would have needed to be replaced again, were he and his brothers to stay.

Matt said, "I have to admit, I'm going to miss this little place."

Johnny nodded. "For a short time, it was home for us."

They mounted up and crossed the valley floor. The stream was again rushing with run-off, but there was a section where the stream widened and got a little shallower. It was two feet deep at this point and the bottom was sandy, with even footing for the horses. They turned the horses into the water and got through.

They climbed a slope and at the top of the ridge, Johnny gave a little tug to Bravo's reins and then looked back and down at the valley.

From this elevation, their valley looked like a mass of treetops rising from a depression between ridges. Their little camp would be off to the other side.

"I wonder if we'll ever be back," Matt said.

Johnny shrugged. He was reminded of when he looked back at the family farm the last time, wondering if he would ever be back.

He said, "I hope so."

Then he turned Bravo away and said, "All right. Let's ride."

PART SIX
California

74

Montana, 1881

THE FIRE WAS crackling away in the hearth. Ginny was in her rocker, and Bree was now on the sofa beside Johnny, with her feet curled under her and a quilt over her lap. Dusty was dropping another chunk of wood on the fire.

Jessica had taken Cora off to bed. Joe was awake again and was sitting in a French carved wing chair Ginny had bought Josh and Temperance as a wedding gift. It stood where Johnny's chair once had.

Ginny said, "I don't think you ever told me about that little valley."

Johnny said, "That was where I first fell in love with the mountains. I always liked the mountains back in Pennsylvania, but it was in that little valley that I started feeling somehow drawn to them. And not just any mountains, but the range that goes from Colorado all the way up into Canada. The same mountains our valley belongs to."

"The Rockies," she said.

He nodded. "There's something magical about the wide-open spaces of Texas. But the Rocky Mountains took hold of my heart like no other place ever has."

Bree said, "So, when you brought us here to this valley, it must have felt a little like coming home."

"Yeah, it sort of did, Punkin'."

Ginny said, "Did you ever get back to that little valley?"

"No. I always wanted to, and one day, I might."

"What about all that desert land, west of those mountains? I remember it, when you brought us all here years later. It encompassed two territories, Utah and Nevada. At that time, we had wagons and supplies. I can't imagine how the three of you crossed it on horseback with just the clothes on your back."

"We crossed it one mile at a time. There's water out there if you know where to look. If you see a canyon and it has trees growing, then you know there has to be a water source. And we brought a little food with us. We made some venison jerky when we were still in our little valley, and we brought some of those roots Joe had been digging."

Joe said, "We stopped at Fort Bridger. An old fur trapper was there, and he was helpful. Drew a map for us."

"I remember that man," Johnny said. "And by early June, we had made it to the second mountain range further west, what they call the Sierra Nevadas."

Ginny said, "Were Utah and Nevada all as desolate then as they were when we traveled through?"

Johnny nodded. "Moreso. When my brothers and I went through, it was still a year before the big gold rush that saw Virginia City and Carson City spring to life. There was a little prospecting going on in the Washoe country, where the gold rush would be, and there was some ranching southwest of that area. That's all there was that passed for civilization. Most of the territory was wide open and empty. Except for the Indians, who lived like they always had. Roaming free. Hunting an area until the game started to get too thinned out then they'd pack up the entire village and move on.

"There was no railroad, like there is now. And the only settlements were around the Great Salt Lake, in the eastern part of the territory. We skirted around them, just to be on the safe side."

Ginny said, "You three must have looked quite rough, having lived all those months in the wild."

Johnny nodded. "We were unshaven and sorely in need of haircuts. Covered in sweat and trail dust. And that's how we rode into the Sierra Nevada mountains, on the California border."

75

The Sierra Nevadas
May, 1858

JOHNNY WAS riding a little ahead, climbing a ridge that was covered with pines. Just like with the Rockies, these mountains were covered with a pine forest, and the pines grew far enough apart so a man could ride a horse through. There was very little underbrush to tangle up a horse's legs. The trees grew tall with most of their green boughs toward the top, so Johnny found no low-hanging branches to catch a rider in the face.

He topped the ridge, and beyond was a grassy glade that stretched for what he guessed to be a mile.

The grass was green and lush, and purple and pink flowers grew. Out in the grass were four antelope.

Johnny gave Bravo's reins a little tug. The horse was more than happy to stop, after climbing the slope.

The way the wind was blowing, the antelope hadn't caught the scent of Johnny or Bravo. Johnny sat in the saddle and watched the animals. They were chewing on grass. Then one would raise its head and look across the field. Probably had heard something. The others would follow suit, then they would go back to grazing.

Matt and Joe came up behind Johnny, and he held up a hand for them to stop.

"One of them would sure taste good for supper," Joe said. "I'm about tired of rabbit."

"Rabbit's all we've found for game for the last few days." Johnny slid his Hawken from the scabbard. "That's about to change."

"Johnny," Matt said. "They've got to be a quarter of a mile away."

Johnny nodded. "I loaded two hundred and fifty grains of powder. Just in case we ran into a bear."

Joe said, "That should cover a quarter of a mile."

Johnny brought the rifle to his shoulder, cocked the hammer back, and pulled the rear trigger to engage the hair-trigger effect on the front trigger.

"Johnny," Matt said. "That's an impossible shot you're trying to make. You're just gonna scare them away. We should try to get closer, maybe move toward them downwind."

Johnny said, "Quiet Matt, I'm drawing a bead."

Matt sighed and shook his head.

Johnny gave the hair-trigger a tap and the gun bucked against his shoulder. The *boom* echoed, and a cloud of gun smoke swirled about them. Through the smoke, Johnny could see three antelope running off.

He and his brothers started their horses forward into the glade. There in the grass was one antelope, on its side. Johnny's fifty caliber ball had caught it just below the ear.

Johnny said to Matt, "What'd you say?"

"Not a thing."

They found a place to make camp near a small creek. They were close to a mile beyond the field where Johnny had shot the antelope. A thick tangle of junipers was behind them, and behind the junipers was a grove of maples. A good stone's throw in front of them was the water.

By nightfall, they had rigged a wooden spit and were roasting a haunch of antelope, and their coffee pot was heating up at the edge of the fire.

Matt was stretched out on his bedroll and his arms were folded behind his head.

He said, "You know, I've been thinking about what we talked about back at our little valley. Once we get to California, doing things a little more intelligently than we did in Texas."

Johnny was standing by the fire. "I think we might actually be in California now. We're on the western side of the mountain range."

"Then it's time we put some thought into what we're going to do."

Joe was sitting cross-legged on a blanket by the fire.

He said, "What do you think we should do?"

"For one thing, we have to think about our names. The reward posters might have made it all the way to California. There's no reason to believe they wouldn't. The posters call for three brothers. You two look enough alike that anyone could tell you're related."

Johnny grinned. "Even with that beard? Joe looks more like a grizzly than my brother."

Joe snorted a chuckle.

Matt said, "Have you looked at yourself, lately? You're not looking all that much different than Joe. When was the last time you shaved?"

Johnny shrugged. The last time he had looked into a mirror had been in the Broken Spur bunkhouse. There had been a broken piece of a mirror held up on the wall between two nails.

Johnny said, "Last time I shaved was Texas."

They had left the Broken Spur five months ago. Johnny's hair now covered his ears and touched his collar in back. His beard wasn't as thick as Joe's, but it was three inches long.

Matt said, "I think the two of you should call yourself brothers. Use an alias. You can't very well use the name O'Brien, because of that arrest warrant back in Texas. We can say I'm not related. Just a friend. We can say we worked together in Texas. I'll use Aunt Sara's maiden name. I'll call myself Matt O'Toole."

Johnny said, "We can call ourselves Reynolds."

Joe grinned again. He said, "Worked for me, once."

Matt said, "I wonder what Taffy Reynolds would say at the thought of being immortalized this way?"

Johnny grinned. "She's immortalized in the memory of many a boy from Sheffield."

The coffee was ready, so Johnny filled their cups.

"So," Johnny said. "We're Johnny and Joe Reynolds. Lately from Texas. Might as well keep it as truthful as we can. The more complicated we make our story, the harder it'll be to keep it all straight. We're lately from the Broken Spur. Breaker Grant died and no one wanted to work for his son, so we all went different directions."

"It's mostly the truth," Joe said. "Goullie, Shelby and the others all left for just that reason. And we would have too, even without the arrest warrant."

Matt nodded. "Another thing I've been thinking about." He said to Johnny, "Those guns you wear. How many cowhands do you see wearing two guns?"

Johnny looked down at his guns. He shrugged and said, "I suppose I don't see many."

"At the Broken Spur, I didn't see any. I didn't in town, either. I saw a couple Texas Rangers riding through one time, and they each wore two guns."

Joe said, "He might have a point. Wearin' them two

guns kind of makes you look like a gunman. Which I suppose you are. The gunman of the Rio Grande."

Johnny shook his head. "I still hate that name."

Matt said, "Is there anything you can do?"

"Not really. This is a two-holster gunbelt. I had it made in a small town just south of the border."

The horses were picketed a little ways from the fire. Bravo's head went up, his eyes on a point out beyond the firelight, and then the other two horses did the same.

"What is it?" Matt said.

"I don't know." Johnny set his coffee down to free both hands.

They heard a stick cracking out in the darkness.

Matt said, "Indians?"

Joe shook his head. He was getting to his feet. "If it was Indians, we wouldn't have heard 'em."

A man called out from the darkness. "Hello, the fire!"

Johnny loosened the right-hand gun in its holster. He called back, "Come on in! The coffee's hot."

Joe moved off to the other side of the fire, so all three brothers wouldn't be in an easy line of fire. He hooked a thumb in the belt buckled around his buckskin shirt, which brought his hand within easy reach of his pistol.

The man came in on foot, leading his horse. He was tall and thin, and he walked with a bow-legged cowhand way. He had leather leggings strapped on over his trousers and a large bandana tied around his neck. His hat was wide-brimmed with a rounded crown. He had a scar that began above one eye and trailed down around the eye to his cheekbone.

He said, "I could sure take you up on that offer of coffee."

Johnny said, "You got a cup in those saddle bags?"

"Surely do." He dug a tin cup from his saddle bags and Johnny filled it from the kettle.

He was about thirty, with some trail dust on his clothes, and he looked like he hadn't shaved in a few days.

Johnny said, "There a ranch near here?"

The man shook his head. "We're out mustangin'. Been out here for a couple of days. We ride for the McCarty Ranch, about a two-day ride west of here."

He held out a hand and said, "Name's Cooper. True Cooper. I'm their ramrod."

Johnny shook the hand. "Johnny Reynolds. This here's my brother Joe. And Matt O'Toole."

Cooper blew on the coffee for a moment. Hot coffee can heat up the rim of a tin cup, and you can scald your lip.

He took a sip and said, "So, what brings you boys out here?"

"Heading on into California," Matt said.

"Mind if I ask from where?"

Odd thing, Johnny thought. Men of the West usually allowed a man his privacy. They didn't ask probing questions.

Johnny said, "Texas. Worked at the Broken Spur for a while."

"The Broken Spur? That's Breaker Grant's place, isn't it?"

Johnny nodded.

Johnny noticed Cooper give a quick glance to Johnny's guns.

Cooper said, "If you don't mind my sayin', you don't really look like cowhands."

"Been on the trail a long time," Johnny said.

"Haven't seen many cowhands wear two guns like that."

Johnny decided to follow the idea of telling as much truth as possible. "I rode with the Texas Rangers for a while. Old habits die hard."

Johnny noticed Bravo and the other two horses were looking off into the night again.

"Mind if I ask?" Cooper said. "What brings you all the way here from Texas?"

Matt said, "Breaker Grant died. His son is running the place now, and a lot of us decided maybe it was time to ride on."

"And you decided to go all the way to California."

Matt nodded. "We had some money saved up, and decided we'd like to see a different part of the country."

Johnny glanced over to the horses. They were all still looking off into the night. Joe had looked toward the horses too, and then his gaze met Johnny's.

Johnny said, "So, you're cowhands, out chasing down wild horses."

Cooper nodded. "That's what we're doin'."

"Well, maybe we don't look much like cowhands, but if

you don't mind my sayin', you don't act much like one."

Cooper had been about to take a sip of coffee, but what Johnny said caught him by surprise.

Johnny said, "Most cowhands I know don't ride into a camp and accept a cup of coffee while they're friends hide out in the dark, with their guns trained on the camp."

Joe looked at him, his eyes in their habitual squint. "How many guns you got trained on us?"

Johnny said, "I assume one for each man, and maybe a couple extra. But keep in mind, whatever it is you want, if one of them fires I'll put my first bullet right between your eyes."

Cooper said, "Your gun ain't even drawn."

"Not yet."

Cooper looked at him. Johnny returned the gaze. Johnny felt the familiar but strange feeling of calmness wash through him. Should anyone fire from outside the camp, presuming the first bullet didn't kill Johnny, then he would be hitting the dirt and rolling to make himself a more difficult target to hit. And he would draw his gun as he moved, and his first shot would go into the man called Cooper.

Joe said, "We don't want no trouble. Tell your men to stand down."

"Whatever it is you want from us, money or horses," Johnny said, "it won't be worth it. Because you'll be dead."

Johnny didn't really think the man was a highwayman, but you never knew these days. And they were a long way from civilization.

Cooper grinned and then held up a hand in a sort of stopping motion. "All right. We don't want any trouble. It's just there've been some problems with rustlers lately. There's also some concern that some of the border violence going on in Kansas might work its way out to these parts."

Matt said, "We're not rustlers. Just honest men lately from Texas. Once we've had a turn in a bath tub and a shave, we'll look a lot more like the cowhands we are."

Cooper called out to the darkness. "Stand down! Come on in."

Four men came in, and they were indeed cowhands. Boots worn so tight it was hard to walk in them, leather leggings strapped to their pants. Wide brimmed hats, and bandanas about the neck.

Johnny said, "I'll put on some more coffee."

76

THE MCCARTY MEN HUNKERED DOWN for coffee and to share the antelope.

"There's a town called Greenville," Cooper said. He was sitting on the ground beside Johnny, with a chunk of roasted antelope impaled on his knife blade. "You boys go in there and get yourselves lookin' presentable. There's four different ranches within riding distance of town. At our place, it's called the Bar M, we might have an opening for a man. There's others, too. The Washburn place, about thirty miles south of town. The Hill spread, about twenty miles west of town. Use my name as a reference."

Johnny said, "Much obliged."

The men rode on. They had a camp five miles to the north.

Once they were gone, Matt climbed into his bedroll. Johnny added some wood to the fire because here in the mountains, it still felt like winter after the sun went down.

Matt said, "So, should we ride straight on to the town of Greenville? We should have a little money left over to make ourselves a little more presentable. I, for one, could use a hot bath."

Joe was sitting by the fire. He said, "I'd be content to roam around these mountains for just a little more. Greenville will be there when we get there."

Johnny nodded. "I have to say, I agree. Maybe tomorrow we can do some hunting. Maybe find a good spot by a stream to camp for a couple of days. But then we probably should be heading down out of the mountains to find that town. I'd hate to deprive Matt of his bath."

"You got a point. He's startin' to smell a little rank."

Matt said, "I've got nothing on either of you."

Come morning, they were riding along a wooded ridge. Pines rose all about them.

They started down the ridge, and the land opened up a bit. They could see the piney slope descending away from them. It looked like a thick, green carpet in the distance. Beyond were some rocks and cliffs.

"Looks like there might be a canyon, a little further down," Joe said.

They continued downward, and Joe was right. A canyon opened up before them. It was long and narrow, and a small stream wound its way along the canyon floor. Johnny figured it was probably from spring run-off and would be about half as wide and deep come August.

Matt said, "I bet geologists would tell us that stream carved out this canyon, over a period of thousands of years."

Joe shook his head. "Sometimes it's best just to enjoy the beauty of God's world and not try to wrap our heads around how He made it all."

"But Joe, it's the normal state of the human mind to be curious. Curious about all things. You see a thing of beauty like this canyon, don't you want to learn all there is to know about it?"

"I want to learn anything that's important to us. Like, can we get down to that water and let our horses have some of it? And fill our canteens? But some things are beyond us. We can wonder about it all day, but we'll never have all the information. We weren't here over them thousands of years you talk about, so we can't really know if that stream had anything to do with it at all."

"But Joe..."

Johnny was grinning. He remembered arguments like this between the two, when they were growing up. He wasn't sure which one of them was trying to egg on the other.

"Come on," he said. "Let's find a way down to that river."

He rode closer to the edge. The canyon looked to be shallow on both ends, but as deep as thirty feet here at the center. Grass and a few trees grew on the canyon floor, but mostly it looked to be gravel and rock.

Then Johnny noticed five riders in the canyon. They had reined up and were positioned a few yards apart. They were facing toward one end of the canyon, as though they were watching something or waiting.

When Joe and Matt rode up behind him, he said, "I think our friends from last night are down there."

Joe said, "Looks like Cooper in the middle."

Matt said, "What do you suppose they're doing?"

But before Johnny or Joe could answer, a gun was fired from one end of the canyon. Then they heard the rumble of hooves hammering into the earth, and twelve wild horses came galloping toward the riders.

Most were bays, but one was a paint horse, and one was a black with three white stockings. It was running slightly ahead of the small pack. Johnny figured it was the dominant stallion. A king in the wilderness with his harem, Johnny thought.

The horses saw the line of riders and came to a stop. But more riders were coming up behind them. Some of the horses spun about, realizing they were trapped.

The men had lassos out and loops were spinning overhead.

However, the black stallion began charging toward the line of riders. Directly at Cooper. The ramrod threw his loop, but it hit the stallion at the side of the neck and fell away.

Cooper's horse reared. The stallion pushed past, and started away toward the far end of the canyon at a full gallop. Cooper turned his horse and was off in pursuit.

"Come on," Johnny said.

He turned Bravo and was off, running along the edge of the canyon wall. He was careful not to get too close because rocks could break away and he and Bravo would go tumbling down into the canyon. But he kept Cooper within sight.

The end of the canyon was closed, and the stallion came to a sliding stop in some loose sand. Then he turned to face Cooper.

Johnny brought Bravo to a stop, and Matt and Joe reined up beside him.

Cooper had pulled in his lariat as he was riding, and he was about to start spinning the loop again. But the stallion didn't look frightened. Johnny thought the horse looked like he wanted to fight.

Cooper got a loop into the air and around the stallion's neck, but instead of pulling away, the horse charged.

Cooper's horse reared up again, and Cooper came loose from the saddle. All except one foot, which was stuck in the stirrup.

Then the stallion was on top of Cooper. Pounding with his hooves. The saddled horse tried to pull away, dragging Cooper along with him, but the stallion followed along and continued to drive his hooves into the man.

Johnny pulled his rifle.

Joe said, "The horse is gonna kill him."

Matt said, "We've gotta get down there somehow."

Johnny cocked the rifle and brought it to his shoulder. No time to play around with the second trigger. He just drew a bead fast, more pointing the rifle than aiming it. He figured about seven hundred feet, maybe less, at a downward angle. No wind. He pulled the trigger and the rifle bucked against his shoulder.

The horse lurched and spun. It then wobbled away and then spun in a circle again.

"Got it in the neck," Johnny said. "Didn't have time to really aim."

He had the powder horn around his saddle horn, and some loose balls, greased patches and percussion caps in a vest pocket. He began to reload as fast as he could.

Matt swung out of the saddle and left the old mare's rein trailing, and he started down the side of the canyon on foot. The canyon wall descended at a small angle, and Matt was able to retain some footing. At least, at first. Then rocks and sand began to slide under the smooth soles of his riding boots. He began to slide with it and kept his balance. He had seen some Filipino boys riding long, flat boards on the ocean surf. They called it *surfing*. He realized he was essentially surfing down the side of the canyon wall.

Joe was right behind him, but not faring as well. He was built stronger than either Matt or Johnny, but was slower on his feet. When the gravel began to slide underfoot, he couldn't react in time and went head-over-teakettle down to the canyon floor.

The stallion had stopped circling, and was now facing toward Matt and Joe. Blood was streaming down the side of its neck and onto one shoulder.

"Don't much like horsemeat," Johnny said, bringing the rifle back to his shoulder, "but you're asking for this."

He didn't have to aim as quickly this time, so he was more able to find his target. Right between the eyes. He drew a breath, let it out slowly, and pulled the trigger.

The horse lurched back a couple of steps, then fell over.

Joe called out to Matt, "I'm all right! Go tend to Cooper!"

Matt ran over to Cooper. The saddled horse was flailing about, taking lots of dancing and turning steps but not going far. What he was doing, though, was dragging Cooper along through the gravel.

Matt had learned a bit about horses at the Broken Spur. He figured the animal was frightened and confused, and having the weight of a rider pulling at one stirrup probably wasn't helping any.

Cooper was flopping like a rag doll on the ground, being pulled along by the horse. His face was lost in a pool of blood, and his leg was twisted like there were no bones in it at all.

Matt approached the horse, stepping gently and trying to make it look like he wasn't in a hurry while he was hurrying.

"Easy, boy. Easy, now."

The horse was rolling its eyes at him and snorting furiously. It took one more step, but then Matt got hold of its reins.

He held the reins in a way that said, *I'm in charge now.* The horse knew it and settled down a little. Matt started stroking its nose.

"Easy, boy. You're all right."

Two riders came along from further down the valley.

They reined up hard and half swung, half jumped out of the saddle and ran toward Cooper.

"What happened?" one of them said. A boy, not much older than Luke.

But the other, an older man with white stubble on his chin and a perpetual squint to his eyes, said, "I'll tell you what happened. It was that danged stallion."

The man had been introduced to Matt the night before as Quint.

Quint brought his head down to Cooper's chest. "He's alive. For the moment."

He looked to the other man and said, "Get his foot out'a that stirrup."

The boy did. He said, "He ain't ever gonna walk on this leg again."

Quint said to Matt, "It's that foolish obsession he has with that stallion. We were out here in the fall, before the first snow. He faced that stallion then. That's how he got that scar on his face. I told him the horse was gonna kill him, but he wouldn't listen."

Johnny was hurrying over. He had left Bravo topside and was running toward them.

He said, "How is he?"

Quint said, "He's alive. But don't know for how long."

"Where's the nearest place? A house, a town? Even a way station?"

Quint said, "The nearest place is the ranch. Two days away from here. The town of Greenville is even further out."

The younger man said, "We can ride and fetch the doctor."

Quint shook his head. "If we can find the doc, if he's not out on some house call. And then we have to bring him all the way out here. Maybe the best way is just get Cooper back to the ranch."

"How? He can't ride."

Johnny said, "We can build a travois for him. There are some pines back there, outside the canyon."

The other rider said, "It'll take a while to build a travois."

"Then you better get on it now. Go back and get the other riders. Tell them to forget about those horses. Do you have an axe?"

The boy nodded. "We got two hatchets."

"Then get to it. And get a rider up there to fetch our horses."

"Yes sir," and the boy was off.

77

JOHNNY DECIDED the terrain was too rough for a travois to be dragged. He had the men rig it so it was suspended between four riders.

These weren't horses trained for pulling a wagon. They were cutting horses, but in Johnny's experience, a good cutting horse could adapt to almost anything. These horses were doing fine.

Even still, it was slow going. They couldn't move any faster than a casual walk without jostling the travois.

Johnny was riding ahead of the procession, with Quint beside him.

By early afternoon, Johnny said to him, "I'm starting to think Cooper's not going to make it back to the ranch at this rate."

Quint nodded. "He's breathin' poorly back there, and we're lookin' at one night on the trail. At the rate we're traveling, maybe two."

"I'm thinking we should send a rider for the doctor, after all. Maybe have him meet us on the trail. Who's the fastest rider here?"

"Evans."

Johnny remembered Evans from the antelope feast the night before. Evans was tall and rangy, with a bushy red beard.

Johnny said to Evans, "I want you to ride for the doctor. Ride like a pack of wolves are on your tail."

"I won't waste no time, Boss."

"All right. Take a second horse. Switch mounts rather than rest one."

Evans took a second horse and was on his way.

Quint said to Johnny, "I'll say one thing for you. You don't give up."

Johnny shook his head. "I may get beaten. But you won't ever see me quit."

Quint nodded with a grin. "I'm startin' to think you're a man to ride the river with."

They built a big fire that night, with men cutting enough wood so the fire could burn tall and hot all night long.

Joe had said he was all right, after his tumble down the slope. But he wasn't. His ankle had caught on something and twisted, and it swelled so much they had to cut his boot off. He was in the saddle all day, and the ankle was held in place with a splint, in case it was broken.

Joe sat by the fire, his splinted ankle stretched out in front of him.

The travois was placed by the fire. They didn't try to move Cooper out of it. They were concerned that moving him any more than they had to might make his injuries worse.

His breathing was shallow and raspy. He had taken two hooves to the ribs and Johnny thought the man's lungs were filling. Hopefully not with blood.

But Cooper was awake.

He said, "Where are we?"

"Trying to get you back to the ranch. We've sent Evans for the doctor. They're gonna meet us on the trail. Riding hard, maybe they'll be here tomorrow."

Cooper nodded. Johnny could tell the motion was causing some pain. At least one hoof had caught Cooper on the head, and he had a purple bruise along one side of his face, and an eye was swollen shut.

"You thirsty?" Johnny said.

Cooper nodded. Johnny called for a canteen, and one of the men brought one over. Corry, Johnny had learned his name was. The one who had come riding with Quint right after Cooper had been hurt.

Cooper reached for the canteen, but he found one arm was trussed up with hand-cut pine poles.

"You've got a broken arm," Johnny said. "Your leg's broken, too."

He decided not to go into detail about how bad the leg was. That Cooper would probably never walk on it again, and he might not even keep the leg.

Johnny held the canteen. Cooper brought his good hand up to steady it, and he took some swallows.

He then gave a wet-sounding cough. Like a man sounds with pneumonia, Johnny thought.

Cooper said, "What're you doing here?"

"Saving your life. I shot that horse that was trying to trample you to death."

"Shot him?"

Johnny nodded. "There wasn't much choice."

"That was a fine animal. Shame it had to be put down. Thank you for doin' what you done."

"I'm just glad we happened to be riding along when he did."

"Danged fool thing I did. Goin' after that stallion. I should've listened to Quint. Too much pride, I guess."

"You get some rest. I'm gonna have us all moving by sunrise."

Cooper nodded.

Johnny walked away, to return the canteen to Corry. But he cast a quick glance back at Cooper's leg. It was trussed up with four pine poles running along it, and spare bandanas to tie it all together. They had straightened out the foot so it aimed in the same direction as the other one. The leg was swollen to more than twice its size from the mid-calf up beyond the knee. Johnny thought it might be broken in two places. And the bone wasn't just cracked, but broken clean. He had never seen a leg broken as bad.

Johnny handed the canteen to Corry.

Corry said, "Is he gonna make it?"

"I don't know. But if not, it won't be because we gave up. I want the travois rigged back with the horses and moving by the first light."

"You want me riding with the travois?" He had been one of the riders with the travois rigged between them.

"Not this time," Johnny said. "I want you to ride ahead. Be our scout. My brother Joe is usually my scout, but he's got that busted-up ankle. I want you to watch for any terrain that might be hard to bring the travois through. Any areas we should ride around.

"I won't let you down, Boss."

Matt stood nearby with a cup of coffee, watching the activity around camp. He was mostly watching Johnny, and he had to admit to feeling a little amazement.

These men had known Johnny no more than a day, and yet he had fallen into a position of leadership as though he was born to it. Some of the men were even calling him *Boss*. It was those natural leadership skills Matt had mentioned in his letter home. The letter he never sent.

Johnny poured a cup of coffee and walked over to him. Johnny said, "I'd like you to be one of the travois riders, tomorrow. You've developed a real natural way with horses. We can't have those horses spooked. If one of them spooks and gets out of control and the travois flips, it might finish Cooper off."

Matt nodded. "That was incredible shooting you did, today. I find myself saying that a lot. But you saved his life."

"You did a good thing, too. I saw you ride that rock slide. If you hadn't, Cooper's horse might have kept on dragging him along."

Cooper was hit with a bout of coughing, then it died down.

Matt said, "Doesn't sound good. He's got fluid in his lungs."

"We'll do what we can, but it's in God's hands."

"I suppose most things are."

Johnny grinned. "Now you're starting to sound like Ma."

"Never a bad thing."

"It sure ain't."

78

THE TRAVOIS HAD a tendency to swing a bit as the horses walked along.

"Keep it slow, boys," Johnny said.

Johnny noticed Cooper's eyes were open, so he held up a hand for the travois riders to stop.

Johnny said to him, "How you doing, old hoss?"

Cooper grinned a little. "Been better."

Cooper was pale, and his face was gaunt. The one eye Cooper could open had a haunted look. Johnny had seen the look when he was with the Texas Rangers. A man who took a bullet and was dying, and was beyond the point where he could be saved.

Cooper said, "That stallion. What happened to him?"

He didn't remember the conversation the night before. Not good, Johnny thought.

Johnny said, "Had to be put down to save your life."

Cooper shook his head. "That's a shame. That was an incredible horse."

Then Cooper was unconscious again.

Johnny motioned for the riders to continue on.

Quint had ridden up beside Johnny. Quint said, "He looks like men I've seen who've lost a lot of blood."

Johnny nodded. "I think he's bleeding inside."

"That old doctor better get here soon, or it'll be too late."

Johnny saw Corry riding into view, through a stand of thick pines.

"Come on. Corry's checking in."

Corry had dismounted and was loosening the cinch. "There's a long narrow draw coming up. It'll be too steep for the travois. We'll have to go around it."

Johnny said, "How much time will we lose?"

"A couple hours. Maybe more. But it can't be helped."

The ravine was a quarter mile ahead, and at the speed they were going, it took them nearly fifteen minutes to reach it. The ridge fell away sharply with rocks and sharp pieces of bedrock jutting out. And in the middle of it all it looked like God himself and taken a huge trowel and just cut a swath through it.

Joe rode up beside Johnny and Quint.

He said, "It's like Corry said. No way you can get the travois down there."

Quint looked off to their right. "The land is less steep over there, on that side of the ridge. Even still, we'll have to go down the slope diagonal-like, so the travois isn't tipped too much. Like Corry said, a good two hours."

Johnny went back to the travois. "I think we should rest the horses a little before we start down the slope."

From here, they couldn't see the ravine.

Matt said, "Is it as bad as Corry says?"

Johnny nodded.

One of the riders was a man named Hardy. Older than most of the riders, but not quite gray, yet. He was in a floppy hat, with a bandana around his neck.

He said, "So that'll add two more hours to our ride. Can he make it?"

Johnny's gaze fell on Cooper. The man was very still, and his eyes were shut. He looked downright gray.

Johnny swung out of the saddle and left Bravo's reins trailing, and walked over to the travois. Didn't look like Cooper was breathing at all. Johnny reached a hand to Cooper's neck, trying to find a pulse. There was none. He then pressed fingers into Cooper's wrist. None there, either.

Johnny let out a load of air he didn't even realized he was holding. He felt a weight of defeat fall onto his shoulders, like it was trying to push him right into the ground.

"Won't matter, boys," Johnny said. "Cooper's come as far as he's going to."

Johnny and the boys wrapped Cooper's body in a blanket. The boys were all emotionally exhausted watching the life of a man they admired dwindle away, so Johnny decided they would travel no more that day.

He said, "We'll make camp right here."

Quint didn't cry. But he stood with the stoic sort of stillness Johnny had seen in many a strong man, when confronting something hurtful.

Quint said, "The man was like a brother to me."

Corry was young and tried to be stoic like Quint. But he couldn't quite manage it. A tear escaped, and he wiped it away.

"Mister Cooper was like a father to me," he said.

Johnny put an arm around the boy's shoulder.

Matt said, "It's a sign of the kind of man True Cooper was, that his passing so hurts the men around him."

Later in the day, Johnny went out hunting on one of the spare horses the men had brought with them mustanging.

He rode down the slope they would have taken with the travois had Cooper not died. He was surrounded by tall ponderosa pines, but at the base of the hill he emerged into a grassy clearing. Toward the middle of the clearing was a tangle of bushes and vines and some reeds. Johnny figured they were probably growing around a small body of water.

Might be a good place to find some tracks, he thought. Or find a good, concealed spot and wait to see what might come on in for some water.

He heard a rustle from inside the bushes. It had been a big noise, but he knew it didn't mean it was necessarily made by a big animal. He had seen more than one squirrel or bird make more noise than a deer. But just in case, he thought he would wait a bit and see what emerged from the bushes.

He decided to dismount. Had he been on Bravo, he would have remained in the saddle, because of Bravo's knack of knowing when to remain still. But this was a cutting horse Johnny had never ridden before, so he pulled his rifle from the scabbard and swung down to the ground.

He cocked the rifle and then released the rear trigger. He then brought the rifle to his shoulder and waited. A Hawken was perhaps the best rifle made for accuracy and distance, he was finding, but it wasn't designed for snapping off a quick shot.

A deer lifted its head from the bushes. It was a mule deer, with a tawny hide and huge antlers. Johnny thought he saw ten points.

He fired the rifle and the deer lowered its head back into the bushes. Johnny thought he had placed his bullet between the eyes.

He started for the bushes, switching the empty rifle to his left hand. If the deer was still alive, he would finish it off with a pistol.

He had covered half the distance to the bushes when the deer raised its head again.

Dang! I missed!

He really thought he had gotten the deer.

He hadn't yet reloaded his rifle, but he was much closer now, less than a hundred feet, so he drew his right-hand revolver like he was drawing on a man. Moving in one fluid motion, cocking the gun as he moved, and bringing the gun out to full extension. He fired and the deer lowered its head again.

He started running toward the bushes. He couldn't have missed twice. Not that he meant to be cocky, it was just that he had made trickier shots. Even just the day before, when he shot the mad stallion.

He pushed through the tall bushes and grass, and on the ground in front of a small water hole were two bucks. Both were lying dead in the grass. One had a ten point rack and the other eight points.

How often do you see this? Johnny asked himself. Two bucks together. The men were certainly going to feast tonight.

79

THE MOOD OF THE MEN LIGHTENED up when they saw Johnny walking into camp, leading his horse and with two bucks draped across the back.

As it grew dark, the men cut spits and began to roast venison over a fire. Laughter erupted, and they began to celebrate the life of True Cooper rather than to grieve his passing.

Quint got out a whiskey flask and began to tell stories of him and Cooper. Some of the stories involved outrageous things that happened while they were working on the ranch. Most of them involved even more outrageous things that happened in the Greenville saloons. Johnny didn't know how much of it was exaggeration, but the whiskey flask was being handed around and the men were smiling and laughing.

Johnny stood by the fire with a cup of coffee in one hand. He looked over at the travois and at the figure wrapped in blankets.

He said, "I wish I had known you longer, True Cooper."

The fire was dancing high, and Johnny could hear the howl of a wolf from somewhere out in the darkness. A chorus of howls joined it.

Then he saw the riders emerging from the darkness into the circle of firelight. Three of them. One was Evans. Another was a man with a wide hat and a gun at his side. He had some age on him, but he sat tall in the saddle. The third was a man with a gnarled, hunched over way of riding. He was in a jacket and string tie, and a narrow-brimmed hat.

They reined up.

Johnny said, "Evans. You made good time. Better'n I would have thought."

The man with the wide hat swung out of the saddle and said, "You must be Johnny Reynolds. Evans has told me about you."

Johnny nodded.

"I'm Frank McCarty. Owner of the Bar M." He extended his hand and Johnny shook it. The grip was firm, just like the man's gaze.

"I'm right pleased to meet you, sir."

"How's Cooper?"

"I'm sorry to say he passed on this afternoon." Johnny

looked back at Quint and the men. "We're having a sort of early wake for Cooper. The men needed it."

"I fully understand. I knew Cooper a long time, and I think he'd be pleased," McCarty said. "I don't generally allow drinking on the job, but I think it's all right in this case."

Then he indicated the man with him and said, "This here is Doctor Marker."

"Looks like I came all the way for nothing," the doctor said. He didn't extend his hand. "The last place I want to spend the night is in a cow camp."

Johnny realized the man was younger than he had first thought. Maybe mid-forties. But he had an old way about him.

He reminded Johnny somehow of a scavenger bird. Eyes that were small and yet intense, and a hawk-like nose. A face that was gaunt and with sunken-in cheeks. His fingers were long and narrow.

Corry came over. "Johnny, them wolves sound closer than I like. Maybe we should move the horses closer to the fire."

Johnny nodded. "Grab Matt and Hardy to help you."

Corry nodded and headed off.

McCarty said, "Evans has told me about you. Once we've gone and buried Cooper all proper-like, I want to talk to you."

"Yes, sir."

McCarty slapped Johnny's shoulder. "But for right now, let's go have a taste of that whiskey."

McCarty slapped Quint on the shoulder too, and said, "Hand that flask over."

McCarty took a pull from it, and then he said, "Have I ever told you boys how I met Cooper?"

A chorus of *no* and *no, sir* rose up. McCarty launched into the story.

After a time, Quint got up and wandered over to Johnny.

He said, "I'm glad you're here. Cooper was a natural leader. Men just seemed to gather around him. You've got those same qualities. With Cooper gone, somehow the empty spot seems a little less empty with a man like him standing here."

Johnny nodded. "My mother always said, God puts us where we're needed."

"Sounds like a wise lady."

The doctor checked Joe's ankle and announced it was just a sprain and it should remain in a splint for a few days. Then the doctor went to the edge of the camp and found a fallen log to sit on. He remained there, looking off into the night, but Johnny realized it wasn't that the man saw something out there worth looking at. He was just looking away from the men. He was sitting with his back erect and his hands folded in his lap.

Johnny said to Quint, "What's the story with the doctor?"

"Him?" Quint said. "Walks around town like he's got a rod shoved up his butt. Not a bad doctor, but no one you want to sit and talk with. Holds hisself above everyone else. Got a right purty daughter, though. Lookin' at her, you'd never know she was related to him."

After a bit, Johnny decided to walk over to the doctor. No reason not to be neighborly, he thought.

Johnny said, "It's too bad you had to ride all the way out here for nothing. But it shows you're a doctor who cares."

"Frank McCarty better realize I still intend to be paid. I am not going to go gallivanting about the countryside and spend the night with a bunch of hooligan cowboys for free. That man you work for, he's got the money, and he's going to part with some of it."

Johnny said to himself, *Okay, that went well.* And he wandered his way back to the fire.

He did find it amusing, though, that the doctor assumed he worked for Frank McCarty. Maybe it was because of the position of leadership Johnny had somehow fallen into with the men.

Johnny hoped there was another doctor in Greenville, because he wanted nothing to do with this man at all. He didn't care how pretty the man's daughter turned out to be.

80

TRUE COOPER WAS buried in a cemetery outside of a Methodist church in Greenville. McCarty had bought a plot for Cooper, and he was paying for a headstone to be engraved and set up.

At the graveside ceremony, once the preacher had finished speaking and led them all in prayer, Frank McCarty walked up to the open grave for a final look at the casket. Johnny walked up to stand beside him.

Johnny said, "I didn't know him long, but I knew right off he was a good man."

McCarty nodded. "Cooper was with me the longest of any of my men. Even longer than Quint. He was like family to me. He was the brother I never had."

Johnny and his brothers had little money with them, but they had decided to spend that money on baths and haircuts. Except for Joe. He partook of the bath, but decided against the shave or haircut.

He said, "Long Indian hair and a beard are the way I am. Folk'll just have to get used to it."

There was also a Chinese laundry in town, and Johnny stood beside McCarty in clean clothes, with his hair cut short and with his jaw clean-shaven. After those expenses and a few beers at one of the saloons, they didn't have enough left for a hotel room, so they were camping by a brook outside of town. But they were doing it in clean clothes and they no longer had to avoid standing downwind of each other.

McCarty said, "True was a simple man. Not complicated. He was straight-forward. The kind of man who said what he meant and nothing else. He was of stout heart. He was more than simply ramrod of the Bar M. He was part of its life blood."

A few upright chairs had been brought out from the ranch. McCarty's wife was sitting beside him, and next to her was their daughter Verna.

Verna was about the age of Becky back home, and she was stealing glances at Johnny in a way that made him uncomfortable. Not that a man didn't want to be looked at by a pretty girl, and Verna was indeed pretty, but there was something about her that made him wary. Something he couldn't quite define.

All of the cowhands from the McCarty ranch were at the burial. There was also the blacksmith and wrangler, a man with hard muscles that made his sleeves pull tight. He had been introduced to Johnny as Moses Timmons.

Standing beside Timmons was his son. Maybe a few years older than Johnny, and he stood as tall as his father. He moved with the presence strong men often have, but his frame was much narrower than his father's. Where his father had pronounced cheekbones, the boy's looked hollow. He had dark hair that grew like a wild bush.

While Verna kept looking toward Johnny and throwing him a smile if he looked her way, the Timmons boy couldn't keep his eyes from Verna.

Johnny wondered why everywhere he went, things had to be so complicated. For the first time, he found himself missing the simplicity of his time with the Texas Rangers. They chased after raiders and renegades. Shot it out with them, then it was on to a saloon. Tequila and women. Work hard, play hard. Nothing complicated. No hidden agendas.

He had found himself caught up in all the twisting tangles of family politics at the Broken Spur. He decided that if he were to take a job at the Bar M—and no job had been offered yet—he would keep away from Verna and the Timmons boy. He would deal with Frank McCarty, only.

McCarty said to Johnny, "Hardy and Quint have talked to me at length about all you did for them out there. All you did for Cooper. It means a lot to me."

"I did what I could."

"Walk with me. I'd like to talk with you in private. One of the men can take Mrs. McCarty and Verna home."

Johnny noticed Corry and Quint nearby. They were facing toward the grave, each with his hat in hand.

Johnny called them over. "Could you boys escort the women back to the ranch? Mr. McCarty will be joining you shortly."

Quint nodded, and Corry said, "Sure can, Boss."

Johnny and McCarty began strolling away from the crowd.

McCarty said, "How old are you, boy?"

"Not quite twenty-two, sir."

"I would have guessed you to be older. You don't seem reckless or rash, like most men of that age."

Johnny grinned. "I've had my moments, sir."

McCarty grinned, also. "As have we all."

McCarty drew a breath and said, "I take it you have some leadership experience."

Johnny nodded. "I was ramrod of the Broken Spur, in Texas."

"Breaker Grant's place?"

Johnny nodded.

McCarty said, "I heard he had passed on. That's too bad. He and I did business together a few times."

Johnny told of his time at the Broken Spur, though leaving out anything that might connect him and his brothers to the incident in Missouri. He also left out any of the details that might cast Maria Carrera in a disparaging light. A gentleman protected a woman's honor, even if she wasn't always the best at protecting it herself.

He finished by saying, "His son Coleman wasn't well-liked, so a lot of us decided to ride on."

"How long were you ramrod?"

"Nearly eight months."

McCarty nodded. "I know some people in Texas. For one, the county sheriff in Clarksville. Harris Newcomb. He and I and Breaker Grant rode together years ago, when I was about your age. If I were to write to him, could he verify what you say?"

Odd question, Johnny thought. In his experience in the West, you took a man at his word.

He nodded. "I know Sheriff Newcomb. He's a good man."

It then occurred to him the folks in Texas knew him under the name O'Brien. He decided to come a little clean about that.

He said, "We didn't use the name Reynolds in Texas. We called ourselves O'Brien. We got ourselves into a little trouble back East."

McCarty looked at him.

Johnny said, "Some of that recklessness and rashness you spoke of."

McCarty chuckled. "Many a man out here is running from something. Leaving his past behind and starting over. That's one thing the frontier has to offer. A new life. A new beginning."

Johnny let his gaze fall on the landscape ahead of

them. An expanse of grass that was mostly brown, and beyond it was a softly rounded hill covered with oak. Not the type of oak he had known in Pennsylvania. These were shorter with branches that reached out all which-way. The bartender in town had referred to them as scrub oak.

McCarty said, "I take it Matt is actually your brother."

"We didn't hide it very well."

McCarty shook his head. "You can tell. The three of you have a bond that you don't find very often outside of a family."

They took a few more steps, then McCarty stopped and looked at him. "I don't normally pry this way. And I normally take a man at his word and would never even suggest trying to verify his statements. But I'm about to make you a job offer, and since I haven't known you long, I need to be careful."

Johnny waited. He wasn't sure where McCarty was going with this.

McCarty said, "On my ranch, Johnny, the ramrod has a lot of responsibilities. He oversees practically everything. Hirings, firings. Expenditure of money on things like supplies. I have to know he can run the place without me watching over his shoulder. It has to be a man I can trust. Quint and Hardy have both been working for me a long time. Quint has been with me almost as long as Cooper was, and he's worked a lot of cow outfits over the years. But neither of them is leadership material. Not like you."

McCarty chuckled. "Even back there, without so much as a second thought, you took charge and had Quint and Corry escort my wife and daughter home. Corry even calls you *Boss*, even though you're not on the payroll. It seems that you're already in charge of the men. You sort of fell into the role naturally, and the men look to you like they are meant to.

"I guess what I'm trying to say is I want you to be the new ramrod." He chuckled. "It looks like the men already consider you the ramrod, so we might as well make it official."

Johnny didn't know what to say. He had been hoping he and his brothers could find work, hopefully on the same ranch. But he hadn't been expecting this kind of offer.

"I don't know what to say, sir."

"Then just say, yes. And you and your brothers can

move into the bunkhouse tonight."

"So, they have jobs too?"

He shrugged. "If you want to hire them. *You're* the ramrod, now."

81

"THE WEATHER SURE IS different than what I'm accustomed to," Matt said.

He was standing outside the bunkhouse with a cup of coffee in his hand. There was a gentle breeze, and the air was dry. It was morning and the day was already growing hot, but it didn't feel hot.

"Different than Texas," Johnny said. "Different than back home, too. A day with this kind of heat back in Pennsylvania, and we'd have sweat dripping from us."

Johnny was standing with Matt. Johnny was in leather leggings and his guns were holstered at his hips.

Joe was sitting in a chair by the bunkhouse wall. His ankle was no longer in a splint, and the scowly doctor said he didn't think the ankle was broken, but Joe needed to be off it for a couple of weeks.

Joe said, "Didn't we start out at the Broken Spur like this? Me unable to work because I could hardly walk, and a woman at the ranch house looking at Johnny?"

Johnny grinned. He said, "The one at this ranch was looking at me for a couple of days, but I decided to just not look back. I saw her at the house this morning but she didn't even look my way once. I'm kind of relieved."

"Good," Matt said. "Because she's looking at me, now. Just this morning, she looked my way and flashed me a shy little smile."

When Matt had finished his coffee, he headed off to the corral where a few of the boys were working on breaking some mustangs they had caught a few weeks earlier.

Johnny still had some coffee remaining, but when it was done he was going to ride out to the line shack at the edge of Bar M range. When he was ramrod of the Broken Spur, he had made it a policy to personally check on the boys who were stationed at the line shacks.

Their job was to patrol the outer reaches of the ranch. Keep any strays from roaming too far and watch out for squatters. They would ride back to the ranch headquarters every month for payday, join the rest of the cowhands whooping it up in town for the night, then ride back out to the line shack with a pack horse loaded with supplies. Johnny had heard them sometimes called line riders. Or

Outriders. Or the *floating outfit* or sometimes just the *floaters.*
Seemed everything out West had three or four terms.
Johnny and Joe watched Matt walk away.
Johnny said, "I hope Matt knows what he's doing with that girl."
"He always seems to act like he does, even when he doesn't."
Johnny nodded. Joe was right. There was a sort of natural confidence in Matt in everything he did.
Johnny said, "There's something about that girl Verna that just doesn't set right."
Joe nodded. "I've noticed it, too."

The boys had gotten a saddle on a wild mustang and were holding the reins tight. Corry was the resident bronc buster, and he was getting ready to ride.
He wasn't wearing a gun. You don't wear a gun when you're on a wild bronc. He was in leather leggings and he wore a wide-brimmed hat that was gray and floppy. It was hard for Matt to figure what kind of hat it had been when it was new.
Matt stood by the corral. Hardy was there, and so was Quint. And a man he now knew as Valdez.
Valdez was the old-school vaquero. He wore black pants with silver conchos down each leg and a short waist-length jacket with all sorts of intricate design along the edges.
Matt felt motion behind him, the way you sometimes do. He looked over his shoulder and saw Verna riding onto the ranch yard. She had dark hair that was tied into a long braid, and it bounced along her back as she rode. She was in a red gingham blouse and a split skirt.
Matt was hoping she would look his way. He wanted to see if he could get another one of those shy smiles from her.
"Verna McCarty," Hardy said. "The only child of Mr. McCarty."
"Does she have any beaus?"
"She seems to have her sights set on a young feller whose father owns a ranch nearby. Ern Cabot. She dances with some of the men from this ranch sometimes, when there's a social or a barn dance. She's danced with Evan and Corry once or twice. But she saves most of her dances for Ern."

Matt's gaze remained fixed on her as she reined up in front of the ranch house.

Hardy said, "Don't even try. You'll be wastin' your time."

"Don't be too sure of that."

Valdez called out, "Ride him, Corry!"

Matt turned his attention back to the corral. Corry was in the saddle, and the men let go of the reins.

The horse humped its back and bucked and jumped. Corry's hat went flying away, and then Corry himself followed his hat.

He landed on the dusty ground, rolling with the impact. Then he was on his feet and ran to the fence to get away from the pounding hooves. The horse was still bucking like it was trying to shake the saddle from its back. Evan was in there, running and grabbing at the reins of the horse.

Quint had a stopwatch in his hand. "That was six seconds. Not bad."

"Not bad? I'd like to see anyone else here do better."

Johnny and Joe were approaching. Joe was hobbling on crutches to keep the weight off his bad ankle.

Matt said, "I thought you were riding out to see the line riders."

Johnny nodded. "I wanted to watch some of this, first."

But then Matt noticed someone else. Verna had left her horse at the hitching post in front of the house and was walking over. Maybe the action in the corral had gotten her attention.

"Had enough?" Hardy said.

"Never," Corry said with a smile. "I'll never let any horse win against me."

He climbed up onto the fence and brushed the dust from his leggings. He looked at the girl with a smile and said, "Mornin', Miss Verna."

"Good morning," she said.

Matt said, "I want a try on that horse."

Joe looked at Matt. "What're you doin'? You'll get yourself killed in there."

Matt said, "I'm doing what I do best."

"What? You plan on talkin' the horse to death?"

Matt ignored him.

Johnny said, "How do we tell Ma and Luke that you got yourself killed doing something like this?"

Joe was grinning. "It's usually Johnny who does the fool stunts."

Johnny gave him a look.

Matt said, "Laugh all you want, you two. But I want a try at that horse."

Corry said, "Go on ahead. Have yourself a try."

Matt unbuckled his gunbelt and handed it to Joe, and then climbed up and over the fence.

Evan had brought the horse back to the far end of the corral. Another man was there, helping control the horse. They called him Chip.

Evan held the reins tight while Matt climbed up and into the saddle.

"You ready?" Chip said.

Matt nodded.

Evan and Chip cleared away, and the horse exploded across the corral. Bumping and thumping. Jumping and then landing hard with its hooves. Matt didn't even know when he lost his hat, because he was too focused on trying to stay alive.

There was one large jarring impact with the back of the horse that rattled him all the way to his teeth, and he found himself in the air and then crashing into the dirt.

Evan and Chip ran after the horse. Matt intended to run from its hooves like Corry had done, but it was all he could do to get to his feet.

He managed to put one foot ahead of the other and got himself back to the fence. He felt pain in his backside and hips and all the way down to his feet. He wasn't sure if it was because of the fall or the ride itself.

"How long did I last?"

Quint was looking at the watch. "Two whole seconds."

Matt looked at him.

Quint said, "I'm roundin' up."

Matt gave him a pained look. Not hard to do, considering the pain he was in.

Verna was laughing.

Joe said, "That's what you do best, huh?"

Matt looked at Verna. He gave her a sort of embarrassed shrug of his shoulders, and she gave him a wide smile.

Matt said, "Yep. It's what I do best."

82

IT WAS dark when Johnny rode up to the barn and swung out of the saddle.

Moses Timmons was there. He said, "Didn't know if you were coming back tonight."

Johnny stretched his arms out and twisted a little to one side, and some kinks in his back snapped.

"Maybe I should have just stayed the night. That was a lot of miles to cover in the saddle in one day."

"There's beans in the bunkhouse, and the coffee's hot."

Johnny said, "How's Matt?"

"Still alive. But not by much."

Johnny found Matt stretched out in his bunk. Johnny said, "It's your own fault, you know."

Johnny unbuckled his leather leggings and hung them on a hook on the wall.

Joe was sitting at a table, thumbing through a deck of cards. Chip was leaning back in a chair with the front legs of the chair off the floor, and a harmonica was in his hands. He was playing something that sounded haunting and mournful. The kind of stuff often played around campfires.

Quint was on the next bunk down from Matt and was snoring away. Chip seemed to be using Quint's snores as a rhythm for his playing.

Joe said, "I still don't get what it was all about. How is nearly gettin' yourself killed tryin' to break a wild mustang what you do best?"

Johnny grabbed a tin cup from a shelf. He blew some dust out of the cup, and then filled it with coffee. "What he's talking about is using some of that natural charm he's been told he has. Maybe he's been told it once too often."

Matt said, "I was making an impression."

Joe looked at Matt like he thought Matt was crazy. "On who? The horse?"

"No," Matt said. "Not the horse."

Joe made an O shape with his mouth, like you do when something dawns on you. He looked at Johnny, and Johnny shrugged. Then he looked back at Matt and said, "So you thought to impress her by breaking your neck in front of her."

"I didn't break my neck, though, did I?"

"Danged near it."

"Danged near doesn't count. Except in horseshoes. And I got a smile out of her and made an impression that wasn't negative. Entirely."

"That was what you meant by doing what you do best?"

Johnny took a sip of coffee. He said to Joe, "Sometimes girls like it when a man makes a fool out of himself in front of her. Never tried it myself."

Joe said, "Looks kind of dangerous."

Johnny walked over to Matt. Johnny's bunk was across from Matt's. He put his coffee on the floor, and then began to tug away at his boots. It took a while, but he got his boots off. Felt good.

He said, "Look, Matt. I know she's a pretty girl. But you've got to look at it from my point of view. I'm the ramrod here, and I don't want to see my men doing something risky like that for no reason. You're not an experienced broncbuster. Corry's in charge of breaking the wild ones. If you hurt yourself and can't do the job I need you to, then the rest of the men will have to pull your weight. It ain't fair to them."

"You're right, Boss. I didn't think about that."

"So you'll stay off the horses that ain't been broke yet?"

"I didn't say that."

Johnny had Ma's temper and was on the verge of a shout. Chip had stopped playing and was looking away, trying not to laugh. Joe was laughing outright.

Matt said, "Riding that bronc might have been a harebrained notion. I'll give you that. But there was something exhilarating about it. Painful but exhilarating. As a cowhand, I want to do the entire job, not just part of it."

"Not all the cowhands ride wild broncs. I don't. That's a specialty job."

"Well, it's one I want. I wouldn't have thought so, until today. Tomorrow, I want to climb back into the saddle. And this time, I'll keep at it until I have that horse broken."

Johnny looked at Joe, and Joe shrugged.

Johnny said, "And I thought among the three of us, you were the sane one."

"Whatever gave you that idea?"

83

MATT'S HAT FLEW from his head as the horse lurched and rocked beneath him. His right hand held the reins and his knees gripped the horse's shoulders.

So much fury beneath him. So much power. He thought it was almost a shame to be trying to tame it.

And yet, he found it was a thrill like no other.

The horse humped its back and jumped, coming down hard with its legs stiff. Once. Twice. Three times. And Matt became separated from the saddle.

He landed in the dirt but rolled with the fall. Then he sprang to his feet, covered in dust, and ran for the corral fence while Hardy caught up with the mustang and grabbed its reins.

Valdez was sitting on the fence with the stopwatch in his hand.

He said, "Five seconds."

Johnny was leaning against the fence with his arms folded on the top rail.

Matt said, "Come to watch me break my butt?"

Johnny shook his head. "Just come to see how my newest bronc-buster is doing."

Quint was standing with him. "He's really come along, the last couple of weeks. I don't think Corry has anything on him."

Matt grabbed a canteen that was hanging from a fence post and took a couple of pulls from it.

He said to Johnny, "You think I'm crazy, don't you?"

Johnny said, "I was starting to wonder, at first. But then I remembered something."

"What's that?"

"A certain Christmas tree, the winter you were fourteen."

Valdez and Quint were looking at him, waiting for him to continue.

Johnny said, "We grew up in the mountains of Pennsylvania. The summer before, we had picked out a fir tree we wanted to cut for Christmas. But it was an extra hard winter. Bitter cold and with more snow than usual. The tree was a mile from the farmhouse, and Pa decided it was too far away to haul back. The temperature hadn't gotten above ten degrees for a week, and there was three feet of snow on the ground.

"But Matt insisted it had to be that tree. Against Pa's orders, Matt left the house before sunup one morning, with snowshoes strapped onto his shoes and an axe in one hand. He trudged all the way out there and cut that tree, and hauled it all the way back."

Quint said, "What'd your Pa say?"

"He was furious," Matt said.

Johnny nodded his head. "That he was. But I remember what you said. What you told Pa."

"I said, I just can't shy away from a challenge."

"As far as I'm concerned, you're now one of our bronc-busters."

Matt nodded. "And I have a horse waiting for me."

He walked back into the corral and snatched his hat from the dirt.

Hardy was holding the reins of the horse.

Matt said, "All right. Let's try it one more time."

The horse tried to throw him off. Matt's hat fell into the dirt again, and Johnny had to wonder why bronc-busters even bothered to wear one.

The horse spun around in circles. It jumped and bucked.

Johnny found himself calling out, "Ride 'im, Matt!"

Then the horse reared up and clawed at the air with its front hooves. Then he came down to all fours and began running. But it was no longer bucking.

It circled the inner perimeter of the corral a couple of times. Then Matt reined up. The horse clawed at the dirt a couple of times but held its ground. Obeying its rider.

Valdez was grinning. He had forgotten to check the stopwatch.

Matt said, "That's how it's done."

Then he looked past Johnny and Quint, and Johnny followed his gaze to the barn. McCarty and his daughter had returned from riding and had reined up there. Probably going to let Timmons handle the horses.

Both were looking toward the corral, and Johnny could see Verna had a grin wider than Valdez's.

Matt threw her a wave, and she waved back.

Matt then had the horse rear up triumphantly. Verna laughed and waved at him again.

Johnny said to Quint, "At the next dance, I think this Ern Cabot I've heard mentioned is going to have some competition for Miss McCarty's attention."

Quint was grinning. "It does look that way, don't it?"

84

JOHNNY GENERALLY STOPPED by McCarty's office on Monday morning. He wanted to give McCarty a general report on how things were doing about the ranch and what his plans were for the week.

Often it meant sitting with a cup of coffee and listening to McCarty talk about his earlier days on the ranch. How he had come west on a wagon train back in 1822. Barely twenty years old, he had signed on with a train of freight wagons taking the Santa Fe trail to New Mexico territory. That was how he first met Breaker Grant and Harris Newcomb. He then got involved in a series of adventures, scouting for the Army at one point, and working at various ranches throughout Texas. It was during those years that he had worked for Breaker Grant for a few months.

Johnny sat with a cup of coffee in one hand. Here at the big house, coffee wasn't served in a tin cup. It was in a cup and saucer. Johnny had learned how to handle a cup and saucer from Ma, a skill he never thought he would have much use for.

He generally offered little when McCarty was talking about his early years. Johnny sat and listened. Pa had once said a man can't learn much with his mouth open. He needs to be quiet and listen.

One morning in July, McCarty said to him, "Oh, before I forget" and slid a leather valise across the desk to Johnny. "I have some things in here that have to be mailed. Could you have a rider take it to town for me? In fact, I'd rather you took care of it yourself. I have some money going out in an envelope."

Johnny nodded. "Consider it done."

Johnny left Quint in charge for the morning and asked Moses Timmons to saddle Bravo.

Greenville was about the size of Clarkston. One long street of businesses, which included three saloons and a couple of hotels. A little smaller than the town of Camanche, which was maybe a two-hour ride away. Beside the town marshal's office was the post office, which was where Johnny was headed.

As he rode along the main street, he saw one horse in

front of the saloon he and the boys from the ranch usually frequented. A sign over the boardwalk read CATTLEMAN'S LOUNGE. It wasn't in the usual hand-painted way of many signs in smaller frontier towns. It was in a sort of flourishing hand. The owner of the place had spent a little money creating a distinctive sign.

Johnny thought he might take Bravo to the livery and have him rest up from the ride into town and maybe have a few oats before they began the ride back to the ranch. Johnny also thought maybe he would do a little resting up himself at the Cattleman's Lounge.

As he rode past the Cattleman's, a man stepped out. Taller than Johnny and maybe forty, but a grisled-looking forty. A tall hat and a tattered vest. A shaggy beard. He wore a gunbelt with a revolver at the left and turned backward. A man who favored a cross-draw.

The man looked at Johnny, and his eyes remained fixed on him as he rode along.

When Johnny swung out of the saddle in front of the post office, he allowed his gaze to swing in a seemingly casual way up the street and toward the Cattleman's. The man was still there, standing on the boardwalk and watching him.

When Johnny was finished at the post office, he looked up the street again. The man's horse was still there, but the man himself was not.

Once Bravo was at the livery, Johnny walked down to the Cattleman's. He pushed in through the batwing doors and saw the man was at the bar with a glass in front of him.

A thin boy with bushy, sandy hair was pushing a mop. He said, "Howdy, Johnny."

Johnny nodded and said, "Artie."

Johnny went to the bar.

The Cattleman's was a little more prosperous than most of the saloons Johnny had known. In many of them, the bar was little more than planks laid across upended beer kegs, but the Cattleman's had a mahogany bar. Behind the bar was a mirror that stretched the length of the bar.

The bartender, a thin man who answered to Slim, said, "Howdy, Johnny. Didn't expect to see you in town this time of the week."

Johnny said, "Yeah, I had some things to mail for Mister McCarty."

"Want a glass of tequila?"

Johnny grinned. Slim knew his preference. "Kind of early for that. Got any coffee?"

Slim nodded. "I'll go to the kitchen and see if there's any left."

The man at the bar was looking at Johnny with a squint.

Slim came back with a cup. "It's a couple of hours old and it ain't hot, but it's warm."

"That's good enough for me."

Slim set the cup in front of Johnny. "It's on the house. Can't charge a man for coffee that's two hours old."

"Thanks, Slim. I appreciate that."

Johnny took the cup with his left hand, keeping his right hand free and within reach of his right-hand gun. Something he normally did.

The man with the cross-draw gun stepped away from the bar. Through the long mirror, Johnny watched the man step around behind him.

Johnny said, "I don't much cotton to men standing behind me."

The man said, "Then why don't you turn around and face me."

Johnny set his coffee down and turned. The man was fifteen feet away. The thumb of his right hand was hooked into his gunbelt.

Slim said, "Now, see here. I don't want no trouble."

The man said, "Stay out of it, barkeep, and you won't get hurt."

Slim moved further down the bar, away from the direction of potential gunfire. He said, "Artie, go get the marshal."

Artie let the mop fall to the floor and scurried out the door.

Johnny said to the man, "I don't know who you are, but I got no beef with you."

The man said, "I know who you are. You might go by the name Reynolds, here. But I know who you really are."

"Like I said, I want no trouble."

"Well, you got it, boy. I've been lookin' for you and your brothers ever since you left Texas. Been on your trail a long time. Now I'm gonna shoot you down and the reward's mine. Whether you go for your gun or not."

Johnny had never been the first to reach for his gun in

a gunfight. He didn't intend to start now.

He focused on the man's eyes. And then he saw the flicker of intent. The man was reaching for his gun, and then Johnny's pistol was in his hand, his arm going out to full extension. Both guns fired, the man's firing first with Johnny's second. The man's bullet missed. Johnny's did not.

The man took a couple of steps backward. But the gun was still in his hand. He raised it to fire again, and Johnny put a second bullet in him. The man lurched as he took the second shot, then his gun fired and Johnny heard glass shattering behind him.

The man dropped to his knees and fell face forward.

"I seen the whole thing," Slim said. "It was self-defense."

Marshal Brannigan came into the saloon just as Johnny was holstering his gun. Artie was right behind him. Brannigan had a rounded stomach and a fleshy face, but he looked to Johnny like he might have been strong when he was younger.

It took ten seconds for Johnny to tell Brannigan what had happened. Then Slim and Artie both said the man had ridden in about an hour before Johnny. He had asked questions, like which ranch the Reynolds boys and Matt O'Toole worked for.

Brannigan said to Johnny, "Have you ever seen him before?"

Johnny shook his head. "Never."

Slim and Artie said the man never gave his name.

Brannigan went through the man's pockets. Since he had come in on horseback, Brannigan went for the vest pockets first. They found nothing.

"A bounty hunter, I would say, since he talked about claiming a reward. Who did he think you were?"

Johnny shrugged. "He never said."

"He thought you were somebody else, I guess."

Slim was looking at the mirror behind the bar. Both of the bounty hunter's bullets had found it. An entire section was now missing, and a crack ran the length of it.

Slim said, "And he cost me my mirror."

85

WEEKS PASSED.

There was little rain, which Quint told Johnny was common in this part of the country. A water hole was drying up at one section of McCarty range, so Johnny and some of the men moved five hundred head to another section where there was a stream that flowed down from the mountains. Now that winter run-off was done, the stream was much narrower and shallower, but it would be enough for the herd.

Then, Johnny took some men and headed back to the mountains to do some mustanging, to give Matt and Corry some wild ones to break. They were gone a week.

Once they were back, there was a storm that provided no rain but gave a few flashes of lightning. One streak of lightning started a grass fire and scattered two hundred head. Johnny took Hardy, Evans and Valdez with him, and they were nearly a week rounding them up.

One afternoon, Johnny reined up in front of the stable. Moses Timmons had the portable anvil set up and was banging away on a strip of iron, bending it into a horseshoe.

He looked up and said, "Hey, Boss. Mister McCarty said he wants to see you."

"All right." Johnny was covered with dust. He had been out on the range all day. Because of the lack of rain, the ground was dry. A horse would kick up a cloud of dust as its hooves struck the earth. All day long, you rode with dust all about you. It got into your nose and your mouth. It got so that was all you could taste, even after a drink of water.

Johnny said to Timmons, "Take care of Bravo for me, will you?"

Timmons nodded.

Johnny hated to go to the main house looking like this. He tried to brush the dust from his shirt sleeves, but it seemed ground in. He looked down at his leggings and boots. Hopeless. But Mr. McCarty wouldn't have asked to see him if it wasn't important.

Johnny decided not to knock at the front door. Mrs. McCarty kept the house rather elegant, with oriental carpets spread across the floor, and chairs with velvet upholstery. Fine doilies here and there. It wasn't quite the palace that had been Breaker Grant's, but it was within shouting distance of it. Instead, he went to the kitchen door and knocked.

A Mexican woman answered. She had an apron tied about her middle and a kerchief about her hair.

He knew her name as Anna, so he said, "Hey, Anna. I was told Mister McCarty wants to see me. I didn't want to track dust and dirt all through the house."

She left him at the doorway and then came back a few minutes later. "Mister McCarty says to go on in. He's in the study."

Johnny found him behind his desk. The study had glass windows that were more like doors, each with a knob that could be pulled open. A man could step through to the yard behind the house.

There was a fireplace with a marble mantelpiece, and a fire was burning low against the oncoming coolness of the night.

"Johnny," McCarty said. "Come on in."

McCarty had a ledger book open on the desk. He said, "There's a mine outside of San Francisco that's up for sale. A town called Lonesome Camp. I'm trying to decide whether or not I should make a bid."

Johnny said, "'Fraid I don't know much about mining."

"Have a seat," McCarty said. "Would you like a drink? Tequila, isn't it?"

Johnny nodded.

McCarty got to his feet and went over to a small table that had four decanters on it. He filled two glasses and brought them to the desk and set one in front of Johnny.

Johnny took a belt. "Sure washes down the trail dust."

"I'll say one thing for you," McCarty said, "you're a hands-on leader. True was too."

Johnny nodded. "I was that way at the Broken Spur. My father used to say a leader has to be willing to get his hands dirty alongside the men he's leading."

"Your father sounds like a good man."

"He was, sir. He's passed on."

"I'm sorry to hear that."

Johnny took another belt of the tequila. "I used to drink too much of this down in the border towns. Brings back memories."

Alongside the ledger book was a white piece of paper Johnny hadn't really noticed until McCarty picked it up.

He said, "I sent a letter off to Harris Newcomb, a while ago. I got his reply today. He thinks quite highly of you and your brothers. But he and I have few secrets from each other. We fought side-by-side more than once in our early days. Saved each other's life a couple times over."

Johnny nodded. "I know how that is. There are a couple of Texas Rangers I feel that way about."

McCarty reached into a desk drawer. "As a result, he told me some interesting things about you and your brothers. I went into town afterward and took this off a wall."

He pulled out a long sheet of paper and slid it across the desk to Johnny.

At the top, in big black letters, was the word REWARD.

Then the names of Johnny and his brothers, and their cousin Thad.

It went on to say they were wanted for murder in Missouri, and the reward was for $1,000 each.

"That's a lot of money," McCarty said.

Johnny nodded.

McCarty said, "Newcomb knew about this, but kept it to himself. He said Breaker Grant knew about it too, the entire time you were working for him."

Johnny decided it was time to tell McCarty the whole story, like he had done with Breaker Grant. He began with his return home and his father's murder, and he followed it with the ride west he, his brothers and their cousin Thad had made in a futile attempt to find the killer. He told of the killing in Missouri and of the journey to Texas.

McCarty said, "So, it was your cousin Thad who actually killed that lawman."

Johnny nodded. "But we were there. We shouldn't have been. We owe that shopkeeper for the goods we took. We'd like to pay him back, but I'm not sure how we can do that without tipping off the law as to where we are."

"Have you had any word from your cousin?"

Johnny shook his head. "Not since we told him to ride on, more than a year ago."

McCarty sat in thought a moment. Then he said, "Tell you what I'm going to do about all of this."

He got out of his chair and crumpled up the reward poster, and he threw it into the fire.

"None of it will ever leave this room," McCarty said.

"I'm beholdin' to you."

"Harris Newcomb is a good judge of character. I'll stand by his judgment."

McCarty went back to his seat behind the desk. "Marshal Brannigan has been asking questions ever since that bounty hunter you had to kill a while back. But I'll hold him off. I was a major contributor to his last campaign, and he knows he won't win again if I don't back him up."

Johnny shifted in his chair. "I hate to be that kind of burden to you."

"It's no burden at all. I fancy myself a good judge of character too. You're a good man, and you're running this ranch with the same efficiency True Cooper did. I don't want to lose a man like you."

"I won't let you down."

86

"DON'T YOU LOOK all spiffed up," Johnny said. "You'll put us all to shame."

Matt said, "I usually do."

He was standing in front of the bunkhouse mirror, adjusting his tie. He had a gray, pinstriped jacket and matching trousers.

Evan was in a clean shirt and had buttoned the top button. He had watered down his hair and was taking a comb to it.

He said, "You wasted good money on them duds. She ain't even gonna look at you twice. She'll be with Ern Cabot."

"But," Matt said, "she'll be leaving with me."

Johnny was using a bandana on his boots in hopes of bringing out a shine. "I hate to see a man so overcome with humility."

Matt was smiling. "I'm not bragging, gentlemen. I'm just stating a simple fact."

The trail to town was a few miles long, and the men from the Bar M were taking it by horseback.

Johnny rode alongside Matt and Joe. Corry and Evan were a little ways ahead.

Matt was on a cutting horse. The old mare from the farm was in a pasture at the ranch.

A year ago, the old mare was about all the horse Matt could handle. Now here he was, Johnny thought, one of the bronc-busters at the ranch. When Matt chose a horse to ride to town tonight, he picked a young mustang with some spirit.

Johnny said, "I've been thinking about Ma and Luke a lot lately."

Matt nodded. "It's been a year and a half since we left."

"And they haven't heard from us in that time."

"Don't seem right," Joe said.

His ankle had long-since healed, and he was in a new pair of boots.

Johnny said, "Matt, since you're the best with words and seem to have all that natural charm..."

Joe said, "At least he thinks he does."

Johnny grinned. "As foreman, I'm assigning you a job to do. Not today, but after the dance. Maybe tomorrow morning. I want you to write a letter to Ma and Luke."

Matt sort of shrugged with his eyebrows. "What can I really tell them?"

"I think it's time we just tell them everything. They're bound to have figured something's wrong by now. We wanted to spare them the truth, but it's been so long now, they might be wondering if we're even still alive. I say, just tell them the whole story. Even the names we're going by, now."

Joe nodded. "I agree."

Matt thought about this a moment. "Tell them the whole story, huh?"

Johnny said, "They might have seen the reward posters by now, anyway. If the posters are here in California, there's no reason to believe they're not being circulated back East too."

Joe said, "They deserve the whole truth, and they deserve to hear it from us."

Matt said, "Even the part about Thad? I'd hate to hurt Uncle Jake and Aunt Sara."

Johnny nodded. "Even the part about Thad."

"All right. It'll have to be Monday, though. I'll have to buy a pen and a bottle of ink and some paper, and the general store is closed on Sunday."

Joe said, "I thought you already had the fixin's for writin'."

Matt smiled at the way Joe phrased it. Matt said, "I left my *fixings* back in Texas. I didn't think the bottle of ink would hold up well on a horse. If it broke, the ink would get all through my saddlebags."

Johnny nodded. "All right. Monday it is."

The dance was being held in the lobby of the hotel, which had a dance floor and a small stage for a band to play. The balcony was decorated with red, white and blue bunting, left over from the Fourth of July celebration.

On the stage was a fiddler, a banjo player, and a man playing a stand-up bass, and they filled the air with the rhythm of a southern two-step. Couples moved about on the dance floor, some twirling and improvising doe-see-does, and others just doing old-fashioned stomping and clogging.

Johnny stood by the punch bowl. Joe and Matt were with him, and so were Evan and Corry.

Johnny held a glass of punch. He wasn't much of a dancer, though a girl at the far side of the room had caught his attention. Blonde hair that was all done up in curly ringlets. She moved with a sort of reserved grace.

"That's Doc Marker's daughter," Evan said to Johnny. "Pretty girl."

Johnny blinked with surprise. But it was Joe who said, "How could that old horny toad of a man have a daughter that purty?"

"Don't know," Evan said. "Accident of nature, I suppose."

The music stopped. The band conferred for a moment, then the fiddler started wailing out a slow waltz.

Matt said to Johnny, "You should go ask her to dance."

But then a man Johnny didn't recognize approached her. Probably a cowhand riding for the Cabot ranch. It was a safe bet in this town if a cowhand didn't ride for the McCartys, he rode for the Cabots. The cowhand took her hand and she gave him a shy little curtsey, and they stepped out onto the dance floor.

Too late, Johnny thought.

"So," Joe said to Matt. "Are you going to go out on the dance floor?"

Matt nodded. "As soon as the right girl gets here."

And at that moment, the right girl got there. Verna McCarty walked in through the open doorway. Johnny thought she had a grandness in the way she moved that said she had arrived. Johnny much preferred the shy girl with the gentle grace even though she was now on the dance floor with another man.

McCarty and his wife were with Verna. And there was a man with her. He was about Matt's age, with dark hair that was combed neatly. He was also in a Sunday-go-to-meeting suit and a string tie, and Verna was on his arm.

"Must be Ern Cabot," Johnny said.

Evan nodded. "That's him all right."

Verna was in a sky blue dress that fell from her shoulders in gentle ruffles. Her hair was tied up on her head in a collection of swirls.

Matt said, "All right, boys, now I'll show you how it's done."

"Matt," Johnny said, "she's with someone already."

"That's about to change."

He took a moment to make sure his tie was straight,

then started across the floor toward Verna and her escort.

He gave a polite greeting to McCarty and his wife and even to Cabot. Johnny couldn't hear what was being said over the music, but he figured polite greetings are all mostly the same. *How are you doing this evening? Why fine, thank you. And you?*

Then he took Verna's hand and gave a little bow. She was grinning and nodded her head, and her hand slipped away from Ern. She and Matt headed out onto the dance floor.

Joe was staring. "I'll be danged."

Johnny said, "Well I guess he showed us how it's done, didn't' he?"

"It ain't braggin' if you can do it."

Evan held out a hand to Corry and said, "Pay up."

87

THE BAND TOOK the crowd through a Virginia reel and then began another waltz. A Strauss melody. The fiddler showed the crowd he could really play the violin. Same instrument, Johnny thought, and yet very different.

Matt was holding Verna close through the waltz, and her head was on his shoulder.

When the music was done, the crowd gave a little applause, like they weren't quite sure if they were clapping for themselves or the band.

Matt then came over to the punch bowl and grabbed two glasses.

Joe said, "If you don't beat all."

Matt dipped one glass into the punch bowl, then the other.

Johnny said, "Ern Cabot doesn't look too pleased."

Matt gave a grin. "I'm not trying to please him."

Matt looked over at the blonde girl. She was standing alone again.

Matt said to Johnny, "You know, there's a time to hold back and a time to move in. You're missing your opportunity."

Verna came walking over. By protocol, a girl should wait for her man to fetch a glass of punch and bring it to her. But Johnny had the feeling Verna was the kind of girl who lived by her own protocol.

"Matthew," she said. "I don't believe I've ever been formally introduced to your brothers."

Matt looked like he was about to go through the song-and-dance of explaining that they weren't brothers. But then he said the heck with it, and just said, "Verna McCarty, Johnny and Joe Reynolds."

"Pleased to make your acquaintances," she said with a nod.

She gave a quick glance in one direction and then the other. There was no one else at the punch bowl.

She looked at Johnny and said, "Or should I say, pleased to make your acquaintance, Mister *McCabe?*"

Johnny glanced at Matt. Matt was looking at her wide-eyed.

Johnny said, "Your father told you?"

She looked from Johnny to Matt. "Don't be silly. Either of you. My father's word is as good as solid steel. But there's not much that goes on in that household that I don't know about, whether anyone is aware of it or not."

Johnny didn't know what to say. Apparently even Matt didn't.

Verna said, "Don't worry. Your secret's safe with me. I promise."

She made a little crossing motion over her chest. "Cross my heart."

She gave Matt a smile that made her face glow. "You can trust me. Really."

"Somehow," Matt said, "I think we can."

Matt glanced across the room at Ern Cabot. It was like Johnny said. He didn't look happy. His arms were folded across his chest and his eyes were fixed on Matt.

Verna followed Matt's gaze across the room and said, "Oh, don't worry about Ern. He and I are just friends."

"Does he know that?" Johnny said.

"Oh, of course he does."

Matt's smile was back. "Well, if he didn't, he's learning it tonight."

Verna laughed. "I do so like you, Matthew."

Joe said, "That's something you and Matt have in common."

Matt and Verna drifted off into the crowd with their glasses of punch.

Joe said to Johnny, "She sure is a purty girl. But there's something about her that reminds me of a rattlesnake."

Johnny nodded. "Or a wolf."

88

JOHNNY WAS GETTING tired of standing idly by the punch bowl, so he made his way over to the door. The music was going, and the banjo player was calling a square dance. He wasn't too shabby at it.

Quint was standing by the door, so Johnny said, "Evenin', Quint."

Quint nodded. He had a glass of punch in one hand. He said, "Having a good time?"

Johnny shrugged. "Actually, I've had about enough of this. I think I'm going to take a break and go find something stronger."

Quint said, "I'm with you."

Johnny didn't realize Joe had followed him over until Joe said, "Lead the way."

The saloon was open, yet the only man in the room was Slim, the bartender. The mirror that had been shattered in Johnny's gunfight with the bounty hunter had been replaced.

"Quiet night," Johnny said.

Slim nodded. "Most everyone's at the dance, I reckon."

"How about a whiskey," Quint said, bellying-up to the bar.

Joe ordered a bottle of beer.

Slim said to Johnny, "Tequila?"

Johnny grinned. "That sounds like what the doctor ordered."

Slim set a glass on the bar and poured. He stood a bottle in front of Joe and pulled the cork.

Joe said, "So, how come you ain't asked that purty blonde girl to dance with you?"

Quint grinned. "Probably afraid of her father, the old buzzard. I don't blame you."

Johnny shook his head. "I don't think it'd be fair to her. I like life on the Bar M. But we don't really know how long we're going to be able to stay."

Johnny was being careful with his wording, but he gave Joe a long look that said, *read between the lines.*

Joe nodded.

Quint said, "You boys can talk open around me. I figured you're runnin' from somethin'. Many men out here are. I was too, when I first come west."

Johnny said, "But you don't know what we're running from."

"Don't matter none. It couldn't be worse'n what I was running from. Killed a man back in Kentucky. It was self-defense, but I knew I couldn't prove it. I busted out of the local jail and ran. I just kept on runnin'. Wound up out West. Worked different places, different jobs. I worked a few months at the Broken Spur, about fifteen years ago. Heard you boys mention that place. Worked the Shannon Ranch further south for a while. Worked at the Goodnight place for a time. Ended up here."

Joe said, "Ain't you worried talkin' about it might get you arrested?"

Quint shrugged. "Changed my name when I started runnin'. Been almost twenty years, now. Figure everyone's pretty much forgotten about it. The boy I was back in Kentucky and the life I led, it was so long ago it's almost like it never happened at all."

Johnny said, "You don't have the sound of Kentucky in you when you talk."

"Prob'ly lost it over the years. That can happen. Years in Texas, years out here in Californy."

Johnny nodded. He understood.

He said to Joe and Quint, "I understand Matt finds Miss McCarty pretty. I can see in his eye that he really likes her. But I don't think he's being fair to her. Our mess that we're running from is only a year and a half ago, and if folks find out, we might have to cut and run."

Quint said, "Are there reward posters out on you?"

Johnny nodded. "Reynolds ain't our real name, either."

Quint nodded. "Maybe you're bein' smart, then, stayin' away from Doc Buzzard's daughter. If you really like her. It wouldn't be fair to her."

"I don't know if I'd really like her. Don't intend to find out."

Joe was chuckling. "That's funny, though. Doc Buzzard."

Quint grinned. "That's what we call him, sometimes."

After they finished their drink, they decided to head back to the dance. They were walking along the boardwalk with the hotel in sight when they saw a crowd of men circling around with their backs facing out. Johnny knew what it meant.

"Looks like there's gonna be a fight," he said.

Johnny shouldered his way into the crowd and saw Matt and Verna to one side of the opening in the ring of men. Ern Cabot was standing at the other.

Cabot said, "I told you, step away from my girl. I'm not gonna say it again."

Verna said, "I'm not your girl. You're making a jack ass of yourself, Ern. Stop it."

Johnny could tell by the heated-up look on Ern's face that he had a little too much to drink. Johnny didn't know where Ern had found it. But Ern had enough to muster up some courage, and sometimes drink can fire up a man's anger. But he hadn't had enough to make him unsteady. A dangerous combination.

Matt said to Verna, "Step back. This is between Ern and me."

"Matthew, no."

Johnny stepped between Ern and Matt. "Hold on. I don't want you getting so beaten up you can't work on Monday."

Matt said, "I won't be the one getting beaten up."

Ern focused his hate-filled eyes on Johnny. "Out of my way, or I'll knock you aside."

Johnny grinned. "All by yourself?"

"Boss," Matt said. "This is my fight."

Johnny looked at Matt, and he realized his brother was right. Out here, a man had to fight his own fights, even if he got whupped. Matt had been a reasonably good scrapper back home, but he had never been hell-on-wheels like Johnny was, or Joe. But the confrontation with Ern belonged to Matt.

Johnny stepped back.

Ern took off his jacket and casually tossed it to one side. But the casualness of the motion was a decoy, because he then charged at Matt.

Cabot swung a fist. Matt was stepping back and turning away from it, and the punch glanced off of a cheekbone. Johnny could tell the way Cabot fought that he had received some training. Cabot then swung a hard left hook, and Matt ducked.

Matt tackled him and pulled him down, and both

rolled in the mud for a moment. Even though there hadn't been rain in weeks, the street still found a way to be muddy. Like streets in most western towns, Johnny figured.

They got to their feet and Cabot shot off another punch at Matt, and it caught him squarely on the cheekbone. Matt's knees buckled and he was down.

"Matthew!" Verna screamed and ran to him.

Matt was getting to his feet, but his knees were a little wobbly.

"I'm all right," he said. His voice was shaky.

"No, you're not." She looked at Ern and said, "What's wrong with you? Get away from us."

Cabot looked at the crowd, and his anger was washing away. He looked like he felt a little foolish.

He grabbed his jacket from the mud, pushed his way through the crowd, and stormed away.

Matt looked like he wasn't going to stay on his feet much longer, so Johnny took one arm and Joe the other.

Verna was placing a hand on Matt's cheekbone. "Oh, Matthew. You're so brave. Let's go inside and put some ice on that."

They got him back into the hotel and into a chair, and Verna ran to the punch bowl to get some ice.

Joe said to Matt, "You gotta learn when to duck."

Matt grinned. "Sometimes it's more important to know when *not* to duck."

89

IT WAS late, and people were going home. But there were still some on the dance floor.

Johnny stood by the door with Joe at his side.

Quint was there, too. He had said, "I'll hang with you boys, if you don't mind. Things get interesting around you."

The doctor's daughter was sitting at the far side of the room. A couple of girls were with her, chatting.

Johnny knew it wasn't wise to get to know her. And yet, there she was. Not dancing with anyone at the moment. Something about her almost called to him. He had never felt drawn to any girl like this. Not even Becky Drummond.

And then she looked at him. From across the room. Their gazes met, and he couldn't pull away.

Joe said, "Be smart."

Johnny said nothing. He started across the floor to her.

Her eyes were on him as he approached.

He stood before her and held his hand out, and she took it and rose to her feet. He said nothing and neither did she. They walked out to the dance floor, like at each other's side was where they were meant to be.

Joe stood with a cup of punch in his hand, and shook his head.

Matt and Verna were on the dance floor. Matt had been watching over her shoulder and was smiling.

The old doctor was also watching, and he was glaring with disgust. His daughter dancing with a cowhand.

But Johnny was seeing none of it. For him, there was no one in the world but himself and the girl in his arms.

After the dance, they stepped outside. Out where Matt's fight with Cabot had been.

She said, "My name's Lura."

The first words she had spoken to him.

He nodded. "Johnny McCabe."

Then he realized, *Dang!* He had given her his real name.

"Johnny *Reynolds*, actually. It's a long story."

"Whatever the story, it's safe with me."

"Lura. That's a nice name."

She smiled, and then looked downward for a second.

As though she was hit with a sudden bout of shyness.

She said, "My last name's Marker. But I know they call me Lura Buzzard behind my back."

Johnny couldn't help but grin. He said, "I'll never call anyone so beautiful a name like that."

That's when the old buzzard called out from the doorway. "Lura!"

She rolled her eyes. "Yes, Papa?"

"Come with us. We're going home."

She gave Johnny a long look, then left to join her parents.

Her mother was about Lura's height and Johnny could see the resemblance. But, he thought, she sure doesn't look like her father.

Doc Marker scowled at Johnny and said, "Stay away from my daughter."

Then he turned and stormed away down the boardwalk.

Lura looked back at Johnny and threw a little wave at him and a look that said, *I'm sorry.*

He smiled at her and gave a return wave with one hand. She smiled.

Joe walked over to Johnny. "Are you being smart?"

"Trying to be. Mighty danged hard thing to do, though."

Joe nodded. "Always seems to be."

Johnny said, "Come on. Let's get out of here."

They fetched their horses from the livery and started along the dark trail back to the ranch.

Johnny said, "I shouldn't have danced with her. It's not fair to her. But it was like her spirit was somehow calling to me. When we danced, it was like…it was like I had somehow known her all my life. Without even a word being said between us. It was like she was where she was meant to be, in my arms. And I was meant to be where I was."

Johnny grinned and shook his head. "Sounds foolish, doesn't it?"

Joe was silent a moment. Then he said, "No. I felt the same thing once. That Cheyenne girl I mentioned."

Johnny nodded.

They rode along in silence, each with his own thoughts.

90

ERN CABOT HAD driven Verna to the dance in a carriage from his ranch, and now she had no ride home.

Matt said, "I have nothing as grand as a carriage to offer. But you can join me on the back of my horse. I assure you, the horse won't turn into a pumpkin."

She smiled. "I assure you, I'm hardly a princess."

"You are in my eyes."

And so Matt let her have his saddle, and he sat behind her. He wrapped his arms around in front of her and held the reins. She nestled back into him as they rode.

"You aren't exactly dressed for horseback riding," Matt said. "I hope this doesn't ruin your dress."

"Don't worry. It'll survive."

As they rode along, they talked, about nothing and everything. The kind of light chatter that fills the time between a man and a woman.

"I suppose a woman as beautiful as you has never been without gentleman callers," Matt said.

"I would hardly call Ern a gentleman. I thought so, until tonight. I'm starting to think he was only interested in my father's money. That's what Mother has said from the start. His father's ranch is successful but nothing like the Bar M."

"I assure you, I'm not after your father's money."

She looked playfully back over her shoulder at him. "Oh? Are you a rich man, then?"

"Not in money, no. But in the things that really count."

"So, what do you want in life? How do you define success?"

He said, "Success to me is a good wife, good children. A hearth to rest by when the day's work is done."

"Do you think you'll know the right girl when you meet her?"

"I might."

She said in a whimsical, teasing way, "Maybe you've already met her."

"Maybe."

He reined up by the front door of the ranch house and jumped down from the horse. Then he reached up and helped Verna to the ground.

He walked to the door with her.

"Verna, I don't mean to be forward, but may I see you again?"

She nodded. "Tomorrow night? For dinner?"

He gave a big smile. "I'll be there."

"Five o'clock."

"Five it is."

She laid a hand aside his face for a moment, then she stepped inside. Matt stood and waited until the door had fully shut.

He took the reins of the horse and began leading it toward the barn. He could scarcely keep from leaping in the air.

Once his horse was taken care of, he walked along toward the bunkhouse with his hands in his pockets. He had a bounce in his step, almost like he was dancing along to the rhythm of his own happiness.

He found Johnny and Joe at the bunkhouse.

"What're you boys doing here?" Matt said. "I didn't think you'd be back yet."

Johnny was pouring a cup of coffee for himself. He said, "I guess we both had enough of the dance."

Joe was sitting at the table, sharpening his knife on a small whet stone.

Matt said, "I rode home with Verna. I told everyone I would be the one leaving with her, and I was."

Joe nodded. He said nothing.

"She invited me for dinner tomorrow night. Can you believe it? I've never felt like this about anyone before. Not even that Filipino girl I mentioned. Johnny, I think Verna could be the one."

Joe said, "Do you think this is smart?"

Matt blinked with surprise. "Smart?"

Johnny said, "She's kind of high profile, Matt. The idea is not to draw any more attention to ourselves than we have to."

"What about that bounty hunter you shot down a couple months ago?"

"Couldn't be helped. But if you go around courting the daughter of the most successful rancher in Calaveras County, you're gonna draw attention to yourself."

"*Courting* her? Why, Johnny," he slapped his hands

together. "I'm going to marry that girl."

Joe looked at him with his perpetual squint. "*Marry* her? You cain't go marryin' that girl."

"And just why not?"

Joe looked at Johnny. A cup of coffee waited in front of Joe, but he said, "I think I need somethin' stronger."

He got to his feet and shambled over to his bunk. His saddlebags were stuffed underneath. He pulled them out, then reached into one of them and came out with a bottle of whiskey.

Johnny said, "How long have you had that?"

"Clearly not long enough."

Joe pulled the cork and took a belt.

Johnny said, "You know, there's rules against drinkin' on this ranch."

"You're the ramrod. Mister McCarty gives you full authority. You can waive the rule for tonight." Joe handed the bottle to Johnny.

"I hereby officially waive the rule for tonight," Johnny said, and he tipped the bottle.

Matt said, "What do you mean I can't marry her?"

"Think about it," Johnny said. He held the bottle out to Matt, but Matt shook his head.

Johnny said, "We have reward posters out there with our names on them. And the reward is for a lot more money than I would have thought. We're only here on this ranch until someone learns our real name."

Joe returned to his chair and stood the bottle in front of him. "Like with that bounty hunter. We're lucky he didn't actually mention our real names."

"Our names get mentioned, and we'll have to pack and run."

"That's why I keep my saddlebags packed. At least with the stuff I need."

"We'll have to run, and then start over again somewhere else. Oregon. Northern Nebraska Territory. Maybe Canada. Or maybe down in Mexico somewhere. Sonora has some good cattle country."

Joe held the knife in his hand and the small whetstone in the other. "It ain't fair to the girl. Start buildin' somethin' with her, when tomorrow we all might be havin' to high-tail it out of here. You might not even get a chance to say goodbye."

Johnny reached for the bottle and took another pull

from it. "You don't think I'd like the chance to do the same? There's a girl in town. She's not like any girl I've ever known before. Not even Becky Drummond."

Matt said, "Doc Buzzard's daughter."

Johnny nodded. "I allowed myself one dance with her. And I know she's the one. The one for me. But it wouldn't be fair to her."

Matt was silent a moment. He started pacing a little to one side and then to the other. Johnny stood the bottle back on the table.

Then Matt said, "No. You're both wrong. There has to come a point when this ends. Mister McCarty knows our real names. You told us so. He said he's not going to do anything about it. Time passes by, and things get forgotten."

Joe said, "When you marry this girl, what name is she going to take? O'Toole? Even her married name will be a lie."

"We'll figure that out when we get there. She knows the truth about us. Apparently she has, all along. We'll figure something out."

"Matt," Johnny said, not sure exactly what to say.

But Matt's ire was getting raised. He said, "No."

Johnny said, "No?"

"That's right. I'm going to take a more optimistic approach. It's time to stop running. A life is being handed to me. An open doorway. All I have to do is step through. You have such a morose way about you, Johnny. Did anyone ever tell you that?"

Matt stood a moment and stared at Johnny.

Then Matt said, "I'm happy. I'm really happy. Can't you just allow me that? Can't you just be happy for me?"

He left the bunkhouse and slammed the door.

Johnny looked at Joe. "Do you think I'm morose?"

Joe said, "Don't really know what that means. But you do seem kind of gloomy a lot."

91

JOHNNY SAID to McCarty, "I'm thinking on taking some men back into the mountains to do a little more mustanging. The Army needs horses, and even though this is a cattle ranch, there's money to be made in horses. It's said I'm a fair judge of horseflesh. Joe is too, and Matt has learned a lot over the past year or so."

It was Monday morning. Johnny was sitting in front of McCarty's desk with a cup of coffee and a saucer.

The old man said, "You taking your brothers with you?"

"I'll leave Matt here. I'd hate to have Miss Verna upset with me."

McCarty grinned. "Don't you worry about her. Leave her to me."

"Besides," Johnny said, returning the grin, "I don't want to risk Matt or Corry getting hurt up there. As you are more than aware, mustangin' can get a little dangerous. If we're going to get into the horse ranchin' business, we need to keep our bronc-busters healthy."

"Horse ranching, eh?" McCarty rubbed his chin in thought. "I always focused my business on cattle. Other ranches in the area always provided their own horses."

"Times are changing, sir. The Army has a bigger presence here, now. And there are a lot of folks in towns like Greenville and Camanche who don't know a lot about horses. Even as far away as Stockton. We get enough mustangs, we can undercut the competition. There's a lot of wild stock in those mountains."

McCarty nodded. "I like the way you think, son. Go to it."

"I'll need some money for a larger corral."

"Just tell me how much."

"I appreciate the confidence you have in me, sir."

Johnny took Joe with him, and Evan and Quint.

Johnny said, "I'm leaving you in charge, Matt."

Matt said nothing. He was at the table in the bunkhouse.

Johnny said, "What, are you not speaking to me, now?"

"Got nothing to say to you. Other than, while you're

gone, I'll get that pen and paper and write that letter to Ma and Luke."

"I appreciate that."

"Well, like you said, they've been too long without hearing from us."

Johnny nodded. He strapped on his leather leggings and then grabbed his bedroll and his rifle.

He said, "You know, Matt, it's not that I don't want you happy. It's just that I don't think you're being careful enough."

"And maybe it's time you started looking to your own affairs and keep out of mine."

Johnny nodded. He opened the door.

"Johnny," Matt said. "Don't get yourself hurt up there in the mountains. You and Joe, be safe."

Matt grinned. Johnny returned the grin. "See you in a few days."

Branching out into horse ranching would bring a lot more money to the Bar M, Johnny thought.

And maybe a week in the mountains would help get his mind off of Lura Marker.

He found it wasn't so.

They roamed canyons and ridges, following the unshod tracks of mustangs. They cornered a few and used the box canyon where Cooper was killed as a natural corral.

By day, Johnny had enough on his mind. Two days in the mountains, and they had six mustangs.

He thought about that stallion Cooper had been obsessed with. They had found the carcass in the canyon where it had fallen, and there was little left of it. Wolves and other critters had torn it apart. It was now mostly hide and bones.

When it had been alive, it was the most magnificent horse Johnny had ever seen. He and Cooper were of one mind on that. But Johnny didn't think that horse could ever have been tamed. It would have wound up injuring or killing the bronc-busters and would have had to be put down anyway.

But at night, when wolves were calling from somewhere in the darkness, and Evan was working on his harmonica and Joe was taking smoke from his Indian pipe, Johnny would sit by the fire and think of Lura.

On their fourth night in the mountains, with eighteen head of horses in the canyon, Joe looked over at Johnny and said, "You all right?"

"Yeah, I was just thinking about tomorrow's work."

Joe said, "I know what you're thinking about, and it ain't tomorrow's work."

Johnny gave a grin that he hoped wasn't as sad as it felt. "No. It ain't."

92

JOHNNY HAD HOPED a week in the mountains would get his mind off of Lura. It didn't work. Being away from her created a pain deep inside him that almost haunted him. He had ridden away from Becky Drummond twice, and neither time had it brought a pain like this.

On the Sunday after Johnny and the others returned from mustanging, Matt rode into Greenville with the McCartys to attend church. Johnny knew Ma would want all of her boys at church on Sunday morning, and Johnny had attended a few sermons at the Methodist church in town. But on this Sunday, he remained behind and drank coffee.

Joe said, "Maybe he's right. You're bein' morose. I found out what that means." He gave a little grin. "But I cain't criticize. I been through the same thing you're going through, and I didn't handle it any better'n you are now."

The family returned from church. Matt announced that he and Verna had picked a wedding date. It would be in September.

Her mother wanted them to wait until the following June. Matt said, "She thinks weddings in June are so romantic. But Verna and I are in love, and we don't want to wait any longer."

Johnny was at the bunkhouse table. His tin cup was empty and he was considering filling it with something stronger than coffee. Waiving that no-drinking rule again.

In Texas, before he had gone home, he had been known for going on what Zack Johnson had once called *spectacular benders*. He was starting to think he was on the verge of such a thing now.

"So," Joe said to Matt. "Where's your beloved now?"

"She decided to go out for a ride. She said she sometimes likes to ride the countryside alone. She'll be back for dinner. Mister McCarty said I'm practically a part of the family now, so I have a standing invitation to dinner."

Johnny didn't know if it was the pain he was feeling over Lura, or the idea of having Verna as a sister-in-law, but the idea of going on a bender was becoming more appealing by the moment.

He decided to instead saddle up Bravo and just ride.

He wore his guns, like he always did, and he tucked

his Hawken rifle in the saddle scabbard.

There was a light breeze, and the air had the dry, light feel it seemed to always have in California.

He let Bravo have his head and just hung on for the ride. Bravo would canter along for a while, then slow to a walk. He stopped at one point, looking about sniffing the air. Then he continued on.

Johnny tried to turn his thoughts to nothing but the terrain about him. Mostly grass, and gently rolling hills. A little scrub oak. He was vaguely aware that Bravo was taking him in a northwesterly direction.

Bravo stopped again and looked around like he had heard something. Johnny guessed they were probably two miles from the ranch headquarters, but he really wasn't paying attention. About a hundred feet to the left was a stand of scrub oaks, and the land was open off to the right. Really beautiful country, but he wasn't in the mood for beauty right now.

He found himself wondering if maybe Matt was right. Maybe he was being morose. He wondered if Matt had the right idea. Just embrace the moment and let tomorrow take care of itself.

That was when he became aware of a rider moving out from behind the stand of oaks and leveling a rifle at him.

It was Ern Cabot.

"Don't move, Reynolds," he said. "Or should I call you McCabe?"

Johnny cursed himself. He always rode along alert, watching the trail in front of him as well as behind. Always, but not this time. He had been too wrapped up in his own miseries.

"Ern," Johnny said. "We haven't heard from you since my brother whupped you in that fight outside the hotel."

"*I* whupped *him,* if I remember right."

Johnny shook his head. "You might have thrown the final punch, and you might have been the one on your feet when it was done. But he was the one who rode home with the girl. He whupped you, and you didn't even know it."

"Well, now it's my turn. There's a reward on you, a thousand dollars. Dead or alive. That's a whole lot of money. I know I'd never get you back to Greenville alive. I know the reputation of Johnny McCabe. But all I have to do is put a bullet in you. Simple as that. They're sayin' Johnny McCabe is the fastest there ever was with a gun. You know that?"

"I wish they wouldn't. It's embarrassing."

"So you don't deny you're Johnny McCabe."

"That rifle looks like a Harper's Ferry."

"It's brand new. It'll take your head right off your shoulders. What about it?"

Johnny was squinting in the sun. "It holds one shot, and you're about a hundred feet away. You have to make that shot count. You ever shoot a man, Ern?"

Ern said nothing.

"I didn't think so. You're a cowhand, not a gunfighter. So let me tell you, from experience. It's hard to make a shot count when your target is shooting back at you. And I'll be shooting back at you."

"How? You don't even have your gun out."

"Because in a few seconds, I'm going to draw my gun and put a bullet into you. Even if you fire first. Even if your bullet hits me, mine is still gonna hit you. Think about that."

A shot was fired from off to one side and back a ways. Ern lurched in the saddle and his rifle went off, but the bullet went wide of Johnny.

Ern had been hit somewhere in the upper chest or shoulder—Johnny couldn't be sure. But it had been fired from a distance and the bullet was partially spent before it hit him.

Ern and Johnny both looked off to the direction of the shot. Two riders were about five hundred feet away, in front of another small grove of scrub oak. One rider was Verna, and the other, the one holding the rifle, was the son of Moses Timmons.

The boy jacked the gun. It was a Volcanic repeating rifle. Johnny had seen a few of them. Jacking the trigger guard chambered another round, and then the Timmons boy sighted in on Cabot.

Cabot tried to raise his rifle to shoot, but realized it was now empty, so he reached for the pistol on his belt.

The Timmons boy fired again.

The second bullet caught Ern in the head, and even though the bullet was partially spent, it was enough to snap Ern's head back.

The rifle fell from Ern's grip. Then he toppled from the saddle. His foot caught in the stirrup and the horse started to run. Ern was dragged a few yards before his foot came free, and he came to a sliding stop face-down in the grass.

Johnny leapt out of the saddle and left Bravo's rein trailing, and he ran to Ern.

Johnny rolled him over. Ern's face was scraped up from being dragged, and Johnny saw there was a bullet hole in his forehead. He knew Ern was dead, but he checked the side of Ern's neck for a pulse, anyway. There was none.

Johnny rose to his feet as Verna and Timmons rode up.

Johnny said, "What are you doing?"

She said, "Saving the life of my future brother-in-law."

"You didn't have to shoot him. You could have just ridden up. You had the drop on him."

"He was going to shoot you. For all I know, he would have put a bullet in you before we could have ridden up." She smiled. "Besides, he had pretty much figured out who you, Matthew and Joe were. He had told me at church, last Sunday."

"You killed him so he wouldn't talk."

"Oh, Johnny. When you put it that way, it sounds so cold. Of course we didn't kill him for that reason. But, if there's a little side benefit to it," she gave a little shrug, "who am I to complain?"

Johnny didn't know what to say.

She said, "We have to talk."

She looked at the Timmons boy and said, "Ride on ahead."

The Timmons boy nodded and nudged his horse on.

Johnny swung back into the saddle. Timmons was soon fifty feet ahead of them.

Johnny said to Verna, "Would he roll over and play dead if you told him to?"

"Timmons is loyal. Actually, he's in love with me. The poor fool. He'd do anything I told him to."

"And, of course, you use that to your advantage."

"Why, Johnny," she said, putting on a look of mock surprise. "Whatever kind of person do you think I am?"

Johnny started Bravo forward at a walk, and Verna did the same with her mount. She was in a shoe-length skirt and was riding side-saddle. She wore a hat with a stiff, wide brim, and the hat was held in place by a chin strap.

Johnny said, "I will admit, that was a good shot he made."

She nodded. "Timmons is useful to keep around."

"So, we leave the body right there? We just ride on?"

She shrugged. "Why haul it into town? We'll have to answer a lot of bothersome questions."

"The remorse you feel at his passing is touching." Johnny let the sarcasm rise to the surface. "He was a suitor of yours at one time. He cared about you enough to be jealous of Matt. Driven to distraction by it, apparently."

"Why, of course I feel remorse. Ern Cabot was a good man." She looked off toward the distance, and she batted her eyes as though there were tears she was blinking back. Except Johnny could tell her eyes were dry.

She said, "Ern was driven to a jealous rage. And I, the naïve little girl that I am, didn't realize how he felt about me until it was too late. Until Timmons and I just happened to be riding along, perfectly by chance, and saw Ern with a gun aimed at the brother of the man I love."

"And Matt is the man you love." His sarcasm was still present. He was starting to think this girl didn't know the meaning of the word *love*.

She nodded. "Why, of course. Matt is the right man for me to marry. He's an eloquent speaker and exudes a charm I simply do not have. I have grand plans for my father's ranch, McCabe. I have a head for business, and I intend to use it. This ranch will all be mine, one day."

"Yours and Matt's."

"Same thing. We are going to build an empire."

Johnny glanced up ahead to Timmons, who was now nearly a hundred feet ahead of them. Timmons had slipped his rifle back into the scabbard and was riding along as though he hadn't just shot a man to death.

She had said nothing that would give Johnny reason to believe she was lying. It was something almost intangible in her voice, something in her energy, that made her statements seem somehow hollow.

He thought again of what he had learned from Pa and Apache Jim. *Trust your gut.* And his gut was telling him somehow Verna knew fully well Ern would be out here.

He couldn't prove it. He doubted he ever would. And there was nothing he could say to Matt without driving more of a wedge between them.

Johnny said, "Is Matt aware that he's going to be building an empire?"

She shrugged. "He will be, as it happens. As it unfolds, one step at a time."

She looked at Johnny again. "You don't like me much, do you?"

He shrugged. "I don't really know you."

"You don't have to. All you have to know is your brother loves me and I love him, and I intend to make him happy. Isn't that enough?"

He nodded. "It should be."

Her words were still ringing hollow. Or like they were somehow manufactured. Like her words were orchestrated to lead Johnny along a certain path.

He could tell by the look in her eye that she knew he wasn't fully convinced.

She said, "Is it true? All of the things that are being said about you? All of the men you've killed?"

"True enough."

"So, you're a dangerous man."

He shook his head. "I've never killed a man that didn't need to be killed. I plan to never do different."

"You're an idealist."

"Miss Verna, quite frankly, I don't know exactly what I am."

She laughed. "Neither do any of us, Johnny."

She called to Timmons, who turned his horse back.

She said, "Timmons, we're going home."

She looked to Johnny and said, "Would you like to join us?"

He wanted to be alone, to deal with the pain of not being with Lura. Of knowing he would probably never be able to have her in his life. But he wasn't sure he wanted to turn his back on these two.

He said, "I'll ride along with you, if you don't mind."

93

JOHNNY HAD Monday morning coffee with McCarty.

"Are you all right, Johnny?" he said. "You seem a little sullen this morning."

Johnny said, "No, I'm all right. Just didn't sleep well."

After their meeting was done, on his way toward the front door, he passed Verna in the corridor.

"Why Johnny," she said. "How pleasant to see you this morning."

She gave him a big, beaming smile. But it didn't seem real. She was like an actress on a stage.

"Good to see you again, Miss Verna," he said, and continued on his way.

He wasn't just trying to avoid her. He needed to get out to the ranch yard. There was work to be done.

It was time for Matt and Corry to get to working with the new mustangs. And Johnny sent Quint and Hardy into town with two buckboards. A load of lumber was waiting for them at a saw mill. Johnny wanted to start expanding the corral.

Evan, Chip and Valdez were on their way to watch the horse-breaking, and Joe was with them.

Johnny said, "Joe, will you hold up? I want to talk with you for a minute or two."

Once they had the bunkhouse to themselves, Johnny told him about Timmons killing Ern Cabot and the talk Johnny and Verna had.

Joe said, "So, what do we do?"

"I'm not staying here. That's for sure. I don't want to be near that girl or the lapdog who follows her around."

"Lapdog?"

Johnny shrugged. "Well, what would you call it? He follows her around like a dog follows its master. Moses Timmons is a good man, but there's something wrong with his son."

"There's something wrong with anyone who can just kill because he's told to. I don't want to stay around here either. But we've got to tell Matt about her."

Johnny held his hands out to either side. "How? You see how starry-eyed he is over her. All we'll do is push him away from us."

Joe thought a moment. He ran his fingers through his beard. "You know, if we ride on, then we're leaving Matt alone with her. If we stay, then at least we'll be here to watch his back."

Johnny let that settle in for a moment. Then he said, "Maybe you've got a point."

There was a knock at the bunkhouse door and Johnny called out, "Come on in."

A man stepped in, a man Johnny had seen at the main house but never in the ranch yard. His name was Juan, and he was about Mr. McCarty's age. He was in a black jacket and a tie. Johnny knew little about the doings and ways of the rich, but it seemed Juan had the role of butler. Like Alfredo, back at the Broken Spur.

He said, "Senor Reynolds. The master of the house has requested you. Both of you."

He and Joe followed Juan toward the main house. Johnny saw a horse tethered by the front door.

They found McCarty and Matt in the study, along with Marshal Brannigan.

Matt said, "Juan went to the corral and got me, too."

"Have a seat," McCarty said.

They did.

Brannigan had a sheet of paper in his hand. "I got a letter from a territorial marshal in Nebraska. It seems a Thaddeus McCabe was arrested there. He confessed to everything about the murder in Mansfield, Missouri."

McCarty said, "The marshal knows who you are. I told him everything this morning, after he rode out here with that letter. He had pretty much figured it out, anyway."

Brannigan said, "You boys are off the hook. The reward has been rescinded, and the murder charge has been dropped. Considering how slow the mail travels, the charges were actually dropped more than three months ago."

Johnny wasn't sure he was hearing this correctly. He looked at Joe and then at Matt. Looked like they were having the same reaction.

Brannigan said, "The robbery charge is still there, but if you pay the store owner back, he's willing to drop those charges too."

It took Johnny a moment to find his voice. "How much do we owe him?"

"Twenty-four dollars."

"It's over," Joe said. "It's finally over. No more runnin'."

Johnny looked at Brannigan. "What about Thad? Where is he now?"

"He was extradited to Missouri. They hanged him for the murder."

Hanged. Thad was gone.

Johnny sat a moment, letting everything Brannigan had said settle on him.

"So," McCarty said. "No more of this Reynolds or O'Toole business. My daughter will be taking the name McCabe."

Matt was giving a big smile. "That she will, sir."

McCarty called out for Juan.

Juan couldn't have been far away, because within five seconds he was in the doorway. "Sir?"

"Drinks. For all of us. Get the glasses. Those wild horses can wait. We're going to celebrate!"

When the McCabe brothers left the main house, it was nearly noon. Johnny had put down three glasses of tequila, and he was feeling it. Not that he was by any means staggering, but he wouldn't have trusted his accuracy with a pistol.

Matt said, "I'm going to go try those horses."

"No you're not," Johnny said. "You have the day off. No need to break your backside on those mustangs today."

"Nonsense," Matt said. "I feel like I could walk on air." He spun in a complete circle as they walked.

Joe said, "That's the tequila talking. You had two of 'em."

Matt ignored him. "I don't want to let Corry have all the fun. I'm no longer Matt O'Toole. Now, the whole world can know, I'm Matt McCabe. Ace bronc buster."

"All right," Johnny said. "Go get 'em. Don't break your neck."

Matt started away toward the corral.

Johnny said, "Oh, and Matt."

Matt looked back at him.

"I want you to know, I'm sorry about the hard words between us. I want you to know, no matter what, I have your back. Always will."

Matt nodded. "I know that, Johnny. I always knew that."

And he was off to the corral.

Joe said, "I'm gonna go watch the action. You coming?"

Johnny shook his head. "I'm heading to town. I'm giving myself the day off. Tell Quint he's in charge."

Joe said, "You're going to town?"

Johnny said, "There's a girl in town. The daughter of Doc Buzzard. And I'm riding in to see her."

Joe smiled. "About time."

Johnny slapped Joe on the shoulder and said, "I'm gonna marry that girl."

Joe watched his brother run to the stable, and he laughed.

EPILOGUE

Montana, 1881

THE WINTER WINDS BLEW strong and hard outside. Snow drifted against the side of the house and rattled the window panes. But the fire in the hearth roared and kept the cold of winter at bay.

Bree was still on the sofa beside her father, and she said, "Gunman of the Rio Grande? I still can't believe they actually called you that."

Joe had gotten another glass of scotch. He said, "They sure did call him that."

Bree said to her father, "How come you never mentioned that before?"

Johnny drew a long, patient breath. "I was hoping people would forget about it."

Ginny was in her rocker, and she gave a little chuckle. "You've been trying for so long to outrun the growing legend, but you've never quite been able to."

He shook his head. "Can't fault me for trying."

"So tell us," Bree said. "What happened when you rode into town to see Ma? Did you start courting her right then?"

Johnny found sleepiness was finally starting to descend on him. "Punkin, that's a story for another day. I'm bushed, and I think we should all get to sleep."

Josh and Temperance headed upstairs. Johnny gave Bree a kiss on the forehead and she followed them. Haley and Jonathan had long since fallen asleep, wrapped in blankets, and Dusty joined them. Joe had spread his bedroll on the kitchen floor.

And yet Johnny found himself still on the sofa, looking at the fire. The sleepiness he had been feeling a few minutes before was now slipping away.

Ginny was still in her rocker. She had gone to the kitchen and poured herself one more glass of wine.

"You're thinking of Lura," she said.

He nodded. "For so many years I felt pain when I looked back on my days with her. But now I feel peace."

"Jessica's good for you. I haven't seen you this happy since your days with Lura."

"Most men never find a truly fine woman to love them.

I have found two. I'm blessed, and I know it."

"Three, I suppose, if you count Becky Drummond, back in Pennsylvania. You never mentioned her."

He shrugged. "No need to, I suppose."

"And four, if you count the woman down in Texas. What was her name?"

"Maria Carerra."

Ginny nodded. "Almost musical, the way you say it. A woman you cared about, and yet it was love from afar."

"I don't know that it was love. There was something about her, something smoky and sensual that almost drew a man in. Like a moth to a flame."

"Like the sirens of old."

He nodded. "But I wouldn't call it love. And with Becky, we were kids. It seemed intense at times, but it was nothing like what I had with Lura, or what I have with Jessica."

A nautical clock on a wooden base rested on the center of the mantel. It had belonged to Ginny's father, and she had long ago sent to San Francisco for it. Even though she had moved into town, she left the clock here because she said the clock was made for this hearth.

It chimed seven times.

"Seven o'clock," Johnny said. "The sun will be rising in half an hour, or so."

Ginny nodded. "We've been talking all night. And even still, you've really told only half the story."

"That I have. But the other half will have to wait for another time."

She said, "When I think of those days, packing up and leaving that little ranch house you had in California, and the group of us making the trek all the way here by covered wagon. And that first winter in this valley. When I think of those times, I realize how far we've all come."

Johnny nodded.

She said, "You have built quite a family, John. That's the true legacy, you know. Not the larger-than-life legend of the gunfighter. The so-called Gunman of the Rio Grande. Your real legacy is right here."

Those were good words. They settled easily on Johnny's heart and he found himself smiling.

He took a sip of coffee and looked at the fire.

He said, "I think about what Matt said, all those years

ago. Calling me morose."

"And how do you feel now?"

He let the question hang there for a moment, while he considered it. How did he feel?

"Happy," he said. "I feel truly happy."

Ginny smiled. "I've longed to hear you say those words. They were a long time coming."

They sat, Ginny with her glass of wine and Johnny with his cup of coffee, and they watched the fire as it crackled in the hearth.

Made in the USA
San Bernardino, CA
19 December 2017